Praise

"Comedy, tragedy and more great sentences than seems entirely fair . . . It's high time he was deified . . . one of America's greatest contemporary storytellers . . . Marvellous"   *Uncut*

"Exhilarating . . . *Drop City* is a marvel of construction with a champion omniscient narrator"   *Independent*

"*Drop City* verges on flawless . . . Boyle has a light, winning touch that never fails. He conveys small details beautifully, and through them encapsulates whole worlds . . . literary bliss. All in all, quite a trip"   *Sunday Business Post*

"Lively, intelligent . . . wonderfully written"   *Observer*

"Boyle has spun a tale of love, lust and communities, set against the backdrop of the great American landscape"   *Harpers & Queen*

"Right from the opening sentence, Boyle shows himself to be a consummate novelist. Utterly stylish prose, humane character-isation, deft attention to detail and graceful plotting: what reader could ask for more? . . . A profoundly satisfying book"   *Scotland on Sunday*

"One of the finest American contemporary novelists, his name on the cover a guarantee of an intelligent and stimulating read . . . Read it and, if you haven't done so already, go away and invest in his fine back catalogue. Don't be a square, man, get hip to the trip"   *Sunday Tribune*

"Boyle, whose prolific fiction outpouring has begun to rival that of such workhorses as John Updike and Joyce Carol Oates, ranks as one of our master satirists"   *San Francisco Chronicle*

also by T. Coraghessan Boyle

drop city

T. Coraghessan Boyle

BLOOMSBURY

First published in Great Britain 2003
This paperback edition published 2004

Copyright © by T. Coraghessan Boyle 2003

The moral right of the author has been asserted

Bloomsbury Publishing Plc, 36 Soho Square, London W1D 3QY

A CIP catalogue record for this book
is available from the British Library

ISBN 0-7475-6807-3
ISBN-13 9780747568070

10 9 8 7 6 5 4

All papers used by Bloomsbury Publishing are natural,
recyclable products made from wood
grown in well-managed forests.
The manufacturing processes conform to the
environmental regulations of the country of origin.

Printed in Great Britain by Clays Ltd, St Ives plc

www.bloomsbury.com/tcboyle

For the sisters

Kathy, Linda, Janice and Christine

acknowledgments

The author would like to thank Chuck Fadel, Jorma Kaukonen, Russell Timothy Miller, Alan Arkawy and Jim Perry for their help and advice.

Think of our life in nature, – daily to be shown matter, to come in contact with it, – rocks, trees, wind on our cheeks! the *solid* earth! the *actual* world! the *common sense! Contact! Contact! Who* are we? *where* are we?

– Henry David Thoreau, "Ktaadn"

Let me tell you about heartache and the loss of god,
Wandering, wandering in hopeless night.
Out here in the perimeter there are no stars,
Out here we is stoned
Immaculate.

– Jim Morrison, "The WASP
(Texas Radio and the Big Beat)"

part one

drop city south

C'mon people now
Smile on your brother
Everybody get together
Try to love one another right now.
　　　　　– Chet Powers, "Get Together"

part one

drop city south

1

The morning was a fish in a net, glistening and wriggling at the dead black border of her consciousness, but she'd never caught a fish in a net or on a hook either, so she couldn't really say if or how or why. The morning was a fish in a net. That was what she told herself over and over, making a little chant of it – a mantra – as she decapitated weeds with the guillotine of her hoe, milked the slit-eyed goats and sat down to somebody's idea of porridge in the big drafty meeting room, where sixty shimmering communicants sucked at spoons and worked their jaws.

Outside was the California sun, making a statement in the dust and saying something like ten o'clock or ten-thirty to the outbuildings and the trees. There were voices all around her, laughter, morning pleasantries and animadversions, but she was floating still and just opened up a million-kilowatt smile and took her ceramic bowl with the nuts and seeds and raisins and the dollop of pasty oatmeal afloat in goat's milk and drifted through the door and out into the yard to perch on a stump and feel the hot dust invade the spaces between her toes. Eating wasn't a private act – nothing was private at Drop City – but there were no dorm mothers here, no social directors or parents or bosses, and for once she felt like doing her own thing. Grooving, right? Wasn't that what this was all about? The California sun on your face, no games, no plastic society – just freedom and like minds, brothers and sisters all?

Star – Paulette Regina Starr, her name and being shrunk down to four essential letters now – had been at Drop City for something like three weeks. *Something like.* In truth, she couldn't have said exactly how long she'd been sleeping on a particular mattress in a particular room with a careless warm slew of non-particular people, nor would she have cared to. She wasn't counting days or weeks or months – or even years. Or eons either. *Big Bang. Who created the universe? God created the universe. The morning is a fish in a net.* Wasn't it a Tuesday when they got here? Tuesday was music night, and today – today was Friday. She knew that much from the buzz around the stewpot in the kitchen – the weekend hippies were on their way, and the gawkers and gapers too – but time wasn't really one of her hangups, as she'd demonstrated for all and sundry by giving her Tissot watch with the gold-link wristband to an Indian kid in Taos, and he wasn't even staring at her or looking for a handout, just standing there at the bus stop with his hand clenched in his mother's. "Here," she said, "here," twisting it off her wrist, "you want this?" She'd never been west before, never seen anything like it, and there he was, black bangs shielding his black eyes, a little deep-dwelling Indian kid, and she had to give him some-thing. The hills screamed with cactus. The fumes of the bus rode up her nose and made her eyes water.

She'd come west with a guy from home, Ronnie Sommers, who called himself Pan, and they'd had some adventures along the way, Star and Pan – like Lewis and Clark, only brighter around the edges. Ronnie stopped for anybody with long hair, and that was universally good, opening up a whole world of places to crash, free food, drugs. They spent one night in Arizona in a teepee with a guy all tanned and lean, his hair tied back under a snakeskin headband, cooking brown rice and cauliflower over an open fire and swallowing peyote buds he'd gathered himself in the blinding white hills. "Hunters and gatherers," he kept saying, "that's what we are," and every time he said it they all broke up, and then Ronnie rolled a joint and she felt so good she made it with both of them.

She was still chanting to herself, the leaves on the trees frying right before her eyes and the dollop of oatmeal staring up at her from the yellowish goat's milk like something that had come out of her own body, blown out, vomited out, naked and alive and burnished with its own fluids, when a shadow fell over her and there he was, Ronnie, hovering in the frame of her picture like a ghost image. "Hey," he said, squatting before her in his huar-aches and cutoff jeans, "I missed you, where you been?" Then he was lifting her foot out of the dust, her right foot, the one with the fishhook-shaped scar sealed into the flesh as a memento of her childhood, and he kissed her there, the wet impress of his lips dully glistening in the featureless glare.

She stared at her own foot, at his hand and his long, gnawed fingers, at the silver and turquoise rings eating up the light. "Ringo-Pan," she said.

He laughed. His hair was getting long at the back of his neck, spilling like string over the spool of his head, and his beard was starting to cohere. But his face – his face was small and distant, receding like a balloon swept up into the sky.

"I was milking the goats," she said.

Two kids – little kids – blond, naked, dirty, appeared on the periphery, flopped down and started wrestling in the dirt. Somebody was banging a tambourine, and now a flute started up, skirling and stopping and lifting away like birdsong. "Good shit, huh?" he said.

Her smile came back, blissed-out, drenched with sun. Everything was alive everywhere. She could feel the earth spinning like a big ball beneath her feet. "Yeah," she said. "Oh, yeah. Definitely."

And then it was night. She'd come down gradually through the course of a long slow afternoon that stretched out and rolled over like a dog on a rug, and she'd worked in the kitchen with some of the others, chopping herbs, onions and tomatoes for the lentil soup and singing along to the Airplane and Country Joe and the Fish. Somebody was passing a pipe and she took a hit or two from that, and she'd kept a fruit jar topped up with Spañada right next to her throughout the cooking and the washing up and the meal that went on like the Last Supper while a guy named Sky Dog or maybe it was Junior Sky Dog played acoustic guitar and sang verses he made up on the spot. The blond kids from the morning were there, naked still, lentil soup streaking their torsos like war paint, and there was a baby in a wicker papoose strapped to the back of a gaunt tall woman with eyes that were like two craters sunk into her head. People were everywhere, people she'd never seen before – the weekend hippies up from the city – and her brothers and sisters too. Smoke rose from joss sticks, from grass and hash threaded

5

meticulously from hand to hand as if they were all collectively stitching a quilt in the air. A pair of rangy yellow dogs sniffed at people's feet and thrust their snouts in the bowls that lay scattered across the floor.

Star was perched up on a throne of old couch pillows in the corner, along with Ronnie and a new girl whose name she'd forgotten. She wasn't feeling anything but tired, and though the whole thing – the whole scene – was fantastic, like summer camp without the counselors, a party that never ends, she was thinking she'd had enough, thinking she might just slip off and find a place to crash and let the sleep wash over her like a dark tide of nothing. Ronnie's leg lay across her own, and she could just barely feel the new girl's hair on her shoulder like a sprinkle of salt or sugar. She closed her eyes, let herself drift. The music began to fade, water sucked down a drain, water that was rushing over her, a creek, a river, one pool spilling into the next . . . but then one of the kids let out a sudden sharp wail and she came back to the moment. The kid, the little boy with his bare abdomen and dangling parts and his missing front teeth that gave him the look of a half-formed little ghoul, slapped something out of his mother's hand – Reba, that was her name, or maybe it was Rena? He let out another shriek, high and mechanical, but that was the beginning and the end of it, because Reba just held a joint to his lips and then sank back into the pillows as if nothing had happened.

Nothing had. No one seemed to notice or care. Sky Dog had been joined by a second guitarist now, and they were working their way through the steady creeping changes of a slow blues. A topless woman no one had ever seen before got up and began to hump her hips and flap her enormous breasts to the beat; before long, a couple of the commune's more or less permanent members rose up from the floor to join her, swaying in place and snaking their arms like Hindu mystics.

"A tourist," Ronnie said, the syllables dry and hard on his tongue. "Weekend hippie." He was wearing a Kmart T-shirt Star had tie-dyed for him on their first day here, orange supernovae bursting out of deep pink and purple galaxies, and when he turned to the new girl the light behind him made his beard translucent. "You're no tourist," he said. "Right, Merry?"

Merry leaned back into the cradle of his arm. "I am not ever going back," she said, "I promise you that."

"Right," Ronnie said, "right, don't even think about it." Then he slipped his free arm around Star's shoulders and gave her a squeeze, and "Hey," he was saying, caught up in the slow-churning engine of the moment, "you want to maybe go down by the river and spread a blanket under the stars and make it – just the three of us, I mean? You feel like it?" His eyes were on the dancing woman, up one slope and down the other. "Would that be righteous, or what?"

And here was the truth: Star *didn't* feel like it. Nor, despite what she'd told herself, had she felt like it that night in the teepee either. It was Ronnie. Ronnie had talked her into undressing in front of the other guy – or no, he'd shamed her into it. "You don't want to be an uptight bourgeois cunt like your mother, do you?" he'd said, his voice a fierce rasp in her ear. "Or *my* mother, for shitsake? Come on, it's all right, it's just the human body, it's natural – I mean, what is this?"

The other guy, the teepee guy – she never knew his name – just watched her as if she were a movie he'd never seen before. He was sitting there yoga style, the very avatar of peace and love, but you could see he was all wound up inside. He was intense. Freakish, even. She could feel it, some sort of bad vibe emanating from him, but then she told herself she was just being paranoid because of the peyote. So she lay back, crossed her legs at the ankles and stared into the fire. No one said anything for the longest time. And when she looked up finally the teepee guy's eyes were so pale there were no irises to them, or hardly any, and Ronnie rolled a joint and helped her off with her blue denim shirt with all the signs of the zodiac she'd embroidered up and down the sleeves and across the shoulders, and he was in his shorts and the teepee guy – *cat,* teepee *cat,* because Ronnie was always correcting her, you don't call men guys you call them cats – was in some sort of loincloth, and she was naked to the waist. The firelight rode up the walls and the smoke found the hole at the top.

"Just like the Sioux camped on the banks of the Little Bighorn, right, man?" Ronnie said, passing the joint. And then time seemed to ripple a bit, everything sparking red and blue-

7

green and gold, and Ronnie was on top of her and the teepee guy was watching and she didn't care, or she did, but it didn't matter. They made it on an Indian rug in the dirt with this *cat* watching, but it was Ronnie, and she fit the slope of his body, knew his shoulders and his tongue and the way he moved. Ronnie. Pan. From back home. But then he rolled off her and sat there a minute saying, "Man, wow, far out," breathing hard, sweat on his forehead and a tiny infinitesimal drop of it fixed like a jewel to the tip of his nose, and he made a gesture to the teepee cat and said, "Go ahead, brother, it's cool – "

Outside, at the main gate to the Drop City ranch, there was a plywood sign nailed clumsily to the wooden crossbars: no men, no women – only children. That was about it, she was thinking, nothing but children, Show and Tell, and show and show and show. Ronnie's arm was like a dead thing, like a two-ton weight, a felled tree crushing her from the neck down. The big topless woman danced. *Got to keep movin',* Junior Sky Dog was singing, *movin' on down the line.*

"So what do you say?" Ronnie wanted to know. His face was right there, inches from hers, the pale fur of his beard, the dangle of his hair. His eyes were fractured, little ceramic plates hammered into the sheen there and then smashed to fragments. She said nothing, so he turned to Merry, and Star watched the new girl's face.

Merry had her own version of the million-kilowatt smile, wide-mouthed and pretty, and she was all legs in a pale yellow miniskirt that looked as if it hadn't been washed in a month. She looked first to Ronnie, then stared right into Star's eyes before letting her gaze drift out across the room as if she were too stoned to care, but she did care, she *did* – Star could see it in the self-conscious way she ducked her head and tugged at the hem of her dress and the dark indelible line of dirt there where she'd tugged at it a thousand times before. "I don't know," she said, her voice nothing but air. And then she shrugged. "I guess."

The two blond kids were dancing now, the vacant-eyed boy of four or five and his little sister, watching their feet, no sense of rhythm, none at all, the boy's little wadded-up tube of a penis flapping like a metronome to another beat altogether. "Cool,"

Ronnie said. And then he turned to her, to Star, and said, "What about it, Star, what do you say?"

She said, "I don't think so. Not tonight. I'm feeling – I don't know, *weird*."

"Weird? What the fuck you talking about?" Ronnie's brow was crawling and his mouth had dropped down into a little pit of nothing – she knew the look. Though he hadn't moved a muscle, though for all the world he was the hippest coolest least-uptight flower-child *cat* in the universe, he was puffing himself up inside, full of rancor and Ronnie-bile. He got his own way. He always got his own way, whether it was a matter of who he was going to ball and when or what interstate they were going to take or where they were going to spend the night or even what sort of food they were going to eat. It didn't matter if they were passing through Buttwash, Texas, the Dexamil wearing off and eggs over easy the only thing she could think about to the point of obsession and maybe even hallucination, he wanted tacos, he wanted salsa and chiles and Tecate, and that's what they got.

"No, come on now, don't be a bummer, Paulette. You know what the Keristan Society says, right there in black and white in the *Speeler?* Huh? Don't you?"

She did. Because he quoted it to her every time he felt horny. Whoever they were, the Keristanians or Keristanters or whatever they wanted to call themselves, they preached Free Love without prejudice – that is, making it with anybody who asked, no matter their race or creed or color or whether they were fat and old or retarded or smelled like the underside of somebody's shoe. It was considered an act of hostility to say no to anybody who wanted to ball, whether you felt like it or not – it's seven a.m. and you're hungover and your hair looks like it's been grafted to your head, and some guy wants to ball? You ball him. Either that, or you're not into the scene because you're infected with all your bourgeois hangups just like your fucked-up parents and the rest of the straight world. That was what the Keristan Society had to say, but what she was thinking, or beginning to think, in the most rudimentary way, was that Free Love was just an invention of some *cat* with pimples and terminally bad hair and maybe crossed eyes who couldn't get laid any other way or under any other

9

regime, and she wasn't having it, not tonight, not with Ronnie and what's her name.

"No, Ronnie," she said, lifting his arm off her shoulder and letting it drop like the deadweight it was, "n-o." She was on her feet now, looking down at him, at the tiny dollop of his face and the girl staring up at her with her smile fading like a brown-out. "I don't give a shit about the Keristan Society. I'm going to bed. And don't call me that."

He was hurt, put-upon, devastated, clinging to the girl – Merry, that was her name, *Merry* – as if she were a crate on the high seas and his ship had just gone down. "Call you what?"

Breasts flapping, the little penis swaying, people hammering tambourines against their palms and the smoke of grass and incense roiling up off the floor like fog. "Don't call me Paulette," she said, and then she was gone, bare feet picking their way through the sprawled hips and naked limbs of her brothers and her sisters.

It was another morning. This one came in over the treetops with a glow that was purely natural because she hadn't been high for three days now because Ronnie was busy with Merry and the big tits woman, who was twenty-seven years old as it turned out and worked as a secretary for some shipping company. Her name was Lydia, and she'd found a welcoming mattress or two and decided to stay on and screw her job and the plastic world and her big straining flesh-cutting brassieres and the hair pins and makeup and all the rest. Star was indifferent. It wasn't as if she was in love with Ronnie or anything, she told herself. It was just that he was from back home and they'd been together on the road all that time, through the big bread pan of Iowa, yellow Nebraska, New Mexico in its shield of crumbling brown, brick-red Arizona, singing along to the Stones, Under My Thumb, Goin' Home, home, home, home. That was something. Sure it was. But as she maneuvered the bucket in under the first of the goats, she realized she was feeling good, clean and pure and good, without hangups or hassles, for the first time in as long as she could remember.

The moment was electric, and she could feel it through the soles of her bare feet, through her every pore: this was the life she'd envisioned when she left home, a life of peace and tranquillity, of love and meditation and faith in the ordinary, no pretense, no games, no plastic yearning after the almighty dollar. She'd got her first inkling of what it could be like back at home with Ronnie, with some people he knew who'd rented a collection of stone cottages in deep woods no more than a mile off the main highway. She and Ronnie would go there most nights, even nights when she had to get up and work in the morning, because she was living at her parents' still and this was a place where you could kick out your legs, drop all pretense and just be yourself. People from the surrounding cottages would gather in the last one down the row – two sisters from Florida had the place, JoJo and Suzie – because it was the biggest and it had a stone fireplace Suzie's boyfriend kept stoked all the time.

JoJo was older, twenty-four or twenty-five, and she'd been part of a commune in Vermont for a while – a place called Further – and on the good nights, when everybody wasn't so stoned they just sank wordlessly into the pillows on the floor and let the heartbeat of the stereo take over for them, JoJo used to reminisce about it. She'd gone there just after high school, alone, with six dollars in her pocket and a copy of *The Dharma Bums* under one arm, hooked up with a cat, and stayed three years. Her eyes would draw into themselves as she talked, and the ash on her cigarette would go white. She'd sit at the kitchen table and tell Star about the way it was when you could live with a group of people who just lit you up day and night, your real appointed mystical brothers and sisters, selected out of all the world just for you, and about the simple joys of baking bread or collecting eggs or boiling down the thin, faintly sweet sap of the sugar maples till you had a syrup that was liquid gold, like nothing anybody ever bought in a store.

Ronnie would be out in the main room – he was into heroin then – nodding and scratching and talking in a graveyard voice about cars or stereos or bands, and JoJo would have a pot of something going on the stove just in case anybody got hungry, and they did, they would, practically every night. This wasn't a commune – it wasn't anything more than a bunch of young people, hip people, choosing to live next door to one another – but to Star it seemed absolute. You could show up there, in any one of those cottages, at any time of the day or night and there'd always be someone to talk to, share a new record with – or a poem or drugs or food. Star would settle into the old rug by the fireplace, shoulder-to-shoulder with Ronnie, and listen to music all night long while a pipe or a joint went round, and when she wanted to just gossip or show off a new pair of boots or jewelry, she had Suzie and JoJo and half a dozen other girls to relate to, and they were like sisters, like dormmates, only better.

That was a taste, only a taste. Because before long the police zeroed in on the place and made it a real hassle even to drive down the dark overgrown street to get there, the flashing lights and out of the car and where are you going this time of night and don't I know you? And it was too dependent on drugs, everybody zoned out after a while, and no real cooperation – they all still had their own jobs in the plastic world. Suzie got busted, and then her boyfriend, Mike, and the whole thing seemed to just fade away. But now Star was here, in California, the sunshine ladled over her shoulders and the goats bleating for her, really part of something for the first time, something important. And how about this? Until two weeks ago, she'd never even seen a goat – or if she had, it might have been at a petting zoo or pumpkin patch when she was ten and her jaws were clamped tight over her braces because she wouldn't dare smile with all that ugly metal flashing like a lightbulb in her mouth – and here she was milking the two of them like an expert, like a milkmaid in a Thomas Hardy novel, Star of the D'Urbervilles, and the whole community dependent on her.

All right. The yellow milk hissed into the bucket. But then the second goat – it was either Amanda or Dewlap, and she couldn't tell them apart for all the squeezing and teat-pulling she'd done for how many mornings in a row now? – stepped in it, and the milk, which they were planning to use for yogurt, not to mention cornflakes and coffee, washed out into the dirt.

"Wow," said a voice behind her, " – an offering to the gods. I *am* impressed."

She was squatting in the shade of the oak tree they tethered the goats to overnight so as to prevent them from stripping every last green and burgeoning thing off the face of the earth, and she pulled up her smile and swung her head round. She was happy –

exalted, ready to shout out and testify, spilled milk and all – because this was what she'd always wanted, living off the land with her brothers and sisters, and fuck Ronnie, really, just *fuck him*. Okay. Fine. But she was smiling at nothing: there was no one there.

Was it that bad, then? Flashbacks were one thing, but aural hallucinations?

"Up here," the voice said, and she looked up into the broad gray avenues of the tree and saw the soles of a pair of dirt-blackened feet, feet like the inside of a tomb, and the naked white slash of a man's thighs and hips and then his bare chest and his hair and his face. He was grinning down at her. Spraddling a branch as big around as the pipes that fed water to the kids-on-bicycles and mom-in-the-kitchen suburban development where she'd grown up amidst the roar of lawnmowers and the smoke of the cooking grills. *Barbecue. Lilac bushes. K through 12.*

What could she say? She automatically raised the rigid plane of her hand to shield her eyes against the glare, but there was no glare, only the deep shadows of the tree and the soft glowing nimbus of the sun.

Behind him – to his left and just above him, and how could she have failed to notice it? – was a treehouse, the very image of the one her father had built for her in the wild cherry tree in their backyard when she turned eight because that was what she'd wanted for her birthday and nothing else. His voice came floating down to her: "Goats being naughty or were you really trying to propitiate the gods?"

Propitiate? Who *was* this guy?

"I was going to make yogurt – for everybody – but Dewlap here, or maybe it's Amanda – doesn't seem to want to cooperate."

"You need a goat wrangler."

"Right. You wouldn't be a goat wrangler, would you – by any chance, I mean?"

He was a naked man sitting in a tree. He laughed. "You got me pegged. But really that's only my avocation – my true vocation, what I was born here on this earth to do, is build treehouses. You like it, by the way?"

His name was Marco, and Norm Sender, the guy – cat –

who'd inherited these forty-seven sun-washed acres above the Russian River and founded Drop City two years ago, had picked him up hitchhiking on the road out of Bolinas. Marco had built the treehouse from scrap lumber in a single afternoon – yesterday afternoon, in fact, while she was taking a siesta, meditating, pulling weeds and scrubbing communal pots – and when he reached down a bare arm to her she took hold of his hand and he pulled her up onto the branch alongside him as if she weighed no more than the circumambient air. She was in his lap, practically in his lap, and he was naked, but not hard, because this wasn't about that – this was about brother- and sisterhood, about being up in a tree at a certain hour of the morning and letting the world run itself without them. "This is Mount Olympus," he said, "and we are the gods and givers of light, and can you see that stain in the dirt down there on the puny earth where the goat girl made sacrifice?"

She could, and that was funny, the funniest thing in the world, goat's milk spilled in the dirt and the unadorned tin pail on its side and the goats bleating and dropping their pellets and some early riser – it was Reba, blowsy, blown, ever-mothering Reba – coming out of the kitchen in the main house with a pan of dishwater to drip judiciously on the marguerites in the kitchen garden. She laughed till her chest hurt and the twin points of oxygen deprivation began to dig talons into the back of her head, and then he led her into the treehouse, six feet wide, eight long, with a carpet, a guitar, an unfurled sleeping bag and a roof of sweet-smelling cedar shake. And what was the first thing he did then? He rolled a joint, licked off the ends, and handed it to her.

2

The roadside was silken with ferns, wildflowers, slick wet grass that jutted up sharply to catch the belly of the fog, and he was standing there in his interrupted jeans with his thumb out. He was wearing a faded denim jacket, a T-shirt he hadn't washed in a week and a pair of hand-tooled red-and-black cowboy boots he'd got in Mexicali for probably a fifth of what he'd have paid in San Francisco, but they weren't holding up too well. The heels had worn unevenly for one thing, and to compound matters, the uppers had been wet through so many times the color was leached out of them. Up under his pantlegs, the boots were still new, but what you could see of them looked something like the rawhide twists they sold in a basket at the pet shop. His guitar was another story. It had never had a case, not that he could recall, anyway, so he'd wrapped it in a black plastic garbage bag for protection. Now, as he stood there, thumb extended, it was propped up against his leg like some lurid fungus that had sprung up out of the earth when nobody was looking.

It wasn't raining, not exactly, but the trees were catching the mist, and he'd tied his hair back with a red bandanna to keep the dripping ends of it out of his face. He had a knife in a six-inch sheath strapped to his belt, but it was for nonviolent purposes only, for stripping manzanita twigs of bark or gutting trout before wrapping them in tinfoil and roasting them over a bed of hot coals. There was water in his bota bag instead of wine (he'd learned that lesson the hard way, in the Sonoran Desert), and the Army surplus rucksack on his back contained a sleeping bag, a ground cloth, a few basic utensils and a damp copy of Steinbeck's *Of Mice and Men*. Just that morning he'd reread the opening pages – George and Lennie sitting by a driftwood fire in a world that promised everything and gave up nothing – while he made coffee and heated up a can of stew over his own campfire, and the dawn came through the trees in a slow gray seep. Marco was thinking about that, about how Lennie kept up his refrain *An' live off the fatta the lan'* despite all the sad dead weight of the evidence to the contrary, as the first of a procession of cars materialized out of the fog and shushed on past him as if he didn't exist.

He didn't mind. He was in no hurry. He wasn't so much running as drifting, anonymous as the morning, and yes, he'd had trouble with the law on a count of misdemeanor possession, dropped out of college, quit his job and then quit another one and another after that, and yes, he'd received the cold hard incontrovertible black-and-white draft notice in the gray sheet-metal mailbox out front of his parents' house in Connecticut, but that was two years ago now. In the interim – and here he thought of his favorite Steinbeck book of all, *Tortilla Flat* – he'd been trying to make things work on a different level, living simple, dropping down where the mood took him. Everybody talked about getting back to the earth, as if that were a virtue in itself. He knew what the earth was – he slept on it, hiked over its ridges and through the glare of the alkali flats, felt it like a monumental set of lungs breathing in and out when he woke beneath the trees in the still of the morning. That was something, and for now it was the best he could do. As for the cars: he hadn't been able to connect the night before either, and he'd found this place – this loop of the road hemmed in by white-bark eucalyptus that smelled of damp and menthol and every living possibility – and he bedded down by a creek so he could waken to the sound of water instead of traffic.

When the cars had passed it was preternaturally still, no sound but for birdcall and the whisper of the dripping trees. He waited a moment, listening for traffic, then slung the guitar over his shoulder and started walking up the road in the direction of Olema and Point Reyes. He got into the rhythm of his walking, feeling it in his calves and thighs like a kind of power, a man walking along the side of the road and he could walk forever, walk across the continent and back again and his face telling every passing car that he didn't give a damn whether they stopped for him or not. Twenty-five or thirty vehicles must have passed by and the sun had climbed up out of the fields to burn off the fog by the time a VW van finally stopped for him. It was practically new, the van, white above, burnt orange below, but as Marco came hustling up the shoulder he saw the peace sign crudely slashed on the side panel in a smear of white paint and knew he was home.

At the wheel was an older guy – thirties, maybe even late thirties – with an erratic beard that hung down over his coveralls and crawled up into his hair. He was wearing a pair of glasses in clunky black-plastic frames, and his smile had at least two gold teeth in it. "Hop in, brother," he said. "Where you headed?"

The slamming of the door, a rattling blast of the tinny engine, kamikaze insects and dust, the rucksack and guitar flung into the backseat like contraband, every ride a ritual, every ritual a ride. "North," Marco said. "And I really appreciate this, man," he said automatically, "this is great," and then they were off, the radio buzzing to life with an electric assault of rock and roll.

The visible world flew by for a full sixty seconds before the man turned to him and shouted over the radio, "North? That's a pretty general destination. What'd you have in mind – Sitka, maybe? Nome? How about Santa's Workshop? Santa we can do."

Marco just grinned at him. "Actually, I was going up to Sonoma – the Drop City Ranch?"

"Drop City? You mean that hippie place? Isn't that where everybody's nude and they just ball and do dope all day long? Is that what you're into?" The man looked him full in the face, no expression, then turned back to the road.

Marco considered. He could be anybody, this guy – he could be a narc or a fascist or a stockbroker or maybe even General Hershey himself. But the beard – the beard gave him away. "Yeah," Marco said, "that's exactly what I'm into."

It couldn't have much been past noon when they rolled through the hinge-sprung cattle gates and lurched up the rutted dirt road to the main house. This was the ultimate ride, the ride that takes you right on up to the porch and in the front door, and Marco had sat there, alive to it all, while Norm Sender roared, "Good answer, brother," and launched into a half-hour treatise on his favorite subject – his only subject – Drop City.

He was stoned on something – speed, from the look and sound of him – but that didn't factor into any of Marco's equations, because everybody he'd encountered for the past two years had either been high or coming down from a high, and he'd been there himself more times than he'd want to admit. At first, when he was nineteen, twenty, it was a matter of bragging rights – *Oh, yeah, so you did DMT and smoked paregoric at the concert? That's cool, but I'm into scag, man, that's all, I mean that's it for me. And acid. Acid, of course. And not to expand my mind or any of that mystical horseshit – just to get rocked, man, you know?* – but now it was just more of the same. How many of those conversations had he had? It felt like ten million, so much air in, so much out. Still, when Norm Sender lit up a roach and passed it to him, he took it and put it between his lips. That was what you did. That was the ritual.

They sat there, staring through the windshield, and smoked. When the roach was burned down to nothing, Norm lit a cigarette and passed that to Marco and Marco took a drag and passed it back. The road was like any road, burning silk in a sheen of fire, the trees like bombers coming in low. Marco settled back in his seat as the van rocked and swerved, even as the smoke climbed up the windows and Norm kept pushing at the frames of his glasses as if they'd been oiled. He was wearing a braided rope belt that couldn't contain the spill of his gut, there were spiky black hairs growing out of his ears and nostrils, and his arms were whiter than any farmer's ought to be. He talked and Marco listened, his voice a hoarse high yelp that plummeted into the noise soup of the radio and careened off the clacking whine of the engine.

"So like my parents?" (This by way of prelude, though Marco hadn't said a word about anybody's parents – they'd been talking nothing, talking good shit and groovy and the like, the radio hissing static as Norm manipulated the dial with his battered blunt fingers.) "Like my mother that gave me suck and my old dirt-blasted redneck cowboy of a father? They died. Bought the farm. Head-on collision with a truck full of Grade A fryers coming out of Petaluma on Route 116, and that might sound funny, the irony and all like that, but it isn't, because the old turd-dropper was blind drunk and my mother deserved better than that, but anyway, the son and heir gets the rancho in the hills – that's me, yours truly – and he's thinking he's feeling some kind of *discomfort* over this whole trip of ownership of the land, because nobody owns the land and he's thinking like Timothy Leary, *Let's mutate, man,* and so I come up with the concept of Voluntary Primitivism, and let me spell it out for you, man, LATWIDNO, Land Access to Which Is Denied No One, dig? You want to come to Drop City, you want to turn on, tune in, drop out and just live there on the land doing your own thing, whether that's milking the goats or working the kitchen or the garden or doing repairs or skewering mule deer or just staring at the sky in all your contentment – and I don't care who you are – you are welcome, hello, everybody – "

Two hours. So it went. Marco was in that phase where every high expectation gives way to something grimmer, darker, older, but when he saw the standing grass flecked with mustard and the oaks drinking up the earth, when he saw the milling dogs, goats, chickens, the longhaired men so attuned to what they were doing they barely glanced up, and the women – *the women!* – he felt something being born inside him all over again. He leaned forward and watched it all unscroll, huts, tents, truck gardens and citrus trees, a geodesic dome – or was that a yurt? Then the van came round a bend and the house leapt out at them from behind a screen of trees. It was there, and then it was gone. When it came into view again, Marco saw a two-story frame house with a sprawl of outbuildings, no different from what you'd see in Kansas or Missouri or any other place where farmers tilled the earth, except that somebody had painted the trim in Day-Glo orange and the rest a checkerboard pattern of green and pink so that the house wasn't a house anymore but a kind of billboard for the psychedelic revolution. The van lurched, dust rose up and killed the air, Norm grinning and flashing the peace sign all the while and a pair of yellow dogs loping along beside them, and then they were pulling into a rutted lot behind the house and Norm was shouting, "Home for the holidays, oh yes indeed!"

Holidays? What holidays? And Marco was wondering about that, about what holiday it might have been in the middle of May – he wasn't sure what the date was, but it couldn't have been later than maybe the fifteenth or sixteenth – when Norm turned to him with a grin. "Just an expression, man – and I want to be the very first to wish you a *Merry Christmas!* But really, every day's a holiday at Drop City, because the *straight* world is banned, absolutely and categorically, do not pass through these gates, Mr. Jones, dig?"

What could he do but smile and nod and lend a hand as his benefactor began to unload supplies from the back of the van, cans of ketchup, peanut butter, honey, sacks of bulgur wheat, sesame seeds, brown rice, raw almonds and rolled oats, tools, a rebuilt generator, a whole raft of bread – "Barter, man, barter, broccoli for bread, cukes for bread, eggplant, and can you say rutabaga?" – and two big brown-paper bags that must have had thirty record albums in them. And where was it all going? In the main house, four steps up onto the foot-worn back porch and into the kitchen, arms full, a homemade table, crude but honest, potted herbs in the window, shelves from ceiling to floor and institutional-sized cans of everything imaginable stacked up as if they were expecting a siege. And women, three of them: Merry, Maya and Verbie.

All three looked up when Marco followed Norm through the door and set his packages down on the table, smiling, yes, but he'd seen those smiles before – at Morning Star, Olompali, the Magic Farm, Gorda Mountain – and all but the last lingering residual flecks of brother- and sisterhood had been rinsed out of them. They were meant to be welcoming, these pale dry-lipped worried-over-the-porridge-blackened-into-the-bottom-of-the-pot brotherly-and-sisterly smiles, but how many had been welcomed already? He was new. A new cat. Another mouth to feed, and would he contribute, would he stay on and weed the garden, repair the roof and snake out the line from the plugged-up toilets to the half-dug septic field, would he be worth the investment of time and breath or would he just work his way through the women, smoke dope and drink cheap wine all day and then show up for meals with a plate in his hand? These were smiles with an edge, and they made him feel shy and unworthy.

He must have come up the steps six or seven times, arms laden with groceries, before anybody said anything to him. It was Merry, tall, dark-eyed, a sprig of baby's breath tucked behind one ear, who lifted her eyes and murmured, "Been on the road long?"

Norm wasn't there to answer for him – he'd wandered off shouting into the next room, tearing at the shrink-wrap on one of the new record jackets, and he left a vacuum behind him. Maya and Verbie were in the corner by the sink, leaning into the mounds of green onions, peppers, zucchini and carrots they were dicing for the pot and talking in flat low voices, and Merry had slipped across the room on bare feet to lift things out of the grocery bags and find places for them on the shelves. She was right there, two feet from him, smelling of garlic and cilantro, her eyes chasing vaguely after the question. Marco shrugged. The correct answer, more or less, was two years. But he didn't say that. He just said, "I don't know. A while."

And that was the end of the conversation. Merry's back was to him, the spill and sweep of her hair that floated on its own currents, the white knuckles of her hands as she lifted cans to the shelves, sun pregnant in the windows, the potted herbs uncurling like fingers and a cat (a *feline*, that is) Marco hadn't noticed till that moment lifting its head from its perch atop the refrigerator to fix him with a steely yellow-eyed gaze. The silence held half a beat more, till it was broken by the super-amplified hiss of a worn needle dropping on immaculate vinyl and a manic blast of drums and guitar filled the house. Two beats more. Then he ducked his head and edged back out the door.

Outside, beyond the dirt lot where Norm had parked the van, there was a more-or-less conventional backyard, with a pair of lemon trees, a flower garden and an in-ground pool that flashed light as a single swimmer – at this distance, Marco couldn't tell whether it was a man or woman – swam laps with the kind of loopy tenacity you see in caged animals. Dark head, tangled hair. Back and forth, back and forth. He had a sudden urge to strip down and plunge in, relieve himself of all the oils and stinks of the road and the lingering funk of the sleeping bag, but he didn't know anybody here and he was tentative yet – what he needed to do, before he got caught up in the rhythms of the place, was to decide where he was going to sleep for the night at least, and maybe beyond. Norm had pointed out a pile of scrap lumber behind one of the outbuildings as they came up the road – "Build," he'd shouted over the radio, "go ahead, build to suit, and I'm not going to be a policeman, I'm not going to be mayor, you do what you want" – and Marco thought he might have a look at it, to see what he might do. He wasn't exactly a master carpenter, but he was good enough, and aside from a couple of days on a construction crew in San Jose, he hadn't done any real labor in weeks. Why not? he was thinking. Even if he didn't stay, it was a way to pass the time.

He left his rucksack and guitar under one of the big snaking oaks in the front yard, then strolled back up the road to inspect the lumber. It wasn't much. A nest of two-by-fours weathered white, a couple of sheets of warped plywood, some odds and ends, most of it charred, and you didn't have to be Sherlock Holmes to see that Drop City had lost at least one dwelling to fire. He was separating the good stuff from the bad when a man in his early twenties came rolling out of the high grass on lubricated hips, walking as if he was dancing, his head too big and his feet too small. "What's happening?" the man said, bobbing up to him, and Marco saw that he was balancing a spinning rod in one hand and a stringer of undersized small-mouth bass in the other. His eyes were glassy and fragile, as if he'd just shuffled out the doors at the very end of a very long concert. What else? Deep tan, choker beads, cutoffs, huaraches, the world's sparsest beard.

Marco nodded, and gave back the tribal greeting: "What's happening?"

The man stood there studying him a minute, the faintest look of amusement on his face. "I'm Pan, he said, or Ronnie, actually, but everybody calls me Pan . . . and you're – ?"

"Marco."

"Cool. Going to build?"

"I guess so."

Ronnie frowned, rotating the toe of one sandal in the dirt. "With this shit?"

"From humble beginnings," Marco said, and he said it with a smile. "Hey, Thoreau paid something like twenty-eight dollars for his place on Walden Pond, and that was good enough to get him through a New England winter – "

"Yeah," Ronnie said, "but prices have gone crazy since then, right?"

"Right. This stuff is free. Talk about deflation, huh?"

But Ronnie didn't seem to get the joke. He stood there a long while, watching Marco bend to the pile of mismatched lumber, the fish already stiffening on the stringer. It was hot. A flock of crows sent up a jeer from somewhere off in the woods. "So what you building, anyway?" Ronnie asked finally.

It came to him then, and it took the question to elicit the response, because until that moment there was no shape before him. He saw the oak tree suddenly, the spread and penetrant shade of it, roots like claws, acorns, leaf litter, and beneath it, his guitar and rucksack propped casually against the trunk. He dropped a board at his feet.

"A treehouse," he said.

3

Pan was taking the day off. Pan was just going to stroke his shaggy fetlocks and blow on his pipes and mellow out, no sex today — he was rubbed raw from it — and no hassles, not with Merry, not with Lydia, not with Star. Not today. The morning had already been a kind of nightmare, nine a.m. and crawling up off the mattress in the front bedroom with a taste like warmed-over shit in the back of his throat, everybody piling into the rusted-out '59 Studebaker he and Star had bombed across the country in and then on into Santa Rosa to the county welfare office to apply for food stamps. It must have been a hundred degrees, the streets on fire, the tie-and-jacket TGIF world closing in, big-armed *mothers* going to the supermarket in their forty-foot-long station wagons and nobody with even so much as a roach to take the pain away.

It was late afternoon and Ronnie was stretched out by the pool, his hair greased to his head with the residue of a whole succession of dunkings in the vaguely greenish water — and shouldn't somebody dump some chlorine in it, isn't that the way it's done? — the sun holding up its end of the bargain, birds making a racket in the trees, the sound of somebody's harmonica drifting across the lawn along with the premonitory smells of dinner firming up in the big pots in the kitchen. Last night — or was it the night before? — it was veggie lasagna with tofu and carrots standing in for meat, and that was one of the better nights. Usually it was just some sort of rice mush flavored with stock and herbs and green onions and whatnot from the garden. He wasn't complaining. Or actually, he was. His food stamps were going into the communal pot along with everybody else's, and that he could live with, but Norm — Norm was insane, because Norm insisted on feeding anybody who showed up, even bums and

24

winos and the spade cats from the Fillmore, who incidentally seemed to have taken over the back house in the past week, with no sign of leaving.

They'd come up over the weekend, seven of them crammed into an old Lincoln Continental with fins right off a spaceship that could have taken them to Mars and back, very cool, very peaceful, just checking out the scene. Ronnie had been on the front porch with Reba, Verbie, Sky Dog and a couple of others, watching the light play off the trees and doing their loyal best to cadge change off the tourists who always seemed so timid and *thankful* to be able to do something to support the lifestyle, because they really believed in everything that was going down here, they really did, but their mother was sick and they were behind in their house payments and the orthodontist was threatening to rip the wires off their kids' teeth, and could they just sit here a minute on the porch, would that be cool? Some of them would bring cameras, and Sky Dog would charge a quarter for a picture with a real down and authentic hippie in full hippie regalia, and the braver ones would stay for supper and line up with a tin plate in their hands and maybe even take a toke or two of whatever was going round once the bonfire was lit and the guitars emerged from their cases. They'd even sing along to Buffalo Springfield tunes or Judy Collins or Dylan, if anybody could remember the words. Just like summer camp. Then they got in their Fords and Chevys and VW Bugs and Volvos and went home.

The spades were different. They didn't so much emerge from the car as uncoil from it, all that lubricious menacing supercool spade energy – and Ronnie wasn't a racist, not at all, he was just maybe a bit more *experienced* than the rest of his brothers and sisters here at Drop City, who, after all, were maybe just a wee bit starry-eyed and *lame* – and they came across the dirt lot in formation, like a football team. Lester was the name of the one in charge. He was soft-looking, small, with a face made out of putty, and he was wearing a red silk scarf and high-heeled boots. "Peace, brother," he said, spreading wide his middle and index fingers and looking Ronnie in the eye. Ronnie didn't say anything, but Sky Dog and the rest flashed the peace sign and made the usual noises of greeting in return. A heartbeat later Lester was sitting on the steps of the porch, taking a hit from the pipe that was going round, his black bells hiked up to show off red socks and the elastic tops of his Beatle boots, while the others milled around in the dirt, looking needful.

"So this is the famous Drop City," Lester said, exhaling. His voice was so soft you had to strain to hear it, and that was a kind of trick, not so much an affectation as a *device* to make you pay attention.

Verbie, who never shut up for long, said, "Yes it is."

"We, uh – me and my amigos here – we heard all sorts of out of sight things about this place, like from the Diggers' soup kitchen? You know, in the Fillmore?" Lester gave a quick glance around the porch, then handed the pipe to one of his amigos, and then it went around to all of them and back again up onto the porch, and it was exactly like two tribes meeting on the high plains, peace, brother, and circulate the pipe. "Is it really as cool as they say it is? Like all brothers are welcome?"

The hippies on the porch fell all over themselves assuring him that that was the case, and everybody was thinking Hendrix, Buddy Miles, Free Huey, except Lester, because he just stretched out his legs and settled in.

Now, though – now Ronnie was crashed by the pool, just taking the day off from everything and everybody, never mellower, the smallest little hit of mescaline wearing down the sharp edges of things. Reba's kids – Che and Sunshine – were making a racket with one of those plastic trikes, humping it up and down the strip of concrete on the far side of the pool, and the communal horse – they called him Charley, Charley Horse, what else? – was stomping and snorting up a storm because some head from Daly City whose name escaped Ronnie at the moment was trying to get him to jump a shrunken sun-blasted strip of oleander at the base of the lawn, but that was all right, that was nothing. Ronnie drank it all in, feeling magnanimous. He was Pan. He was stoned. The sun was in the sky and the earth was a good place, a groovy place, a place designed by some higher power – *higher* power – for the sensory awakening and spiritual uplift of every one of his brothers and sisters.

Until nightfall, that is. The night came seething and festering up out of the shadows that bunched themselves in circus shapes at the feet of the trees and in the clotted scrub that chased the hillside round and round. He was feeling a little – well, a little *jittery*. There'd been an interlude there where he'd let things slide, a second hit of the mesc, a bottle of red wine and a couple of hits of something somebody had been smoking after dinner, and he hadn't even made dinner, had he? Dinner. Big pots full of mush, women with their tits hanging, health and simplicity and the good rural life. The pool glistened like oil, like blood, in the fading light. He wasn't hungry.

He had a sudden urge to see Star, to just sit with her someplace quiet and talk about home, the little routines and reminiscences that had kept them going all the way across the flat shag of the Midwest and into the Rockies and beyond – Mr. Boscovich and tenth grade biology and how he would call everything *material,* as in *these cells are constructed of cellular material,* the way the books in the school library smelled of soap and burning leaves, the afternoon Robert Stellner, the straightest kid in the school, stuck his head in a bag of model airplane glue and carved the mysterious message *Yahweh* into his chest with a penknife while standing in front of the mirror in the boys' room, all of that – but Star was up in the tree with the new guy all the time, and that rankled, it did, all the shit about Free Love and the Keristan Society notwithstanding. He pushed himself up off the pavement, but that was a bit much, so he sat back down again. The pavement was warm still, and that made him think of the rattlesnake somebody had seen out here just two nights ago. "They come for the warmth," that's how Norm had put it, " – and you can deal with that or you can kill 'em, skin 'em and eat 'em, but then you'll have bad snake karma your whole life and maybe into the next one, and do you really want that?"

From the main house, the sounds of laughter, conversation, music, all blended in a murmur that was like some sort of undercurrent, as if that was where the real life was, the only life, and this out here, this nature and this crepitating dark, was for losers – losers and snakes. Lydia was in there, and Merry, Verbie and the rest of them. Maybe he'd get up and go inside, just for the human warmth and companionship, because that's what Drop City was all about, companionship, a game of cards maybe, or Monopoly – but then the image of Alfredo clawed its way into the forefront of his brain, and he thought maybe he wouldn't.

Alfredo was one of the founding members of the commune, one of Norm Sender's inner circle, one of those sour-faced ascetic types, twenty-eight, twenty-nine, Reba's old man. He was always going on about natural childbirth and how Reba had cooked up the afterbirth and everybody shared a piece of it and how Che and Sunshine had been born outside under the moon and the stars, but he was an uptight, tight-assed jerk nonetheless, and two days ago Ronnie had gotten into it with him over some very pointed criticism about *volunteering* to do wash-up or haul trash or dig a new septic field because all these *people* were clogging up the commune's only two working toilets until they were rivers of *shit,* and he wouldn't mind, would he? Hell, yeah. He minded. He didn't come all the way out here to California to dig *sewers*. Jesus Fucking Christ.

That was what he was thinking, sitting there on the warm snake-loving pavement with the night festering around him, just a little shaky, but pissed off too, royally pissed off, when Lester and one of the other spade cats – Franklin, his name was Franklin – appeared out of nowhere with a jug of wine. "Hey, brother," Lester breathed, easing himself down beside him, " – what you doing out here, swimming?"

"I don't know. Yeah. I guess. I was swimming before – earlier, you know?" The words seemed to be stuck in his mouth, like the crust at the bottom of a pan. "Kind of cold now, I guess. But what's happening with you?"

Franklin was just standing there, the jug of wine – Cribari red – dangling from his fingertips like a big glass bomb. Lester grinned. "Same old shit," he said. "We're having a party in the back house, brother, and you're welcome to join us – we'd be real pleased about that, in fact; I would, at least – how about you, Franklin?"

Franklin said he'd be pleased too.

"By the way," Lester said, and they were already gathering themselves up, "you wouldn't happen to have a couple of hits of that mescaline I heard you got left, would you?"

Well, he did. And two minutes later he was in the back house and there were six or seven cats sitting around listening to Marvin

Gaye out of a battery-powered portable stereo with a blown bass, thump, thump, *blat,* thump, thump, *blat.* Sky Dog was there, cradling his guitar, somebody had lit a couple of scented candles because there was no electricity in the back house, and there was a new girl there – a chick – and she couldn't have been more than fourteen or fifteen. A runaway. What was her name? Sally. Where was she from? Santa Clara. And what was her father like? He was a son of a bitch. They probably got twenty a week just like her, and none of them stayed more than a night or two, as if this whole thing – Norm Sender, Alfredo, Reba, Drop City itself – was no more than a kind of extended slumber party.

Ronnie introduced himself as Pan, gave her a little brotherly and sisterly squeeze, and then settled in on the floor against the back wall and took it upon himself to make sure the jug kept circulating. All was peace. Silken voices murmuring, Marvin Gaye, Sly and the Family Stone, Hendrix, thump, thump, *blat,* and Pan was in the middle of an elaborate story about a free concert in Central Park and the good and bad drugs he'd done that night and how somebody had vomited all over the wind-shield of his mother's car, which he'd borrowed with every warning and proscription attached, when Sally, the skinny-legged fourteen-year-old runaway in the patched jeans and stretch top, cried out. Or she screamed, actually. "Get off me, you freak!" she let out in a piping wild adolescent vibrato that shot up the scale like feedback, and Ronnie glanced away from his story to see Lester simultaneously pinning her down and going at her breasts with both hands and the pink slab of his tongue, and Sky Dog – *Sky Dog,* Mr. Mellow Peace-and-Love himself – stripped to his tanned buttocks and working hard to peel her jeans down the flailing sticks of her legs.

Ronnie was right in the middle of a story, his voice droning on through the standard interludes and rich with the twenty nasal catchphrases of the day, and he was so *mellowed out* he could barely keep his head up off the floor, but this – this scream, this scene going down in the corner – sent a shock wave through him. *"Get off, get off!"* the girl kept screaming, and now her legs were bare and Sky Dog's buttocks were clenching and thrusting in a way that hurt to watch, a way that was wrong, dead wrong, and Ronnie tried to get up off the floor, tried to say, *Hey, man, what do you think you're doing,* because this wasn't right, it wasn't – but by the time he got to his feet he realized everyone in the room was looking at him with eyes that had no brotherly or even human spark in them.

In the morning, which came hurtling out of the sky like a Russian missile aimed straight at his brain, Pan opened his eyes on the stiff tall grass and the golden seedheads drooping over him as if he were already dead and decomposed. He seemed to be lying supine in the weeds beyond the back house, and this was a nasty little surprise, speaking of snakes, rattle or otherwise. His hair was stiff with dirt and bits of twig and chaff, and when he rubbed the back of his skull he felt an unevenness there, as if some essential fluid – *blood,* that is – had leaked out of him and coagulated in a bristling lump. He felt bad. Bad in every way. But most of all, he felt thirsty, and he saw himself rising up out of the sun-blasted weeds and staggering first to the hose on the back lawn and then to the pool, where the dried blood – and there seemed to be a rough granulated gash over his cheekbone too – would dissolve and boil up around him in a dull brown cloud of cellular material gone to waste.

It must have been noon or maybe even later, because people were gathered round the lawn and the pool coping with metal plates of lunchtime mush in their hands, eyes shining, hair flowing, all the colors of their sarongs and T-shirts and burnished flesh aglow as if everybody was a lightbulb and they just kept shining and shining. A couple of people made comments – "Rough night, huh?" – and laughed and joshed him in a brotherly and sisterly way when he bent to the hose and let the silver liquid flow in and out of his mouth in a long glowing arc. He couldn't figure out what was wrong with him, or what was most wrong – hangover, drug depletion or blood loss, and had he been in a fight, was that it? He tried to focus, tried to bring up the image of that girl on the floor in the back house, but the only thing that came into his mind was a phrase he'd used a thousand times, two truncated monosyllabic words that did nobody or no thing justice at all: *Free Love.*

Reba's kids were there, nice day, lunch outside, not enough seats in the meeting roomdining hall anyway, and they were chasing each other around the pool as if they'd never stopped, their cheeks distended with corn mush and cauliflower, their bodies naked and brown and stippled with cuts, contusions, poison oak, dirt. He dropped the hose and moved toward the water like a zombie. Then he was in, the green envelope, the cessation of sound, his limbs moving under command of the autonomous system, pump and release, pump and release, till he cracked his head on the far side of the pool and heaved himself streaming from the water.

Somebody else was in now, cannonballing and shouting, the two yellow dogs barking at their heels, Lydia – was that Lydia? – and the greenish water lapped at his knees and he was feeling he ought to shake the water out of his hair and get himself a plate of mush just for the ballast, when he locked eyes with Alfredo across the lawn. Alfredo gave him a look, niggardly little eyes, his mouth like a wad of gum stuck up under a desk at school, and Ronnie gave him a look back. He wasn't going to take any shit. He had as much right as anybody to be here – LATWIDNO, right? – and he wasn't about to apologize to Alfredo or Norm Sender or anybody else. Then he felt a hand on his knee and it was Lydia, her breasts bobbing, the hair pressed flat to her head. "Where you been?" she said. "We looked all over for you last night." The water lapped, dragonflies hovered. And then: "Did you hear what happened?"

No, he hadn't heard.

She blinked the water out of her eyes, snaked a hand up his leg, and he felt himself go hard against the rough wet folds of his cutoffs. "A girl got raped."

"Raped? What do you mean *raped?*"

"I mean she was some runaway – fourteen, she was only fourteen – and Norm's freaked about the whole thing, running around the kitchen jabbering about the man – the man's coming, the man's coming – and hide the dope and all, and clean this shit up, and do this and do that, and Alfredo's right there with him. They want Lester out. And Sky Dog and the rest of them."

Ronnie considered this, the water lapping at his legs, Lydia's breasts bobbing at his ankles, her hand crawling up his thigh. His normal response would have been something like "Bummer" or "Heavy," but the moment was huge and hovering and his head wasn't clear yet, not even close, so he just stared down at the white ghosts of her legs kicking rhythmically beneath the surface.

"What I hear is they got her stoned, and then they pinned her down, and it wasn't just Lester and Sky Dog either. It was all of them." She paused, kicking, kicking, the slow fluid rhythm of her legs. Che threw something – a scarred Frisbee – at his sister and she let out a shriek, and then the dogs started barking and Reba, at the far end of the pool, went off on a laughing jag, ha-ha, ha-ha, ha-ha. Lydia's hand was cold. She clutched him tighter. "Somebody said you were there," she breathed, and then trailed off.

He was there. Sure he was. And he'd gotten into it with a couple of them too, hadn't he? Sure, sure. He must have. Because he didn't care how stoned he was or how voluntarily primitive it got, he wasn't about to stand by and watch something like that . . . And the thought of it, the thought of that cheap little acidic moment in the back house with all those null and void faces and the thump, thump, *blat* of the stereo and the girl with her stick legs flailing just made him feel so black inside he wished he'd never left home himself. What could he say? How could he explain it?

"Yeah," he said, "yeah. I was there."

Lydia seemed to consider this a moment, her eyes glittering like planets in the uncharted universe of her face. She was a big girl, big in the shoulders and the hips, big all over, black hair, everted lips, flecks of eye shadow caught in her lashes like drift washed up on a beach. Her legs kicked beneath the surface. Her hand tightened on his thigh. She blinked the water out of her eyes and gave him half a smile. "You want to rape me too?" she said.

4

Alfredo was the one who called the meeting, eight p.m., the supper dishes mostly washed, or soaking anyway, and everybody feeling lazy and contented, six pans of brownies cooling on the kitchen table and the promise of a movie afterward (Charlie Chaplin, one Star hadn't seen – something about Alaska, was that possible?). A few people had dressed for the occasion, Verbie in particular, because a meeting was really the template for a party, everybody already collected from their huts and yurts and the back bedrooms and all those acres of strung-out woods, and why not, Star was thinking, why not? Party on. If you thought about it, even peeling potatoes for the veggie stew or hacking the weeds out of the garden was a kind of party. It certainly wasn't work, not in any conventional sense, not when you were surrounded by your brothers and sisters and nobody was standing over you with a time clock.

By half past seven, Verbie was parading around in a lime green cape over a pink ruffled blouse, her face painted the color of the cracked saltillo tiles Norm had inexplicably dumped on the west side of the house one morning before anybody was awake. Jiminy was right there with her, wearing a high hat and tails with nothing underneath but a pair of Donald Duck briefs, some new guy was playing bongos, rat-a-tat-tat, the dogs and even the goats were in a high state of alert, and Maya swept in the door in a Goodwill wedding gown that looked as if the moths weren't done with it yet. And Ronnie? Ronnie was Ronnie, keep it simple. Star settled for a little face paint – a peace sign on each cheek and a third eye, replete with false lashes, centered in the middle of her forehead.

It must have been eight-thirty or so by the time Reba came in and lit some candles and set two pots of chamomile tea and a tray of thick ceramic mugs on the big table at the front of the room. That was the signal, or so Star thought, and she settled in on the floor beside Marco, Ronnie, Merry and Lydia, but it was another half hour before Norm Sender showed up and Alfredo lifted an old circus-prop megaphone to his lips and began saying, "All right, people, all right – can I have your attention up here for just a minute, and we're going to make this as painless as possible, I promise you – "

Star was feeling good, very good – blissful, even – as she sank into the pillows and Marco put his arm around her and one of the yellow dogs threaded its way across the room to settle at her side and prop a big yellow head on her knee. Everything seemed to converge in that moment, all the filaments of her life, the tugging from one pole to another, Ronnie, Marco, the teepee cat, her parents and the job and the car and the room she'd left behind, because this was her family now, this was where she belonged. She stretched her legs, gazed up at the drift of cobwebs stretched out across the ceiling like miniature cloudbanks and the craneflies straining against them. Until Drop City, she'd never belonged anywhere.

Who had she been in high school? Little Miss Nobody. She could have embroidered it on her sweaters, tattooed it across her forehead. And in smaller letters: i am shit, i am anonymous, step on me. please. She wasn't voted Most Humorous in her high school yearbook or Best Dancer or Most Likely to Succeed, and she wasn't in the band or the Spanish Club and when her ten-year reunion rolled around nobody would recognize her or have a single memory to share. The guys noticed her, though. In college they did, anyway. They noticed her big time, noticed her in the hallway and the cafeteria and downtown in the claus-trophobic aisles of the record store, their eyes glazed with lust and a kind of animal ferocity they weren't even aware of. She dated a few of them, but she'd never had a serious boyfriend, and though she was pretty – she knew she was pretty – she couldn't figure out why that was, except that something was out of sync, as if she'd been born in the wrong era and the wrong place, especially the wrong place, where nothing ever happened and nobody ever got anywhere. That's what it was, she decided, that had to be it, and the notion comforted her through all her disappointments and the cardboard array of days and months and years, each as stiff and unyielding as the one that preceded it. She sat through the banal Education classes, Psych 101, faced down the six primary causes of World War I, algorithms and the internal anatomy of the earthworm, thinking there had to be something more.

She graduated, put on a face and started teaching third grade in the very elementary school she'd attended ten years earlier, living in her girlhood room in her parents' house like a case of arrested development, and she was just like her mother everybody said, because her mother taught kindergarten and wore cute petite-size pantsuits and mauve blouses with Peter Pan collars and so did she. But she didn't want to be just like her mother. When she got home at night she balled up her pantyhose in her own petite-size pantsuits, flung them on the floor in her room and lay stretched out on the floor with a speaker pressed to each ear, staring at the flecks and whorls of the thrice-painted ceiling while Janis Joplin flapped and soared over the thunderous changes of "Ball and Chain." Her mother chattered through dinner, the lace curtains from Connemara hung rigid at the windows, her father guarded his plate as if someone were about to take it from him. She could barely lift the fork to her lips, peas, meat loaf, cod in cream sauce, Brussels sprouts. *And what about Tommy Nardone, is he behaving in class, because I had his brother Randy, and believe you me,* her mother would say, and she'd nod and agree and go back up to her room and study the sneers of the Rolling Stones on the jacket of the *Out of Our Heads* LP. And then she went to buy makeup at Caldor one rinsed-out dead bleak soul-destroying October afternoon and ran into Ronnie in the record section – Oh, yeah, he'd dropped out, all right, and he was hustling records just until he could save the *bread* to get out to California, because that's where it was happening, there and no place else. Oh, yeah. *Miniskirt. Head shop. The Haight. Lucy in the Sky with Diamonds.*

"There's been some problems," Alfredo was saying, "and I'm sure everybody's hip to them, but we all – I mean, me, Norm, Reba and like everybody that was working the communal garden this morning? – we all felt things had come to a head . . ."

"Which head?" Ronnie said, propping himself up on his elbows. "I think there's more than one here, man."

"Uneasy lies the head – " Merry chimed in.

Ronnie swung round, playing to the crowd: "Heads of the world, unite!"

There was some foot-stomping, a spatter of applause and a whinny or two of laughter that might have had a bit too much fuel behind it. Alfredo merely sat there, slumped over the table, his eyes burning into every face in the room. When the noise died down, he continued: "Yes, but you all know that two toilets are inadequate for a commune this size, not to mention the fact that we're swamped with visitors every weekend, and with summer coming on it's just going to get worse – "

"Put up a sign," Jiminy said. He was skinny, nineteen, with a beard that might have washed up out of the sea, and he'd been here no more than a week or so. Star liked his style. She'd been sitting outside on her stump, snapping the tops off of green beans and talking bands with Merry, when he came winding up the road on a unicycle, a black Scottie dog levitating over the bumps behind him. I have *arrived!* he sang out, and *Scottie* too! Somebody ran over the dog two days later, and Jiminy had sat there in the tall weeds crying like a child. " 'Keep Out, No Trespassing, That Means You!' " he shouted now, oblivious to the irony. "That's what they did at the original Drop City, in Colorado. And Thunder Mountain too."

"Yeah, right, and who's going to decide who comes in and who doesn't? What, are we going to like hire pigs, is that it?" This was Verbie, swirling green-pink like a fruit drink in a blender. "Norm, what do you think? You going to be our policeman?"

Norm Sender was sitting cross-legged on the table, a cowbell suspended from a suede cord round his neck. He didn't even look up. "No way."

"The problem," Alfredo was saying, and his voice was strained now, as if he were trying to hold something back and it was choking him, "the problem is the shit in the woods. And everybody in this room is guilty – "

"Including the dogs," a voice boomed.

"Right, including the dogs. But it's unsanitary, people, and I mean, people aren't even bothering to bury it, that's our own people, the Drop City people – the weekend hippies just fling their trash – and their excrement – anywhere they feel like it.

And, speaking of which, there was that incident last night, in the back house, and you all know what I'm talking about."

There was a murmur of agreement. Verbie said two words – "Sky Dog" – and then somebody called out: "It was the spades."

"Really?" Alfredo let his eyes creep over the faces in the room. "Well, I don't know, maybe we better ask Pan over here – he was there, weren't you, Pan? Why don't you tell us about it? Come on, *Ronnie,* enlighten us all – tell us about peace and love, huh?"

Ronnie had been lying there limp amongst the pillows, his feet skewed at the nether ends of his stretched-out legs, but now he came up off the floor so fast he startled her – and startled the dog too. Suddenly he was standing there trembling in his cutoffs and tie-dye, and she was wishing she had a hit of something, anything, because this was Ronnie when the finger was pointing at him, this was Ronnie the victim, Ronnie the crucified saint. "I told you once, man, and I'm telling all of you now, I had nothing to do with it – "

"Yeah, right. It was Sky Dog, wasn't it?" Alfredo hissed. "And the *spades.*"

Ronnie let his eyes bleed out of his head, cool Ronnie, poor Ronnie, and he spread his palms wide in extenuation. "I mean, it's me, Pan, you all know me. You really think I would do something like that, no matter how stoned I was – ? Fourteen, she was only fourteen, jail bait no matter how you slice it. I'm not like that, I'm not that kind of person. You all know me, right? Right?"

Somebody up front, one of the founding members, stood up now too. Star couldn't see him at first, so she lifted her head up off the pillows and felt Marco adjust his position beside her. It was the guy – *cat* – everybody called Mendocino Bill, two hundred fifty pounds of hair wedged inside a pair of coveralls you could have used as a dropcloth. "Listen, people, this isn't the issue, and I'm with Pan, he's my brother and I believe in him – I mean, what is this, a kangaroo court or something? No, look, the issue is our black brothers out there. They've been intimidating people, and all they want to do is drink cheap wine and score dope and have one big nonstop party – and it's at our expense. Because they sure don't miss a meal, do they?"

"Racist," Verbie said. People began to hiss.

"It's not like that at all, man, and that's not fair" – Mendocino Bill's voice went up a notch – "because I of all people was in Selma and Birmingham and I wonder where the rest of you were cause I sure as hell don't remember seeing any of you down there, and I'm telling you I don't care who it is, we've got to police ourselves, people, or the Sonoma County sheriff'll come in here and do it for us – and I don't think there's anybody here wants that."

That was when everybody started talking at once, accusations flying, people making bad jokes, somebody hitting a sour note on a harmonica over and over and Ronnie slipping out of the spotlight and settling back into the nest of pillows like a lizard disappearing into a crevice. Lydia took hold of his hand and Merry gave him a million-kilowatt smile, but he reached over to her, to Star, to make his plea. He was shaking his head, and this was for Marco too, because Marco was right there with his eyelids rolled back and his ears perked: "I swear," Ronnie said. "I swear I didn't do a thing."

"Bum's rush!" Jiminy shouted. "Kick 'em out!"

"Who?"

"The spades! Kick 'em the fuck out! Norm, come on, *Norm* – "

All eyes went to Norm Sender where he sat Buddha-like in the center of the table, and for a fraction of a moment, everyone exhaled. But Norm was having none of it – he ducked his head and shrank down to half his size. "Land Access to Which Is Denied *No* One," he said.

"Somebody's got to do something – it's like *Lord of the Flies* out there, man."

"Oh, yeah, sure it is – and what's it like in here, then?"

"Hey, fuck you."

"No, fuck *you!*"

The whole thing was too much. Star lay there, propped up on her elbows, wishing they'd all just shut up, wondering where all the harmony and joy had gone to and why everybody had to hassle all the time, and then she looked at Ronnie, looked into his eyes, and saw a cold hard nugget of triumph there, sealed in, impervious to all things hip and the brotherly and the sisterly too. She was going to say something to him, she was going to call him out, when she felt the warmth leave her side as if it had evaporated and she was looking at Marco's frayed jeans and the dead bleached leather of his boots planted on the floor. "Hey," he was saying, "hey, everybody," and he put two fingers to his lips and produced one of those nails-on-the-blackboard sort of whistles you hear at ball games and rock concerts.

The room went quiet. Everybody was watching him. "Listen," he said, "why doesn't somebody just go talk to them?"

"Talk to them?" Alfredo was incredulous. "If they wanted to talk they'd be here now, wouldn't they? But no, they're up there drunk as usual, looking to ball some other fourteen-year-old chick." He glanced round the room. "Who's going to do it? You? Are you volunteering?"

"Yeah," Marco said, nodding slowly. "I guess I am."

That first day, the day when he lifted her up into his tree as if the breeze was blowing right through her, she'd felt like the heroine of some fairy tale, like Rapunzel – or no, that wasn't right. Like Leda maybe, Leda all wrapped in feathered glory. *Leda and the Swan.* That had been her favorite poem in Lit class, and she'd read it over and over till it was part of her, all that turmoil and fatality spinning out of a single unguarded moment, and that was something, it was, but what made her face burn and her fingers tingle was the weirdness of the act itself. Picturing it. Dreaming it. The flapping of the wings, the smell, the violence. All the other poems in the anthology were about flowers or death or Grecian urns, but this, this was about fucking a swan. She remembered her amazement, wondering how that could be – did birds even *have* penises? – and not just the mechanics of it, but the scene itself. Did he carry her off into the sky, or did it just feel that way? How big was he? And whose seed was he carrying – Zeus's, the professor said – but how did that work out, and wouldn't Helen be half-bird, then?

Marco had handed her a joint and she'd taken it reflexively. She'd had three days to clear her head, nothing stronger than Red Zinger running through her veins, Maya peeling onions and rattling on in her thin spidery voice about getting beyond drugs to a natural high, the oneness of the gurus, pure bliss in an overheated kitchen, but three days was enough. She needed something to kick-start her again, a quicker way to alter her consciousness than chanting *Om Mani Pema Hung* a thousand times, because her consciousness was clogged like a drain with all the residue of Ronnie and the dregs of back home. Plus, she had to admit she felt awkward in the presence of this new *cat* with his clothes off and his red-gold hair swinging like a curtain across his face and masking his eyes, because now that she was actually up there in his aerie, everything had changed. He didn't know what to say, and neither did she. The joint was an offering. It was the great equalizer, the holy communion, get wrecked and stare off into space and who actually needed to talk? They smoked it down to the last disintegrating nub of a roach, pressing it finger to finger, lip to lip, and neither of them said a word.

The air was sweet with the smell of it. Birds lighted on the split-wood railing and peered at them as if they were just another extension of the tree, some unlooked-for fruit or shell-less nut, or maybe some canker working its way out of the bark. She lay back, dissolving into herself while the sounds of the stirring commune – soft voices, the splash of the pool, music on the radio – drifted up to them from what seemed like miles away.

"Laundry day," he said, appending a strained little chuckle that was meant to set them both at ease, and it might have if it hadn't turned to dust in his throat. Behind him, a limp array of jeans, T-shirts, ragged underwear and mismatched socks lay spread-eagled over the branches as if they'd dropped down out of the sky. She pictured a sudden cataclysm, a whirlwind that had ripped the clothes off people's backs and spared the flesh beneath. Or bombers, high overhead, on their way to Vietnam, dropping soggy underwear instead of death.

"Yeah," was all she said, but it seemed as if the word stretched to eight syllables.

"It's been a week, at least. I was beginning to smell like roadkill."

"Tell me about it," she said, and suddenly all her burners were on high, "because when Ronnie and I drove across country it was exactly like that – you know Ronnie? *Pan,* I mean? Every town, we were trying to get our quarters together for the laundromat, but we either got lost or they'd never heard of washing machines and dryers and those little one-scoop boxes of

Tide and bleach – remember those? They just say *Bleach,* that's it. No brand name or anything, just *Bleach.* Don't you hate that?"

"Yeah," he said, staring at a place just over her shoulder and nodding as if he'd been there with them through every turning in every soulless gloom-blasted dead-end town Oklatexahoma could offer. "I guess. But isn't that what's wrong with the whole consumer society – brand names? – as if my soap's better than yours? See the U.S.A. in your Chevrolet. Buy, buy, buy, kill, kill, kill, eat, eat, eat. That's what the war's all about – products, brand names, keep the economy going and who gives a shit if a couple hundred women and children get napalmed every day?"

She sat up and put a hand on his arm. "Whoa," she said, "whoa. I'm just talking, that's all."

"That's okay," he said, and he was looking into her eyes now, no problem at all. "So am I."

"All right," she said, "all right, if we're just talking, then I was just wondering what you think about being nude in front of a girl you've never met before, and stoned on top of it at something like half past eight in the morning. Is it a statement or something, or are you just out of clothes?"

She'd expected him to laugh, but he looked away from her. He shrugged, eloquent shoulders, hard muscle, a cord flashing in his neck. "I don't know," he said, and caught her eyes again. "Does it embarrass you? The human body, I mean?"

All the leaves held steady, then jumped, as if somebody had slipped a new slide into the projector that was the world. "Maybe," she said. "Sometimes."

They were silent a moment, the bleating of the goats rising up to them, a distant shout, the rumble of a car on the dirt road. Then he said, "Why don't you take your clothes off, see what it's like?"

"I know what it's like – I was naked in the shower at six o'clock this morning. Why don't you put yours back on?"

"They're wet."

She laughed then – he had her there. His clothes *were* wet, pasted to the branches like papier-mâché and dripping arrhythmically on the goat party below.

"Listen," he said, "Star," and he used her name for the first time since she'd given it to him, "you want to maybe just hang with me up here for a while, kick back – "

"And ball?"

He shrugged again, rubbed at an imaginary spot on his calf. "Sure. If you're into it."

She gave it a minute, thinking of Ronnie and the new girl, Merry, and the big tits woman and everything that was hers to taste at Drop City and in the redwood forests and anywhere else she wanted to go outside the rigid stultifying confines of the straight world, and she considered Marco, his smile, his manner, the way he put things, and then she said, "No, I don't think so."

He dropped his head, let his voice go loose till it sounded like something that had pitched out of a basket and rolled across the floor: "I was just asking – "

"What am I trying to tell you?" she said, and she propped herself up on one elbow and took hold of his arm just above the wrist. "I'm involved with somebody right now, I guess, okay? That's all."

She watched him gather up his legs, two balls of muscle flashing in his calves, and even as he stood he was careful to keep himself turned from her. "I don't know," he said, and he was apologizing now, "you never know unless you ask, right?"

She gave a laugh, but it wasn't the kind of laugh she'd intended, because it had Ronnie and the teepee cat all tangled up in it. "No," she said, "you never know."

The night was darker than any night had a right to be, no moon, no stars, the sky locked up tight with the fog seeping in off the river. She couldn't see Marco or Ronnie, though they were three feet ahead of her, feeling their way around the trikes and tools and discarded saltillo tiles, but she could smell the dust beneath her feet and the fishy stagnant odor rising from the pool somewhere off to her right, and she could hear the goats softly rustling their chains as they changed position beneath the oaks. A lone cricket kept opening and shutting a tiny door in the deep grass. There was nothing else.

Verbie had decided to come along, as referee, and Jiminy, adamant Jiminy – he was ten feet behind them, cursing softly in the dark. "Shit. Fuck. I can't see a thing. Hey, Verbie, where are you? Verbie? Star?"

There was a hiss from just in front of her and Ronnie swung

round on them, the pale ball of his face hanging there in the night like a broken streetlight. "Keep it down, will you?"

"Why?" Verbie's voice bloomed in the darkness. "What do you mean keep it down? Why should we? You think this is a raid or something? What are we, commandos? These are our brothers we're talking about here, and this is our place, all of it, free to everybody, power to the people – why should we have to keep it down, huh? *You tell me, huh?*"

Lydia and Merry were back in the main house, sitting round the scrapwood fire Norm had made to take the chill off the night, curled up, out of it, hunkering down with the rest of them to watch Charlie Chaplin eat his own shoe ("No, no, it's really a gas, like he boils it in a pot and serves up the laces like *spaghetti*"). People were helping themselves to brownies and tea, settling into little groups, stretching out on quilts, thumping the taut bellies of the dogs as if they were drumskins. Nobody made a move as the posse formed behind Marco (and Ronnie, who had no choice but to go if he was going to have any credibility with anybody), because it was too much trouble, let's plead laissez-faire and kick back and let the problem take care of itself. Star didn't want any hassles either – she hated confrontation, hated it – but this was something she had to do, not just for the family or because Marco had stood up and taken it all on himself, but for the girl, for *her*. Because it had to stop someplace.

Star hadn't even seen her. She'd been baking, scrubbing, gardening, dreaming. People came, people went. Half the time she didn't recognize the faces round the dinner table, especially on weekends. It didn't matter. She might not have seen her, but she knew her from the inside out, somebody's little sister, skin the color of skim milk, the orthodontically assisted smile and the patched jeans and R. Crumb T-shirt, grubby now from the road and the leers and propositions and big moist hands of all the *cats* who'd stopped for her out-thrust thumb and she didn't even need to turn and face the traffic because they would stop for her hair and the shape and living breath of her. Her boyfriend was an asshole. Her mother was a clone. There was verbal abuse, physical abuse maybe. She didn't fit in. She wanted something more than diagramming sentences and *Mi casa es su casa,* and she'd come to them, to the hip people, the people she'd heard about till they were legends of redemption and hope, and found out that in the end she was just another *chick,* so roll over and make it bald for me, honey.

Star stretched her hands out before her, red light, green light, moving forward one step at a time. It couldn't have been more than a couple hundred yards between the two houses, but it seemed like miles, their footsteps shuffling through the beaten dust and the clenched brown leaves of the oaks that were like little claws, everybody quiet for the first time since the door had shut behind them. "Man, it's dark," Jiminy muttered after a moment, just to break the silence, but now there was the low thump of music up ahead, and they moved toward it until two faintly glowing windows floated up out of the shadows. Ronnie tripped over something and kicked it aside in a soft whispering rush of motion. Candlelight took hold of the gutted shades in the windows, let go, took hold, let go.

This was it, the back house, a place the size of a pair of trailers grafted together at the waist, with a roof of sun-bleached shingles and an add-on porch canted like a ship going down on a hard sea. Migrant workers had been housed here in the days when Norm's father ran the place, or so Alfredo claimed, pickers moving up and down the coast with the crops, apples in Washington, cherries in Oregon, grapes in California. Star could believe it – the place was a crash pad then and it was a crash pad now, the single funkiest building on the property. The windows were nearly opaque with dirt, there was no running water or electricity, and somebody had painted drop city dropouts over the door in a flowing swirl of Gothic lettering. She'd been inside maybe half a dozen times, attached to one movable feast or another – until Lester moved in, that is.

Marco didn't knock. He pushed the door open and they all just filed in, more like tourists than an invading army, and she tried to put on her smile, but it failed her. It took a minute for her eyes to adjust, a whole flurry of movement over the stale artificial greetings of the tribe, *what's happening, bro,* candles fluttering, the soft autonomous pulse of Otis Redding, sitting on the dock of the bay. Who was there? Lester, Franklin, three cats, two black and one white, she'd never seen before, even at mealtimes when everybody tended to get together, and – this was a surprise – Sky

44

Dog. It was a surprise because he hadn't shown up for the noon meal or dinner either and everybody assumed he'd gone back to the Haight, or Oregon – wasn't he from Oregon originally, and what *was* his real name, anyway? She looked at him sitting there cross-legged on the floor, bent over his guitar and playing along with the record as if he didn't have a care in the world, as if nothing had happened, as if forcing yourself on fourteen-year-old runaways was no more sweat than brushing your teeth or taking a crap, and she felt something uncontainable coming up in her.

"Hey, man," Verbie was saying, "how's it going? All right? Yeah? Because we just, you know, felt like dropping in and seeing what the scene was over here, you know?" She was five foot nothing, red hair clipped to the ears, with a tiny pinched oval of a face and a black gap where her left incisor should have been. The face paint clung like glitter at her hairline and she was twirling the cape and shuffling her feet as if she were about to tap dance across the room. "I mean, is it cool?"

No one offered any assurances, and it didn't feel cool, not at all. It felt as if they'd interrupted something. Star edged into the room behind Ronnie.

There was no furniture other than a plank set atop two cinder blocks, and everyone was sitting on the floor – or not on the floor exactly, but on the cracked and peeling vinyl cushions scavenged from the rusty chaise longue out by the pool and a khaki sleeping bag that looked as if it had been dragged behind a produce truck for a couple hundred miles. Someone had made a halfhearted attempt to sweep the place, and there was a mound of brown-paper bags, doughnut boxes, shredded newspapers and broken glass piled up like drift in the far corner. The only light came from a pair of candles guttering on either end of the plank – calderas of wax, unsteady shadows, a hash pipe balanced atop a box of kitchen matches – and as the jug of cheap red wine circulated from hand to hand it picked up the faintest glint, as if a dying sun were trapped in the belly of the glass.

"So what is it," Lester said, looking up from the floor with a tight thin smile, "Halloween?" Beside him, Franklin ducked his head and gave out a quick truncated bark of a laugh. "It's trick or treat, right?" Lester said. "Is that what it is?"

"Yeah," Franklin said, and he lifted the jug to his lips but had to set it down again because the joke was just too much, "but we ain't got no candy."

Ronnie found a spot on the floor and eased himself down as if he belonged, and maybe he did, but the others just stood there, shifting from foot to foot. "It was a meeting," Ronnie said, and then Verbie, who never knew when to shut up, started in on a blow-by-blow account of who had said what to whom, going on about the shit in the woods, the weekend hippies, the septic fields that needed to be dug, and she was just working her way around to the point of the whole thing, trying to soften the impact, when Marco spoke up for the first time.

He was leaning against the wall, arms folded against his chest. He was wearing a clean white T-shirt and a pair of striped suspenders that stretched taut over his chest. "We want you out," he said, "all of you." He gave Sky Dog a look. "And that includes you, my friend."

Sky Dog never even lifted his head, but Lester made a face. "Ooo-ooo, listen to you," he said, "and what's your sign, baby – Aries? Got to be – the ram, man, right? Ram it on in, huh? Ram it to 'em. Or is it that other *Ares* I'm thinking of, god of war, right? Is that it? God of war?"

There was a snicker from Franklin, but the others just sat there. The record rotated. The jug wine went from one hand to another.

"But listen, you want to know about war, and I don't mean this SDS shit and setting the flag on fire on your mother's back lawn while us niggers go on over to Vietnam and smoke gooks for you, you talk to my man Dewey here" – and he indicated the man seated to his left – "because Dewey was dug in at Khe Sanh for something like eight fucking months and he can kick your white ass from here to Detroit and back."

"That's not the point," Verbie was saying.

"Nobody wants to get violent," Jiminy put in, and he loomed over Verbie like the representative of another species, all bone and sinew, the white shanks of his legs flashing beneath the cutaway tails and Donald Duck grinning in endless replication from the hard little knot of his little boy's briefs, "it's just that we all, I mean, for the sake of the community – "

46

This was hard-going, very hard, and Star couldn't contain herself any longer. "You raped that girl," she said, and it was as if she'd ripped the wiring out of the stereo or shot out the candles with a pair of smoking guns. The room fell silent. She looked at Lester, and Lester, hands dangling over the narrow peaks of his knees, looked back at her. This wasn't peace and love, this wasn't brothers and sisters. This was ugly, and she could have stayed home in Peterskill, New York, if she wanted ugliness.

"Come on, Star," Ronnie said finally, but Lester cut him off. "I didn't *rape* nobody," he said, "because if anything happened here last night it was consensual, know what I mean? Shit, you were here, *Pan* – you know what went down."

"Fuck it," Marco said. "You're out of here, all of you."

"Right," Jiminy seconded the motion. "Look, I'm sorry, but we all – "

"All what?" Lester snarled. "Consulted the *I Ching*? Took a vote, let's get rid of the niggers? Is that it?" His voice was like the low rumble of a truck climbing a hill, very slow and deliberate. "Shit, you're just trying to tell me what I already know – peace and love, brother, do your own thing, baby, but only if your precious ass is white."

5

The pick rose and fell, rose and fell. Marco was out in the heat of the day – a hundred-plus, easy – stripped down to his jeans and boots, sweating, working, feeling it in his upper arms and shoulders. Jiminy had been working beside him all morning, tearing away at the skin of the soil where the new leach lines for the septic tank were going in, but when the sun stood up straight overhead he'd set down his shovel as gingerly as if it were a ceramic sculpture and shambled across the yard in the direction of the swimming pool. He'd been good company, rattling on about books and records and all the places he wanted to visit – Benares, Rio, Nairobi, some town in Wisconsin that featured the world's biggest wheel of cheese, and if it had already gone moldy by the time he got there, well, he was sure they'd just make another one – but Marco didn't mind working alone. All the communities he'd been part of, or tried to be part of, had fallen to pieces under the pressure of the little things, the essentials, the cooking and the cleaning and the repairs, and while it was nice to think everybody would pitch in during a crisis, it didn't always work out that way.

And this *was* a crisis, whether people seemed to realize it or not – the toilets in the main house were overflowing and there was a coil of human waste behind every rock, tree and knee-high scrap of weed on the property, and that was primitive, oh yes indeed. *In*voluntarily primitive. Nobody even had the sense to bury it, let alone dig a latrine. They didn't think, didn't want to get hung up on details. They'd dropped out. They were here. That was enough, and the less said about it the better. But before long, as Marco knew from experience, the county health inspector would have plenty to say, and it wouldn't reflect a higher consciousness either.

He was down in the trench, waist-deep, flinging dirt, when Alfredo came across the yard with a fruit jar of lemonade in one hand and a spade in the other. Marco saw him coming, but he kept digging, because for the moment at least digging was his affliction, his tic, the process that made his blood flow and his brain go numb. Simplest thing in the world: the pick rises, the pick falls; the shovel goes in, the dirt comes out.

"Hey," Alfredo said, and he was showing his fine pointed teeth in a smile that cut a horizontal slash in the wiry black superstructure of his beard, "I thought you could use something to drink – and maybe some help too."

Well, he could. And he appreciated the three precious ice cubes bobbing in the super-sweetened fresh-squeezed lemonade too, but there were probably twenty people at Drop City he'd rather spend the afternoon with. Nothing against Alfredo, except that he lacked a sense of humor – it was as if someone had run a hot wire through his brain, fusing all the appreciation cells in a dead smoking lump – and when he did manage to find something funny, he ran it into the ground, repeating the punchline over and over and snickering in a bottomless catarrhal wheeze that made you think he was choking on his own phlegm. He was older too – twenty-nine, thirty maybe – and that was a problem in itself, because he used his age advantage like a bludgeon any time there was a difference of opinion. His favorite phrases were: "Well, you were probably still in high school then" and "I don't want to tell you what to do, but – "

Alfredo got down into the trench, stripped off his shirt to reveal a pale flight of ribs, and started digging, and that was all right. They worked in silence for the first few minutes, the penetrable earth at their feet, the smell of it in their nostrils like the smell of fossilized bone, bloodless and neutral, the sun overhead, sweat pocking the dust of their shoes. At some point, there was a sudden high whinnying shout from the direction of the pool, a splash, two splashes, and then Alfredo, in the way of making idle conversation, was asking about his name. "Marco," he said, "is that Italian?"

"Yeah, I suppose – originally, that is." Marco straightened up and swiped a forearm across his brow, and what he should have done was dig a bandanna out of his pack, but it was too late now. He'd cool off in the pool, that's what he'd do – but later. Much later. "My father named me for Marco Polo."

"Really? Far out." There was the crunch of the shovel cutting into the earth. "What'd he name your brother – Christopher?"

Marco acknowledged the stab at humor with a foreshortened smile – he'd been responding to that joke since elementary school. "I don't have a brother."

"My father's Italian," Alfredo said, and he grunted as he heaved a load of dirt up over his shoulder. "My mother's Mexican. That's why I can take the heat – like this? This doesn't bother me at all."

Right. But Marco was thinking of his own father, the man he'd known only as a voice over the long-distance wire these past two years and counting. *Where you now?* his father would shout into the receiver. *Twentynine Palms? Hell, I was there during the war – desert training. For Rommel. Paradise on earth – in winter, anyway . . . Your mother wants to know when you're coming home – isn't that right, Rosemary? Rosemary?*

There were no hard feelings. It wasn't the usual thing at all, the sort of adolescent fury that goaded his high school buddies to ram their screaming V-8s down the throat of every street in the development and answer violence with violence across the kitchen table. In fact, he missed his father – missed both his parents. There were times, hefting his pack, sticking out his thumb, waking in a strange bed or in some nameless place that was exactly like every other place, when it infected him with a dull ache, like a tooth starting to go bad, but mostly now his parents were compacted in his thoughts till they were little more than strangers. He'd skipped bail. There was a warrant out for his arrest, the puerile little brick of a misdemeanor compounded by interstate flight and the fugitive months and years till it had become a towering jurisdictional wall – with a charge of draft evasion cemented to the top of it. Home? This was his home now.

Sorry, Dad, but the answer is never.

European history – that was what defined Marco's father, and he'd taught it, chapter and verse, out of the same increasingly irrelevant textbook to an endless succession of unimpressed faces for thirty years, thirty years at least. *This new class of tenth graders?* he'd say at the dinner table, still in his brown corduroy jacket with the elbow patches that shone as if they'd been freshly greased, the only father in the whole development of two hundred and fifty-plus homes to wear a mustache. *They're more like the Visigoths than the Greeks. Not like in your day, Marco – and what a difference five years makes. You people were scholars!* he'd roar, as if he meant it, and then he'd laugh. And laugh.

"We're Irish, mainly. My last name's Connell. Everybody thinks it's Mark O'Connell, but my father was a joker, I guess. And I guess he saw me going to distant lands."

"Really? Ever been out of the country?"

Marco set down his shovel to work at an embedded stone with the business end of the pick. He glanced up and then away again. "Not really."

And then Alfredo was onto travel, the names of places clotting on his tongue like lint spun out of a dryer, no two-thousand-pound Wisconsin cheeses for him – it was London, Paris, Berlin, Rome, Venice, Florence – he was an art student at one time, did Marco know that? Yeah, and he'd sketched his way across Europe, from the Louvre to the Rijksmuseum to the Prado. That was the only way to do it, like a month in every city, just living there in some *pension* or hostel, meeting people in cafes, scoring hash on the street and going straight to the bakery after the cafes close for your *pane* and your baguette. He must have talked without drawing a breath for a solid fifteen minutes.

Somewhere there, in the space between Amsterdam and the Place de la Concorde, the crows started in, a bawling screech that came out of the trees and circled overhead as the big glistening birds dive-bombed an owl they'd flushed from its roost. "The owls get them at night when they're helpless, did you know that?" Marco said, glad for a chance to change the subject. "That's what that's all about. Survival. And imagine us – imagine if there was another ape species here to challenge *us,* and I don't mean like gorillas and chimps, but another humanoid."

Alfredo didn't seem to have anything to say to that – he believed in universal harmony, brotherhood, vegetarianism, peace, love and understanding. He didn't want to know about the war between crows and owls, let alone apes, or the way the crows mobbed the nests of lesser birds – sparrows, finches, juncos – to crush and devour the young. That had nothing to do with the world he lived in. "Heavy," that's what he said finally. *Heavy.*

They bent to their work, the silence broken only by the persistent slice of the shovels, the tumult of the birds running off the edge of the sky until the pedestrian murmur of Drop City began to filter back in: the goats bleating to be milked or fed, the single sharp ringing note of a dog surprised by its own hunger, the regular slap of the screen door at the back of the house – and underneath it all, like the soundtrack to a movie, the dull hum of rock and roll leaking out the kitchen windows. "Listen, I really appreciate your doing this," Alfredo said, pausing to straighten up and arch his back, the fine grains of dirt clinging to the flesh in a dense fur of sweat. "Taking the initiative, I mean. I know you've only been here like two weeks or whatever, but this is a trip, it really is – it's what we need more of around here."

"Sure," Marco said, "no problem," and the shovel never stopped working. It felt good to be doing something, making something, putting his back to it till there was nothing left to clutter up his head. Drifting was fine. To a point. Lying up in a treehouse with a book, that was fine too. And dope. And women. And music. But right now, in this ditch, under this sun, it was the tug of the physical that mattered, only that.

"You know, I was at Thunder Mountain before this – me and Reba, that was before we had the kids. Or no, Che was like one or maybe a year and a half, I don't know. But mainly what happened was everybody just wanted to ball and do dope, which is okay, don't get me wrong, but it got to the point where nobody wanted to tend the garden or make the food. The chicks, I mean. Because they're the key to the whole thing. If the chicks don't have any energy and don't want to, you know, wash the dishes, sweep up, cook the meals, then you're in trouble, big time. There's nothing worse than having all the dishes piled up and the pots and pans all crusted and dirty, and then everybody milling around like what are we going to do about dinner, man, and that's where it all breaks down, believe me."

Marco had no chance to respond, even if he'd wanted to, because when he looked up he saw Sky Dog sauntering across the lot with Lester and Franklin in tow. Or no, it wasn't Franklin – it was the other one, what was his name, Dewey, the war hero. They didn't say anything, didn't wave, didn't smile, just kept coming across the weed-strewn lot in a slow, sure amble, miniature explosions of dust riding up the heels of their boots. Alfredo looked up too, just as the three of them reached the far end of the ditch and stood there staring down like executioners. The phrase *Digging your own grave* popped in and out of Marco's head. This wasn't going to be a happy occasion.

"Hey, Alfredo," Sky Dog said, "I wanted to talk to you."

Alfredo spread one palm flat at the top of the ditch and came up out of it then, wiping both hands on the bleached-out fabric of his jeans, trying for a grin. "Hey," he said, as if he were happy to see him, "what's happening, man?" and he snaked out a hand for the soul shake that never came.

And what was Sky Dog? Five-ten, five-eleven maybe, a hundred seventy pounds, tanned till his skin was a sheath of gold, a single blue vein painted down the biceps of each arm, his eyes lighter than his face. He wore a Fu Manchu mustache that trailed a good three inches below the line of his jawbone. Usually he was in jeans and an embroidered blue jeans jacket with the sleeves removed at the shoulders, the humble hippie farmer adorned in humble hippie chic, but today he was a dude, dressed up in a paisley shirt and a silver scarf fed through a little gold hoop at his throat and a pair of elephant bells that swallowed up his feet. "I want to tell you I'm pissed off," he said, and his face went the color of liver before it hits the pan, "because if you think you can just vote me out of here or whatever, you're crazy. And to send this fucker" – a gesture for Marco – "to be your errand boy because you don't got the balls – "

"Come on, Bruce, come on, you know I wouldn't do anything against you, me of all people" – Alfredo had his arms spread wide in renunciation – "but you've got to know we can't run the risk of the law coming in here, and whether you had anything to do with that girl or not, she could still go straight to the Sonoma County sheriff and say anything she wants, and we don't even know who she is or where she is – "

"Aw, fuck it, man, listen to you – you're nothing but a hypocrite. I mean, listen to yourself – *if you had anything to do with that girl*. Yeah, I did. And so did Lester and Dewey and a couple of other guys – including that little shit, Pan, or whatever his name is. She was asking for it – no, she was begging for it, like let's get stoned and ball and get stoned and ball some more, and do you guys have any weed? – and I'm not apologizing to anybody. There isn't a cat on this property that wouldn't have done the same thing, am I right?"

Lester said he was right. Dewey said nothing, but his eyes were lying in wait.

Sky Dog – or Bruce, that was his name, *Bruce,* and to know it was to know the shibboleth that would cut him down to size – let his voice ascend the scale into the upper register of complaint. "I've been here, what, eight, nine months? And you send this fucker here" – again a finger stabbed at Marco, down in his hole – "who's been here like a week to tell *me* I got to go? Well, I'll tell you, I'm not going anywhere, not even if Norm himself comes knocking on the door, and you want to know why, I'll tell you why – "

That was when Marco stopped listening. He was thinking about a dog his uncle once had, a husky, one brown eye, one blue, the single wildest canine ever domesticated, like no other dog Marco had ever seen. It didn't want to chase a ball or do tricks or go for a ride in the car, it never fawned or licked your hand or begged at the table, and when it was thrust into the company of other dogs at the park or on the broad humped lawn out back of the school, it wouldn't budge, barely deigning to lift its leg or take the exculpatory sniff. But when it was pushed, when another dog crowded in too close with a ratcheting growl and a thrust of its shoulders, the thing erupted – no warning, just a pure fluid rush of violence so sudden and absolute you couldn't be sure you'd seen it. The other dog, no matter how big, wound up on its back, and his uncle's husky – *Lobo,* that was his name – was locked at its throat.

Twice now, in the space of sixty seconds, Marco had been called a fucker to his face, and twice was two times too many. Before *Bruce* could air the remainder of his grievance in his high nasal wallop of a voice that was absolutely pitched to the key and tenor of the blues – *and no doubt about it, the boy could sing* – Marco reached up and took hold of his left foot, right at the heel of his boot, and jerked it out from under him. In the next instant, Sky Dog came down hard on the edge of the ditch, and in the instant after that he was sputtering and thrashing at the bottom of it, and Marco, with all the calm deliberation in the world, watched his own right fist rise and fall like a piston as he bent to retool this particular *cat's* features in the most unbrotherly way he could imagine.

If he'd thought he was ending something, he was wrong, and he should have known better, should have calculated and looked to his best chance, but none of that mattered now. What mattered was Dewey, who clapped an arm around his throat and snatched his head back as if he were rebounding the ball after an errant layup; what mattered was Lester, puff-faced Lester, in his platform boots and wide-brimmed pimp's hat with the silver chain flashing at the crown, who gathered himself atop the mounded dirt and shot two clean balletic kicks to Marco's midsection as Marco fought the hammerlock at his throat and Sky Dog – *Bruce!* – came up out of the trench with both fists flailing. Ten seconds passed, twenty, all three of them going at Marco where he stood immobilized, caught up in Dewey's grip like a man of straw, Alfredo shouting "Break it up! Break it up! Come on, man, *break it up!*"

Marco had no illusions. It was power against power, what they wanted against what he wanted, and what he wanted was Drop City, nothing less. He twisted, churned his legs, kicked out at Sky Dog and fought the arm clamped round his throat. It was a dance, that's what it was. A jerking, twisting, futile dance punctuated by the wet dull thump of one blow after another. Sky Dog was sloppy, near tears, half his punches glancing off muscle or bone, but Dewey was made out of hammered steel and Lester kept stepping up and aiming his kicks, one after another, as if he were climbing a ladder. "Motherfucker," he kept repeating, softly, almost tenderly, as if he'd confused the act and the epithet, "you motherfucker."

It might have gone on even longer than it did, no usual end to this, blood on top of blood, the knife in its sheath, the sheath on the belt, the wet slap of flesh on flesh, if it hadn't been for the tourists. Two of them – a couple, denim and leather, bronze peace signs dangling from their throats, just in the night before to see how the counterculture lives, maybe write an essay or a book about it, promiscuity and peace, granola, goat's milk, marijuana under the stars. Marco had met them that morning – they were from Berkeley, he was a professor and she was a poet, and they'd donated two dollars each for runny oatmeal and scones that were like loofahs, and it was worth every penny because they were making the scene. The professor was bald on top, but he'd wrapped a bandanna round his head and greased up the long stiff hairs at the back of his neck so they trailed down over his collar in what must have been a royally hip display for his colleagues in the Sociology department. The poet was forty maybe, nobody he'd ever heard of, with a pair of big collapsing breasts in a sleeveless T-shirt, bird feathers for hair, a parsimonious mouth and mean little inquisitive eyes that dug and probed everywhere, because everything was a poem in the making. Well here was another one unfolding right before her eyes, and what would she call it – "The Fight for the Leach Field Ditch"? Or maybe just "The Ditch"? Marco wasn't thinking. He dodged and writhed and absorbed the blows as best he could. But yeah, "The Ditch" sounded just about right. "The Ditch" said it all.

What happened was this: they were out for a stroll, professor and poet, grooving on the heat, the dust, the fence lizards puffing up their tiny reptilian chests in the blissed-out aura of peace and love and communal synergy, when suddenly she – the poet – let out a scream. And this was no ordinary scream – it wasn't the kind of semi-titillated pro forma shriek you might expect from a female poet announcing a fistfight among hippies in a half-dug ditch in a blistering field above the Russian River; no, this was meant to convey shock, real shock, a savage tug at the cord strung taut between the two poles of existence. The poet's scream rose above the heat, airless and impacted, and everything stopped right there. Dewey let go, Lester snatched back his foot, Sky Dog and Alfredo swung their heads first to her, then to the dense stand of woods at the edge of the lot. And Marco, unsteady on his feet, riding the adrenal rush till it was a hot cautery run through his veins, Marco was the last to turn and look.

What he saw was Ronnie – Pan – staggering out of the shadows in a suit of blood, wet blood set afire by the hard harsh light of the sun, and something slung across his shoulders, swallowing him up in the fresh red wetness. It was – it was a living thing, or no, a dead thing, clearly dead. And bleeding. *The girl,* Marco thought, *the girl,* and it wasn't enough that they'd raped and humiliated her, now they'd – but this wasn't a human form at all. What did he see? Fur, dun fur. Had he killed one of the dogs, was that it?

"Hey, man," Ronnie's voice came stunting across the field, weak with excitement, "we got *meat!*"

"Meat?" Alfredo said, already moving toward him – they were all, all of them, moving toward him. "What are you talking about? What is that?"

Marco climbed up out of the ditch. Ronnie was closing now, a hundred feet, maybe less, staggering under his burden of blood, meat, hair, bone. "The fuck you mean, man? I got me a deer!"

6

You would have thought he'd shot *Bambi* or something the way some of the chicks carried on, and Merry was the worst – or no, Verbie, Verbie was even worse than that, as if she hadn't spent the first eighteen years of her life cruising the meat department at the supermarket and gorging on fifteen-cent burgers and pepperoni pizza like every other teenager in America. And *Alfredo,* with his meat-is-murder rap and how could you just slaughter one of your fellow creatures and live with that kind of karma, and *blah, blah, blah.* It was a joke, it really was. All they talked about was going back to the land, living simple, dropping out, and yet if there wasn't a supermarket within ten miles they'd have starved to death by now, every one of them. There were fish in the river, there was game in the woods, and so what if it was out of season, so what if he'd wound up with a doe that couldn't have weighed more than ninety pounds dressed out? It was meat, free meat, and it could feed everybody on the place for a week at least. Did they really expect to go through life choking down soy patties and eggplant on rye? Falafel? *Tofu kabobs,* for Christ's sake? Shit, they should have given him a medal.

As it was, he spent the whole afternoon skinning and quartering the thing, slippery, ugly work, no doubt about it, and the only one who'd give him a hand was Marco, because Marco understood what going back to nature was all about – he'd been hunting and fishing since he was eight years old, grouse, rabbit, squirrel, duck blinds on a morning made out of ice, standing waist-deep in water that shot by like a freight train and nothing but two stunted half-developed swaybacked hatchery trout to show for it, and you'd better hope your mother made meat loaf. He'd been there – there and back. Just like Ronnie. Like *Pan.* And while Che and Sunshine stuck their fingers up their noses and stood there gaping and half the commune seemed to just drop what they were doing and drift by to scold and kibitz and feature the way a few nice venison steaks might look sizzling on a grill over a bed of hot coals, Ronnie tugged at the hide in a blizzard of flies – he was thinking he might make a doeskin jacket maybe, with a fringe – and Marco bent to sever the thin tegument that held it all together with the slick glassy edge of his hunting knife.

"What happened to your face?" Ronnie asked in the course of things, his hands dipped in gore, the sun quavering in the trees like some novelty item from Japan. The butt end of a joint clung to his lower lip; a quart of beer, slick with bloody palm prints, tilted out of the stiff yellow grass beside him. It was late in the afternoon, and the smells from the kitchen were strictly vegetarian.

Marco looked up, grinning, but it was a lopsided Floyd Patterson sort of grin. His left eye was swollen up like a sausage in a pan and a crusted-over gash dropped down into the facial hair below it. "A difference of opinion," he said, and that was all right, because Ronnie wasn't prepared for any heavy trip about the spades and Sky Dog and who did what to whom in the back house night before last, so he just nodded and let it go.

The two of them kept sawing away, first one side, then the other, and before long the hide pulled back from the flesh like a wet rug, but didn't you have to salt it or rub it with lye or something? And for leather, you had to get the fur off too, and that was a drag, a lifetime sentence, no less . . . That was what Ronnie was thinking as the fat bluebottle flies scorched the air and the voice of Tracy Nelson, strong and true, rose up high over the currents of the main house. They were out behind the pool on a dead bleached strip of grass, and they'd hung the carcass from a branch, to bleed it, but just for an hour – they were both afraid of the heat, because who'd ever shot a deer this time of year? Nobody. Nobody but Pan. Yes, and here it was, in the flesh. This morning it had been down by the river, pawing around in the mud, pulling up tender shoots of this and that, off on some trip of its own no one could ever have imagined or predicted, and now it was dead, now it was his.

Pan was feeling it – the grass, the beer, the pure streaming uncontainable *rush* of accomplishment, his *deer,* his *first deer* – and

58

he began to sing along with the music, *When it all comes down, you got to go back to Mother Earth.* Oh, yes. And he let it rip too, no reason to be shy about it because everybody told him he had a nice voice and you couldn't hold back when you were trying to sing any more than you could when you were trying to talk French or bring a ten-speed bicycle down Portrero Hill with a full pack and a load of groceries on your back. *I don't care how rich you are, I don't care what you're worth* – he threw his head back, really getting into it, on a roll, unbeatable, when the record choked off with a screech and almost instantaneously somebody put on some frantic self-congratulatory raga that was like *compulsive masturbation* or something. "Fuck," he said, "I hate that. I really hate that."

Marco took the joint from his lips with two bloody fingers. "Hate what? Ravi Shankar?"

"No – I mean, yes. Shit, yes. It's utter crap. But what I mean is when you're really like into a song, you know, and somebody just" – he waved a hand, his own bloody knife, as if to say *You know what I mean,* and Marco did, because he nodded in sympathy, say no more.

They listened in silence to the blooming sitar and the tablas that seethed under it like rain on a tin roof, Marco squatting beside him, inhaling, holding it in, then taking a good churning hit from the bottle. The beer sizzled yellow, so warm at this point it was like carbonated piss, but when Marco passed him the bottle Ronnie put his lips to the aperture and tilted his head back. The knives slashed, the flies rose. They were cutting out crude steaks now, and this was a learning process for both of them. "You've got a good voice," Marco said.

"Oh, that? You like it? I mean, that was just singing along with a record. You should of heard me with this band I almost got into back in New York – I mean, I sang with them a couple times at rehearsals, the guitar player and I were like really tight, and the drummer was this cat I went to high school with . . ." He went on in that mode for a while, enjoying himself, thinking of Baracca and Herlihy and the other guys in the band and the sense of flying without wings he got every time he stood at the microphone with all that electric surge of the band behind him and Eddie Herlihy's voice twisting round his own like two *veins* out of the same body. How could he ever explain that to anybody? Yeah, sure, and the scag that went with it, in the three- and five-dollar bags you got from the spades out back of the burned-out, boarded-up storefronts downtown, taste it, cook it, shoot it, just to come *down* from the rush of the music, and that was brotherhood, the brotherhood of the syringe copped from somebody's old lady the nurse that was so dull you had to hammer it into your arm –

"So what do you think," Marco was saying, "should we try smoking the rest of the meat – have you ever done that? Or salt it. I hear you can salt it."

"What about the freezer?"

"Are you kidding? It's full of Tofutti and six kinds of ice cream and cookie dough and what, fifty trays of ice? If we can squeeze three roasts in there it'll be a miracle, and I don't know how many people are going to want steaks tonight – but I say we grill up as much as we can."

"Right on," Ronnie said, and he was already picturing it, the smoke rising like a forest ablaze, the sweet meat scent permeating everything, another joint maybe to mellow out and goose the appetite, and all of them – even Alfredo – lined up at the grill with their tin plates and a shriveled-up pathetic little scoop of rice and veggies, and Pan, magnanimous Pan, hunter and gatherer, essential cog, man of the hour, dishing it up.

As it turned out, it was nearly dark by the time the coals had died down enough to do the steaks without igniting a firestorm on the grill, and Ronnie, who was feeling pretty loose by then, really heaped them up. A little salt, a little pepper, a smear of *Pan's* famous barbecue sauce (two parts ketchup, one part mustard, garlic powder to taste and upend the bottle of apple cider vinegar over the whole mess for ten seconds, *glug, glug, glug*), and that was that. Before he'd got the job in the record department at Caldor, he'd worked at a steakhouse called the Surf 'N' Turf, two days a week on the grill, three behind the bar, and he had a pretty good idea of what to do with meat, once it looked like meat, that is, and he kept the steaks moving with all the flair of a pro.

He was feeling expansive, flipping steaks with both hands and talking everybody up, accepting the odd hit from this pipe or that, and then he was telling Jiminy about this hitchhiker who'd invited Star and him to a party one night in Iowa, he thought it was – yeah, Iowa – and there were maybe ten or twelve improbably hip people gathered round a big picnic table in the middle of a field, crickets going at it, the moon rising fat over the horizon, very calm and soulful. All the plates – tin plates, just like these, exactly, *and isn't that a trip?* – were nailed to the table, just crucified there with a single nail dead center all the way down both sides of the table. When the party was over, when they were all done gnawing on their pork bones and corn cobs and the rest, the hitchhiker's brother – he was the host – just stood up and hosed off the table.

"Really? And how was that?"

"Utterly fucking cool."

"No problem with like grease and germs and all that?"

"The ants would be at it next day, the birds and the flies and whatnot. The sun. Rain."

"Let nature take care of it, right?"

"Yeah, that's right: let nature take care of it."

Most of the brothers and sisters had already eaten – dinner was at six – but they lined up nonetheless, all except for Merry and Alfredo and a couple of the hard-core vegetarians like Verbie. (That hurt him – *Merry* – but she was adamant, every creature is sacred, wouldn't slap a malarial mosquito if it was perched on her wrist, and did he know about the Jains in India who went around with gauze over their faces so they wouldn't inadvertently inhale so much as a gnat?) Norm was there, though, glad-handing and effusing, ripped on something and shouting "Loaves and fishes! It's a miracle!" every two minutes. Somebody dragged the big speakers out onto the back porch and dropped the needle on *Electric Ladyland,* and pretty soon people were dancing out across the lawn in a kind of meat frenzy, and by the time it was over the steaks were gone, and a good time had by all.

At one point, stretched out on the grass with his plate, a transient joint and the dregs of a jug of wine he kept swishing round the bottom of his fruit jar in the hope a little *circulation* would make it taste less like recycled lamp oil, Ronnie found himself hemmed in by the professor and his old lady, the one who'd let out that stone-cold shriek when he'd come staggering out of the woods with the deer wrapped round his shoulders, and if anybody thought *that* was fun they were out of their minds. Star was there too, and Marco, Lydia, Jiminy, a whole little circle of people off the main circle, and they'd been discussing weighty matters like is Hendrix an alien and how many heads fit on the pin of an angel. And suddenly here was this *professor* sitting right there at his elbow with a plate full of gnawed gristle, and the professor was saying things like "So, when did you drop out?"

Ronnie wanted to tell him to fuck off and go back to Berkeley with the rest of the tourists – *Can't you see we're having a party here, man?* – but there was something about the guy – the gray in his beard, the fruity rich mellow tenor that brought back all those somnolent afternoons in English class – that just made him duck his head and mumble "A year and a half." And it wasn't just that he was mumbling, he was exaggerating too – six months was nearer the truth. But the professor didn't want any six-month hippies, he wanted the genuine down-in-the-trenches peripatetic lifetime dirtbags he could awe and thrill the *reading public* with. He had a notepad. He had a – no, yes – tape recorder.

"You mind if I tape this?" the professor was asking.

Hendrix rode the night, supreme, astral, totally mind-blowing, and Ronnie mumbled *Sure* and the professor's old lady moved in, thick legs in a long skirt and the joint pinched in her fingers like a deadly writhing South American bushmaster with its fangs drawn. Did she take a hit? Yes. And then she passed it on.

"You're how old? Here, talk into this."

"Into this?"

"That's right, yeah."

"I'm twenty-two."

"Family problems?"

"No more than usual."

"Ever run away from home?"

"Not that I can remember. Or maybe once. Or twice."

"You were how old then?"

"I don't know – nine. I went to the bowling alley and hid behind the pinball machine."

"Both parents alive?"

His parents were alive, all right, but so was Lon Chaney Jr. in *The Mummy's Ghost.* They were just like that, staggering from one foot to the other and grunting out hostile messages to the world and the trashed wind-sucking son they saw only at dinner because he needed that dinner to stay alive. Might as well wrap them up in mummy's bandages too, because they were both walking disasters, his father's nose like a skinned animal pinned to his face with the shiny metallic tackheads of his eyes, his mother a shapeless sack of organs with a howling withered skull stuck atop it. Come to think of it, she could have starred in *Screaming Skull* herself. And they nagged. Nagged and grunted. Pan looked into the professor's eyes and then away again. "Yeah," was all he said.

"Any abuse? You use marijuana? Hard drugs? Booze? What about Free Love? Any social diseases? You vote in the last election?"

Pan fell into it. He warmed, grew effusive. He told the professor about scoring dope on South Street and cooking it up in whatever semi-clean receptacle that happened to be handy and wouldn't catch on fire, a spoon usually or one of those little cups they poach eggs in, an example of which he'd had and prized for about a week until it got lost, and he laid out both his arms like exhibits at the morgue to show the professor his tracks that were six months gone because the truth of the matter was heroin scared the shit out of him and he was never going to do anything other than maybe snort it ever again. Drew was dead. And Dead Mike, he was dead too. "But Free Love – oh, man, don't get me started. That's what this is all about – the *chicks,* you know what I mean?" That was when he realized Star was watching him, her knees pulled up to her chin and locked tight in the clasp of her arms, the firelight like hot grease on her face and that smirk she had, that smirk that was more of a put-down than anything she could ever say.

"What about VD?" the professor was saying, leaning in close with the microphone, his face hanging there at the end of his veiny blistered old man's throat like a piñata, the gift-shop peace medallion dangling like a rip cord below that and his eyes like two wriggling leg-kicking toads, and Pan – Ronnie – felt so *embarrassed,* so fucking mortified and put-upon, he actually jerked the microphone out of the professor's hand and then, not knowing what to do with it, flung it into the fire in one smooth uncontested motion.

"What the hell you think you're doing?" the professor wanted to know, and his old lady – the poet – said, "American Primitive," and laughed a long-gone laugh.

Ronnie was on his feet now, not much kicking power in a pair of huaraches, but enough to send the rest of the apparatus – the big silver-and-gray box with the knobs and dials and slow-turning *spools* – into the fire too, and the professor shouting and grabbing for the machine amidst the coals and the black and quiescent remains of the deer.

"You crazy son of a bitch!" That was what the professor said, but it was nothing to Ronnie, he wasn't even listening. He heard Star laugh though, a hard harsh dart of a laugh that stuck right in him as he went off into the night, looking for something else altogether.

Later, much later, after sitting around a campfire with some people he didn't recognize – or maybe he did recognize them – he thought about going up to the back house and seeing what Sky Dog and the spades were up to, but then he thought he wouldn't. Better not press his luck. There were people who wanted him gone – and here Alfredo's face loomed up out of a shallow grave in the back corner of his mind, followed in quick succession by Reba's and Verbie's – and what happened the other night had split the place down the middle. Lester and Sky Dog and the rest had been voted out, and that meant they didn't show for meals and kept strictly to themselves, running the Lincoln down to the store for wine, cigarettes and processed cheese sandwiches every couple hours, but they might as well have been in another county for all they had to do with Drop City. They'd smelled the meat – Ronnie had seen them out on the porch of the back house as the light faded, and he almost wished they would have come down and joined the party so he could show them what he'd done with a .30-06 rifle and two shining copper-jacketed bullets, but they weren't interested, because it was war now, and you had to choose sides. And that was no contest as far as Pan was concerned. He was for the side in control, the side that had all the chicks and the food and the big house with the KLH speakers and all of those five hundred or eight hundred or however many records that were lined up on the shellacked pine bookcases in random order and was there a radio station in the *country* with a better collection?

The night deepened. Shouts and laughter ran at him across the lawn and the music pulsed steadily from the back of the main house. He was standing there in the bushes, where he'd just zipped up after responding to the call of nature, and he could feel a headache coming on. It had been a *day*, all right, and he felt pretty glorious, all things considered, but what he needed was maybe a little of that sticky Spañada Star was always drinking – or Mateus, if anybody had any. Sure. That's what he needed, to knock down the headache and put a mellow cap on the evening, and he headed back across the lawn, toward where the shadows danced round the cookfire.

Star wasn't there. She wasn't up in the treehouse either, because he hoisted himself up the ladder to see, and she wasn't in the main house where half a dozen people shushed him because they were watching some silent movie Norm had got out of the library for the sheer appreciation and *uplift* of it. Ronnie stood there a minute in the darkened room, watching the light play over a frozen landscape until an Eskimo appeared, two slits for eyes, the wind tearing at the ruff of his parka, and began building an igloo out of blocks he cut from the snow. He had a knife the size of a machete, and he wasted no time, because you could see the way the wind was blowing and his breath froze into the wisps of his beard, each block perfect, one atop the other, and when he fitted the final block into a gap in the roof of the thing, everybody burst into applause. "Fuckin' Nanook," Norm said, and there he was stretched out on the floor with a comforter drawn up to his chin, "you want to talk about living off the land, man . . ."

In the morning – or no, it was the afternoon, definitely the afternoon – Ronnie woke with a lurch that set the whole room rocking like a boat, and the dream, whatever it was, was gone before he could resuscitate it. Just as well, because he could feel the veins inflating in his neck with the frantic scramble of his heart – he'd been trying to escape something or somebody, dark twisting corridors and howling faces – and now, suddenly, he was awake in the apparent world, a fine sheen of sweat greasing his body and leaching into the sleeping bag that each day stank ever more powerfully of mold and ammonia and creeping decay.

Beside him, breathing through her open mouth with a faint rattling snore, was Lydia, her arms stretched out as if she'd been crucified. The dark nipples were like knitted caps pulled over the white crowns of her breasts, and her breasts were like people, two slouching fat white people in caps having a conversation across the four-lane highway of her rib cage. A fine line of glistening dead black hair measured the distance from her navel to her bush. There was hair under her arms, hair on her legs, a faint stripe of it painted over her upper lip. She was sweating. Her eyelids trembled. He lay there contemplating her a minute, letting his heart climb back down from the ledge he'd left it on, feeling as if he'd been assembled from odd scraps during the night. His head throbbed. His stomach made a fist and relaxed it. He needed to find some toilet paper, *fast*.

Pan rose from the sleeping bag that was stretched over a double mattress on the floor in the far corner of the back room of the main house. He rose slowly, warily, his bones as heavy as spars, and began silently shuffling through his backpack and the cardboard box that between them held everything he owned. He didn't want to wake Lydia. He definitely did not want to wake Lydia. Because Lydia would want one thing, and that thing, in his present condition, he was unwilling to give her. In fact, as he studied her out of the corner of his eye while rummaging for any last overlooked and forgotten quarter or eighth or even sixteenth of a roll of toilet paper his brothers and sisters might not already have got to, she struck him as being fat, too fat, not at all his type. His type was Merry. His type was Star – and where was she?

He hadn't been able to find her the night before, though he'd looked everyplace he could think of except the back house, where the spades and Sky Dog were nursing their grudges and washing down their Velveeta cheese sandwiches with sour red wine and snuffing the last fading vestiges of grilled venison on the thin night air, but she wouldn't be there, he knew that and the spades knew that and everybody in Drop City knew it too. He'd run into Merry – she and Jiminy were reading poems out loud to each other in Norm's bedroom upstairs – but Merry said she didn't feel in much of a festive mood because the whole *idea* of a barbecue went against everything she believed in, and then she'd called him a carnivore, or maybe it was a cannibal, but she said it with a smile, as in all is forgiven but don't bother me now I'm reading poetry. Out loud. To Jiminy. So Ronnie found some other people and continued to abuse various controlled and illicit substances until the whole day went into extra innings and he wound up in the shadowy deeps of this room with a stick of incense and a single phallic candle burning and Lydia naked and hairy and wet and taking hold of his prick as if she owned it.

And now he needed toilet paper. Desperately. He found his cutoffs and stepped into them, and forget the shirt, forget the huaraches, he was in the grip of something urgent here. He was thinking *Leaves, I'll just use leaves,* when Lydia's purple Elizabeth Taylor eyes flashed open. "Oh," she said. "What? Oh, it's you." And then she was on her hands and knees, stretching, her great pumped-up tits suspended beneath her like airships, like zeppelins, and she was saying "Come on over here, Ronnie, *Pan,* come on, just hold me, just for a minute, huh? You got a minute, don't you?"

He didn't have a minute. He didn't have fifteen seconds. The deer, all that gamy protein and wild hard gristle and backwoods fat, was having its revenge. His stomach clenched again, the image of gas rising in a beaker in Chemistry class set up camp in his brain, and he was out the door, through the house – startled faces, oh, it's Pan and what's the hurry? – and out across the blistered lawn and into the nearest clump of bushes he could find. And then, finally, he was squatting, no thought of septic fields or clogged toilets or luxury accommodations in mind, and it was all coming out of him in a savage uncontainable rush.

What he thought was that he'd feel better as the day wore on, but he thought wrong. His head throbbed, his insides kept churning. And though he made his slow careful way through a plate of rice mush, grain by grain, *that* went right through him too. He wound up lying beside the swollen green carpet of the pool through the late afternoon and into the evening, refusing all attempts at conversation and invitations to eat (Merry), ball (Lydia) or inhale drugs (half a dozen people, cats and chicks alike). Every once in a while, hammered by the sun, he'd wallow lethargically in the pool, but even that made his brain pound and his gut clench, and he didn't really rouse himself till somebody pulled the shades down over the day and dusk came to sit in the trees like a vulture and everything went gray. Then he had a few shaky hits from a bottle of Don Ricardo special reposado tequila he kept under the seat of the car and went out across the lawn to inspect the remains of the deer. There was no one around, and the fire he and Marco had made – the smoking fire, not the barbecue, because the meat had to be preserved somehow – wasn't even warm. It was a circle of white ash flecked with cinders, and you could lay your palm on it and feel absolutely nothing. The deer – the unchoice cuts, the parts they hadn't bothered with in the rush to get the blood off their hands and the party under way – dangled from a thin strand of wire like the leavings of some twisted vigilante squad, its head skewed at an impossible angle, backbone gnawed to a blue-black ripple of bone. While he'd been asleep, while he'd been lying up beside the pool as if he'd been gutshot himself, the flies had been busy making a playground of the thing, and he saw that now, but it didn't affect him one way or the other. He didn't even bother to raise a hand and flick them away. It was getting dark. And the meat – the deer, his triumph – had already begun to stink.

part two

the thirtymile

The wife hath not power of her own body, but the husband: and likewise also the husband hath not power of his own body, but the wife.

– St. Paul, 1 Corinthians 7:4

7

Cecil Harder was fortifying himself at the bar of the Three Pup Roadhouse, half a mile down the Fairbanks Road from Boynton. He was on his third Oly and his second shot of Wild Turkey, and in about three minutes he was going to slam his way out the screen door, get into Richard Schrader's pickup and drive the remaining hundred fifty-nine and a half miles into the city. There were a few things he needed for the cabin – a new axe handle, duct tape, kerosene for the lanterns, rice, .22 cartridges, beans, yeast, sugar – and Richard had given him a whole long list too, but that wasn't the reason he was going.

He gazed up from his nested hands. The air in the roadhouse was as thick as a wall with residual dimness and the dust that was nailed to it in two thin streams of sunlight. Mosquitoes faded in and out of it, all but stationary, and they beat at both sides of the windows as if it were some kind of contest, as if all they'd ever subsisted on was glass. He threw back the Wild Turkey and took a long pull at his beer.

There was a new woman working the place, a summer person, a tourist, as lean and tall and plain-faced as a warden – a male warden out of a Jimmy Cagney movie, that is – and she came out from behind the bead curtain that masked the grill from view with his ham and cheese on very old rye wrapped up in a sheet of waxed paper. Her name was Lynette, she was in her fifties, and it would be a long cold night of a long cold winter before anybody looked at her twice. Skid Denton was sitting at the other end of the bar. Sess knew him as a denizen of the Nougat, the only other place where you could get a drink in Boynton, population 170. "Hey, Lynette," Skid said, "Sess is going into Fairbanks for a little shopping, did you know that?"

She set the sandwich down as if it weighed a quarter of a ton, gave a smile that barely wrinkled her lip and took a drag of her cigarette. She only worked here. She'd only just started. She was trading free rent on a shack out back for zero wages and zero tips and all she could eat and drink when Wetzel Setzler, who owned the place, was away. As he was now. "That so?" she said, glancing from one of them to the other.

Sess looked away. He was impatient. Time to go, oh yes indeed, and he could already picture the wide familiar planed dirt road rolling under his tires, and then the first pavement he'd have seen in eight or nine months stretched out as smooth as black ice coming into the city, and then the stores and the houses and the saloons. He drained his beer, shrugged.

"Going to get him a wife, isn't that right, Sess?"

He remembered in that moment why he didn't like the man – he talked like a tourist's idea of a sourdough, though he'd been raised in Los Angeles and had a degree in French literature. "You know, pick up some flour, eggs, milk, a new wife, that sort of thing – "

Lynette was wearing a faded flannel shirt buttoned up to her throat, blue jeans and boots. Her hair was cut short as a man's, she'd driven up from Seattle in a brand-new Pontiac station wagon and nobody knew whether she was married, divorced, a spinster or an ex-nun. She wore a pistol in a snug leather holster that looped over her belt, and to Sess's mind that marked her as a particularly dangerous brand of oddball, the kind who come into the country to play out their Technicolor fantasies of the Wild West. "What you wearing that gun for?" he'd asked when he ordered the second beer. She gave him a defiant look. "Protection," she said. "Protection?" he'd echoed. "From what?" The stony look now, the look of a thousand bars and dancehalls and another thousand nights alone staring into the black hole of the TV. "It's not bears," she said. "Or moose or wolves either. It's the two-legged beast worries me."

Now she said, "New wife? I didn't even know you had an old one."

Could he dignify the question with a response? Was it worth the time and effort? Did he want to act inappropriately, act out, tell her to go fuck herself and then maybe bounce Skid Denton's head up and down off the bar as if he were dribbling a basketball downcourt through a swarming defense? No. No, he didn't. The fact was that he'd never had a wife of any kind, new or old, because the last woman – Jill – who'd spent a lush summer and a sere and brokenhearted winter in his twelve-by-twelve log cabin with all the appointments, or at least necessities, had embarrassed him. People still talked about it. People still shook their heads, as if it were some kind of joke, some kind of routine he'd gone through – and Jill had gone through – just for their amusement. A soap opera. A TV show.

He scraped his change up off the bar, having a little trouble with the dimes because he'd chopped off the tips of his fingernails with a penknife just this morning as part of a general effort to spruce up his image. He tucked in his shirt, wheeled and headed for the door. Where he paused, the door open a crack so that the outside mosquitoes and the inside mosquitoes could change places, the agenda they seemed most intent on throughout the duration of their brief bloodsucking lives. "If I get lucky," he said. "Real lucky. So wish me luck."

He let his mind drift during the long drive in, watching in an abstracted way for game, rolling down the window so he could smell the country and the chill coming up off the Chatanika River. A handful of cars passed him going the other way, a camper or two, but this wasn't a busy road, even in the best of times – like now. In winter, once it snowed, the road was closed, drifted in, iced up, landslid and buckled, and Boynton was like a ship at sea with no land in sight. If you wanted out, you flew. In a bush plane that had no paint on it because paint added an unnecessary thirteen pounds to the total load. You flew, that is, unless the temperature had dropped past forty below, the range at which fuel lines tended to freeze, and if you didn't have fuel to the engine you came down out of the sky like a big winged rock. But that was life in the bush, and to his mind, it was a small price to pay for what you got in return.

When he reached Fairbanks he was amazed at the traffic, two cars to the left of him, three lined up at a light, pickups pulling in and out of gravel lots as if they were coming out of the gate at the Indianapolis Speedway, women, children, bicyclists, dogs. He had to remind himself to be careful, because he wasn't used to driving and didn't much like it – in fact, he was more than a little suspicious of people who did.

Plus he was drunk, or residually inebriated, though most of the effects of what he'd downed at the roadhouse had dissipated during the drive and the long slow gnawing at the ham-and-cheese sandwich Lynette had made for him with all the care of a veteran hash-slinger. The city clawed at him. The traffic lights made him frantic with impatience. But he knew right where he was going, and nothing – absolutely nothing – had changed since he'd been here last, in September of the previous year.

She was waiting for him at a table out on the deck of a restaurant on the riverfront, the nicest place in town, and it was nice for people to be able to sit outside and take advantage of the sun and the views. He saw her before she saw him, and he held back a moment so he could compose himself. In profile, against the river and the broad slap of the sun on the water, she was like a figure in a dream. Her bare legs and arms gleamed, her hair shone. She was wearing khaki shorts and hiking boots with thick gray socks rolled down over the tops and a pink T-shirt three sizes too small that pulled tight across her chest. Her name was Pamela, and he'd met her twice before, but that didn't make him any less nervous. He tucked in his shirt all the way round, slicked down his hair with two saliva-dampened fingers, and walked out onto the deck.

At that moment, the very moment his boots hit the planks, she turned to slap a mosquito on her upper arm and saw him. A quick burn of puzzlement went through her face, as if she hadn't been expecting him or had forgotten all about him, what he looked like even, but then she was on her feet and he was there and they went through that awkward man-woman greeting business with a restrained hug and a touch of her cheek to his as she stood up on her tiptoes and pulled him down to her. "Sit down," she said, showing off her perfect white teeth, the teeth of a dental hygienist or a stripper, teeth that said *hello* and *watch out* at the same time. "Sit down and join me, Sess, and don't be so bashful. God," she said, and she let out a laugh, "you're like a little lost boy on the playground."

He fumbled into the chair across the table from her and murmured something like "Nice to see you, Pam," but before the words were out she'd already corrected him: "Pamela," she said, smiling still, smiling so hard, so persistently, so radiantly, that he began to feel a little afraid of her despite himself. Was there something wrong with this picture? Or was she as nervous as he was? He gave an inward shrug – either way, she was beautiful. God, she was beautiful. And what cabin in the bush couldn't use an ornament like that, perfect teeth and all?

The waitress saved him. She was there, short skirt, two breasts and a face, hovering over him. She wanted to know if she could get him something to drink. And was he going to have lunch today?

Pamela was drinking iced tea. The menu lay facedown beside her plate.

"I think I'll have a beer," he said, "an Oly," and for some reason he was looking at Pam instead of the waitress, as if he were asking permission or trying to calibrate her response. "And – I'm sorry, did you order yet?"

"No," she said, "but go ahead. You know what you want?"

He had a cheeseburger, medium rare, with everything on it, fries, and a salad with ranch dressing. She glanced up at the waitress without even lifting the menu from the table. "I'll have the same," she said, with a grin. "And a beer sounds good."

"Oly?" the waitress wanted to know.

"Yeah," Pamela breathed, and she was looking at him now, at Sess, looking right into his eyes, "Oly." As soon as the waitress was out of earshot, she said, "So, are you prepared to turn right around and drive back this afternoon, because I'm all packed and ready and there's no sense in wasting any time – you know, another night in the city when we could be out in the bush, in your cabin, I mean. You're on the Thirtymile, right?"

He just stared. Things were moving way too fast – but wasn't that the way he'd envisioned it in his fantasies, she lying naked on the bed beneath his window, her skin as white as Ivory soap against the deep pile of his furs, her limbs spread wide in invitation? "I was going to pick up a few things at the hardware and the grocery, and I was supposed to . . ." He drifted off a moment and gave her a strained smile. "For Richard, Richard Schrader. You know, because he let me borrow his truck – "

The waitress arrived with their beers and there was a moment of silence as they watched her go through the ritual of tipping and pouring. Someone let out a bark of laughter from the next table over. A pair of silver canoes slid by on the far side of the river.

"I know Richard," Pamela said, and his heart froze inside him.

"You don't mean – was he one of the ones?"

"No," she said, as abruptly as if she were taking a bite out of something, and she shook her head emphatically. "Not Richard, no way. Remember, I'm a practical girl here and the whole point of this is I want somebody to love me, sure, but somebody who can take *care* of me, know what I mean? In the bush. Somebody – *like you* – who knows his way around, who has the survival skills, who's a real woodsman and not just some townie wanna-be."

Was he blushing? The compliment went right to him. He lifted the beer to his lips, took a sip and watched her eyes as if they were fish under the surface of the ice or ptarmigans in a clump of willow, something he was hunting, a brace of geese or old squaws. Suddenly he was Mr. Confidence. Suddenly he wanted to get up from the table and lift the whole deck, the whole restaurant, right up on his shoulders, just to show her what he was. "Is it fair to ask who I'm up against then? And what seed I am in this tournament?"

The smile drew down to nothing. "Richie Oliver and Howard Walpole," she said. "Just them. And you. And you know what, Sess?" Her hand was on the table now, lying there, palm up, like a double-spring Victor trap with the snow blown bare of it. And what did he want? He wanted to be caught, he did, he was praying for it every day and night of his life, and he reached out and slipped his fingers through hers. "No, what?" he said.

"You've got nothing to worry about."

He didn't remember much of the ride back, just a sensation of floating over the road as if he were in an airplane instead of a car, Pamela in the lotus position on the seat beside him, her bare legs glistening in the sun through the window. They were both feeling good, convivial and full of high spirits, and just about everything he said made her laugh and show her teeth. The country unfurled before them like a camouflage jacket, gray and green and brown, and they saw goshawks and Brewer's blackbirds wheeling overhead. At one point, just before the turnoff for Boynton Hot Springs, they stopped to watch a fox hunting in the bush alongside the road and he had to fight down the impulse to shoot it with the .22 Richard kept under the seat for just such an opportunity as this – the fur was worthless this time of year, but it would have been fresh meat for the pot, and he *was* on trial here, after all.

"Look at the way he pounces," she said, leaning out the window so far he thought she was going to fall. "Just like a dog playing with a ball."

"What he's doing," Sess said, and he slid across the seat to look over her shoulder, so close now he could smell the soap she used on her skin, "he's trying to scare up whatever might be hiding under the bushes, you know, voles, grasshoppers, maybe a fat juicy wood frog or two – "

She turned to him now, and she was right there, her face inches from his, and he had to back off, he had to, and she could chalk that up in the credit column under his name. Let her make the first move. Sure. Let *her*. "Sounds appetizing," she said, smiling wide.

Reddening, he slid back across the seat and put the truck in gear. "You hungry?" he asked. "Not for frog legs, I mean, but something like a steak or a sandwich, maybe a couple more beers to celebrate? Because by the time we get to the cabin, I mean, and unload all this stuff, feed the dogs and see what the garden looks like, I don't know if we're going to have time to – " He trailed off. With her here, actually here, living and breathing and watching him out of her eyes that were like two guided missiles homing in on his, he couldn't really get much past the picture of walking her in the door of the cabin. After that, the screen went blank.

But she said sure, sure she was hungry, and twenty minutes later he was escorting her up the bleached wooden steps of the Three Pup, as proud as if he'd made her out of clay and breathed the life into her himself.

It was eight o'clock in the evening and the sun was right there with them, showing all its teeth. The trees were staked to their shadows, the guest cottages that hadn't housed a guest in ten years sank quietly into the muskeg, birds flitted over the decaying snow machines scattered across the yard. There was the rattle of the generator, and beneath it, the whine of the mosquitoes – they were there, of course, always there, ubiquitous, but by now the daytime crew had gone home to sleep off the effects of breakfast, lunch and dinner, and the night shift had taken over. He swatted half a dozen on his forearm and flapped a protective hand round the crown of Pamela's head as they pushed through the screen door and the perpetual gloom of the place rose up to envelop them.

Half the town was gathered at the bar, including Richard Schrader and Skid Denton, who must have gone home in the interval because even he couldn't manage to drink straight through for nine and a half hours – or could he? As soon as they walked in, a general roar went up, people showing off their wit with comments like "Look what the cat dragged in," and a couple of the guys whistled at the sight of Pamela. Who whirled round, her hands outstretched, and did a little pirouette for them. Reticence was not one of her drawbacks, that was for sure.

They had a beer at the bar, and he luxuriated in the sweet proximity of her, in the blond bundle of her hair all coiled up in a no-nonsense braid, in the grip and complexity of the muscles of her legs, in her smile. He bought her Beer Nuts, Slim Jims, pickled eggs, and they each had a shot to go with their beers while Lynette fried up a pair of steaks for them, the holster riding her hip like an excess flap of skin. It was a moment, all right – so glorious and pure he never wanted to let go of it.

Over their steaks, which they ate at a table in the corner, she told him what he already knew or suspected or had heard elsewhere. She'd been born and raised in Anchorage, but every summer of her childhood her father had taken the family – her and her sister and mother – to live out of a tent in the Endicott Mountains of the Brooks Range while he prospected unnamed creeks in nameless canyons and reappeared every third day or so with something for the pot. They'd contract with a bush pilot to drop them off just after breakup, and the pilot would come back and pick them up again at the end of September, and so what if they missed a whole month of school? She and her sister Priscilla would fish and roam and scare up birds, listen to the wolves at night and have face-to-face encounters with just about every creature that made its living north of the Arctic Circle. And now, now that she was a college graduate and twenty-seven years old and sick to death of working nine-to-five in a city of concrete and steel, she wanted to go back to the bush, and not just for a vacation, not as a tourist or part-timer, but forever. That was it. That was the deal.

He'd begun to feel the effects of the long day – the two-way drive, the alcohol, the excitement that burned in the back of his throat like a shot of Canadian on a subzero night – when he looked up from her eyes and saw Joe Bosky across the room. "Shit," he said. "We got to go."

"Already? Aren't you going to ask me to dance? At least once – one dance?"

The jukebox was going – "Mystic Eyes," one of his favorite songs, but hardly the sort of thing you could dance to. "Next time," he said.

She let out a laugh then. "You're just like all the rest of them, afraid of their own two feet. How about if we wait for a slow one?"

And now he was hedging. "But I wouldn't want you to have to spend your first night in my shack in town, and you wouldn't want that either, would you? Because don't forget, we've got a three-hour paddle, upstream, to get to the cabin – "

She told him he was cute. Told him she liked the way the two parallel lines creased his brow when he worked himself up. And she smirked and stretched out her legs so he and everybody else in the place could admire the full shimmering length of them, and agreed with him. "You're right," she said. "I do want to see the cabin, I mean, that's the whole point, isn't it? Or half of it, or part of it, anyway. It's just that I was really enjoying this."

That was when Joe Bosky butted in.

He was hovering over their table like a waiter, stinking of something – fish, vomit, B.O. – and he was grinning like some sort of trapped animal from the deeps of his beard. He was wearing a fatigue shirt that had U.S.M.C. stenciled across the pocket and a khaki cap with the brim worked flat. His jeans looked as if they'd been salvaged from a corpse. And smelled like it too. "Hey," he said, leaning into the table and ignoring Sess, "I hear you're the lady that's looking for a man, is that right?"

Pamela didn't know him from Adam, and she was the kind of person who had a smile for everybody, so she gave him his grin back and said, "That's right. But I didn't realize I was so famous."

Sess was up out the chair. "We got to go," he repeated.

"I was just wondering if I could get in on the action," Joe Bosky was saying, ignoring him still. "You know, I'm a pretty good man in the bush myself – and I'm building a cabin up Woodchopper Creek even as we speak – and I was just wondering if, you know, there might be any free tryouts?"

Pamela's smile faded.

"I mean, I've got a sleeping bag out in the car if you've got maybe fifteen minutes to spare – "

Sess hit him – or attempted to hit him – square in the side of the head, but Bosky had been watching him out of the corner of his eye and had time to get his forearm up and deflect the blow. In the next instant, they were at each other, flailing across the floor, and there was some small damage done to the glassware and one of the rickety dried-out chairs before they were separated. Bosky made some ugly comments – shouted them, raging in the grip of three men, threats, accusations and promises, and there was no law up here unless you got the sheriff to fly in from Fairbanks to inspect the corpse – and Sess threw them back at him. He hadn't meant to, hadn't meant to show that side of himself in front of Pamela – cursing and the like – but of all the men on earth Joe Bosky was the one who could make him boil over till the lid rattled against the pan.

Out in the lot, as the mosquitoes dive-bombed them and they slammed back into the truck for the half-mile drive down to the shack on the river and the canoe that awaited them, Pamela looked shaken, and he felt sorry for that, he did. "What was that all about?" she said. "That guy – I mean, I've seen some bush crazies in my time, but that guy was scary."

In the front seat now, the truck rumbling to life beneath him, Sess just stared out the window a moment. Joe Bosky was what was wrong with the world. Joe Bosky was what people came into the country to escape. And Joe Bosky, hammered, polished and delivered up by the U.S. Marine Corps, was right here at the very end of the very last road in the continental United States, going one on one with the world. Sess was breathing hard, upset despite himself. "You don't know the half of it," he said.

And then they were on the Yukon, the big nineteen-foot Grumman freighter loaded down to the gunwales, the ten o'clock sun picking its way through the rolling black shadows of the debris on the surface, and he was calm again, in his element, off the road, out of the bar and into the embrace of the country. He watched Pamela's shoulders dig at the paddle, studied the heavy braid of her hair, the beautiful locus of her back muscles and the sweet place where she sat the seat. The birds were there, the spruce marshaled along the banks and climbing up into the hills like an emperor's army, naked bluffs, a million cords of driftwood flung up against the shore waiting for the river to decide what to do with them. A breeze came up and took the mosquitoes away. They saw moose in the shallows, a black bear with two cubs hurtling up the far bank as if she'd been shot out of a cannon. They spoke in low tones. They were silent, and the country spoke for them. And then she said something, and he said something, and it was as natural to him as if he were speaking to himself.

It must have been around midnight, the sun hovering on the horizon, when they swung into the mouth of the Thirtymile River and the cabin came into view. Already the five dogs were up and yammering, dust rising round their feet in a distant cloud, the proto-barks drifting off into wolfish howls of greeting. "Hear that?" Sess said, digging into the paddle. "That's your welcoming committee."

She turned to look over her shoulder. "Oh, really? And what are they saying?"

" 'Pam-e-la, looooooove youuuuu!' "

And she laughed, even as a pair of loons went racketing up off the water. "You sure they're not saying, 'Here we are, now feeeeeeeed us'?"

"Well, Pamela," he said, and he winked at her because he was feeling so light in his bones and his organs he might have been a bird that could sail right up out of the canoe and across the flux of the water in a single wild rush of feathers, "to be truthful with you – and I'm going to be truthful with you, always, whether this lasts the weekend or till you're a hunched-over old lady and I'm an old man – I think you do have a point there." He let the paddle trail an instant and cupped a hand to his ear. "Yep. Now that I concentrate, I think I *can* detect maybe just a trace of hunger in that chorus – but that's Bobo, that sharp contralto in there, and he's always hungry. So don't blame him for spoiling the surprise."

Then it was dusk and the canoe was up on the gravel bar, the dogs straining at their chains, and he and Pamela were walking hand in hand up the path that beat through the weeds to the cabin. He wished he could show her something grander – the rambling spread of outbuildings, the smokehouse, sauna and enclosed dog runs he planned to put up once he found the time and the money, not to mention a more spacious cabin – but he was proud of what he'd already accomplished, and he could feel the pride beating at his rib cage as he took down the bear-proof shutters and unlatched the door for her. The door faced south, of course, as did the two double-paned windows set on either side of it, but before they were in the cabin proper they had to go through the five-by-five dogtrot – or mud room, as somebody who lived in town might call it. "This," he said, breathing hard in the dimness and taking in the familiar smells of oil, gasoline, ancient bait and bloodied traps and mold and whatever else had awakened out of the dirt, "this is the mud room."

She was right there, a good eight or ten inches shorter than him, her pale hair and white arms ghostly in the half-light, and she wasn't saying anything, just staring wide-eyed, like a girl on a school trip. He guided her through the inner door and into the cabin itself, dodging round her to put a match to the lantern he kept on a hook just inside the door. "And this," he said, his voice almost strangled in his throat with the sheer tension of the moment, "this is what I call home."

She stood in the middle of the room and she didn't say a word. Her hair was luminous, her shoulders squared. He wanted to say something, wanted to ask her if she liked it, but he couldn't find his voice. After a moment she drifted toward the shelves on the near wall and idly fingered the things there, his few grease-slick books *(Tanning: From A to Z; How to Stay Alive in the Woods; Arctic Wilderness; The Home Brewer),* a bottle of Pepto Bismol set beside a string of dried habanero chiles, Three-In-One oil in a rusted can, a candle six inches around he'd made from the wax of the bees he'd mail-ordered last summer, the odd tool. Still, she didn't say anything.

How long she stood there, picking up one thing after another and gently setting it down again, he couldn't say – no more than a minute or two, certainly, but it was the longest minute or two of his life. Was she in shock, was that it? For all her talk, she was a city woman, and maybe she had a whole different idea of what a cabin in the woods really was, a whole unspooling romantic fantasy of a big Ponderosa TV cabin with forest green shutters and a wide veranda and a kitchen with a tile floor and a hand pump for water. His heart was hammering. He couldn't seem to swallow. Outside, the dogs howled. And never had the place seemed so close, so dingy and confining, so much like a cell, like a bum's palace, like the meanest, crackbrained idea of a tumbledown shack in the world. The floor was caked with dirt. It was cold as a grave. He wanted to get down on his knees and sob. What had he been thinking? What in God's name had he been thinking?

"I'm going to put a coat of varnish on the floor," he said. "That's the next thing. The very next thing."

And then she turned to him, and the tears were in *her* eyes. "Oh, Sess," she said, "it's so, so *beautiful*."

Together they fed the dogs – pots of cornmeal mush with dried chum salmon and the odd greenish scrap of last fall's moose stirred in – and then he got the stove going and made her coffee with evaporated milk and so much sugar the spoon stood upright in it. Down came the table and the bed, both of which folded up against the wall when they weren't in use and rested on dowels of white spruce when they were – "Space management," he told her, "nothing to get in your way and trip over." She perched on the bed, on the thin single mattress he'd hauled upriver in the canoe two years ago, and on the sleeping bag he'd sewn from the hides of a hundred ground squirrels. Within minutes the stove had driven the chill from the place and conquered the lingering odor of dampness and mold.

He sat on the far edge of the bed from her, cradling his cup in his hands. "It's a tight cabin," he said, selling its virtues. "Even at sixty below. You'd be surprised. I mean, you would."

She'd taken off her jacket now, and she stretched and leaned back into the pile of furs – lynx, fox, wolf – he'd heaped up around her. Her eyes were feasting. "That's nice to know," she said. "But with all these furs, and this beautiful sleeping bag – very neat stitchwork, Sess, by the way; I'm impressed – with all of this you'd be warm without the stove."

He was thinking he'd be even warmer if he had somebody inside it with him, and before he could stop himself, he'd said as much. He said it, and then he looked away.

Her first response was a laugh, musical and ringing, a laugh that made the place swell till it was like a concert hall. He brought the coffee mug to his lips so he could steal a look at her. Her face grew serious. She shifted herself closer to him and reached out her hand for his. "That'd be nice," she said, her voice gone raw in her throat. "But I don't want you to get the wrong idea here, because it would be easy to, I suppose, you know, with me advertising for a man and all – "

He held her hand across the expanse of the bed, flesh to flesh, his every cell on fire. He didn't know what to say.

"Because I'm not that kind of girl, not the kind you hear about – or read about in the magazines. I'm old-fashioned, Sess, and I'm sorry, but that's the way it is. I've waited twenty-seven years for the right man and I guess I can wait a few weeks longer. Till I'm married. Can you understand that? Can you?"

He was thinking about Jill, her hair cut short with a pair of shears till it stood out from her head like a clown's, her legs hard-muscled and short, the heavy gravitational pull of her breasts as she swung into the sleeping bag naked, always naked, even on the coldest nights. Jill. He was thinking about Jill. "Yes," he said. "Sure."

And finally, when they thought of sleep with the sun propped back up in the sky and the night as still as a dead man's dream, he was the one who gave up the bed and went out into the pale drizzle of light to pitch his tent amongst the dogs.

8

At eleven-thirty the next morning she was sitting on the edge of the bed, combing out her hair and watching the way the muscles rearranged themselves in his shoulders as he leaned into the stove and cooked her breakfast. He was wearing patched jeans and a sun-faded workshirt that might once have been blue or maybe green. His hair, movie-star black and thick as a wolf pelt, stood up off his head as if he'd been hanging by it all night long in a closet someplace. He was barefoot. The sleeve of his shirt was gutted under the left arm and both cuffs were furred with dangling threads. "Moose sausage," he said, giving her a look over his shoulder, "and your extra-super-special Sess Harder flapjacks with last year's sugared blueberries. What do you think of that?"

Through the two windows came a soft white layered light and both doors stood open to the sun and the sunstruck haze beyond. She could see his bees moving in golden flecks among the birch and aspen in the yard and she could smell the new-made scent of the Thirtymile where it joined with the Yukon and drew wet sparks from the rocks. Her hair was a travail, especially when she was out in the bush, and she'd meant to leave it braided – but when she woke and saw him there at the stove, laying on wood, fussing with the draft, she thought she'd comb it out and let it hang like a flag of surrender. Or enticement. Because she was on trial too, and she wanted to show him what she had, and not only mentally, not only verbally, but physically as well.

"That," she said, giving him a smile, "sounds like just the thing. Because, I mean, anybody could have offered me eggs Benedict, caviar and truffles and the like, but if I'm going to paddle three hours for breakfast, the least I could expect is the super-special flapjacks. With, what did you say, *moose* sausage?"

He didn't answer, because he was executing some sort of arcane maneuver with a cast-iron skillet so black it might have been unearthed from a tomb. There was the sound of hot grease snapping in the pan, and suddenly the cabin was dense with the smell of it, and with smoke too. He stabbed the sausages with a long-handled fork, danced round the coffeepot, flipped the leaden dark cakes with a rolling snap of his wrist. "I ought to get you a toque," she said, and he said, "What's a toque?"

They ate outside in the sun at a picnic table he'd fashioned from black spruce and varnished till it was the color of old leather, and they made use of his entire complement of dishware in the process: two tin plates and two tin mugs. In the center of the table, set in a can, was a sprig of wildflowers he'd gathered while she slept, and that touched her, the effort he'd put out and the essential sweetness it implied. He poured coffee, spooned up blueberries. "You know what I bet the best thing about living out here must be," she said, mopping up her plate. "Aside from the beauty, I mean?"

He shrugged and grinned, tried not to look too pleased with himself. "Tell me," he said.

"Safety. You've got to feel safe here, don't you?"

"Sure, as long as I don't have to perform any emergency appendectomies. On myself, that is. Or you."

"The auto-appendectomy," she said, and they both laughed.

"Or dental work. Imagine trying to pull your own tooth?"

They were silent a minute, contemplating the horror of that particular image, and then she said, "I'll pull yours if you pull mine," and they were laughing again. It was laughter that took a while to subside, and when he got up, still chuckling, to scrape the plates and wash up, she told him to sit down and let her do it, because she'd seen enough – enough, already. What did he think, he had to wait on her hand and foot? "What I meant," she said, sliding the dishes into the tub of water he'd heated on the stove, "was the kind of safety you could never feel in the city, or at least I couldn't. It got so I didn't want to go out at night, not alone."

He'd followed her back inside and was sitting on the edge of the bed now, rolling a cigarette and watching her as she moved amongst his things. "Okay," he said, "sure, I'll grant you that. As a woman you've got to be especially careful – "

"As a man too. The whole society's breaking down, assassinations, drugs in the schools, hippies – I know this guy from my office who used to like to walk his dog before he went to bed . . . just that, walk his dog. And you know what happened?"

Sess lit the cigarette. "Somebody jumped him?"

"You bet they did. Two guys with a knife, longhairs, and they weren't content to just take his wallet – they stuck the knife right up his nose and slit his nostril, and you should see it, it's like a permanent disfiguration, like a tattoo or something. And the dog. It was this sweet little thing, a cockapoo – Berenice, he called her – and she tried to protect him and they just turned on the dog and kicked her and kicked her till there wasn't hardly anything left of her. That's what I mean. That's what society's coming to."

He'd risen from the bed and was standing beside her now, and she was aware of him in a way that made her skin prickle, the breadth of him, the smell of the tobacco, a tentative hand on her shoulder and his voice pitched deep: "You don't have to worry about any of that out here. Bears, maybe. Wolverines. But we know how to discourage them. Believe me."

Her hands were in the water and it was as hot as she could stand it. The scrub pad moved mechanically against the crust of the blackened pan. "That's what I mean," she said. "You have freedom out here, and not just freedom to do what you want, but freedom from that kind of crap – he was just walking his dog, for God's sake." For some reason she couldn't name, she was on the verge of tears, and she wondered about that, about how she could let herself get so wrought up when this was what she'd wanted all her life, this place, and maybe this person, and the rest of the world, with its nose-slitters and dog-kickers, could sink into the ocean for all it mattered.

"Pamela," he was saying, "come on, Pamela," and she felt him lifting her arms out of the sudsing water till she was open to him and he pulled her close. "You're never going to have to think about any of that ever again, not for the rest of your life."

People said she was crazy, wanting to live out in the hind end of nowhere, ten or twenty miles from the nearest store, church, roadhouse or post office, and another hundred sixty from anything even approximating civilization, if you could call Fairbanks civilized. And they said she was crazier still for willingly putting herself in the hands of some grizzled, twisted, sex-starved fur trapper with suet-clogged arteries and guns decorating his walls – in fact, that was exactly, word for word, the way Fred Stines, the man she'd been seeing in Anchorage, had put it – but she begged to differ. What they didn't understand – what Fred couldn't begin to imagine – was that everything they knew, the whole teetering violent war-crazed society, was about to collapse. On that score, she hadn't the slightest doubt. And the riots in the streets were just a prelude to what was to come, because if nobody worked and they all just sat around using drugs and having promiscuous sex all day, then who was going to grow the food? And if nobody grew the food, then what would they eat? To her, the answer was obvious: they'd eat your food, and when they were done with that, they'd eat you, just like in that science fiction book where all the dead and dying were made into potted meat. Sure. But you could work in an office building every day and go to the store in your new shiny car and then come home to your gas heater and your woodstove, and never think twice about it, and that was where the Fred Stineses of the world would be when it all came crashing down. Not her, though, not Pamela. She was going to live in the bush, and she was going to be one hundred percent self-sufficient. Anything less, to her mind, was a form of suicide.

On the afternoon of the second day, after breakfast and the embrace that became a clinch and then a kiss that went on till the blood was singing in her ears, Sess walked her around the place, showing it off. He demonstrated the clarity of the Thirtymile where it crashed into the opaque Yukon, which ran heavy with its freight of glacial debris, showed her where he planned to build a sauna and a workshop, lectured her on the garden that was already showing green against the black plastic he'd laid down for heat retention. He was growing cabbage, cauliflower, turnips, kohlrabi and Brussels sprouts, potatoes, onions, peas, lettuce, Early Girl tomatoes, basil, cucumbers, squash. "Everything has to be in the ground by the first of June," he was saying, "though you risk a frost, which is why I keep that wood stacked up over there, just as a precaution, because we get a growing season out here of maybe a hundred five or so days, what with the influence of the river keeping things a tad less frigid, and every day counts, believe me, and round about February you'd kill to have a little pickled cabbage or stewed tomatoes with your six thousandth serving of moose – "

She was listening, because this was the information she needed, this was the knowledge that was proof against anything, but most of what he said drifted right through her – it was his voice she was listening to, not the words. His voice mesmerized her in a way Fred Stines's never could. It spoke to her in a tone that was like a current flowing through her, like the electric charge in a wall socket or the balky lamp she'd clumsily rewired when she was in college. He talked – and he wasn't shy anymore, not shy a bit – and she listened. "So," he said finally, and they were down at the river staring into the canoe, "should we maybe go upstream a bit and see what we can scare up for dinner? You like duck, maybe? Duck with scallions and a super-extra-special Sess Harder spicy homemade barbecue sauce?"

The canoe rode the river as if it were floating on air, the strewn rock of its bed transformed into puffed and emboldened clouds, the fish like the black silhouettes of birds flitting past. She was on the river with Sess Harder, in the wilderness with Sess Harder, and she was in love with everything. They paddled hard, upriver, into a breeze. She could feel the weight of him behind her, the canoe a seesaw on the playground of the water, and she could feel the thrust of his paddle as they dodged rocks and downed trees and cut across the riffles where the current boiled around them. This was silent work, and for the first time since he'd stepped out onto the deck of the restaurant yesterday afternoon, neither of them felt compelled to talk. It was only when they swept round a bend and she was startled to see a building standing high atop the far bank that she broke the silence. "Good God, Sess," she said, turning to look back at him, "what is that – a cabin? Way out here?"

Yes, it was a cabin. Obviously a cabin. Notched logs, the flash of window glass, sun on the skin of an overturned aluminum skiff laid in tight against the near side. It had a sod roof, and there were trees eight or ten feet tall sprouting from it as if it were the picture of a troll's den in a children's book. Sess kept paddling, the steadiest stroke in the world. "That's right," he said.

"But you didn't tell me I was going to have to live in a subdivision." She tried to inject a note of humorous disparagement, but she was shocked, genuinely shocked, because what was the sense of it all if there was a cabin around every bend?

"Don't you let it worry you, Pamela," he said, the cabin already drifting out to the margins of her peripheral vision, " – nobody lives there. Nobody's lived there for over a year now."

The paddle worked and she could feel it in her shoulders, feel herself toughening already. "But who – ?" she said.

"An old guy, one of the old-timers, a real authentic cranky tattered river bachelor who stank of the goose wings soaked in beaver castor he used to bait lynx, the kind of guy who only bathed when he fell in the river, which was about twice a year." He paused, but the paddle kept working. "The kind of guy – or coot – I'd become if it wasn't for, well, if it wasn't for you."

She let the hopefulness of that sink in a minute, and then she said, "So where is he now – I mean, did he die?"

"Oh, no, no – he was way too cranky to die. He retired. Hung up his snowshoes and rinsed his gold pans for the final time and went on down to Seattle to live with his brother in a rooming house someplace. You know: central heating, color TV, washer and dryer. A little strip of macadam to park your pickup on."

"That's horrible," she said.

"Oh, yeah," he said, and she looked back to see him grinning at her. "Nothing worse."

Then they were beaching the canoe on a strip of gravel and hiking through a sweating dense tangle of birch, aspen and cottonwood that was held fast by the sheer mass of the mosquitoes that swarmed through it in all their regiments and brigades. She was wearing long sleeves and jeans and she'd rubbed herself like a leg of lamb in 6-12, but the mosquitoes got her in the one place she'd missed – the tip of her nose – and the swatting of them became automatic. "Five minutes more," Sess whispered, a shotgun in one hand, a .22 slung over his shoulder. "I'm taking you to this series of little lakes where there's more ducks than mosquitoes even, if you can believe it." And then he went on to tell her that the natives didn't call the season late spring or early summer, but just that – Ducks – because there were so many of them flown up from the south to nest and raise their young. It was like an open-air meat market. You couldn't miss.

But then they got there and he did miss, three times, and the lake that was once a stretch of the river in years gone by – an oxbow, they called it – was first a pandemonium of squawking and flapping ducks, and then it was duckless, a flat black expanse of duckless water. Sess took it hard. He made apologies – but no excuses, because that wasn't the way he was. "Wait here," he said, and she waited the better part of an hour while he slipped off into the undergrowth as quietly as a breeze and the mosquitoes swarmed and the silence finally ruptured with the distant thump of three more shots, and when he came back to her he was still duckless and looking frustrated and angry. He gave her a tense smile. "Don't you worry," he said, "we just – well, I hate to say it, but we just have to be patient. Can you appreciate that, Pamela? Can you?"

She was going to say that she *could* appreciate it, of course she could, and that he didn't have to worry on her account because anything he wanted to cook was just fine with her, when the dark water at her feet began to move as if it had come to life, trailing an even darker *V* across the flat surface, and he grinned and unslung the .22, and a moment later he was wading out of the muck with a dripping naked-tailed black thing depending from one hand, and she said, "What is it, a beaver?" and he said, "It's a rat."

For dinner that night, and she was hungry, ravenous, all her cells crying out for fuel, he cooked her a fricassee of muskrat in a sauce of stewed tomatoes from the can with rice and greens and a sweetish yellow dollop of the prime fat the guest of honor wears under his coat while enacting his murky rituals in the ponds and sloughs of the backcountry. To wash it down, they each had two bottles of homemade beer so strong it was like the depth charges she used to drink in college. It was the best meal she'd ever had. And she told Sess that as she sat on the bed and grinned while he washed the dishes at the stove – "I insist," he said, "because you did them this morning, and that's only fair" – and then he pulled out a harmonica and serenaded her and they wound up harmonizing on three separate run-throughs of "Oh Susannah," "You Are My Sunshine" and "She Loves You" (Yeah, Yeah, Yeah).

It was past midnight and they were both giddy with the singing, the beer and the company that just kept lighting them up and lighting them up again, when she said, "So tell me about Jill."

That stopped things right there. He was tipping a beer to his lips, having just concluded a story about the night last winter when the thermometer showed sixty-two below and he went out to dump the dishwater and it froze before it hit the ground with a sound of marbles spilling out of a bag, and now he pulled the beer back and looked past her to the little window and beyond. "You don't want to hear about that," he said.

"Yes," she said, "I do."

"It's nothing much. Nothing like you must have heard."

"I haven't heard anything," she said, and then, to be truthful, because she *had* heard at least three versions of the story, the most disturbing and unfavorable of which had dripped like acid from the prejudicial lips of Howard Walpole, she added, "or hardly anything."

"She was nothing like you," he sighed. He got up from the table, took the lamp down from its hook and lit it. All his muscle seemed to have migrated to his neck, hard and attenuated, stripped away from the flesh. His face was heavy.

"Go ahead," she said. "I want to hear it."

Jill was young, just twenty-one, and he was young too – twenty-eight, at the time, and this was three years ago. He met her in Fairbanks, when he was tending bar in the winter after working a summer in the bush as a firefighter. He was drinking too much, sleeping late, living in a town that was like any other town and hardly even getting out to the Chena or the Nenana for fishing. He didn't know what he wanted. Jill was a college girl, or had been before she met him and dropped out of the University of Alaska, and they spent the winter sleeping together and talking about the country, about getting away from every-thing and just living free.

She came with him, just after breakup, to the very cabin they were in now, helped him build it, in fact. Neither of them knew what they were doing, but they learned by their mistakes and they had a cache of store-bought food to get them through the winter of the first year, until they could fish and garden and hunt on their own – sixty-pound sacks of rice, lentils and cornmeal, butter in one-gallon cans, smoked fish, that sort of thing. And it was good for a while. But Jill just wasn't built for the country – psychologically, that is. Once winter set in and the sun winked out she started to climb the walls, and anybody would have thought she was in prison, tried and condemned and held against her will. "I'm in for life," she'd say in a voice that was dead and cremated to ash, "I'm a lifer. I'm a San Quentin drudge." He was out, even in the coldest weather, stalking the woods for ptarmigan, porcupine, lynx, anything for the pot, but she just sat there by the stove, staring into the glow, reading the same books over and over – she must have read *Silas Marner* twenty times, and that would put anybody round the bend. She played solitaire till the cards wore out and fell to dust. And then she started carving the days into the wall, four vertical lines and a slash, just like a prisoner.

Pamela let him go on. It was therapeutic, she could see that, and the air had to be cleared, because if things worked out, she was going to take this girl's place, and it would have been intolerable not knowing. Still, when he told her about the marks on the wall, he got up and leaned over her to run his finger across the bulge of the log she'd been resting her head against, and there they were, like cicatrices in a savage skin, the etchings of despair. The best she could do was throw out a question like a lifeline and cling to it: "So she was clinically depressed?"

"Cabin fever," he said, sinking into the furs beside her, "a fatal case." She offered her hand, but he wouldn't take it. "It happens to a lot of people in the bush. Women especially. Women seem to need the company of other women more than men need other men – we're more solitary. Like hermits or something. But you – you need to gossip and whatnot, right?"

She shrugged. "I suppose."

"Of course, the men get pretty squirrelly out here too. You ever hear the one about the two trappers living in the high country outside of Eagle? Two coots, the kind that talk to themselves even when you see them in town for their semi-annual visit? No? Well, anyway, it was February of a bitter winter and the one was half-mad for company, so he harnessed up his dogs and mushed thirty miles to where the other one was and the other man came to the door of his cabin and nodded at him in an inviting way and left the door open a crack. Well, the first man saw to his dogs and then came in without a word, shook out his parka and sat in a chair by the fire and just looked into the other man's face for an hour or so until the other man put a pot of moose stew on to boil and they ate in silence. Then they sat and smoked their pipes and when it was time for bed the first man unrolled his sleeping bag on the floor and conked out. In the morning they had breakfast together – more moose stew, biscuits and coffee – and then the first man went out, harnessed his dogs and waved goodbye while the other man stood at the door of the cabin. And you know what? Neither one of them spoke a word the whole time, not hello or goodbye or mighty tasty stew or I hate the sight of your grizzled ugly face, you son of a bitch."

"Instructive story," she said. "Are you trying to scare me?"

Sess looked surprised. "No, not at all. Why would I want to do that?"

"So Jill," she said, after a moment. "She got out?"

The stove creaked and sighed. The last of the sun laminated the back wall with the faintest, rinsed-out ribbon of pink. "What have you heard?" The voice was harsh in his throat. "That I'm some kind of Bluebeard or something?"

She trusted him. She liked him. She could even love him – she did love him, loved him already. "No," she said in a voice so soft she could barely hear it herself.

"You know where I showed you the garden?"

She nodded.

"Jill went out there where we'd cleared all the trees and she stomped these huge letters in the snow, I mean letters ten feet high and five feet across. You know what they read – from the air, that is? jill wants out. Jill wants out. You know how that humiliated me?" He went to the stove to pour another cup of coffee, and he even got so far as to lift the pot to his cup before he set it down again. "A week later this Cessna 180 equipped with skis lands on the frozen-up river and it's Joe Bosky. He comes to the door. 'You people having any trouble here?' he says."

"And that was the end of Jill."

His voice had gone soft now, all the harshness washed out of it. "I never laid eyes on her again."

The sun faded from the wall. From outside, thin with distance, came the cry of a wolf that died out in a feverish glissando until the dogs took it up. She could see them beyond the window, erect at their chains, noses pointed to the sky, and the sound they made was inharmonious and raw, expressive of some deep unquenchable sorrow, the sorrow of the stake and the chain and the harness. Sess said something then, and she didn't hear the words, only the sound, till he repeated himself: "Do you really have to go?"

"I promised," she said.

"The hell with your promise," he said, and the dogs sent up a howl so plaintive it must have had the wolf smirking from his mountaintop.

"Howard Walpole," she began, but Sess cut her off.

"Howard Walpole is shit," he said, "and you know it and I know it. I'm the one. Tell me I'm the one."

"It's only three days," she said. He wouldn't look at her. He looked at the coffeepot, looked at the wall. The dogs howled. "Three days, Sess. Then I'll know for sure."

9

Framed against the high dun bank and the random aggregation of shacks and cabins that composed the riparian view of Boynton, Howard Walpole stood rooted in the mud in a pair of gum boots and grease-slick chino pants. He was waiting for them as they came round the broad bend of the river that gave onto town, and from the look of him, Sess figured he'd been waiting for hours, though the agreed-upon time was twelve noon and it couldn't have been more than eleven-fifteen or eleven-thirty yet. It was an ugly day, overcast and close. The river was the color of the sky and the sky was the color of the primer you saw on pickups and wagons awaiting the benediction of paint. It was drizzling. The air smelled tainted, as if everything in the water, the woods and the sky had fallen down dead and gone to rot.

All the way down in the canoe Pamela kept chirping away about this or that – a moose in the shallows, an explosion of ducks, her mother's bad feet and her sister's reprobate of a boyfriend – but if he'd given her six words back it would have surprised him. He was feeling sour, sour and hateful, and he didn't care if she knew it. He dug savagely at his paddle, sprinting the last two hundred yards as if he couldn't wait to get rid of her, and in one compartment of his mind he was thinking he ought to take Howard Walpole aside and tell him what a pain in the ass she was, what a complete and utter screwup and bitch, but he knew it wouldn't work. Howard – he was thirty-eight years old, with a head that was almost perfectly flat in the back as if he'd been hit with a board the moment he popped out of the womb – Howard was the sort of man who never threw anything away and never took anybody's word for anything.

The canoe scraped gravel and Pamela hopped out, then let him sit as she lifted the bow up on shore. Howard was grinning, yellow teeth in a grizzled beard, and he'd shoved his begrimed engineer's cap up off his eyebrows so you could see the pale band of flesh to his hairline where the sun never touched. "Howdy, Pamela," he crowed, "enjoy your stay at the Harder palace?"

She said she had and he said, "Howdy, Sess," and then he took Pamela's backpack from her, tossed it onto the front seat of his big flat-bottomed boat with the twin Evinrude engines and held out a hand to help her aboard. "No sense in standing here in the rain," he added, "when there's a whole world out there to show you, and I don't know what you got used to up there at the Harder palace, but my place is like a four-star hotel in comparison, so don't you worry about a thing."

Then he shoved off, the engines roared to life, and Pamela was a receding speck of color on the broad gray back of the river.

He knew he shouldn't start drinking, knew he should turn around and paddle back upriver to his cabin, go out and clear brush along his trapline for the next three days, fish pike in the oxbows, put away some duck, but he found himself ambling past his shack and the various cabins of various people he knew and liked or disliked or was indifferent to, on up the main street, past the frame post office and the Nougat and the general store, in the direction of the Three Pup. He brought a whole new nation of mosquitoes with him, and while they sorted things out with the indigenous population, he ducked inside. Lynette was behind the bar, her eyes squinted against the smoke of the cigarette clenched between her teeth, and she was dealing cards to Richard Schrader as if dealing cards were the chief activity of the human species on this planet and why hurry to the end of the deck when you'd just have to deal them all over again? "Hey," Richard said, without looking up. And then Skid Denton, who was in his usual seat at the end of the rectangular bar that doubled as a luncheonette counter, said, "Satisfaction Guaranteed or Your Money Back. Get your satisfaction there, Sess? Or you looking for a refund?"

Sess told him to shut the fuck up and the tone of it was warning enough to everybody in the place – this was no laughing matter, no subject for lickerish grins and elbow prodding and the kind of behind-your-back laughter he'd had to endure over the

Jill situation. Everybody, at that hour, included Richie Oliver, who was sitting at a corner table with a woman nobody had ever seen before, and Richie Oliver wasn't going to say anything because he'd already had his three-day trial with Pamela, and they were both in the same boat. Besides which, the woman he was with was no beauty, and no girl either, and there was only one thing Richie Oliver or anybody else could have wanted out of that relationship. Sess put a quarter in the jukebox and played "Mystic Eyes" three times running and he ordered a shot and a beer and when he was done with it he ordered another and sat at the window studying a two-year-old copy of *Time* magazine he'd already read cover to cover at least six times.

People came and went. Two middle-aged tourists in a white station wagon with three inches of grit plastered to it chatted him up a while and he told them some creative lies about the country and what they could expect from it. ("Moose? Really? You mean they'll actually charge the car?") Around six he had Lynette make him a tuna sandwich and a plate of fries for ballast, and then he moved over to the Nougat to see who was around and maybe shoot a couple games of pool, and there were two Hungwitchin Indians there he knew from upriver, beyond Eagle, and he drank with them for an hour or two until one of them vomited on the table and Clarence Ford, who was bartending, asked them to leave. The Indians stumbled into their pickup, fired it up and waved a clumsy goodbye, but wait a minute, could they give him a lift up the road to the Three Pup because his legs didn't seem to want to work right? And sure, sure they could.

That was where things got hazy. Joe Bosky was there, that much was certain, and he got into it with him all over again, and who said what to whom or who started it was beyond irrelevance. He did seem to recall Lynette unholstering her pistol and maybe even firing it once or twice in the lot outside, but the upshot of it was that he was eighty-sixed while Joe Bosky stood tall at the bar with ten or twelve people and drank in dignity the rest of the night. But what Joe Bosky hadn't figured on, or anybody else, for that matter, was the fact that Joe Bosky's car, his white fastback Mustang with the blue racing stripe he rented a special garage for and only drove in the summertime, was parked right there amongst the weeds of the lot. Right there, like a steel-and-glass wall, for Sess to stumble into. And it was nothing, a matter of a few fleeting drunken minutes, to pop the hood and relieve himself on the black shining stump of the distributor cap and then wander off toward the river with the vague idea of settling in for the night.

To say he woke with a headache was to say nothing. He was crushed, poleaxed, transfixed on a stake of hurt and regret and the simple dull physical enervation of alcoholic excess. He hadn't quite made it to his shack, and he woke to the sun in his eyes and the gentle prodding of the toe of Richard Schrader's boot. "Sess," Richard was saying, and his face was a shining planetoid orbiting the sky, and there was a moon there beside it, and the moon was the too-white face of the woman Richie Oliver had been with the night before – or maybe a clone of her. He sat up. He was fifteen feet from the door of his shack, nestled in a heap of tires and rusting machine parts just off the south end of Richard's porch. The river humped by behind him. Everything was wet and cold. "Jesus," the woman said, "look at you."

He was a monk. He was a penitent. He refused coffee, Band-Aids, calamine lotion for the damage the mosquitoes had inflicted on him, and he got in his canoe – no fresh supplies, nothing, not even a bottle of water – and headed upriver. He dipped water and drank as he went, and he found a couple of slivers of caribou jerky in his day pack and chewed them in shame and abnegation as he stabbed at the current with the knife of his paddle. It was drizzling still, and he shivered, then pulled over in a quiet eddy against the far bank to beach the canoe and start a fire to warm up, though it was probably sixty-five degrees out – when you're wet and you've got a breeze in your face, it wouldn't matter if it was eighty-five.

The fire was a small, good thing. He had his spinning rod with him, always had his spinning rod, and he figured he'd make lunch simple. Three casts with an orange Mepps spinner and he had a grayling to toast on a stick, and that was so good he switched to a heavier rig and a silver spoon with a bit of green glitter in the center of it to represent the eye of some half-formed oblivious creature of the shallows, and flung it out in the hope of pike for dinner back at the cabin. Out it went with a hiss and a distant splash, and it came back with a whisper, over and over, and all he could think about was Pamela, Pamela in Howard Walpole's three-room cabin with the blond grizzly rug in front of the stone fireplace he used to supplement his stove because he liked the aesthetics of an open fire for all his grease and the raw-boned stink of him. But Pamela would never choose a man like that, skinny, flat-headed, dumb as tar, no matter how much he'd made on a lucky placer strike two years back or how many conveniences he built into his cabin, would she?

It was a question that tormented him all the dilatory, headachy way back up the river, and it tormented him even after he got a pike as long as a Louisville Slugger to rise up out of a hole under a cutbank and take the silver lure in its spiky dentition and leap clear of the water half a dozen times. Maybe he forgot about it – about her – for the space of five minutes there as he worked the canoe into shore and wrestled the thing up out of the shallows like one long whipcrack of muscle, but he thought of her again when he slipped the knife from the sheath and inserted it between the pike's eyes and drove it in till the muscle went slack.

That night he nursed two beers, fed the dogs and set snares for rabbit where there was sign along the far verge of the garden. It was warm, and he didn't bother with a fire. For dinner, it was cold beans and petrified biscuits the mice had gnawed around the edges – he didn't feel up to the smell of fish frying in a pan. He woke once in the middle of the night to a frenzy of barking and stepped out on the porch with his rifle in the pale half-light of three a.m. to see a bewildered moose – an old cow, something under eight hundred pounds and fallow, from the look of her – planted in the center of the garden, her legs like saplings growing out of the sea of black plastic. His first impulse was to shoot her, but he resisted. You didn't shoot moose during Ducks, didn't shoot moose until fall, when the meat would keep. Not to mention that it was out of season and the country was just beginning to set the table for the big summer-long banquet of ducks and geese and salmon and berries. So what did he do? He wasted a bullet and scared the thing off in the fond hope that she would avoid this place like the plague. Until fall, anyway.

In the morning he fired up the stove and made himself coffee and two pike fillets rolled in flour and bread crumbs and fried in an inch of snapping Crisco, and sat in the doorway of the cabin slapping mosquitoes and watching the rain clouds gather and swell over the river. He didn't feel right, and it had nothing to do with the tear he'd been on the other night either. What it had to do with was Pamela. He could smell her, a lingering female aura that was caught in the furs of the bed, in the ambient odors of the place, and if he looked over his shoulder to where she'd been sitting two mornings ago, he could almost see her there too. Pamela. She was his, no doubt about it. *You've got nothing to worry about, Sess,* isn't that what she'd said? But then Howard Walpole's grinning fleshless face rose up before him, superimposed over Richie Oliver's solemn bearded gaze: What if she'd been lying to him? Mollifying him? What if she was just being polite?

Before he knew what he was doing, he was back on the river, moving with the current, moving fast, the near bank racing along beside him and the wind rushing at his face. Howard Walpole's place was below town, near the mouth of Junebug Creek, and it was set back on a bluff that commanded a hundred-and-eighty-degree sweep of the river. Worse, it featured double-insulated windows shipped all the way up from Oakland, California, that gave Howard a full, unobstructed, breakfast-lunch-and-dinner view of anything moving along the shore or out on the water, and Howard always kept a good pair of Army surplus 7x42 binoculars ready to hand. Sess was thinking about that as the rain started in and the wind begin to flail his face and hands with cold hard stinging pellets that were less like rain and more like sleet than he'd care to admit. No matter, he thought of Pamela, and kept close to the bank where the wind wouldn't discover him as readily.

It would be a major embarrassment – life-quenching, horrific – to be caught anywhere within ten miles of Howard's place, the kind of thing he'd never live down, not in a thousand years. If anybody saw him out there – if Howard saw him, or Pamela – he'd have to move out of the country altogether, go find himself a room in the heart of some run-down collapsing urban jungle like Cleveland or Brooklyn or some other godforsaken place where the rumor of it would never reach him. But there was no turning back now, and as the morning rectified itself into afternoon, he slipped past Boynton on the far side of the river in a heavy shroud of weather.

He didn't know what he was doing, didn't know what he expected, didn't have a plan or hope. He had binoculars of his own though, and he was as good on the river and in the woods as any man in the country, except for some of the old-timers, and the old-timers were too old to be good anymore. When he passed Ogden Stump's fish camp, deserted this time of year, he knew the next bend would take him within sight of Howard Walpole's place, so he trailed his paddle and pulled into shore. He didn't have to hide the canoe, but he did – what if Howard was taking her for a scenic ride upriver or somebody went by collecting driftwood and saw it there? – and then started along the mud bank with his ancient .30-06 Springfield rifle in one hand (for bear discouragement, only that) and his binoculars in the other.

It was raining hard now, raining as if it were water human beings breathed and not air, and though he was wearing his olive green poncho and a cap under the hood of it, he was wet through to the skin from the waist down. And shivering, shivering already, and there was no way to make a fire anywhere near here without Howard Walpole nosing round to warm his hands and feet, and jaw about the weather and wondering if he couldn't help out with a piece of meat for the spit and inserting the sly observation that Sess was pretty far afield of his cabin, wasn't he? So he shivered and edged closer, keeping to the dense growth along the riverbank, tightroping a game trail through the willows that no human being had traversed in the history of mankind, or at least since breakup. He saw moose track, black bear, wolverine, wolf. Moose droppings, bear scat. The rain was steady, the leaves dripped.

When he got within a hundred yards of the cabin, he dropped to hands and knees, because there was no sense in putting Howard's dogs on alert. The crawling calmed him – being down like this took him back to the deer stalks he'd made as a boy through grown-over burns in the Sierra foothills, and it gave his elbows a chance to get as wet as his knees. Crawling, he thought about that, about the dairy farm outside Porterville where he'd been raised, where he'd worked beside his father day by day, slowly acquiring the muscle he could have put to use on the football field, but the coach was a jerk of the first degree and he quit that before he'd hardly got started, and he'd quit college too, because he couldn't see boxing himself in behind a desk. His every free moment was spent roaming, hunting, fishing. He was good at it, good at concealment, good at *this*.

Fifty yards out, he eased into a clot of highbush cranberry and raised the binoculars to his eyes, and he didn't feel low or cheap at all. He didn't feel like a hopeless, sick-at-heart, unmanly, voyeuristic *creep*. Not him. No, he felt more like a – well, a commando, that was it. A commando on a secret vital mission essential to the well-being of the entire country, not to mention a very specific plot of painstakingly husbanded bush at the mouth of the Thirtymile.

The only problem was, there was no one home. Or at least that was the way it appeared. From the angle he'd chosen, he could see up and in through the eastern window of the main room, across an inconvenient slice of vacant space, and out the southern windows. All was still, but for the sizzle of the rain. The dogs were huddled at the ends of their chains, deep in the miniature log houses Howard had built for them. Sess watched the windows, and then he watched the doghouses, the dark drawn-down faces of the dogs themselves, a squirrel, a robin, and he studied the way the rain dripped from the eaves in a long gray linkage of individual beads.

Where could they be? There was no smoke either from the stovepipe or the chimney, no movement, no sound. Howard's boat was there, tugging at its painter, and his floatplane too. Could they be out for a hike? Asleep? In bed? That was a possibility he didn't want to entertain – it made his digestive tract broil just to imagine it – but it was a possibility that grew into an inevitability as the day wore on. They were in bed. Fucking. That's what they were doing. They were fucking and she'd lied to him and Howard Walpole was the chosen one all along because Howard Walpole had money and credibility and Sess Harder had neither, and right now, right now as he crouched here shivering and wet in the bushes like some heartworn adolescent, Howard was trying out his new toy, his squeeze box, his jelly roll. Isn't that what they called it in the old blues tunes, *jelly roll?*

Suddenly he was in a rage. It was all he could do to keep

himself from just opening up on the place, blowing out the windows, making meat of the dogs as they came yowling and bewildered out of their houses, cutting down Howard Walpole in his greasy long johns and worn-out carpet slippers. How had he ever gotten himself into this mess? What had he been thinking? A woman – a good-looking woman, a stunner, with strong hands and a stronger back – advertises for a man? What kind of world was that? And how could he ever have expected anything other than heartbreak and humiliation out of the whole mess?

He was standing then, standing up to his full height and damn the subterfuge – he was going to march up to that cabin and bang on the door till it opened and demand an answer of her, right then and there: *Is it me or him? Me or him!* But when he came up out of the bush he detected the faintest shadow of movement through the front room window, and before he could think or act the dogs were rushing at their chains in a froth of champing teeth and bitter startled yips and howls. Was there a face in the window? Was it her? Was it Howard? He fell to his hands in the liquefying mud and began a mad scrambling retreat even as he heard the door swing open on rusted hinges and Howard's voice ringing out, "Who's there?" and her voice answering, "It's probably a moose, that's all," and Howard saying, apropos of what, Sess could only wonder, "Didn't I tell you? Didn't I?"

Two days later, at twelve noon on the dot, Howard Walpole's flat-bottomed boat planed round the gravel bar off the Boynton beach and drifted in on the crest of its own wake. Sess was standing there in the mud in his boots, just like Howard before him. He hadn't slept. He hadn't eaten. He was as hopeless and ragged and pie-eyed as a beggar on the streets of Calcutta. When the boat touched shore with a scrape of gravel and a single sharp cry from one of the gulls overhead, Pamela – she was wearing shorts and a T-shirt under a cotton jacket and a wide-brimmed floppy hat that masked her eyes so he couldn't gauge a thing – sprang out so lightly and gracefully it was as if a breeze had propelled her. He hung his head. Sucked in his breath. "Well?" he said.

She gave him a smile, she gave him that. "I've got to go back to Anchorage for a few days," she said, and there was Howard, behind her, dragging the painter up the shore with the intention of looping it round any convenient boulder or tree stump.

Sess just looked at her. "Why?"

She stopped there, right in front of him, and she never flinched or looked away. "Why? To get my wedding dress, what do you think? And my sister, who's going to be my lone bridesmaid, and my mother – she's going to have to fly up from Arizona. I always did want to be a June bride."

Still nothing. Still it wasn't sinking in. He was dangling in the wind, no more able or sentient than a river-run salmon split down the middle and hung out to dry.

A long moment ticked by, the longest moment of his life, and then she said, "How about the twenty-first, Sess? Will that work?"

10

Pris brought the cake all the way up from Anchorage in the back of her station wagon, and it was a cake the likes of which Boynton had never seen, at least not since the days of the gold rush, when all sorts of excess had bled in and out of the country: five tiers, alternating layers of pink and white glacé royal frosting, princess white cake inside and the plastic figurine of a veiled bride on top standing arm-in-arm with a bearded trapper in a plaid shirt. Pamela's mother arrived by bush plane, two hops and a jump out of the Fairbanks airport, no weather to speak of, her smile uncrimped and blazing like a second sun on everybody in town, even the bush crazies and the Indians. And Pamela herself, established with Pris in the back room of Richard Schrader's cabin to get into her makeup and the white satin gown trimmed with Brussels lace her mother had worn on a similarly momentous occasion two weeks after the Japanese let loose on Pearl Harbor, couldn't seem to stop smiling either and didn't want to. "Give me a drag on that," she said, fixed before the mirror and gesturing at the mirror image of the pale white tube of a Lark that jutted from her sister's lower lip.

"What?" Pris said, feathering her hair with a tortoiseshell comb, both her arms lifted and bare.

"A drag. Your cigarette."

"You? But you don't smoke."

She was smiling past herself, her eyes in the mirror fastening on her sister's, and it was like being ten years old all over again. "Today I do. Today I'm going to do everything."

And then they were gathering in the communal yard that wedded Richard's cabin to Sess's shack, most of the errant junk — the worn-out tires, rusted machine parts, discarded antlers, crates, fuel drums and liquor bottles, fishnets, tubs, traps, derelict

Ski-Doos and staved-in boats – having been hauled around the far side of the buildings, out of sight for the time being. Sess was in a herringbone jacket he'd borrowed for the occasion and a tie so thin it was like a strip of ribbon, and the white of his shirt could have been whiter and the sleeves of the jacket longer, but this was no fashion show and the photographers from *Vogue* seemed to have stayed home on what was turning out to be a fine, sunshiny afternoon. The bride and her sister had shared the better part of a pint of crème de menthe as well as half a dozen Larks, and Pamela was feeling no pain as she picked her way down the weather-blasted steps at the back of Richard Schrader's cabin and into the void left by her peripatetic father.

Since there was nobody to give the bride away, Sess had asked Tim Yule, the oldest man in town, to serve in that capacity, and now Tim looped his arm through hers and they started across the yard to the strains of "Here Comes the Bride" as rendered on Skid Denton's harmonica. Tinny, wheezy, flat, the music insinuated itself into the texture of the day, riding the refrigerated breeze coming up off the river, orchestrating the rhythm of the gently rocking trees. Tim smelled of bourbon and aftershave, and his boots shone with gobs of wet black polish. Stooped and white-haired, with a dripping nose and cheeks aflame with drink, he led her at a pace so stately it was practically a crawl. There was a murmur from the crowd. All her senses were alive. She didn't feel faint or nervous or sad, but just eager – eager and vigorous, ready to get on with the rest of her life. She'd waited twenty-seven years and there was no going back now.

Smoke from the barbecue pit crept across the yard. Every dog in town howled from the end of its chain, goaded by the sour repetitive wheeze of the harmonica and maddened by the wafting aroma of moose and caribou ribs, of broiled salmon and steaks and sausage lathered in barbecue sauce. At the far end of the yard, derealized in the sun off the river, Sess stood waiting for her with Richard Schrader, his best man, at his side. Her mother was there, just to the left of him, tear-washed and clinging to Pris as if she were trying to pull herself up out of a pit of shifting sand.

Wetzel Setzler, proprietor of the Three Pup and the general store, postmaster, mayor, undertaker and local representative of

Prudential Life, presided over the ceremony. Three-quarters of the population of Boynton stood there amidst the weeds and wildflowers, bottles of beer and plastic cups of bourbon and vodka clutched in their hands, to watch her take the vows in her white heels with the smears of mud lapping up over the toes in a fleur-de-lis pattern. She saw Richie Oliver in the back of the press, hand in hand with a plain-faced woman in a red shirt and jeans, and Howard Walpole too, good sports, good sports all, though she could have done without Howard. The harmonica left off and the silence blew in. Even the dogs fell quiet. She could hear the river sliding over its riffles and sinking into its holes. Do you take this man? I do, she said, I do.

Then there was hilarity, the kind of unbridled, unself-conscious, rollicking, full-bore, take-no-prisoners hilarity that only a bush town sunk deep in its ruts could generate. Somebody had a guitar, somebody else a fiddle. A banjo appeared. A washboard. There was dancing, drinking, eating, the cake dwindled through its layers and disappeared in a pale picked-over detritus of frosting and crumbs, the steaks and ribs fell away to fragments of gnawed bone, bottles went clear and gave up the ghost. She stood there beside Sess, her arm round his waist, drinking river-cooled champagne out of a plastic cup, while people she didn't know came up and talked in her face and she thanked them for their gifts of smoked sheefish, nasturtium seeds, fish gaffs and motor oil, and the more practical things too, like a fifty-pound sack of cornmeal and a nightie the size of three slices of bread cobbled together.

"Sess, I know you're the outdoors type," her mother was saying, "just like my Victor, but that doesn't mean you have to be out traipsing through the woods for days at a time while my girl lays up lonely and heartbroken in that tiny little cabin, does it? Because I worry. I do."

"I worry too," Sess told her with an even smile, "but you can bury any fears you might have on your daughter's account . . ." He was about to drop her mother's name into the void at the end of this little declaration, but Pamela could see he didn't know quite what to call her yet, whether "Mom" would float or if he should fall back on "Mariette" or "Mrs. McCoon" or maybe just clear his throat instead. That was cute, that little glitch. It was endearing. And Pamela was right there with him, heart and soul, tucked in under his arm like a text he hadn't read yet but meant to get to directly, and she hadn't stopped smiling since she'd woken up this morning.

"My wife's going to have plenty to keep her occupied," Sess said, a hint of slyness creeping into his voice, "what with skinning out carcasses, tanning hides, hauling ice up out of the river for water, cutting wood for the stove, sewing, mending, feeding the dogs – feeding me, for that matter. Isn't that what wives are for?"

Her mother had been drinking vodka for three hours. The sun pounded at her face, beat cruelly at the thin flaps of skin the plastic surgeon in Tempe had worked like hide over her cheekbones and firmed round the orbits of her eyes. She gave a little laugh and took Sess's other arm, the free one, and leaned into him. "If you ask me," she said, and she paused for effect, "a woman needs to be good, really good, at one thing only – "

Sess colored, and her mother, enjoying herself, went on: "And I don't think I have to tell a grown man like you just what that might be, now do I, Sess?"

That was when Pris, in the middle of the crush of dancers, let out a whoop and they all three turned their heads to see her in the grip of something uncontainable, a romping flailing black-headed blur of motion that might have been a bear going for her throat but wasn't. It took Pamela a minute to understand, because she was new here and she was caught up in the whirl of her own drama: Joe Bosky had crashed the party. He was wearing an old faded military shirt and the blue jeans that were a second skin to him, and he was flapping his feet like a spastic and leaning in to twirl Pris under the eggbeater of his right arm. And Pris, pretty in lavender satin and with her hair piled up atop her head, had no idea who he was or what his motives might have been or that he was the sole resident of the town and its environs who was here uninvited. Expressly uninvited. Adamantly uninvited. She had that wild look on her face that Pamela knew only too well, the cigarette look, the vodka look, the look that said the party had only just begun and there was no stopping her now. Joe Bosky brought her to his chest, spun her away, pulled her in close again. "Yee-ha!" she shrieked, and you could hear the piping breathless cry over the clash of the band like the mating call of some exotic bird.

Pamela felt Sess stiffen. Her mother said, "Looks like my youngest is not to be denied either. But I don't like her hair up like that. Do you like her hair up, Pamela?"

Pamela didn't answer. Her arm was thrust through her husband's – my *husband,* she was thinking, my *husband's* arm – and she was the stake in the ground, she was the chain, because there was going to be no violence on her wedding day, not today, no. "Sess," she warned him, "Sess," and then she moved flush into him and wrapped him up in her arms. "I want to dance, Sess," she said. "Come on. Let's dance."

But then she was jostled from behind and a man she didn't recognize – fisherman's hat with an eagle feather thrust up out of the band, frayed blue dress shirt, beard, yeast breath, hair growing out of his ears – wrapped them both up in a titanic embrace and just squeezed and rocked. "Sess!" he shouted in her ear. "Pamela! Congratulations! Many happy returns! Et cetera, et cetera!"

"Ogden," Sess said, and she could feel him pulling back, trying to get loose, trying to get to the blood-spilling part of the ceremony. Pris let out another shout. Ogden tightened his grip, and then Pamela understood.

"We'll take care of it," he said in a voice that rasped like the hull of a skiff plowing over a sandbar, "me and Richard and Iron Steve. Relax. Okay? Just relax." And then he let go and he was gone, wading through the crowd of dancers on a collision course with Pris and Joe Bosky. She saw a tall, big-headed man closing in on them from one side, and Richard Schrader, looking grim, from the other. "Son of a bitch," Sess spat, and still she held him. "Son of a fucking bitch."

"Well, what – ?" her mother began, her smile uncertain. "You sure do have enthusiastic friends, Sess – I thought he was going to crush the two of you – "

Joe Bosky was oblivious, or at least he pretended to be. She couldn't help watching – couldn't take her eyes from him – as he whirled and shimmied and flung Pris around as if he were one of the teen heartthrobs on *American Bandstand,* all style, all limbs, his eyes bugging and hips thrusting. And Pris. She was lit up – here was the kind of man she'd been looking for, his quotient of animal spirits so far above the average you couldn't begin to put a cap on them. She made two moves for his every one, the gown riding up under her arms, her hair coming down in a slow soft tumble. All in fun. All in good fun. Except that the man was Sess's enemy, here to spoil the day, and make no mistake about it.

The tall man with the big head – Iron Steve, she presumed – caught Bosky under the arms as he rocked back from Pris's white-knuckled grip, and then Richard and Ogden Stump converged on him like tacklers on a football field. She watched his features draw down in surprise, a heartbeat's respite, Pris's empty hand and awakening face, and then he seemed to detonate. He flung himself in four directions at once, screaming like a woman, a long tailing high-pitched shriek that had nothing but fakery and hate in it, and then the four of them were rolling around in the weeds and the mud, good clothes spoiled, the crowd giving way and the band freezing out the chorus of Hank Williams's "Cold, Cold Heart."

In two minutes it was over, black-headed Joe Bosky trussed in arms and Iron Steve's elbow pinned to his throat, the eight-legged walk to the verge of the property and the necessary threats and imprecations hurled back and forth, the band lurching again into the defeated chorus and Sess's eyes gone cold as a killer's. "Good God, Sess," her mother was saying, "but you've got some excitable friends. Too much to drink, I guess" – with a laugh – "or maybe Pris was too much for him to handle. My daughters are like that, you know."

And here came Pris, flustered, blotched, her hair a mess and the hem of her dress stiff with mud. "What was that all about?" she said, extracting a cigarette from her purse. "I was just starting to warm up there. Who was that guy, anyway – an escapee from the mental ward or something? I mean, I kind of liked him. His spirit, I mean."

Sess wouldn't say a word. Her sister looked to him, her mother, but he just stood there rooted to the spot, rigid as a fencepost. "It's all right," Pamela kept telling him, "don't let it spoil the day. It's all right, it is – "

But it wasn't. Sess wouldn't soften, wouldn't give. They danced, they drank champagne, received congratulations and gave thanks in return, and one after another people came up to them, lit with hilarity and goodwill, but it wasn't the same after Joe Bosky had put in his appearance. This was her wedding day, her wedding *night,* and her husband was as distant and impenetrable as some alien out of a spaceship in one of those corny B movies she'd watched as a kid. *Wake up, Sess,* she wanted to say. *Wake up and snap out of it, your bride's here – remember me?*

It must have been around ten when the party began to wind down, people gone off in pairs, migrating to the Nougat and the Three Pup, falling unconscious in the gravel on the bank of the river. Tim Yule was seated on an overturned bucket in a stripe of sun, stirring a plastic cup of Everclear with a big-knuckled finger and holding a sotto voce conversation with himself. Howard Walpole and Richie Oliver had long since drifted off, shoulders slumped in mutual commiseration. Pamela's mother was in the back of Pris's station wagon – "A little catnap, that's all I need, don't worry about me" – and Pris was holding court for the benefit of three drunken bush crazies who would have stripped the flesh from their bones for just a touch of her, while the band had been reduced to a single fiddle sawing away at the melancholy traces of a classical education. The hour had come. She pressed her husband's hand and felt the blood start in her veins. "Sess," she said, her voice echoing oddly in her ears over the strains of the violin – saddest thing she'd ever heard, and what was it, Borodin? Shostakovich? Something like that. "Sess," she said, "don't you think it's time the bride and groom went in and – "

"Went to bed?"

They were on the back porch of the house Richard Schrader had magnanimously vacated for the night. Mosquitoes sailed into their faces, softly rebounded from their lips, their eyelashes. She'd changed into a pair of jeans and a long-sleeved hooded sweatshirt, but she was conscious of the underthings she'd picked out in Anchorage with Pris, lacy satin panties and a brassiere that clung to her like a man's spread fingers. He leaned in close and they kissed, easeful and sweet, all the rage and the woodenness gone out of him finally, finally, and she murmured, "Yes, to bed."

The drone of an outboard came to her then, to both of them, a speedboat planing up the river in the slanting sun of ten o'clock at night, droning closer, a glint of churned water trailing away from the stern and the bearded face of Joe Bosky, black-crowned, at the helm. Joe Bosky, back for one final thrust. Sess rose up off the porch even as the bow leapt out of the current and careened for shore. "Hey, Sess Harder, fuck you!" Bosky roared over the engine, dancing at the throttle. "Fuck you and your dog-faced woman too!" And then the bow cut back and the boat shot past and was gone.

Richard had left them a pair of vanilla-scented candles, one on each side of the bed, tapering pale phallic things rising up out of matching ceramic dishes his ex-wife had shaped and fired herself. The cabin was four rooms, two of which Richard closed off in winter, and it featured a kitchen sink with a hand-pump for water and a bathroom replete with a flush toilet that generally worked, at least in warm weather. As in most of the cabins and frame houses in Boynton, aesthetic considerations had been sacrificed to practicality, and all four rooms were lined floor-to-ceiling with flattened cardboard boxes – Birds Eye Peas, Rainier Pale Ale, Charmin Toilet Tissue – to provide a last line of defense against the winds screaming down out of the polar barrens in the dead of winter. The bedroom was constructed as a kind of loft, four steps up from the main room and the top-of-the-line Ashley stove Richard's ex had insisted on. There was no need of the stove tonight. It was as warm inside as a cabana on a white crescent beach in the Bahamas.

She was sitting on the bed, taking her hair down. She'd lit the candles and set aside the plastic cup of lukewarm champagne – the taste had gone saccharine in the back of her throat, and she didn't need any more. The cabin was still. The sun held. She could hear the sound of her own breathing, the tick and whirr of the blood coursing through her veins. After a moment she got up and pulled the shades over the two slits of the windows.

Sess was busy in the main room, fooling with something, his shoulders so squared-up and rigid you would have thought the vertebrae had fused in his neck. Something clattered, fell to the floor. He was struggling for control, she could see that, but Joe Bosky had poisoned the day, the moment, the night to come, and she didn't know what to say or how to defuse it. In her bag was a paperback her mother had given her, *The Bride's Advisor:*

100 Questions and Answers for Your Wedding Night, but there was nothing in all its three hundred pages and appendices to address the situation at hand. Her husband was in no tender mood. He was twenty-five feet away, his back turned to her, and he might as well have been on another planet. There was a dull thump as some other object fell to the floor.

She stood up then, where he could see her when he turned round, and pulled the sweatshirt up over her head and dropped the jeans down round her ankles and stepped out of them. She was in her underwear, in her sixteen-dollar-and-ninety-nine-cent silk panties and matching brassiere from Oswalt's department store, and she wanted him to see her in them, to be turned on, to see her flat abdomen and the curve of her hips and her long, tapered legs. Her voice was caught in her throat. "Sess," she was going to say, "Sess, why don't you turn around," but she couldn't do it. A long deracinated moment shuddered by and she was thinking about high school, making out with Gary Miranda in the den of her parents' house while they were away at work, the Platters and the Ink Spots dripping honey from the hi-fi and the heat of his tongue and how it made her feel. His tongue was wet and thrusting and insistent, and he took her own tongue into his mouth and sucked it as if it were a peppermint candy or a jawbreaker, and it made her feel abandoned, made her feel wild, but she never let him touch her breasts or anything else, because she didn't believe in that. In college there was petting, the furious dry friction of it, the boys all sprouting second sets of hands and grinding against her like windup soldiers, the rhythm and movement as automatic as the pounding of their hearts, and half her sorority sisters going all the way with their steadies and not a bit shy about it either. Her panties were as wet as if she'd fallen in a lake, her jeans, her skirts, but no boy, even Eric Kresten, and she dated him for almost two years, ever got her to take anything off but her bra. And then she was in her twenties and Fred Stines came to her apartment and she stripped to her panties for him while he stroked her everywhere his fingers lighted and sucked at her nipples like an underfed puppy and she felt herself giving way time after time but she never did.

Howard Walpole was different. The three days with him were part of the compact, the program she'd set herself, and though she knew Sess was the one, knew it even before she climbed into the canoe with him and felt his weight there behind her like the perfect counterpoise to her own, she had to go through with it, because that was the kind of woman she was. You make a promise, you keep it. That was how she felt. That was who she was. But Howard – Howard was stiff as a board. He shook her hand when she got in the boat, as if they were signatories to a solemn truce between two warring factions, and he never thought of brushing his cheek to hers or clasping her shoulders in a welcoming hug. He just gave her his hand, took a minute to taunt Sess and then cranked the throttle on his twin outboard engines.

The day was biting and sharp, flecks of foam riding the wavelets, a spatter of windblown rain in her face. She was up front and Howard Walpole was in back. The fiberglass hull slapped at the water, over and over again, slap, slap, slap, and the noise of the engines made conversation a chore. She held on, thinking how much nicer the canoe had been, the pace of it, the silent liquid progress that was no intrusion on the day, the river, the hovering birds and furtive mammals. "Nice boat!" she shouted back over her shoulder, just to be polite, just to say something, and Howard, a plug of tobacco distending one cheek and his smudged cap pulled down tight against the wind so that his head looked as if it had been preshrunk to fit it, just nodded. The trip took an hour. She didn't say another word the whole way and neither did he.

When they got there, though, when the bow of the boat slid up the bank beneath his house and the dogs stammered out their elaborate greeting, Howard had a whole speech prepared. It was equal parts disclosure, pep talk and closer's spiel, and he never looked her in the face the whole time he was delivering it, and he went on delivering it for the better part of the three days and two nights she was to spend in his company. He told her about his boat and his airplane and his house, about his gold claims and how he'd lay a moosehide in the sluice box so the hairs could pick up the finest particles, showed her a mayonnaise jar with thirty-two thousand dollars' worth of gold flecks in it and asked her to lift it from the table and laughed to see her strain to do it. He talked through the dinner of black bear stewed in a mash of dried apples and prunes with a side dish of kippered salmon and pan-fried potatoes, talked till she yawned on the couch and kept talking as he laid a blanket over her and her eyes fell closed.

In the morning he woke her with talking, talk about his ailments – he'd broken his leg in three places just two years back, did she know that? – and talk about his dogs, the individual quirks and dietary predilections of each one, though he didn't really mush dogs anymore like Sess Harder and some of the other throwbacks because the snow machine was a real hoot, didn't she think so? Over breakfast it was his mother in Minneapolis; automobiles he'd owned; the evil, meretricious ways of his ex-wife, Irene; the insurance business – two years of his life down the drain with that laughable fraud of a con man's scheme, and could she ever see anybody taking out term life and betting against their own death? – and an hour-long tirade against the United States government and the land grab they were about to perpetrate on all Alaskans in the name of the black gold at Prudhoe Bay.

He was a bore. A windy, ignorant, opinionated, half-cracked bore with real staying power and the lungs of a packhorse. And he was unattractive too, now that she got a good long look at him, with his dodging red-flecked eyes, the wispy hair poking out from beneath the cap and his hands laid out on the table like slabs of boiled meat. All right, she was resigned to it, resigned to three days and two nights of boredom, and by the second hour of the first day she'd begun to see it as a kind of purifying ritual, a mortification of the flesh and the spirit to make herself worthy of Sess Harder, who was before her now like a shining promise. She ate the food Howard Walpole gave her. She looked at his dogs, his snow machines, his floatplane, his boat, his cache, his smoke-house. She answered when he paused at the end of a paragraph to put a rhetorical question to her and she fought off his advances. "Sex," he said to her after dinner on the first night, and to the best of her recollection they'd been talking about two-stroke engines to this point, "you like sex? Because I do. And that's the thing I miss out here most of all – just that, sex." He paused a moment, his eyes charging round the room like scattershot. "And I'm very sex-u-al, if you know what I mean."

On the last day, no more than an hour before they were

scheduled to plow back up the river so she could get on with the rest of her life, he appeared in the doorway of the main room where she was sunk into the easy chair reading a back issue of *Argosy* for the second time in as many days and enjoying the briefest respite from the sound of his voice. "Pamela," he said in a low glottal wheeze, "Pamela, look at me." She glanced up, and she saw that he was naked but for his socks and the greasy cap, naked and erect and pulling at himself like a dairy farmer working at the long maculated teat of a cow. It took her a minute, the shock of it settling into her legs like a burden of the blood, and then she was up out of the chair and reaching for the fire poker. All she said was, "Put that thing away," and in the next instant Howard was ducking out of sight, the bulb of his hand blooming with the waxy sheen of the stuff he'd dredged up out of himself as if it were gold dredged from the tailings of an abandoned claim.

And why was she thinking about that now? Because now it was appropriate, now was the time. She was a married woman and that man with the rigid back and the neck like a fireplug fooling with something in the other room was her husband and she could indulge her wildest fantasies, do anything she wanted – stroke him, suck him – and not feel dirty. This was her wedding night. This was the consummation of all those groping, panting hours and the rigor of self-control that was fiercer than any desire. "Sess," she said, and she unfastened the brassiere and dropped it to the floor too, "Sess, look at me."

He turned round then, her husband, and in his hand the thing he was fumbling with, shiny foil, the skin-like droop of plastic. "I was just – " he said, and she watched his face, watched his eyes, as he warmed to this new vision of her standing there in nothing but the thinnest pearly evanescent flap of Oswalt's silk. "I couldn't – I mean, I tore the thing getting it out of the package . . ."

She wanted to laugh. "You don't need that thing," she said, spreading her arms wide, "you'll never need it, ever again. Don't you realize? I'm your wife."

They were up early, both of them, bags packed, the canoe loaded to the gunwales with wedding gifts, and they breakfasted on whatever came to hand (Sess had a ham, Swiss and caribou-tongue sandwich on half a loaf of the French bread her sister had brought with her from Anchorage; she had a plate of leftover three-bean salad, marinated artichoke hearts, a wedge of iceberg lettuce and a scoop of potato salad to round it off). She hadn't slept – or she had, off and on, but in a way that was more like a waking dream than any sleep she'd ever experienced, and she couldn't stop reaching out for him, running a hand down the slope of his arm or over the mysterious topography of the shoulder that lay pressed to hers. She was an explorer, that was what she was, learning the lay of the land, creating it anew all over again, and then again.

He'd made love to her twice under the influence of the tireless copper sun that refused to set on her wedding day, the sun that irradiated the squared-off edges of the shades and painted the foot of the bed as if it existed for them alone, and he was nothing like Fred Stines or Eric Kresten or the straining intent hot-faced college boys whose idea of love was a purely mechanical thing, a kind of exercise, like squat thrusts or push-ups. No. He was patient. Loving. Grateful. He made her feel more than just wanted – he made her feel as if she were the center of the universe. She watched him sleep as the sun dipped behind the hills and the shades went gray with the dusk that wanted to be night, and then she woke him when it came back up and he made love to her again.

But now it was seven a.m. and they straightened up the cabin, made the bed, stowed the leftovers in Richard's icebox and went out hand in hand to the canoe. The sun flooded the trees, the river was a cauldron of light. Birds nattered. A pair of geese shot up off the water and Sess pointed to the black burr of a porcupine caught in the crown of a birch up the shore. And then they were paddling, in concert, the easy rhythmic accommodation of man and wife, paddling as if they'd been a team forever.

Everything looked new to her, every leaf, every turning, the river that resisted her paddle and re-created itself moment by moment. Her brain was flooded with endorphins. She was lighter than air. They talked in a hush, their soft, unhurried voices carrying out over the water, and they talked of practical things, of building a fish wheel, expanding the cabin, putting up a greenhouse for the tomatoes, of scattering seed for zinnias, marigolds, pansies and snapdragons. And the dogs. "The first thing I'm going to do is teach you to mush," he told her, "so you can run the trapline with me, be my partner. You always wanted to be my partner, didn't you? Right from the start?"

Her answer was a smile, delivered over her right shoulder as the paddle slid back from the stroke. Sure she was his partner – she'd chosen him, hadn't she? Wasn't that what this was all about? She'd feed the dogs, she'd mush them, she'd stretch and tan hides, repair the rags of his clothes, feed him, keep him warm at night, and he'd hold her and take care of her in turn. That was her life, spinning out into the future, and it was as fixed and certain as anything on this earth ever can be.

After a time the churning milk of the Yukon gave way to the pellucid Thirtymile, and the cabin – their home – came into view like the last outpost of civilization in a world gone over to nature. The canoe cut across the current and the cabin loomed larger. Everything was still. Still and lush. She wanted to feel the silence, wanted to relax into it, but suddenly Sess was digging at the paddle in a kind of frenzy, out of sync with her for the first time, fighting it, ramming the canoe forward as if the river had caught fire. "The dogs," he said.

And then it came to her: the dogs were silent. Two days at their stakes and no one home – they should have had their noses to the sky, expressing their impatience and their joy. But they were silent. Worse: they were lying still in the weeds, the chains like nooses at their throats. And when she and Sess got there, when they'd beached the canoe and sprinted up the bank with no breath left in them, the carcasses were already stiffening round the ragged dark openings where the bullets had gone to shelter.

part three

druid day

One pill makes you larger,
And one pill makes you small.
And the ones that mother gives you
Don't do anything at all.
 – Grace Slick, "White Rabbit"

11

Star didn't have a mantra on this particular morning, no nonsense syllables or song lyrics ricocheting around her head while the sun sang in the windows over the sink and thirty-two fresh-cracked and beaten eggs fluffed in the pan. Or pans. Four of them, cast-iron, black as char – four pans, four burners, all balky. Posters climbed the walls, four Beatles, three Youngbloods, five Rolling Stones. Basil, rosemary, tarragon and lemongrass. Clay pots. A big spill of green. She was crumbling goat cheese over each of the pans, the fragrance rising, the spatula working, fold and stir, fold and stir. At her elbow, the chopping block, and this morning it had a wet sheen to it, the residue of the tomatoes, peppers and onions she and Merry had diced while Lydia squeezed oranges and Maya pulled biscuits from the oven. On the table, the tin plates were stacked high and the silverware awaited the rush in two big plastic tubs that had once held Blue Bonnet margarine. For napkins, there was a roll of paper towels, just like at Camp Minewa.

Numbers were important this morning, that's what it was – she was into numbers, two dogs stretched out on the floor, four women in the kitchen (and she wasn't going to call them *chicks*, because that was just stupid, that was demeaning and belittling, no matter what Ronnie said), two goats under the tree, forty-three people lined up for breakfast and one sun, fat and glowing, making a magical thing of the flat black grid of the screen door. She scrambled the eggs, one pan, two pans, three pans, four, the scent of the onions competing with the biscuits until the whole room was dense with it and Jiminy stuck his head in the door. "Ready yet?" he wanted to know. "One more minute," she said, and she loved this, this place and this moment, more than she'd loved anything in her life, "sixty short tiny little expiring seconds – you can start counting them off on your fingers."

To Merry, at her shoulder, she said, "Cats and chicks, whoever invented that – I mean, those terms? Isn't it stupid? I mean cats are predatory, they're tough and – "

"Unreliable?" Merry said, leaning in with a smile and the crudely rolled, fat-in-the-middle joint they'd been sharing. She held it to Star's lips while Star plied the spatula and finessed the pans. "Always catting around? Spraying the furniture? Sharpening their claws?"

"Right, that's what I mean. They name sports teams after cats, the Tigers, the Nittany Lions, but what are chicks? Little fluffy helpless things that come out of eggs."

"But cute, right?"

"I don't want to be cute."

Merry was cutting bread into inch-thick slices. Her hair was involved with her hands, the cutting board, and she whipped it back with a flick of her neck. "What do you want to be, then – tough?"

The eggs tumbled out of the pans and into a matching pair of big fluted ceramic bowls lovingly fabricated by Harmony and Alice, Drop City's resident potters. Star shifted her face away from the swirl of steam and called out, "It's ready!" then tuned back in. "Yeah, sure – I'll settle for tough. It's a whole lot better than helpless. Or predatory, maybe. Predatory's even better."

"Like a cat?"

But that was too much, and they were both giggling and rubbing at their eyes and the suddenly itching tips of their noses as they served up eggs, first to Jiminy, and then to all the rest of their brothers and sisters, as Drop City and special guests filed by, tin plates in hand. Jiminy was almost always first in line because he was the hungriest, skinny as a concentration camp survivor but he could out-eat anybody Star had ever seen, including her brother Sam, who played left tackle on the high school football team and wore size fourteen shoes. Two total strangers were next in line, and then it was Reba and Alfredo and the kids, Reba looking hard and *old* in the morning light, her hair like dried weeds, her eyes blunted and lifeless. When she smiled – and she wasn't smiling now, because her lips were two dead things pressed one atop the other – a whole deep rutted floodplain of lines and gouges swallowed her eyes, as if she'd already used up her quotient of joy and from now on out every laugh was going to cost her. "Che doesn't like eggs," she announced, " – I think he's allergic to albumin. Maybe just give me some toast and I'll smear it with honey or something."

Che stood there beside her, looking numbed-out, dirty T-shirt, dirty feet, a frizz of wild sun-bleached hair and two eyes that were like blips on a radar screen. "That what you want, baby," Reba said, bending to him, " – honey and toast?"

"*I* want honey," Sunshine said in a voice that was like the scratching of a scab, rough and low, with no real expectation of relief. She was three years old. She stood just behind her brother, close enough so that the bulge of her bare abdomen brushed the hem of his shirt. Her eyes were soft, brimming, hopeless. Star tried to give her a smile, because that was what you were supposed to do when you came across a kid – *And isn't she cute, or is it a he? Or an it?* – but children made her feel awkward and uneasy, unnatural even. How could she, a woman, tell anybody she didn't want children, didn't relate to them, didn't even really like them? Children were nothing but dead weight as far as she was concerned, red-faced yowling little aliens that sucked the life right out of you, and if you ever had any dreams of living for yourself, you could forget them when you had kids, because from then and forever you were just somebody's mother. And what was wrong with birth control? The Pill? Ball all you want, but just don't forget to take your pill every morning. Star didn't get it. She really didn't.

At any rate, she tried for a smile, and Reba gave her an exasperated look before swinging round on her daughter and plucking at her arm with two fingers molded into pincers, just like Star's mother, just like everybody's mother, and that brought her back, way back, as if she were trapped in a home movie. "You eat your eggs and don't you dare start in because I'm in no mood this morning," Reba hissed, "let me tell you – "

The girl, the kid, Sunshine – there she stood, not in the least moved by the unstated threat. Her brother fell into himself, utterly deranged by the hour, the place, life on this bewildering turned-on planet, and she looked at him as if she didn't recognize him. In her tiny hopeless scratch of a voice, she said: "I want juice."

"Milk," Reba responded automatically. People at the back of the line were drifting along in their own planetary orbits, bells, beards, beads, morning jokes, easy soothing rhythms, but even they began to look up to see what the delay was.

The tiny voice: "Juice."

And now Star intervened, because the juice – well, this was Druid Day, a celebration for the summer solstice, and the juice, fresh-squeezed by Lydia and as pure and sweet and organically salutary as anything you could ever hope to find anywhere in the whole golden sun-struck state of California, was laced with acid, LSD, lysergic acid diethylamide, because everybody at Drop City was going to commune with their inner selves today, all of them, in a concerted effort to raise the consciousness of the planet by one tiny fraction of a degree. "But honey, the juice isn't good today, you won't like it – "

Naked, her legs slightly bowed and her features dwindling in the broad arena of her face, the kid held her ground. "Juice."

"Oh, shit," Reba said. "Shit. Fuck. I don't care. Give her juice."

Lydia was there, Merry, Maya, all looking on with washed-out smiles. They were the chicks, and they were serving breakfast. Tomorrow it would be somebody else's turn, another group of chicks. But this morning it was this group – Star's group – and there was a celebration going on, or about to go on. Star hesitated. "But it's, um – you know, the juice is *special* today, Reba. Did you forget?"

"Summer solstice."

"Right."

"Druid Day."

She could feel the grass tugging at her body as if she were about to lift off, gravity suddenly nullified as in a dream, the gentlest subtlest most persuasive full-body tug in the world, and then it let go. "Yeah," she said finally, "and so we, Lydia, I mean, already – "

" – laced the OJ with acid, as if Alfredo and I didn't like *invent* Druid Day year before last, and where were you then, back home with Mommy and Daddy? You really think I'm that far out that I don't know what I'm doing? You think my kids haven't been turned on?" Reba shot a withering look round the kitchen, then dropped her face to confront her daughter. "See the trouble you're causing? You want juice? Okay, have your juice – but don't you come crying to me if you get onto some

126

kind of kid trip like you did last time – remember last time, when you curled up in that cabinet under the sink and wouldn't come out all day?"

Sunshine didn't nod, didn't say yes or no, didn't even blink.

"Okay," Reba breathed, straightening up and smiling now, her face a cauldron of tics and wrinkles and wildly constellating moles, "give her the eggs, and *milk*, and if it'll keep her out of my hair because I need a day off sometimes too, believe it or not, just half a glass of the juice, okay?"

Alfredo was deep in conversation with Mendocino Bill – "Hobbits are three feet tall, just the size of kids, because it's a kids' book, so get over it, already" – and he had nothing to say. He turned a blank face to Star and the line shuffled forward. Sunshine took her plate of eggs and her juice over to the table, set them down, and came back for the milk. When Star looked up again, all the seats at the table were taken, and Jiminy was holding forth about something, waving his fork and jerking at the loose strands of his hair as if they'd come to life and started attacking him. Sunshine was nowhere to be seen. Her plate, barely touched, had been pushed to one side. The glass of milk was there beside it, a yellow stripe of cream painted round the rim, but the juice was gone.

Star registered that fact, made a little snapshot of it in her head – crowded table, a surge of tie-dye, saffron eggs on a dull tin plate, forks gleaming, teeth flashing, and no kid present in any way, shape or form, and no juice – but the snapshot never got printed because Verbie was there in line with a girl who could have been her twin except she wore her hair long, and Verbie was introducing her as her sister Angela from Pasadena, and the plates moved, the biscuits retreated, the orange juice dwindled in the stoneware pitcher. Verbie helped herself to a double scoop of eggs, accepted biscuits and a full glass of juice. Star had already had *her* juice, and she could feel the first crackling charge of it leaping synapses up and down the length of her, and she momentarily tuned out Verbie, who was in the middle of a complicated story about her sister, something about the Whiskey, too many Harvey Wallbangers and a go-go dancer. The sister seethed with joy. This was a story about her, and Verbie was telling it, at breakfast, on Druid Day in Drop City.

"You know, I guess I'll take a full glass too," the sister said. "It isn't that strong, is it?"

"Two hundred mics," Verbie said. "Three, at most."

And who was next? Ronnie, looking chewed-over and cranky. He had his head down and his eyes dodged and darted behind the oversized discs of his sunglasses, *fish,* but not in a net, little fish, *minnows,* trapped in a murky aquarium. He took a glass and held it out. "Eggs?" she said, and it was a peace offering. She'd cooked the eggs, and here she was to scoop them up and serve them, the hard-working, self-effacing and dutiful little *chick,* and what more could anybody ask for?

"Skip the eggs."

"Toast? Biscuits?" She tried for a smile. "Fresh-baked. By Maya."

"Just the juice." He watched her fill the glass. The breakfast roar surged round the room, spilled out the door and into the courtyard. "So where you been the last couple of days?" he said. "I've been looking all over for you."

She shrugged to show how casual everything was, no big deal, but it wasn't easy to shrug and pour at the same time. Juice dripped down the sides of the glass, puddled on the table. "We were down backpacking round Mount Tam," she said, "in the redwoods there? It was a trip. It really was."

"You and Marco, right?"

She nodded.

"Like the night I got my deer – I looked all over for you that night too." He took the glass from her hand and held it out away from him, the juice foaming like a witches' brew, neon orange and *drip, drip, drip.* "Just you and Marco, right?"

"Yeah, well I'm sure you had Lydia to comfort you, and what about Merry and that new girl I saw you being all friendly with the other day, what's her name, Premstar – the one that's so tripped-out she can barely talk? I'm sure they must've kept you from feeling too sorry for yourself."

"Just you and Marco, right?" he repeated.

She just stared at him.

"Okay, fine." He drank off the juice in a single gulp, snatched the pitcher from the counter and filled the glass back up to the rim. "Don't even talk to me," he said, and he was saying it over his shoulder, because he was already out the door and into the coruscating light that exploded all around him like colliding stars.

Lydia was sitting on the counter by the sink, gazing off across the room as if she were oblivious to the whole thing – off on her own trip, and don't you confuse your trip with mine – but Merry came round the table and stood there till Star acknowledged her. "What was that all about?"

Star was feeling it, right down to her toes, the first fluttering euphoric rush of the drug. She didn't want hassles, she didn't want possessiveness, jealousy, anger, bad sex and bad feelings – she wanted to let loose and watch the day play itself out, one swollen luminous minute after another. She looked at Merry, and it was as if Merry were underwater, her hair floating in gentle undulations, her face, her eyes, seaweed riding the currents and seahorses too. "I don't know," she heard herself say, "I guess Pan's having a bad day."

That was when Lester's face hove into view, big smile, gold in his teeth, his skin as slick and worn as the leather on the speed bag Sam had hanging in the garage back at home. His eyes were huge, as if he'd been groping in the dark his whole life – and what were they, a lemur's eyes, an owl's – and his hair was teased out till it stood straight up off his head like Jimi Hendrix's. Franklin was with him, and they both had their shoulders hunched, as if they were stalking through a rainstorm. "Hey, Star, Merry, what's happening?" Lester said. "Just wondering if, uh, you might have some of that *juice* left for a couple of hermits? Maybe some eggs too – wouldn't some eggs be nice, Franklin?"

"Sure would," Franklin said.

Star couldn't seem to summon a response – try though she might, no response was forthcoming, not right then, not a yes or a no or a see you in hell first, nothing. Zero. She was drawing blanks. Sky Dog had moved on, as had Dewey and most of the others, but Lester and Franklin had persisted, though everybody treated them like lepers. They hadn't showed up for a meal in weeks, and hardly anyone ever saw them. But they were there, and everyone was aware of it, whether they pretended differently or not. Go out to the parking lot, and there was the Lincoln, dusted over till it could have been some spontaneous excrescence of the earth itself. Take a stroll at night, and the music came at you from the back house, deep-bottomed and mysterious. And every once in a while you'd look up from what you were doing, and there they'd be out on their tumbledown porch, stripped to the waist and passing a joint or a cigarette or a jug of wine from one adhesive hand to another.

Merry spoke up first. "I don't think so," she said.

Lester turned to Franklin, as if to interpret for him. "You hear that, Franklin? The girl doesn't think so. What do you say to that?"

Franklin stood a head taller than Lester. He was wearing a wide-collared polka-dot shirt, yellow on black. He had bags under his eyes, as if he'd been up for a hundred nights straight, and he was letting his processed hair grow out in reddish wisps. He looked at Lester when he spoke. "I don't say nothin'."

"Well, I say it's a bunch of racist hippie-dippy shit," Lester said, swinging round on them. "What's a matter, us niggers ain't good enough for you?"

"Fuck you, Lester," Merry said, and there were faces at the door now, people jerked up short as if they had leashes fastened round their throats. And where was Marco? In Santa Rosa, with Norm, getting supplies.

Lester thought this was funny. "Fuck me, huh? There's peace and love for you."

Irate, that was a word, wasn't it? Star was irate – first Ronnie, and now this. "Look," she said, stepping into the breach, "you know perfectly well this has nothing to do with whether you're black or white or, or – "

"Red or yellow?"

Somehow, she had the spatula in her hand. Or no, it was the serving spoon, a stick of dried-out tessellated overcooked pine, and she was waving it like a conductor's baton. "Norm said – "

He threw it back at her, but softly, softly, his voice a whisper: "'Norm said.' Listen to her. Norm didn't say shit. Norm said everybody's welcome here, and if you're so hot on niggers, you tell me how many more brothers you got hiding out there in the woods just in case we do decide to move on out of here one of these days? Huh? How many? Ten? Fifteen?"

She could feel her heart going into overdrive. She dropped the spoon on the table and backed away from it. "I'm not going to argue with you, I'm not going to get involved in your trip at all, because you can just do what you want and I don't care, I really don't."

"What about *Marco* – he care?"

And now she said it too: "Fuck you, Lester. Just go fuck yourself."

But Lester was pouring juice, Lester was scooping up eggs and biscuits. He took enough for three people, mounded it up on a plate till it was spilling over and handed it to Franklin, then served himself, and no one said a word. One scoop of eggs, two, three. He took his time, and he wore a tight little smile on his face that made her feel nothing but sad and ashamed. Had it really come to this? Were they fighting over *food?* Or was it something else, something ugly and dirty, something that made Drop City the biggest joke in the world?

So go ahead and define your bad trip, because here it was. She just turned and walked out of the kitchen, through the meeting room and out the front door, no eggs for her, no washing up with her sisters, no dancing and joy and flowers in her hair, no bonding with the clan and letting the acid strip her clean, inside and out. She crossed the pale dirt drive to the treehouse, climbed the ladder and pulled it up after her, and she lay there on Marco's sleeping bag, staring up into the leaves till she could identify each and every one of them individually and her heart slowed through all the gears from overdrive on down to neutral.

Later – it might have been five minutes or five hours, she had no idea – she pushed herself up and looked around her. There was a dragonfly perched on the rail, a single bolt of electric color like a driven blue nail, and beneath it, a built-in shelf aflame with the spines of the books Marco had been collecting – *Soul on Ice, Ficciones, Cat's Cradle, Trout Fishing in America, Steppenwolf* – and a Coleman lantern in a shade of green so deep it cut a hole through the wall. The books were incandescent, burning from the inside out. She picked one up almost at random, for the color and the feel of it, and she opened it on words that tacked across the page like ships on a poisoned sea. She couldn't make sense of them, didn't want to, hated in that instant the whole idea of books, literature, *stories* – because stories weren't true, were they? – but the books reminded her of Marco, and so they were good and honest and valuable, and she stroked the familiar object in her hand as if it were a cat or a pet rabbit, stroked it until the paper became fur and the living warmth of it penetrated her fingertips.

Small sounds came to her, intimate sounds, as if she'd lifted out of herself and become an omnipresence – a cough, a giggle, a sigh, the faint soughing of Jiminy's breath catching in the back of his throat as he rocked against Merry's sweat-slick skin in the downstairs bedroom of the main house a hundred yards away. She could hear the leaves respiring and the sap creeping through the branches in the way of blood, slow blood, blood like paste. Termites whispered in the duff, the hooves of the goats grew and expanded with a sharp-edged sound that teemed and popped in her ears. And then the book, the one in her hand, rematerialized in a ripple of color, pink and yellow and a single human eye staring out of the page, and she knew it at once, Julio Cortázar's *Blow-up and Other Stories*. It was a book Ronnie had turned her onto, back in New York, and she in turn had bought it for Marco – there was the imprint of the secondhand book shop in Sebastopol, freewheelin' books, 25¢, right there in a faded pink blur on the inside page. All right. At least she had that, and though the words still wouldn't cooperate, though they grouped and regrouped and pitched and bucked across the page and every mouth in the forest buzzed in her ears with tiny voices that kept burning and screaming out their testimony till it was all just a blur of white noise, she could dream the stories, dream of the axolotl and the man who kept vomiting up bunnies, and she did, until she had to pull out all the books, one after another, and let the stories infest her.

And then she was down out of the tree, barefoot in the biting leaves, scattering an armload of books like glossy seeds, because that's where they'd found them, she and Marco, on a dense hot sweating afternoon that went off like a time bomb, and where was he now when she needed him? He was with Norm, she reminded herself, that's where he was. In Santa Rosa. Getting supplies. He'd promised to drop his acid at the same time she dropped hers, so they could ride the wave together, and she saw him doing that as the van lurched down the road and Norm bellowed along with the radio in a voice that was like a long sustained shriek from the house of pain, but Santa Rosa wasn't

Timbuktu, and they should have been back by now, shouldn't they?

With a sweep of her instep, she interred the books beneath the clawlike leaves. They'd smashed his guitar, torn his clothes, eviscerated the books, and now she'd laid them to rest again, but carefully, carefully, with proper obsequies and all due respect. New books, with fiercer colors and truer stories, would sprout up to replace the tattered ones, a whole living library growing out of the duff beneath the tree, free books, books for the taking, books you could pluck like berries. Or something like that. She lingered there a moment, struggling for focus, then found herself drifting toward the main house, a knot of people sunk into the front porch, music rising up out of unseen depths, joy and sisterhood, but it didn't feel right, not yet, and she struck off into the woods instead. Here she was on her own – on her own trip – the earth gripping her feet like custom-made shoes, *hello and goodbye, hello and goodbye,* and the trees giving way like a parting crowd all along the path down to the river.

The air was thick, the sun tortured the water. Birds dropped like meteors out of the sky. She sat on the bank, listened to what the current said, dipped her fingers and her feet, and still she didn't feel right. She couldn't seem to catch her breath, that's what it was, as if she'd overdosed on espresso or taken one too many white crosses in a long streaming night behind the wheel and the Rockies rising up out of the wastelands like a big gray impenetrable wall that could have stopped whole armies. Was she afraid? She was. Afraid of nothing and everything, of things that weren't there and things that shifted and mutated just beyond the range of her vision. She closed her eyes and watched the images play across the dark stage of her eyelids in a careening spastic dance she couldn't slow or stop.

She'd been with Marco the day they trashed his things – out in the field behind the main house, where he was laying the pipe for the leach lines. She'd come out with a pitcher of Kool-Aid, barefoot, in shorts and a peasant blouse with blue quetzal birds stitched into the bodice she'd picked up at a secondhand store in New Mexico – a blouse that made her smile even now to think of it – and she'd sat watching the way the muscles gathered in his back every time he bent to fling a shovel of gravel into the ditch.

He said she was beautiful. She said he was beautiful himself. "So we're a mutual admiration society," he said, flinging gravel. There was another shovel standing there all by itself, thrust right up out of a mound of loose stones as if it were a gift of nature. "Want me to help?" she asked, pulling the shovel from the gravel with a sound like grinding teeth, then striking a pose for him, one bare foot poised on the edge of the blade, both arms digging at the haft.

"Barefooted?" he said, straightening up to wipe the sweat from his face with a wadded-up paisley scarf that doubled as a headband. "You must be one tough woman."

And she was. For the better part of an hour she worked beside him, pitching and thrusting, her movements matched to his, the gravel rising in the ditch like a gray tributary cutting across the dun chop of the field, and she could feel it in her hamstrings, her arms and lower back, and her feet – her feet especially, which couldn't have ached more if they'd been pounded with bricks the whole time – but she never let up. She wanted his praise, and more: she wanted to outdo him.

"All right," he said finally, "all right – Christ, you're like a demon here. Alfredo was right."

"About what?"

He looked off across the field to where the trees staggered down to the river. "I don't know. You want to take a swim?"

The water was a living thing, animated in every rill and ripple, and she entered it in a smooth knifing motion that started with her prayer-bound palms elevated over the arch of her neck and ended with a fillip of her ankles and feet. Marco's splash was muffled by the sound of her own, the cold immediate shock, and then they were racing to the far bank, her crawl against his butterfly. He came on strong at the end, pounding the surface to a froth with the spread wings of his arms and the dull hammering explosions of his kick, but in her mind she was back home at the lake, thirteen years old all over again and the strongest swimmer in her age group, out to the raft and back, and she never lost once, not all that summer. She touched the rocks on the far side and turned to face him. Two beats, three, and he was there, naked against her in the flutter of the current, and he took hold of her as if he'd been chasing her all his life.

Later, when the sun wore a groove down the middle of the river and fell off into the trees, they swam back in tandem, pulled on their clothes and started back up the hill. Her feet glided over the dirt of the path. She felt clean and new, the way she always did after a swim, her muscles stretched taut and then stroked and massaged till they were like the veal her mother used to pound for cordon bleu, first one side, then the other, *whack, whack, whack*. They'd made love in a cool dimple of grass on a sandbar, Marco taking his time, using his tongue and his fingers to pry each soft gasp from her, and she arching her back, taking him in, making love to him every bit as much as he was making love to her. Then they lay there in the grass a long while, watching the cobalt sky and a single hawk on fire with the sun, and then Marco nuzzled her, and she rolled herself on top of him, every square millimeter of her skin lit from within, and she thought of a film she'd seen on TV one late night when she was in high school and her parents were asleep and dead to the world – *Hiroshima, Mon Amour,* that was it, a French movie – and the thrill it gave her to see the two lovers just like that, skin to skin, her breasts to his chest, their loins pressed tight, their legs, their feet. She didn't feel dirty. She felt clean. Pure. Felt as if she'd never lived in her parents' house, never gone to religious instruction or holy communion or listened in red-faced horror as Mrs. Montgomery took the seventh grade girls aside and told them about the penis and how the blood flowed to it to make it erect and what that would mean to them if they couldn't keep their knees together till they were married. She didn't think of Ronnie. Didn't think of the teepee cat. Didn't think of anything at all.

Nobody saw anything. Nobody knew anything. But she came up from the river with Marco, her hair trailing wet all the way to the small of her back, her hand swinging in the grip of his and nothing but pleasure and peace in the world, and there was the guitar, the strings crawling loose in the leaf litter and the fretboard splintered into glittering shards that were no better than souvenirs now. They crossed the road and saw what looked like the remains of a rummage sale laid out beneath the tree, his books, his clothes, even his toothbrush. Marco never said a word. He didn't stoop to examine the books or try to reassemble the pages or tape the covers back together – all that would come later. He just turned and started for the back house, his shoulders set, arms rigid at his sides, and she didn't say anything either – or maybe she did, maybe she gasped out some crumpled little wad of nonsense like *Who?* or *Why?* – but she followed along behind him.

Sky Dog was out on the porch, and Sky Dog saw them coming. What he did was get up out of the swaybacked kitchen chair he'd been sitting in and call out to somebody inside the house – to Lester, Franklin, Dewey – but no one answered the call, and now Marco was coming up the steps in a furious headlong rush and Sky Dog, all hands and extruded eyes, was backing away from him. "I got no problem with you," he said, narrowing himself in the corner, ready to flinch and duck and throw out a warding arm. Marco went straight at him.

She didn't know how long it went on, but there was never any doubt as to the outcome. It took Alfredo, Jiminy and Mendocino Bill combined to pull Marco off Sky Dog, who went down in the first rush and never got up again. Standing there in the dirt with a cored-out shaft of sunlight hammering at her head, she could hear the impact of each blow, relentless, bone on flesh, bone on bone, and it was almost as if Marco was giving him a massage too, very thorough, very diligent, with special attention to the head and throat. But this was no massage, this was murder. Or the closest thing to it. There was blood where there wasn't supposed to be blood, on the dried-out floorboards, on the bleached walls, imbued in the fabric of Sky Dog's denim vest and smeared like finger paint across the cavity of his breastbone. Her own blood was racing. She hated this, hated it, but she couldn't take her eyes away and she never once called out for help.

But that was then, and then didn't count for much.

Now was what counted, and she flashed open her eyes on the nodding trees, the festival of the river, a pair of kingfishers swooping low. It was just a day, a kind of garment you could crawl inside of and use for your own purposes, and it was brightening now, brightening till all the colors stood out in relief against the shadows gathered along the far bank. Numbers, she told herself, numbers, not stories. Two birds, one river, three hundred and sixteen trees, seven thousand wildflowers, one earth, one sky: there was nothing to be afraid of here, nothing to get hung about. *Strawberry fields forever.* She pushed herself up and started back.

12

Norm had a pocket watch that had been in the family for three generations, a tarnished silver disc on a tarnished silver chain he kept tucked away in the front flap of his overalls. By Marco's count, he must have consulted it at least once every thirty seconds since they left the ranch, his free hand draped casually over the wheel, the radio giving back static and the van skating through the curves on River Road as if the usual forces in operation – gravity, velocity, wind resistance – had been suspended in honor of the day. "What I want," he was shouting, "is to coordinate this so we're in tune with everybody else, I mean, right on the stroke – and don't call me crazy because it's a karmic thing, is all. And for the rush. I mean, what's the sense of tripping if you're not having a blast? Am I right?"

He didn't need Marco to tell him he was, but Marco told him anyway.

"All right. So ten o'clock is what we're shooting for, one cup of OJ for me, one for you, then we pick up the stuff for the feast – cream soda, that's what I'm into, man, I really *crave* cream soda, especially when I'm tripping – and then we're back like by eleven-thirty, twelve, you know, and let the party commence, longest day, man, longest day. Whew! Can you believe it?"

They'd just pulled into the parking lot at the supermarket, life beating around them, kids on bikes, old men crawling out of pickup trucks like squashed bugs, planes overhead, dogs scratching, mothers pushing shopping carts as if they were going off to war, when Norm's watch gave out. It froze at five of ten, the hands immobilized as if they'd been soldered in place. "I can't believe it," he muttered, tapping at the crystal. He put the watch to his ear, tapped it again. "I just wound it this morning."

"Well, there you go," Marco told him, "too much attention to detail. Go with the flow."

Norm looked puzzled. He squinted at Marco out of the depths of his walled-in eyes as if he couldn't quite place him. He murmured something unintelligible, some sort of prayer or chant, and then, out of nowhere, he said, "You know, not that it's any of my business, but just out of curiosity – you've been getting it on with Star, haven't you?"

The question took Marco by surprise – *Star? Who was talking about Star?* – and right away, it filled him with suspicion. He looked at Norm, at the feverish brown eyes dodging behind the distorting lenses, and wondered, What does he care? Was he even paying attention? And if he was, what was he really asking? As chief guru and presiding genius of the ranch, he recycled women pretty efficiently – at one time or another practically all the Drop City chicks had slept with him. Lydia had gone around for a week talking about his lingam and what a perfect fit it was, Verbie called him "Pasha Norm" behind his back and Star – well, Marco couldn't speak for Star, but from what he knew about her and what he felt for her, he doubted she and Norm had got it on, but anything was possible. Of course, either way it was all right, because everybody was enlightened and the flesh existed to be celebrated, didn't it? If anybody was jealous, if any of the usual bourgeois hangups festered beneath the surface of the long irenic dream that was Drop City, Marco never saw it. But then he wasn't all that observant, as he'd be the first to admit. "I think we're really attuned to one another," he said, and his voice seemed to be caught in his throat. "Star and me."

Norm, leaning in close: "You mean like in a spiritual way? Agape instead of eros?"

"What do you mean?"

"Are you balling her?"

"What kind of question is that?"

"A practical one." Norm's breath was stale, or worse than stale – rotten. The teeth were rotting in his head and his head was rotting on his body. He didn't believe in dentists – only shamans – because it wasn't caries that caused your teeth to fall out, but the evil spirits of dentists gone down, and he had the gold in his mouth to prove it.

"What," Marco said, and he felt his face flush, " – you interested?"

Norm shifted his weight in the seat, gave a shrug. "She's a groovy chick."

Sure she was. Everybody was groovy, every*thing* was groovy. This was the world they were making, this was the new age, free and enlightened and without hangups, climb every mountain, milk every goat. "Yeah," Marco heard himself say, "yeah, she is."

There was a moment's silence, the van's engine ticking off to sleep somewhere beneath and behind them. Norm made no move to get out. He pushed the glasses up his nose and they slid back down. He sighed. Lifted his hand as if in extenuation, then dropped it. "You know, there's something I never told you," he said. "Or anybody, really, except for Alfredo. And it's not good, not good at all." He tapped the watch again, then gave it a rueful glance, as if it were the source of all the world's sorrow and misery.

"What do you mean?"

"They don't like heads in this town, is what I mean – in this whole fucking fascist county, for that matter, and you better pay up now and worship the rules and regulations or you are *fucked*, believe me. They don't want to see people living in harmony with the earth and each other – they just want Daddy, Mommy, Junior and Sis, all shoved into a tract house with a new blacktop driveway and a lawn that looks like it's been painted right on the dirt."

"You having trouble with the county?"

"Bet your ass I am."

"Board of Health? Fire and Safety?"

Bent over the watch, his head lolling weakly on his shoulders as if it were floating on the upended mass of his hair, Norm just nodded. "Bunch of shit," he said finally, but all the animation was gone from his voice. "I didn't sign on for this, no way in hell."

They sat there staring bleakly out the bug-spattered windshield on the fruits of life in the land of plenty, *Wonder Bread, Skippy Peanut Butter, Oleo Margarine,* and while Marco sucked in his breath and idly traced a finger up and down the face of the glove box, Norm heaved a sigh and filled him in. The situation was worse than he'd suspected. Far worse. The county health and sanitation people had been looking to close up Drop City for over a year now, and the fire and building inspectors were close on their heels. Norm had been in and out of court all through the past fall and into the winter; lately, he'd been using the summonses to light the fire in the incinerator out back, because he was through with all that, fed up to his ears, so pissed off and rubbed raw he just wanted to give it all up and let the bureaucratic pencil-pushing bastards take the ranch and pave it over if that's what they wanted. And it got worse still: the county had ordered him to clear the property of all persons and all substandard dwellings or face a fine of five hundred dollars a day. "Like as if I was a slumlord or something," he said, staring out the window of the van on a row of piggybacked shopping carts and the bold bright ads for detergent, meat and liquor that crowded the windows of the supermarket.

"What's so bad that we can't fix it?" Marco said. "The leach lines are in, aren't they? Shouldn't that make them happy?" He was talking just to hear himself, just to say something. He knew the way it worked. Nobody wanted a free-form community in their midst, because free-form meant anarchy, it meant a cordillera of trash a mile high and human shit in the woods, it meant Sky Dog and Lester and a guitar smashed like an eggshell – even if Drop City were on a mountaintop in Tibet the people in charge would steer their overworked yaks right up the face of the cliffs to shut them down. And maybe that wasn't all bad, maybe somebody somewhere had to put the brakes on.

"They've been garnishing my account at the B. of A." Norm was watching a miniskirted blonde lift brown-paper bags from a cart and set them with soft precision in the trunk of the low-slung Cutlass in the next row over. She had two kids with her – a baby with its bare fat legs dangling from the slots cut in the cart, and an older kid of five or six who gave them an even stare and then flashed the peace sign. "Jesus, look at that kid, the baby, I mean," Norm said. "He looks like Alfred Hitchcock, doesn't he? But I guess all babies look like Alfred Hitchcock. Or Mao. Maybe Mao. Maybe that's who he looks like."

Marco didn't have anything to say. He was calculating, pluses on one side, minuses on the other. He'd gotten too comfortable, and he should have known better. He'd settled in, built himself a treehouse, dug the leach lines, found a girl – and here the image of Star, smiling as if in some faded yearbook photo, rose up to take hold of him – but it was all so ephemeral, and nothing lasted, whether you fought for it or not. Sky Dog was gone, that was a plus, and it was just a matter of time before Lester followed him. Alfredo he could take or leave, and Pan could be an irritant, but at least he could be controlled. Not that it mattered. Not with the authorities involved. It was over, and if he had any sense at all he'd dump what he'd accumulated in the past five weeks and hit the road.

Norm shifted around in the seat to face him. "People would say to me, 'Norm, you can't just let everybody in because that's going to ruin it for the rest of us,' but what are you going to do? Everybody wants out of this fucking consumer-freak society and I'm not going to stand in their way, I mean, nobody elected me God." Norm pushed the glasses up the bridge of his nose, and they slid back down. It was getting hot in the cab. "Besides, and I don't have to tell you this, man, if you start to like *limit* the community, then it becomes static, like the Shakers or the Amish or whatever. They die out. Just like that. You've got to have an open community, and in the purest Gurdjieffian sense you let God be the selector, you know what I mean?"

"What about Sky Dog? Or Lester?"

"What about them?"

"Oh, come on, Norm, are you kidding me? – they bring the whole thing down. And there's a million more just like them, and they keep coming till the county drives a stake through your heart or the whole scene collapses. Or even Jiminy. Or Star, or me, or any of us. It just doesn't work unless you have some kind of standards – "

"You want rules, go work in the bank. Which brings me to my point here – motherfuckers are into me for something like three thousand dollars already because of these ridiculous – do I want to say contemptible? Yeah, *contemptible* – fines, and all that money is from the insurance settlement. Get to the end of it and there's nothing left, see what I mean, man? It's over. All she wrote. Good night and goodbye."

The moment drifted past them. On the radio it was nothing but bright little bubbles of pop trash, "I Got You Babe" filtered through a thunderstorm of static and speakers that were already rattling though the van couldn't have been more than six months old.

"That's why I bought this vehicle," Norm said, as if Marco had been thinking aloud. "Spend some of my own money on something *I* want – or we all want, not to mention we all can use – instead of just giving it up to the dickheads with the slide rules and the building codes they must've fucking committed to memory. But fuck it. This is the day, isn't it? Aren't we on a serious mission here to score cream soda?"

They were. And Marco hadn't just come along for the ride – he was building a corral for the horse, a pin-headed, wild-eyed, fat-flanked monster of a thing that didn't seem to appreciate concepts like two-lane blacktop and cement trucks with bad brakes, and he'd been planning on picking up a roll of barbed wire at the hardware store – on Norm's dollar – but that all seemed pretty useless now. He ducked his head, depressed suddenly, and scratched at his beard, wondering vaguely if he'd caught ringworm from the big orange cat that lived atop the refrigerator. He'd wanted to build something – he was twenty-four years old and past the age of butting his head up against the establishment – but it wasn't going to happen at Drop City. He felt heavy all of a sudden, immensely heavy, as if he could crush the car beneath him and plunge down through the blacktop and into the ancient rivers that ran under the earth. He wanted to kick something, wanted to get out and clear his lungs or maybe his tear ducts, and he had his fingers on the door handle when Norm grabbed him by the wrist.

Hot in that van. And Norm: the black clunky plastic-frame glasses, gold teeth flashing in his grin like a prospector's dream. He was holding up the thermos as if it were the solution to every problem they'd ever known, the key, the prize, the grail brought back home on a silver salver. Marco relaxed, accepted the smudged white cup with the screw tread worked into the rim. "One for you," Norm said, pouring till the cup would hold no more. "And one," he said, tipping the thermos back so that the white plastic aperture was swallowed up in the dark accumulation of his beard, "for me."

On the way back, Marco didn't feel stoned at all, and then abruptly he did. There was no tingling in his extremities, no dislocation, no sudden infusion of light or loss of personality – it came over him as if he'd been draped in a blanket, swaddled and pinioned and laid out in a crib, as if it were night and he was dreaming somebody else's dreams for them. Norm, for once, was quiet. And Marco – he couldn't have spoken if he'd wanted to. He wasn't in the front seat of a VW van hurtling down a country road with the river trailing along behind him like a bright fluttering banner, but in a room, in a farmhouse or a rent-controlled apartment maybe, and the room was swollen with inherited and hoarded things, sideboards, stuffed chairs, a chest of drawers, quilts, antimacassars, bibelots, bric-a-brac. There was a bed in the room – a four-poster swamped with blankets – and in the bed, an old man, wasted and white, with a nose that climbed up out of his face as if it didn't belong to him. It was a conventional scene, a deathbed scene, somebody's future or past, utterly conventional, but for the single incongruity of a pair of snowshoes fastened to the wall above the bed. The conscious remnant of his mind drew him back: Was this a photo he'd seen somewhere? A scene from childhood? TV? Or was he outside of himself and powerless to get back in? That was the thing with acid. He didn't like acid, had never liked acid, even when he liked drugs a whole lot more than he liked them now.

Norm murmured something – a snatch of nonsense, or no, he was singing, soft and low, lyrics like a private language – and here they were again, under the trees and then out in the open, moving through the sensory world as if they owned it. "You feel anything yet?" Norm wanted to know. "Because I don't feel a thing, or maybe just like the *beginning* of something, but what I'm wondering is did they forget to juice our juice or what?"

Marco was about to tell him he was feeling plenty himself, feeling possessed almost, feeling stacked up and wrung out, but he never got the chance – another vision sprang right up alongside the road and flung itself in front of the van, a huge dark blur of motion that wasn't a hallucination at all but the real and actual thing that was suddenly defeating Norm's white clenched hands and seriously dislocating his intentions. What was it? The horse. Charley Horse. The very animal, laying claim to the road and shivering its head stupidly as Norm ran his hands helplessly round the wheel and the van did a kind of stock-car trick on two thin wailing tires.

There were two lanes to that road, and the other one, the oncoming lane, instantly became a place of violent contraction, Norm's sidelong van and a pickup truck featuring a pair of startled faces, one male, one female, closing fast on the same space. Thunder and lightning: the van skewed violently to the left and Marco saw the horse loom up on his right before he felt the jolt of the first collision, the one that swatted the animal off its feet with the open palm of a big steel hand, and then the more substantial one, the one that screamed with contorted metal. The pickup truck – there was an old man in a feed cap at the wheel, his face fallen away into a deep pit of astonishment and outrage – caught the van just athwart the passenger's side door and then shook itself loose and continued on into a tree, into several trees, and the horse lost all its legs and then found them again, even as Norm's van rebounded from the collision, described a long slow arc and came to rest in the center of the road.

"Okay," Norm was saying, "okay, everything's okay," as if he'd planned it, as if the whole thing were just another stunt he'd orchestrated to enliven the day. He was bleeding from a gash under one eyebrow, a bright reservoir of blood pooling in the orbit of his eye before draining off into his beard. His glasses had been snapped across the spine and the windshield featured a spidery mandala set in the glass like an ornament, and how clever of those German engineers, Marco was thinking, how clever – but shouldn't there be one on his side too?

Marco was all right, or that was his first impression, anyway. No blood, no broken bones. His right shoulder had a certain rigidity to it where he'd been flung against the dash three times in succession, and the acid seemed to be boiling up in his veins till he could hear the sizzle of it in his ears, but he was all right. All right, and out of the car – kicking open one very reluctant door and setting both his feet on the pavement, which hardly seemed to be moving at all. The horse – Charley Horse – was just standing there, trembling all over as if he'd been hosed down with ice water, Norm was a statue at the wheel of the van, and the old man – and his old wife – were camped out in the woods twenty feet from the road. Everything was still.

Until the next car – a monster of a thing, a Buick, or maybe it was a Pontiac, staggered in the rear by the weight of the blue-flecked fiberglass runabout it was hauling – came shearing round the curve and Charley Horse bucked twice, put his head down and tried to leap it. Marco heard himself shouting, but he was shouting over the adrenal surge and the successive rippling shore-battering waves of peaking acid, and no other living thing seemed to hear or heed him, least of all the horse. Which immediately laid its thousand pounds of horseflesh across the crumpling hood of the Buick – or no, it was a Pontiac, because there was the chrome V with the stoic chief welded into it – and began a slow futile drumming of its hooves against the fenders on either side. The boat was part of the act now too – it rode up the back of the trailer, then relaxed an instant before gracefully spinning across the road till it came to rest against the bumper of the van.

Somebody was cursing. The sound of it arose from between the clenched teeth of the crash like an incantation, the same three monosyllables repeated over and over with increasing vehemence till the curses were screams and Marco was moving toward them through a scrim of what was real and what might have been. What did he see? A woman pinned behind the wheel of the Pontiac, her hair in curlers, her face distorted. Charley Horse had managed to tear himself open on the fulcrum of the hood ornament, and he'd collapsed the roof. Marco was fighting the drug, willing his mind to retake control of his body. He ducked away from the horse's hooves, from the horse's hundred buckets of blood and its looping gray intestines, and forced open the back door of the Pontiac. He had the woman – one long shriek of a woman – by the shoulders and dragged her into the backseat as if she were a piece of furniture, and then he had her out of the car and onto the shifting pavement. She wore her mouth like a badge, all that noise and violence, and he stood beside her, an arm round her shoulders, while Charley Horse thrashed himself off the car and slid across the shoulder of the road like a slick black sea lion leaving the shore for good. This time the horse didn't get up again.

"Marco!" Norm was shouting. "Marco, do something! Shit! What is this, blood?" He was standing in the road now too, and so were the old man and the old lady, squinting into the light as if they'd come in late to a movie and were trying to find their seats. Norm looked strange without his glasses – inhuman, or no: non-human. He'd found a rag in the car – a torn T-shirt that must have belonged to one of the children – and he pressed it to his face to stanch the bleeding. "Fucking horse," he muttered, and there it was, on its side and heaving in the ditch.

"I just hope for your sake, mister," the old man was saying – and there *he* was, like a pop-up doll at Norm's elbow, with a white strained face and teeth that didn't seem to fit in his head (borrowed teeth, and that was a concept) – "I just hope you got insurance is all I got to say."

Next thing Marco knew, he was running. Half a mile down the streaming blacktop to the Drop City turnoff, and then up the rutted dirt road to where the main house stood rippling against the trees. "Get help!" Norm had shouted in his face. "Get Alfredo! Get anybody!" And suddenly Marco was running, heaving himself down the road in a kind of pure white-hot acid-fueled panic, his boots flapping first at the pavement, then the dust. Somebody, anybody! He vaulted a rotting fence and pounded across an open field, thinking he'd better calm himself, better do whatever it was people were expected to do in a situation like this – shake it off, wake up, take responsibility – but the drug wouldn't let him. It was in his throat, in his head, it was strangling his heart, eating his lungs.

There was nobody on the front porch, nobody in the front room. The music was there, though, playing all on its own, loud, raucous, a clash of metal like a whole marching band falling down the stairs, and why didn't he recognize the tune? He saw plates of half-eaten food perched on the arms of chairs, the still-wet chopsticks like evil insects crouched over a splay of rice, beans, tofu; he saw record jackets come to ground like wind-swirled refuse, and in the back corner of the bookshelf, the black glistening puddle of a record working its way round the turntable. And that was strange, the music living a life of its own in a house with no human occupants. It was like a ghost story. A fairy tale. Nobody home and the porridge still warm on the table. The meeting room presented more of the same. Ditto the kitchen. He looked up and the square-headed orange tom looked down on him from its perch atop the refrigerator.

And then, beneath the music – or threaded through it – he heard the human noise in the backyard, a wailing, a hush, then a clamor of voices, repeating now, slight return: wailing, a hush, clamor of voices. He took himself out the screen door and there they were, the whole tribe, gathered round the swimming pool and what appeared to be a very wet cloth doll stretched out on the flagstone coping. That was when the acid let go of him just long enough to record the scene: it was one of the kids, one of Reba's kids, and Jiminy was pumping at the kid's chest like a Marine Corps medic on the evening news and everybody else was wringing their hands and jumping in and out of the green murk that was the pool. He saw Ronnie inflate his cheeks and go down, and then Alfredo bobbing to the surface in a maelstrom of hair. "What's wrong?" he wanted to know, snatching at the first person his hand led him to, but he was so full of Norm and the accident he didn't recognize her, not at first.

"It's Che," Merry told him. She was naked to the waist, shivering. She wore body paint, red and blue tendrils striating her limbs like extruded veins. Her eyes didn't seem to be in her head – they were just floating there, three inches to the left of her face. "He drowned, or he fell in or something, and we can't – I mean, nobody knows where *Sunshine* is."

A shriek cut the air, every mother's nightmare. "Sunshine!" Reba wailed, drawing out the last syllable till it caught in the back of her throat. "Sunshine! Come out, baby, come out! It's not funny!" She flung herself across the yard, beat at the stiff brush of the chaparral with angry hands. She was puffed up, furious, just coming on to boil. "It's not a game. Come out, goddamnit! Come out, you hear me, you little bitch!"

"She's not in the pool," somebody said, and in the confusion, Marco couldn't see who it was.

"The river, what about the river?" He glanced up to register

Verbie – she was perched on the wet coping, her eyes dilated, hair glued to her head. "Did anybody search the river?"

A look of helplessness swept over them, lost eyes, mouths agape, the slumped shoulders and agitated hands, and how could anybody be expected to do anything at a time like this? It was Druid Day. They were wiped, all of them. They didn't want to save children, they wanted to *be* children. "What do you mean, the river?" Merry wondered aloud.

"I mean the *river*." Verbie flung out her hands as if she were taking a bullet on a dark stage. "She could've drowned. Down there, I mean." Up to this point, she'd been going fine, but now she seemed to falter. She looked to her sister, then to Marco. "I mean, right?"

That was when Star appeared out of nowhere, parting the crowd like a prophet, her face ironed shut, quick bare feet on the flagstones, her naked limbs, wet T-shirt, wet shorts. And then she was bent over the limp form of Che, clearing his tongue with a sweep of two fingers, pinching his nostrils and breathing her life into him. *CPR. Junior Lifesavers. Mouth-to-Mouth.* It all came back to him in that moment, but all he could do was stand and watch, his arms dangling as if they'd been attached with pins, and what he felt was awe. He watched Star's knees grip the flagstones, watched her balance on the bridges of her feet. And her hair. It was a miracle, spread out over the child's head and torso like an oxygen tent, each curl like a finger, each finger willing him back.

People were pounding the bushes now, shouting out Sunshine's name as if it were the only word in the language, and Norm was down there bleeding like an animal somewhere on the road with the sheriff on his way and the citizenry up in arms, and still Marco didn't move. He watched Star's hair, watched her lips fasten to the boy's. Fasten and release, fasten and release. A year went by. A decade. And then Che's left foot began to dig at the flagstones, and Marco was released. In the next moment he was running again, generating a breeze all his own, the sweating cables of his own hair beating around his head, the cords of his legs fighting the descent that sent him hurtling down the bank of madrone, bay and knobcone pine to where the river took its light from the sky. He said it too, then, pronounced the name all the others were pronouncing, as if it were involuntary, called it out till his lungs burned and his throat went dry, "Sunshine! Sunshine!"

There was no answer. He took a path north along the bank, straining to see into the water, but the water was murky with its freight of sediment and deep here where the current sliced round a long garrulous bend. The water spoke to him, but it didn't calm him. Birds called out. The sky rose up and slapped down again. What had he expected to see – a pale arm waving amongst the river-run debris? The ghostly body pressed against a wedge of rocks six feet down? "Sunshine!" he called. "Sunshine!"

He was still calling when he found her. He was calling, but she wasn't answering. She was crouched at the foot of a deep arching bush hung with berries, a red stain of juice painted on her chin and exaggerating her mouth till it was like a clown's. Her red hands moiled in her lap. She was wearing a dirty white dress, no shoes, beads at her throat and wrist, and her hair was in two lax braids bristling with bits of twig and leaf. "Sunshine," he said, just to hear himself say it again. She was staring past him, crouched there, just crouched. Maybe she was singing to herself, maybe that was it, because she was making some sort of noise in the back of her throat, and the noise made him uneasy. "Are you all right?" he asked her.

She didn't answer.

"Look," he said, and the words were hard to extract, "everybody's been worried about you – your mother, she's been worried. And your father. And Norm and me and everybody." He paused to let the breath go out of him, just for an instant, just to escape the tedium of breath-in and breath-out. "Been picking berries, huh?"

She didn't look at him, but she nodded her head, or at least he thought she did.

"Well, I'm going to take you back now, is that okay? I'm going to lift you up on my shoulders and take you back – you want a ride? You want to go piggyback?"

He came out of the woods to a hero's welcome, the whole clan gathered round him with their slow shy smiles and spooked eyes, yet another tragedy averted, and let's stir up the pot of mush and get it on in a major way, sure, and crank the music too. It surprised him to see the sun fixed overhead – it was early afternoon still, though it felt much later, felt like midnight in his mind. Reba came across the yard, slid her daughter from his shoulders without a word and carried her into the house as if nothing had happened. Che was gone – presumably he was in the house too, in bed, fluttered over by half a dozen women, and that was an image Marco wanted to hold – but the blurred outline of him still clung to the wet flagstones as if it were a piece of some elaborate puzzle to which no one had the solution. Jiminy settled into one of the chaise longues with a pair of bongos and started a slow lugubrious slap-palmed beat. A beer – still cold from the tub – appeared in Marco's hand, and then Star was at his side. She didn't say a word, just leaned forward and kissed him and held her lips there until he came back to life.

13

When the black-and-white sheriff's cruiser came nosing up the drive like some sort of mechanical hound, sniffing out the curves and drawing a bead on the main house, Pan didn't feel much of anything. The day had careened right by him. There was all that hassle and hysteria, diving and diving again till he damned near wound up drowning *himself,* and then a lull that smoothed out all the wrinkles like a hot iron. Reba's brats had been saved and resurrected and either punished or rewarded or both – of that much he was sure, or at least he thought he was – and then at some point Norm had appeared with a bloody strip of cloth pressed to one eye and his glasses cobbled together with a white knuckle of masking tape. Norm was wearing his ask-no-questions look and went straight for his room at the top of the stairs, so that little drama was over before it began, and after a while the party or communal navel-gaze or whatever it was had recommenced in all earnestness.

But that was hours ago. What Pan was concerned about now was meat, and to that end he'd sequestered a package of Safeway hot dogs in the depths of the refrigerator and stashed an eight-pack of spongy supermarket buns under a pile of dirty clothes in the back bedroom, and as the cruiser worked its slow sure way up the road – moving so slowly, in fact, it barely even spun the dust off its tires – Pan was thinking he'd be building a little fire soon, after which he'd have a couple of hot dogs slathered with mustard and sweet pickle relish, and anybody who happened to be around, weekend hippies and part-time heads included, would be welcome to join him.

He was sitting on the front porch, Merry, Maya and Mendocino Bill settled in beside him and some new cat in a serape and high-crowned straw hat sprawled on the steps (*his* trip was

Krishna and there was no way to shut him up about it unless you took a claw hammer to the back of his head, and for the past half hour Pan had been giving it some real consideration). Merry wasn't going to eat any meat, or Maya either, that was for sure. Maybe Mendocino Bill, but Ronnie really didn't give a shit about Mendocino Bill one way or the other so it hardly mattered. "Krishna is love," the new cat said, and the cruiser eased into the space in front of the railing like a foot slipping into a shoe. Two cops, each a replica of the other, got out.

They stood there in the dirt a moment, shifting their eyes around, two almost-young men, and what currents were *they* floating on? Lean, narrow-hipped, all but hairless, they looked as if they'd been specially bred in some police kennel somewhere, and Ronnie could picture it, the women staked out on chains and the bull-headed men going at them till they got the litter just right. *Woof-woof.* He studied their faces, but their faces gave away nothing. Their eyes, though – their eyes lit up every particle of dust, alive to every gesture, every nuance, eyes that could see through walls, through clothes, through flesh, and you'd have to be crazy not to feel the heat of them.

As the car doors slammed in unison, the two yellow dogs slunk out from beneath the porch to sniff at the cops' boots, and Freak, the one with the hacked-off tail, seized the opportunity to lift a leg and piss against the sidewall of the near tire. The cops never so much as shrugged. They took a minute to square their shoulders and adjust their belts, running their hands idly over the butts of their guns and truncheons and the rest of their head-cracking paraphernalia, then turned their attention to the porch. "You live here?" the one to the left asked, addressing Ronnie but letting his cold blue eyes jump to Merry, Maya, Mendocino Bill and beyond, where the depths of the house stirred with a thick, lazy batter of activity.

Though half of Drop City had melted off into the woods at first sight of the cruiser, Ronnie played it cool. He had nothing to fear. He'd never been in trouble with the law – his luck had held through every transaction, every furtive hit and airless squeeze of the plunger – and his father's cousin the psychologist had gotten him a 4-F on the grounds of mental incapacity. Which is not to say he didn't recognize the pigs for what they were. "I live on the green planet earth," he said, showing all his teeth.

"That's right, man," the new cat put in, "and it was Brahma that put us here – and Lord Vishnu that preserves us."

"Right on," Maya said, and then Merry, flinging her hair back to expose her painted breasts, said, "You live here too. We all live here. On the planet, dig?" And everybody on the porch, even the new cat, flashed the peace sign.

The cop lifted one shining boot to the dried-out blasted paint-stripped plank of the porch's second riser, and rested it there, leaning into his knee and focusing tightly on Pan. "Who's in charge here?" he wanted to know, and his voice was reasonable yet soft and reasonable, as if he were addressing a clutch of fourth graders or maybe the town drunk stewing in his own juices. "Who's the landlord? The owner?"

Dale Murray stepped through the screen door then, just in time to field the question. Dale was a head of the old school – No moment on this earth was rich enough to risk forgoing drugs for, that was his motto – and he'd blown into the ranch one night last week on a fig green Honda motorcycle that sounded as if he'd attached grenade launchers to the muffler pipes. He was wearing a pair of blue-and-white-striped bell-bottoms, he was shirtless, rigidly muscled and deeply tanned; bells and beads and the yellowed teeth of some unlucky carnivore dangled from his neck, and a guitar was fixed at his waist like a big wooden cummerbund. He gave each of the cops a hallowed look and said, "Listen, I'm not going to give you the runaround and say God's the owner here and we're all mutual on this earth, you and me and your wife Loretta and Richard Milhous Nixon too – no, I'm not going to insult your intelligence and waste your time because I know how hard you guys work and the kind of shit people are always laying on you." He paused. The cops' faces hardened, and the near one, the one who'd been asking the questions, drew his leg back and stood up square. "I won't lie," Dale Murray said, " – I am. I'm in charge here."

The talkative cop glanced at the top sheet in his summons book, then brought his eyes back up to drive them like staples into Dale Murray's. "You must be Norman L. Sender, then, is that right? Owner of an orange-and-white VW van with a peace sign painted on the driver's side panel and the California plate O-W-S-L-E-Y-1? Is that right?"

Dale Murray tugged at the loose ends of his hair. Ronnie could hear him breathing, a ragged intake and outflow that sounded like a machine in need of oil.

"Wanted for leaving the scene of an accident," the cop went on, "in an obviously intoxicated state. That wouldn't be you, would it?"

"No, sir," Dale Murray said, and there wasn't a flicker of recognition from anybody on the porch. "No, sir," he repeated, and his accent — what was it, cowboy? Southern redneck? — seemed to thicken, "I didn't say that."

The second cop had moved in to close the gap. "You got ID?" he wanted to know, and his voice wasn't reasonable at all — it was the standard-issue no-nonsense truncheon-swinging voice they must have handed out with the badges. "All of you," he snarled, "I want to see some ID. Pronto."

Nobody moved. Out on the periphery of the dried-up lawn, too far away for it to matter, Verbie was juggling three or four grapefruits in a shaft of sunlight while her sister danced round her like a mental case, strutting and writhing to some unheard melody. There was dogshit everywhere, piles of it like miniature termite mounds marching off into the distance. Two staved-in cars listed over their ruined springs to the side of the house, amidst a midden of old lumber and shingles. From the back, the sounds of festivity, rock and roll, the odd splash and shout.

"Anybody here own a horse?" the first cop asked, posting the soft missive of his question in the slot left open for him by his partner.

That was when Mendocino Bill, all two hundred fifty pounds of him, shot up out of his chair as if he'd been launched, a question of his own on his lips: "You got a fucking warrant, man?"

Before it was over, everybody on the porch had to do penance, Ronnie included. As soon as Mendocino Bill opened his mouth, both cops went for him, even as Merry, Maya and the Krishna cat began chanting "Peace and Love, Peace and Love, Off the Pigs, Peace and Love." Ronnie — *Pan* — gave the cops as wide a berth as he could, but he found himself crushed up against the railing as they dragged the big man from the porch, kicked his legs out from under him and forced his pale blubbery arms behind his back for the wedding of the cuffs. "He's not here," Maya squeaked, "Norm's not here!" The cops ignored her. They weren't even breathing hard, and what they were scenting now was a kind of freedom they'd only dreamed of: hippies, a whole parade of them, resisting arrest.

Mendocino Bill – he was a loudmouthed know-it-all like Alfredo, up to his ears in *Popular Mechanics* in high school, no doubt a ham radio operator and an eagle scout on top of it, and here he was writhing in the dust on the fulcrum of his belly like a bowling pin set spinning by a strike right down the middle of the alley. So what if he'd been to Selma, so what if he could eat four plates of mush to anybody else's two, so what if he was one of the brothers and sisters of Drop City and the cops were the pigs? Despite himself, Pan felt something soar inside him to see the loudmouth brought low – until the second cop, the silent one, herded everybody off the porch and lined them up, hands against the wall and legs spread.

"What's the problem, Officer?" Dale Murray was saying as the first cop patted him down. "I mean, what'd we do? A little kidding? Is that it? I mean, I was only joking. Can't you take a joke? You want to tell me jokes're against the law now?"

"Norm's not here," Maya kept repeating in her thin strand of a voice. She had her head down, her hands framed on the wall and the dried-out ends of her hair dangling, and she was talking to the ground. She was no beauty, and if it weren't for the very loose scene at Drop City, and all those strung-out horny cats like Mendocino Bill and Jiminy, she'd never have gotten laid in a million years. "He's not. I mean, *really*. He went to Santa Rosa for like supplies and things and he never – "

"What was he driving?" the cop wanted to know, the first one, the talker. "VW van, right?"

"Don't tell him anything," Merry said, and Ronnie saw that she'd clenched her face against the whole world, even as her eyes bled out of her head with the residue of the acid. He felt something for her then, something that took in her straining legs, her arched back and the painted breasts that stood up firm

155

under the pressure of her out-thrust arms, and it wasn't just lust. She was all right, and more than all right – she was like Star, only better.

"You got ID?" the second cop repeated. "You? And you?"

Ronnie showed him his New York driver's license – *Ronald Daniel Sommers, 8 Crestview Avenue, Peterskill, New York, D.O.B. 12/2/48, eyes hazel, hair brown, 5'10", 162 lbs.* – and kept his mouth shut. They weren't interested in him. They were interested in Dale Murray, who had the better part of a lid of grass tucked down the front of his pants in a crotch-warmed plastic bag, and they were even more interested in Merry, who was wearing nothing but body paint from the waist up. If Norm had been in the house when the commotion started up, he was long gone by now – out the back door, across the yard and into the trees – and whatever he'd done with the van, the cops weren't going to find it here. They weren't going to find anything beyond Dale Murray's pot, Mendocino Bill's sweating carcass and Merry's tits – which was plenty, for one day – and as the people out back began to drift round the house and surround them, the cops lightened up noticeably.

Ronnie was still flying high, way up there at thirty-five thousand feet, cruise control, the billowing clouds – *leavin' on a jet plane* – and none of it really affected him, though he resented the prodding and poking. Resentment, that was what he was made of, and the realization made him bristle inwardly, just a bit. He resented the cops, resented Mendocino Bill and Alfredo and Reba and her tripped-out filthy little suicidal brats, resented his parents and Star and Marco and maybe even the teepee cat out in the desert. Standing there in the late sun, with his hands spread flat against the outside wall of the house and his brothers and sisters gathered all around him and the cops starting to hedge their bets, he drifted back to that aching sorrowful high-crowned day when he went looking for Star, just to see her, to be with her, and his resentment took him across the yard and up the ladder and into the treehouse. How long had it taken him – five minutes? Ten? The space was empty, neat, rug on the floor, books on the shelves, guitar in the corner, backpack, clothes, Marco's hairbrush, his nail clippers, his toothpaste. The whole world was holding its breath. Pan didn't stint. He let the resentment come up in him till it was a kind of spew, and when he spewed, the violence of it surprised even him.

But now it was Druid Day and everybody was coming down in the fading afternoon and the cops were tucking Dale Murray's head into the black-and-white cruiser as if it were some precious object they were returning to its rightful owner. They let their eyes burn into the crowd for a long moment, Mendocino Bill rubbing at his liberated wrists and Merry jeering without opening her mouth, and then they ducked into the car, fired it up in a rapture of turbocharged power and made their slow sure way back down the dust-laden road.

The evening wore on. The light grew denser. Pan was roasting hot dogs on the slim green wand of a willow stick, woodsmoke tearing at his lungs and Lydia propped up on a log beside him, already eating, when Norm came loping out of the woods. *Norm,* he thought, *here comes Norm,* and something tightened inside him. Ronnie always felt at a loss with Norm, because Norm was older – *an older cat* – a kind of guru whose approval he sought, though he was hardly aware of it himself. He always straightened up when Norm was around, though, and he found himself trying to exaggerate his own grasp of things, as if the only way he could relate to the man was through an intervening lens of cool. Was he trying to impress him? Sure he was. Trying to get him to take note, lean on him, single him out? Sure. So what did he say now but "Hey, Norm – man, hey, you want a hot dog?"

Norm didn't answer right away. He looked dazed, as if he'd been lost in the woods for a month. There was a crust of dried blood over his left eyebrow. His glasses clung awkwardly to his face. "The man," he said, and he was gasping or wheezing or both. "The man was here, right? Looking for me?"

Lydia glanced up from her hot dog. Her bare feet were splayed out in the dust and you could see up the crotch of her cutoffs. She was sloppy, that was what Pan was thinking, sloppy and overweight. She said: "They took that new guy, what's his name – Dale? – and nobody's been down to bail him out or whatever. Alfredo said to wait for you."

"Dope," Ronnie said, and he sucked at his cheeks. Serious

business. He was standing here by the open fire talking serious business with Norm Sender.

"Dope?" Norm's face dropped. "You mean they searched him? Right here, on private property? Right on my front lawn, for shitsake? Is that what you're telling me?"

The sky was lit with tracers of fire from the setting sun and bats had begun to hurl themselves through the air. The first mosquitoes were making their forays. A jay screeched from the line of trees behind them.

"They searched us all, everybody on the front porch."

Norm gazed off toward the shadow of the house as if he could detect them there still. Ronnie gripped a bun, squeezed a hot dog from the willow stick and handed it to him. "You want mustard?" he asked. "Relish? We got relish too."

"Jesus," Norm murmured, and he took the hot dog without comment, no mustard, no relish, just meat and bun, and lifted it to his mouth. "Jesus," he repeated, and it sounded as if he was praying, "they're killing me here, that's what they're doing, they're killing me."

The smoke shifted then and came back at them, twigs snapping in the flames, and both Ronnie and Norm had to step to one side.

"It was Bill," Ronnie put in, and he couldn't help himself. "If he didn't go and open his big mouth, nothing would've happened. He pushed them. 'You got a fucking warrant, man?' That's what he said."

Norm was eating, his gaze vacant, the hot dog bun an extension of his face. Lydia scratched her inner thigh, slapped idly at a mosquito and contracted her shoulders in annoyance. "Fucking bugs," she said. And then, musing: "I wasn't there. I missed the whole thing."

"You didn't miss much," Ronnie said, and he was wondering where she'd been – on her back someplace, no doubt, tripping her brains out and balling anybody who could manage to get his zipper down. "What do you think, Norm – think they'll be back?"

It was a stupid question, and Norm didn't respond – and if he had, it probably would have been with some put-down like *Where do you think they'll come looking for me, city hall?* He didn't respond because he hadn't come down all the way yet – he was just a little too jittery and bug-eyed – and in a rare moment of empathy, Ronnie saw how the day must have cut through him, what with the accident and watching the horse breathe its last and then having to hightail it into the woods. *Hightail it. And where had that expression come from? Some cowboy movie?* Pan had a brief glimmer of Hopalong Cassidy spurring a big white horse through the sagebrush, a round black-and-white screen the size of a fishbowl and his father screaming from the kitchen because some ingrate – that's what he used to say, *ingrate* – had used up all the ice in the tray without filling it again. Norm just stood there. He fed the rest of the bun into his mouth and chewed mechanically, and when Ronnie handed him a second hot dog nestled in a fresh bun, he took it wordlessly.

It was a moment, and Ronnie was enjoying it. But then Reba came dragging her six-hundred-pound face across the back lot like some sort of bled-out zombie, already complaining from a hundred feet away, and the moment was gone. "Norm," she was hollering, "did you hear? The cops. They were here. They're looking for you."

Norm had heard. He'd been crouching in the woods in an acid coma for three hours with the blood crusting on his face and his glasses snapped in two, hadn't he? What did she think – he was hiding out there for the sheer thrill of it? They watched her, all three of them, as she made her way toward the flash and snap of the fire. "You heard about Che?" she called from twenty feet away.

Norm grunted something in response, something vaguely affirmative, and then she was right there, swaying over the balls of her feet, her pigtails unraveling round twin ligatures of pink rubber bands. "He's all right, he's going to be cool, but I tell you, he really freaked us out . . . I mean, for a while there he wasn't even breathing." There was a pause, and nothing filled it. Her eyes were like grappling hooks, tearing at them, tugging and heaving and pulling. "But Charley Horse," she said, "what a bummer."

Lydia said, "Yeah, bummer," and nodded her head.

Norm looked at his feet. "You know what you do with a dead horse?"

"Beat it," Ronnie said.

"Render it. They use it for dog food, glue, whatever. I never liked the thing anyway. It was just this big, stupid, four-legged sack of shit my ex-wife just had to have. *You got a ranch, don't you? Well then you gotta have a horse.* Brilliant logic, huh?"

Reba stood there, hard-eyed and pugnacious, her feet splayed, braids coming undone, already hurtling into middle age. Ronnie saw the two vertical lines gouged into the flesh between her eyebrows, the parentheses at the corners of her mouth: married too young, knocked up too soon, that's what she was all about. And what did she want? Answers. She wanted answers. "So what are we going to do, Norm? You know they're going to come back with a search warrant. You know they're going to close us down. What then? Where we going to go? I mean, Alfredo and me, we've given like two years of our *life* to this place – I mean, this is it. This was where we were going to stay for the rest of our lives – and Che's life, and Sunshine's." She looked away, as if she couldn't bear the sight of him with his slumped shoulders and bloodied face and taped-up glasses, and then she lifted her head and came right back at him. "So what's it going to be, Norm? What are we going to do now?"

Pan skewered another hot dog on his willow stick and thrust it into the flames. *Close the place down?* He was just getting comfortable. Sure, some of his brothers and sisters might have been a pain in the ass, but they all knew him, and for the first time in his life he had a purpose, whether anybody wanted to admit it or not – he was the provider here, or one of them. One of the main ones. He'd got the deer, hadn't he? And quail – he'd shot quail too. And fish – that's all he did was fish, and even the vegetarians couldn't complain about that. They ate for free, and that was the whole point of going back to the land, wasn't it?

Reba's words hung on the air, accusatory, demanding, tragic, self-pitying: *What are we going to do now?*

Norm wasn't staring at his feet anymore. He straightened his shoulders as if he'd just woken up, tucked the remains of the second hot dog in his mouth and slicked back his hair with the palms of his hands. He was thirty-seven years old. There was gray in his beard. His toes were so twisted they looked as if they'd been grafted on. "What are we going to do now?" he echoed. "We're going to have a meeting, that's what we're going to do."

14

This meeting wasn't anything like the last one. All the air had gone out of the day, a slow insidious deflation that was so wearying it wasn't even worth thinking about, and by the time Norm put out the word, half the population of Drop City had already crashed and burned. People were stretched out on sofas, stained mattresses, sleeping bags, on mats of pine boughs and the backseats of cars, their faces drawn, hair bedraggled, sleeping off the effects of simultaneously opening all those doors in their minds. Star was asleep herself, her face pressed to the gently heaving swell of Marco's rib cage, when Verbie came up the ladder to the treehouse and told her to get up, it was an emergency, and everybody – everybody, no exceptions – was due in the meeting room in fifteen minutes.

Star didn't know what to think. She was in the treehouse, with Marco, and she'd been asleep – that much was clear. Beyond that, everything was a jumble. It felt like the middle of the night, but it was light out, and for the life of her she couldn't have said whether it was dawn or dusk. The light had no source, no direction – it just held, as gray and dense as water, and the limbs of the oak were suspended in it like the superstructure of a dream. But she hadn't had any dreams – she couldn't even remember going to bed. She looked up into the branches of the tree for clues, but it was just a tree, hanging over her with all its ribs showing. It gave off a smell of gall, astringent and sharp, and whether it was a morning smell or an evening smell, she couldn't say. Birds came to the branches like dark, flung stones. Marco slept on. She couldn't find her panties – or her shorts – and something seemed to have bitten her in a series of leapfrogging welts that climbed up her naked abdomen and then vanished beneath her breasts. Where were her shoes? She sat up and looked around her.

Suddenly she was frightened. Emergency? What emergency? She summoned up a picture of the little boy then – Che – his hair kinked and wild, skin the color of olive oil thickened in the pan and his eyes sucked back into his head as if they were going to hide there forever, and she felt the impress of his cold lips on hers, lips like two copulating earthworms, like flesh without fire – but hadn't all that been settled? Hadn't she saved him? Saved the day?

It wasn't morning. That would be too much to hope for. It was dusk, and she knew it now. She could taste it on the air, hear it in the way the birds bickered and complained. It was Druid Day, the longest day of the year, and the worst, by far the worst – and it was still going on. Marco lay there beside her, his hair splayed across his face, his right fist balled up over his temple as if to ward off a blow. She listened to him breathe a moment, absorbed in the slow sure weave of it – ravel, unravel, ravel again – and then she shook him awake.

"What?" he said, propping himself up on his elbows so she could see the full spill of him.

"It's Norm. Some kind of emergency. Norm called a meeting – "

"Emergency? Now? What time is it?"

"Nine, maybe – I don't know. I thought it was morning."

"What kind of emergency – did the pump burn out in the well or something? Or let me guess: Reba lost her kids again. Or Pan, what about him? Did he fall into his wienie fire and get all singed around the ears?"

"Verbie didn't say. But she sounded freaked out."

"She always sounds freaked out."

He was reaching for her, to pull her back down into the sleeping bag, but she pushed his hand away. "I'm scared," she said. "After today . . . the kids, the horse, I mean. The whole thing. We're out of control here, Marco – everybody's out of control."

"Yeah," he said, giving her a smile so faint it was barely there. "But isn't that the point?"

The main house was ablaze with the power company's light, the light Norm and Alfredo were always hassling them to conserve – *Candles, people, use candles!* – and when she and Marco came up the worn steps and onto the porch, the floorboards seemed to fall away beneath her feet, as if the whole place were on the verge of collapse. She saw the gouged wood of the doorframe, the tattered mesh of the screen door, the worn spot where the embrace of ten thousand hands had abraded the paint round the latch and replaced it with dirt, human dirt – saw everything with utter clarity, though she could feel a headache coming on, a pounding, relentless, newly awakened shriek of a headache that threatened to burst her skull from the inside out, and that was what acid did for you, that was the price you had to pay. Open up your mind, feed your head. Sure. And wind up feeling like something washed up on the beach and left for dead. She took hold of Marco's arm for support, and then the screen door was slapping behind them and they were standing uncertainly in the front room that was like a funeral parlor – no music, no candles, nobody playing chess or checkers or settling into one of the grease-slicked armchairs with a book. There was litter, though – newspapers, magazines, unwashed plates, cups and glasses, some-body's striped shirt, a pair of muddy boots – and where there was litter, there was life. As if to underscore the point, the dogs chose that moment to waggle into the room and nose at her hands even as the faintest hushed murmur of voices seeped in from the room beyond.

Nearly everybody was there already, most of them sitting cross-legged on the floor, their faces blanched, eyes vacant. People were rubbing their temples, circulating a pitcher of iced tea or Kool-Aid, she couldn't tell which, picking idly at their ears or toes and sprawling in the sea of all that massed flesh as if they were learning to float – or maybe levitate. Alfredo and Reba were up front, and Reba had a cigarette going, lecturing her old man about something and painting the air with the glowing ember at the tip of it. Ronnie was all the way across the room with Merry and Lydia, melting into a heap of pillows, and Jiminy was slouched over the table with Verbie and her sister and Harmony and Alice.

Star wondered how she looked – she hadn't been near a mirror in days – and as she stepped into the room she tried to part her hair with her fingers, forcing it down like a cap over the crown of her head and looping the odd strands behind her ears.

She was wearing a pair of ceramic earrings – blue dolphins with painted-on grins – that seemed to grow heavier by the minute till they felt like bricks tearing at her lobes, but she couldn't muster the energy to pull them out. She hadn't been able to find her sandals, but most of the tribe went barefoot most of the time anyway so that was all right, yet her T-shirt and cutoffs seemed damp, clammy almost, and when was the last time she'd washed them? Washed anything? Her head was pounding, and suddenly she was afraid again – for herself, for Marco and Drop City, for all the lost neurons and miswired synapses of a whole continent full of dopers and heads and teepee cats. *Boom,* the blood pounded in her temples, *boom, boom, boom.*

She exchanged murmurs of greeting with a couple of people, thought of crossing the room to Merry and felt so weak suddenly it was as if her bones had dissolved. "Let's just sit here," she said to Marco, and they sank to the floor just inside the doorway, because really, what difference did it make? Norm didn't call emergency meetings for nothing – this was going to be bad news, and it didn't matter if you took it standing up or sitting down, at the periphery or at the red-hot glowing center.

She watched Alfredo rise to his feet, turn and face the gathering. His eyes glowed with a dull sheen, as if they'd been painted on and hadn't quite dried yet. The overhead light stabbed at his face, hollowing out his cheekbones and giving him the look of the crucified Christ in the big fresco over the altar in the church back at home. He was long-faced at the best of times, but now he appeared nothing less than tragic. "Listen, people, we've got a problem here," he said, and his voice was a dirge. "It affects all of us, Norm especially, but all of us ultimately, and Norm asked me to get everybody together, because he wanted to say a few words – "

She could barely hear him for the throbbing in her head. It was as if a pair of pincers had come down from the ceiling and clamped onto her temples and was slowly and inexorably drawing her up into the air, and all she could think of was one of those arcade machines where you try to extract a prize from a heap of trinkets. She was the prize, the gold ring that was really brass, and the jaws had hold of her, squeezing and pinching, and what she needed was a Darvon, or better yet, a

Seconal, something to kill the pain. She'd ask Ronnie once the meeting broke up – he was usually good for something, and he always had his own little stash hidden away somewhere. She stared at her folded hands and tried to concentrate on looking normal. Or human. Just that.

Alfredo was rattling on – "Brothers, sisters, *people,* we're all in this together, and now, of all times, we need to *stick* together . . ." She leaned into Marco, and a flare of irritation leapt up in her. "What's he talking about? The accident? Is that it? Can't Norm just pay a fine or something?"

Marco tucked a coil of hair behind his ear, smoothed his beard with a ringless hand (he didn't believe in jewelry, not for men, though she saw he was wearing the string of painted wooden beads she'd given him, and for a fraction of a moment that made everything balance out). He was sitting in the lotus position, legs folded, back arched, as perfect as an illustration in one of those pamphlets by Swami Kriyananda Norm was always handing out, *Yoga Made Easy, Eight Steps to Enlightenment, The Swami Speaks.* "No," he said, shaking his head, "it's gone way beyond that. It's – I don't know. I didn't want to tell you this, at least not till tomorrow, anyway, but you want to know the truth? It's over, is what it is. He was trying to tell me this morning, when we went for the cream soda and the rest of it – and the wire for the horse, which is still in the back of the van, by the way, wherever the van is. Not that it matters."

"Over?" She sought out his eyes, but his eyes dodged away. "What are you talking about?"

That was when Norm's voice rang through the room and everybody looked up to see him standing there in the kitchen doorway, his arm around Premstar. "A horse!" he cried. "My kingdom for a horse!" That was all it took – two phrases – and the pall Alfredo had cast was dissolved, and they all, everybody – even Reba, even Alfredo and the Krishna cat – laughed aloud. "Or a match," Norm said, pulling a number the size of a cigar from the inside pocket of his jacket. "Anybody got a match? Or did you forget about the bonfire? Longest day, man, longest *day*!"

The bonfire. Of course. A buzz went through the room. Norm could do that – he could wake people up, turn them on, change the vibe of a whole room just by striding through the door. And Star saw that he'd dressed for the occasion too, emergency or no, in a wide-brimmed suede hat with a chin strap and a fringed jacket cut from the same material. The suede was a deep amber, the color of honey at the bottom of the jar, and he'd cinched a blue bandanna round his throat to set it off. That wasn't all: his glasses were taped together and a slash of white sticking plaster bisected his right eyebrow, not in a way that made him look like a victim or an invalid or anything, but somehow – Star couldn't think of the word, and then she could – *jaunty*. And Premstar. She'd been here all of a week, and she'd done nothing but giggle and play up to Norm as if she was some kind of sex toy or something, and here she was dressed up in a sheer white nightgown like the ingenue in some vampire movie. And her hair – it was braided in two blond ropes that rose up off her brow like a layer cake.

Star turned to Marco, and for just an instant she felt the clamps let go of her. "That hair," she whispered, feeling buoyant suddenly, feeling stoned all over again, "that's what *I* call an emergency."

The whole room watched as Norm led Premstar to the table, where he pulled out a chair for her with the kind of exaggerated gallantry that announced to everybody they'd been balling ten minutes ago, handed her the joint and leapt up onto the worn oak planks. "People," he shouted, "brothers and sisters, this is my rap and I'm like more than grievously sorry to have to lay it on you tonight of all nights and even before we light the bonfire and dance, and I mean we *are* going to shake it out, believe me, we are going to *dance* like nobody has ever danced, I mean we are going to *reinvent* the whole trip of dancing for now and forever, but this has been coming down a long time now and there's no denying it, no postponing it anymore, and I've just *got* to get it out, so bear with me . . ." He stopped right there, and nobody said a word, nobody so much as breathed.

Star found Marco's arm and pulled it up over her shoulder like a cloak. Her heart was pounding now too, along with her head, a little hammer there striking over and over like in the TV commercials – she wasn't going back to Peterskill no matter what happened, not if Drop City closed down tonight. She was going to stay here, right here, and she didn't care what Norm said or how bad it was.

Norm bent low to light the joint for Premstar, and Premstar took a hit and Norm watched in a proprietary way as she passed it on to Reba before he straightened up again and looked out over the room. "I'm telling you the bad news first, but remember what the *I Ching* says – 'Perseverance Furthers' – and you are all, every one of you brothers and sisters, going to *know* that the good vibes outweigh the bad and that we *will* persevere in our mission and our philosophy and all the love and truth and the beautiful vibes of Drop City and everything we've accomplished here in spite of the fascists beating at the door." Another pause. His voice dropped. "Only we won't be here. Not on this property."

If there was any air left in the room, it was gone now, sucked right out the window. Not here? What was he talking about?

"The fuck we won't!" Jiminy jumped up out of his chair, his hair windmilling round his shoulders. His fist was balled, and he brought it down on the table at Norm's feet, and then rocked back into himself, trembling all over. The day hadn't been kind to him either, Star could see that.

"It's over, people," Norm sighed, and he never even glanced at Jiminy, just let his gaze seek out each face in the crowd, one after another, like beads on a string. "The bureaucrats've won the war. The pencil-pushers, the accountants, the *man*. We're history here, and you better get used to it, because the straight world is moving in."

Everybody was aroused now. Or no: they were incensed. "Bullshit!" a voice shouted from the far side of the room. "We won't let them!" "No!" Maya joined in, nothing to her voice but textured air, her glasses flashing in the glare of the overhead lights like a shield, and what was with the lights, Star was wondering, why feed PG&E? Was Norm staging this? Was that it?

And then a voice she recognized, knew so intimately it was as if she were speaking herself: "Come on, Norm, come on, man, don't let us down." It was Ronnie, across the room, his face pinched and his eyes swollen in his head. He looked terrible. Looked as if he'd been buried a week and dug up again. But that voice, that tone – there was something raw and desperate in it, a quaver she recognized from all those late-night disquisitions on

God, the futility of life and how impossible it was to find a good FM station in the flatlands, and she understood in that moment how much all this meant to him. Ronnie. Pan. He needed Drop City as much as she did. "Come on, Norm," he nagged. "Come *on.*"

Norm bowed his head a minute, as if all the fuss were too much for him. He dug at his beard, pushed the hat brim up off his brow so that the bandage flared out like an accusation. "The bulldozers'll be here inside of a week. And that's whether the pigs come back and lock me up or not, because let me give it to you straight, people – by order of the *judge,* and you can look it up, Judge Vincent T. Everard, the Right and Honorable, they're going to take down every substandard dwelling on the place, and that's their words, not mine, because I say *substandard,* my ass."

"Right on!" Mendocino Bill shouted, and then they were all shouting, a dizzy reeling tightly wound gabble of voices – no, they wouldn't budge, they'd fight, they'd chain themselves to the gates – but all Star could think of was the naked hills and the rubble of the yurts and huts and plastic sheeting all rolled up like a frayed blanket, and would they spare the treehouse? Would they see it, even?

She drifted in and out of it then, because that was when the joint worked its way to her and she touched her lips to it and tasted her brothers' and sisters' communion in the wetness of it and filled her lungs with the dense sweet smoke that was going to knock her headache down and out for the count and fill her every cell and fiber with bliss, the bliss she needed and deserved and wanted because that was what this life was all about, wasn't it? Norm went on and on, ranting about the county, about Mr. Jones and the plastic society that spawned him, about conformity and hate and love and the *I Ching.* He must have talked nonstop for half an hour, his voice dipping and raging and looping back on itself until it was a kind of white noise and the words couldn't touch her – she'd had enough bad vibes and negativity for one day. Enough. Enough, already. And she was about to get to her feet and say just that – *Enough, and let's sleep on it and see what the morning brings* – when the room fell silent.

She looked round her, and it was as if she'd just awakened. Norm was still up there on the table, the artificial light bleeding from his face. He'd just delivered the good news, the promise that was going to redeem them all and resurrect Drop City, and it came in three interconnected syllables that didn't sound like a promise at all – it was more like a joke, or maybe a dream. She couldn't even be sure she'd heard him right, and before she knew what she was doing, she was raising her hand, raising her hand and flapping it at the end of her wrist as if she were wedged behind a tiny shellacked desk back in elementary school. "Norm, Norm!" she cried amidst a tumult of voices, everybody talking at once, everybody shouting, but she was on her feet now and he was looking right at her through the clear hard lenses of his taped-up glasses as if she were the only one in the room. "Norm, did you say *Alaska?*"

Yes. That was what he'd said: Alaska. He repeated it for her, the whole long strung-together Normed-out sentence that ended with the noun that hit her like a body blow, the name of that alien, icebound afterthought of a place that had no deeper association for anyone in the room than *Sergeant Preston of the Yukon,* and the Yukon wasn't even in Alaska, was it? No matter. Norm had the stage, Norm was their leader and guru and though he'd never led them before, he was leading them now, his feet dancing and his arms beating time to the silken swoosh of the suede fringe, and he was selling Alaska as if he owned it. "No rules," he shouted, "no zoning laws, no taxes, no county dicks and ordinances. You want to build, you build. You want to take down some trees and put up a cabin by the most righteous far-out turned-on little lake in the world, you go right ahead and do it and you don't have to go groveling for anybody's permission because there's no-fucking-body there – do you hear me, people? Nobody. You can live like Daniel Boone, live like the original hippies, like our great-grandfathers and great-grand-mothers – off the land, man, doing your own thing, no apologies. Do you dig what I'm telling you?"

Silence, stunned silence. Everybody was seeing sled dogs and tracts of rippled snow. They were seeing – what? – king crab, bears, Eskimos, Mount McKinley rising up out of a wall calendar like a white planet tearing loose from its moorings. He was joking. He had to be.

"Are you fucking crazy?" Star turned her head and Mendocino Bill was right there beside her, tottering on his swollen white feet, his beard draining the color from his face. "Are you out of your fucking mind? Alaska? It's like sixty below up there. What are we going to do, make igloos like Nanook? Eat snow and icicles and what, seal blubber?"

"Longest day, man," Norm said. "The sun won't set up there tonight. I've seen it. For three years I saw it. And you know what that means? That means strawberries the size of apples, that means tomatoes like watermelons and zucchini you could hollow out and *live* in. And this" – he reached into his jacket pocket and produced another communal joint, gaudily rolled in red-white-and blue-striped papers – "this shit grows like giant redwoods up there, like sequoias, I mean, get me to the *lumber* mill, man.

"My uncle Roy – and I don't know how many of you know this, I mean, you do, Alfredo, and probably you, Verbie – he's got a place up there, just outside of Boynton, on the Yukon River, farthest place you can drive to in the continental U.S., the last place, I'm telling you, the last frontier, and what's the whole town built out of? Logs. You know what I'm saying? *Logs!* I lived there three years after I dropped out of high school in my junior year because I couldn't take the plastic bourgeois capitalist fucking bullshit *brainwashing* anymore, and I know what I'm talking about." He flipped off his glasses, wiped them on his sleeve and clapped them back on again, and then he was shaking out a folded piece of lined yellow paper and holding it up to the light.

"You see this, people? See it? This is a letter from my uncle. From Uncle Roy himself, dated two months ago, and I've been carrying it around ever since. You know what it says?" He paused to look out over the room. "It says he's in Seattle, living with my other uncle, Uncle Norm – my namesake – because he's seventy-two fucking years old and he's got arthritis so bad he can hardly wrap his fingers around the pen. He's not going back, not ever, and you know what that means? That means the cabin is ours, people, fully stocked and ready to go, traps, guns, snowshoes, six cords of wood stacked up outside the door, pots and pans and homemade furniture and all the rest, and it's going to be an adventure, it is. We're going to take down some *trees,* because that's the way you do it – lumber is free up there, can you dig that, *free* – and we're going to build four more cabins and a meeting house and we're going to build right on down to the river because the salmon are running up that river even as we speak and they're running in the *millions.* You dig smoked salmon? Anybody here dig smoked salmon? And the blueberries. The cranberries. You never saw anything like it. You want to know what we're going to eat? We're going to *eat the land* because it's one big smorgasbord. And there's nobody – I mean *nobody* – to stop us."

Everyone in the room was on their feet now, and it was like a rally, like a concert, and Star was thinking about the time she'd seen the Velvet Underground live in a downtown loft that was wall-to-wall people – there was that kind of excitement, that kind of energy. A current was burning through the room, and it was burning through her too, and never mind the headache, never mind the bulldozers, this was something new, outrageous, beyond anybody's capacity to imagine or envision, and when Norm scrambled down from the table they buried him in an avalanche of hands and shoulders and hair, and the questions never stopped. When? Where? How? That was what they wanted to know, and so many people were talking at once they might as well have been speaking different languages entirely. Verbie was right there at his shoulder, and Jiminy wedged in beside her, his eyes shining. Even Reba looked upbeat.

"Details!" Norm cried over the tumult. "Petty details, people." He was already in motion, dismissing every rational fear and practical concern with a casual swipe of his hand. He had Premstar by the arm and he was leading her through the crush and into the kitchen, and through the kitchen and out into the darkened yard, shouting over his shoulder like an agitator leaving the arena: "The bonfire! On to the bonfire!"

"Man, has he lost it or what?" somebody said, and Star felt herself jostled from behind. "I mean, do you believe this shit?"

She looked to Marco, only to him, and he was watching her out of hooded eyes as they moved toward the door and the scent of the damp night air. He met her gaze and then he grinned and shrugged his shoulders. "You know," he said, and he put his arm round her shoulders and locked his hip to hers, "I've always wanted to see the northern lights."

Later, as the flames leapfrogged into the black vault of the sky and the hiss of Alaska sizzled up from the coals – *Alaska, Alaska,* the only word anybody needed to know tonight, the touchstone, the future – Star relaxed into the grip of whatever it was that was happening to her. She sipped at a fruit jar of Spañada and stood at the edge of the fire, watching the tracers rise up into the night. She felt calm, centered, as if a weight had been lifted from her shoulders, the way she always felt when she came to a decision. Like with Ronnie. She remembered leaving home with him, books and records and brown bleeding bags of food piled up in the backseat, sleeping bags, kitchen things, the only home she'd known for three-quarters of her life receding in the rearview mirror, and then her mother raging barefoot down the street shouting out for the world to hear that she was throwing her life away. Her mother's face hung there in the window even after they'd reached the end of the block, and she could see it now, the wet sheen of her eyes and all the gouges and wrinkles of a long day and a long week mobilized in grief – *Paulette! You're throwing your life away, your life away!* – but she was calm that day too. She'd made up her mind to go, and that was it.

The sweet cold wine massaged her throat and condensed her headache till it was a hard black little India rubber ball come to rest somewhere in the backcourt of her mind. She was standing in a knot of people – Marco, Norm, Alfredo, Reba, Harmony, Deuce, all of them talking at once, talking logistics, talking *Alaska* – and she closed her eyes and rode the wave of exuberance that was washing over Drop City even now, even as Druid Day became something else – the day after Druid Day – and that was a holiday too. Sure it was. Didn't they have a bonfire? Didn't they have drugs, wine, beer? And weren't they going to dance till they dropped?

Just before the fire went up, when everybody was gathered in the field to watch Norm wave the ceremonial torch and make another of his rocket-propelled speeches – *Part of ourselves, people, let's all just step up and throw some part of ourselves on the funeral pyre of old Drop City* – Merry had retrieved the atlas from the high shelf in the kitchen where it was wedged between *The Whole Earth Catalogue* and *Joy of Cooking*. Star had come in to refill her glass, and Lydia and Maya were there too, mashing avocados for guacamole, and they all stood round the kitchen table as Merry traced her finger across the map of Alaska to the black dot on the swooping blue river that was Boynton. "There it is," she said, "Drop City North," and they all leaned forward to see that it was real, a place like any other, a destination. "And look," she added, measuring out the distance with the width of a fingernail, "there's Fairbanks. And wow, *Nome*."

No one said a word, but they all seemed to have caught the same fever. They'd all traveled to get here – that was part of the scene, seeing the country, the world, before you were shriveled up and dead like your parents. Lydia was from Sacramento originally, but she'd been to Puerto Vallarta, Key West and Nova Scotia, and Maya had hitchhiked all the way out here from Chicago. Merry was from Iowa, and Star had been across the Great Plains, through the Rockies and the high desert – all those rambling brown dusty miles – and that was nothing, nothing at all. Here was the chance to fall off the map, to see the last and best place and lay claim to bragging rights forever. *So you went to Bali, the French Riviera, the Ivory Coast? Yeah? Well, I was in* Alaska.

But where was the music? Weren't they going to dance? Wasn't that what Norm had said – *We are going to dance like nobody's ever danced?* Her eyes snapped open on the thought, and the first thing she saw was Ronnie, standing shirtless beside Dale Murray on the far side of the fire, a beer in one hand, a poker in the other. She was wondering what Ronnie thought about all this, because he was still her anchor to home no matter what happened, and the sight of him, of the neutral, too-cool-for-human-life look on his face, made her doubt herself a moment – was he in for this, was he going to commit? Or would he put them all down with some sort of snide comment and slip out the back door? She leaned into Marco. "I'll be back," she whispered, but Marco was already in Alaska, at least in his mind – *Mud and moss? You mean that's it for insulation?* – and he never even heard her.

She skirted the fire as people rushed up out of the dark to

throw branches, scraps of lumber and trash into the flames. Jiminy and Merry came out of nowhere with a derelict armchair that had been quietly falling into itself under the front porch, and she could see the guy they called Weird George – all shadow and no substance – laboring across the yard with the crotch of a downed tree.

And here was Ronnie, lit like a flaming brand, his face a carnival mask of yellow and red, twin fires burning out of the reflective lenses of his eyes. She stood at his side a moment, watching as the glowing skeleton of the fire revealed itself like a shimmering X ray, and then she said, "Hey," and Ronnie – in chorus with Dale Murray – returned the greeting.

"Wow, you're out," Star said, looking to Dale Murray. "We were worried."

"Right," he said, and he leaned over to spit in the dirt. "But it's no thanks to you, is it? Any of you. If it wasn't for my buddy here" – he jerked his head and Sky Dog's profile emerged from the warring shades of the night, a beer pinned to his lips like a medallion – "I'd still be shitting bricks in the county jail. He's the one that went to the bail bondsman. I mean, what does that take? A genius?"

Star didn't have any response to that, because everything froze up inside her at the sight of Sky Dog. She'd thought all that was done with, thought he'd gone on to infest some other family with ego and selfishness and the kind of love that was no love at all, just words, empty words. He didn't acknowledge her, just drained his beer and flung the bottle into the fire.

There was a pop like a gunshot. The flames snapped and roared.

Ronnie said, "So what do you think?"

"You mean Norm?"

"Yeah. Norm. Like as if there's anything else to discuss tonight."

"We looked it up on the map – Boynton. It's a real place. I mean, just like all the places on the map when we were coming across country." And she couldn't help herself – she laughed. "A dot. A little black dot."

"What's it near?"

She was the expert here, the old Alaska hand, but she'd already reached the limits of her knowledge: "Fairbanks. Like maybe a hundred fifty, two hundred miles?"

"The fishing up there," Ronnie said, and he wasn't really talking to her now. "Grayling, char, king salmon as long as your leg. You could shoot a moose. A bear. In fact, you know they have to shoot a bear, everybody does, every year? You know why? The fat. I mean, it's not as if you can just stroll down to the grocery store and pick up a tub of margarine or Crisco or whatever – "

"What about the goats," she said, and she had an image of them crammed into the back of the Studebaker, shitting all over everything, stinking, drooling, making a zoo of the place. "We're taking the goats, aren't we?" And there it was, a fait accompli: *we*.

"Hey, man, you want another beer?" Dale Murray leaned into them, his face swollen in a stabbing flash of light. Ronnie held his bottle up experimentally, shook it twice and drained it. "How about you, Star?" Dale Murray wanted to know, and his voice had softened till it was reasonable, seductive even. Was this a peace offering – after all, she hadn't put him in jail; she hadn't even been there – or did he just want to ball her like all the rest of the *cats?*

"I'm okay," she said, and Dale Murray moved off into the shadows. She took a sip from the fruit jar and turned to Ronnie. "So what happened to your shirt?"

Ronnie pulled his eyes back and stared off into the distance. He shrugged. "I tossed it in the fire. Norm said to get rid of the bad shit, right? The shit with the negative vibes? Leave it all behind, isn't that what he said?"

It took her a minute. "The shirt I made for you?"

His eyes came back to her, dwindling and accusatory. He fingered the beads at his throat. "So what did you throw in the fire, like a little voodoo effigy of me or something? Or that turquoise bracelet I bought you in Sedona? I don't see that. I don't see you wearing that anymore – "

"Okay, look: I'm sorry. I love you, I do, but you have to understand – "

"Understand what?"

"Marco. I'm with Marco now, that's all."

"And who the fuck is he? I've known you since *junior high*. Christ, we came out here together, we had all those adventures, remember? Doesn't that mean anything?" He bent forward to fling his empty bottle into the flames, and there was another pop as the heat took the glass down. "Shit, I don't even know if I want to go to Alaska if it's going to be like this – I mean, are we taking the Studebaker or what? And Marco, what about him – he doesn't even have a car, right? Not to mention all the rest of them. How are we going to get there, even?"

And what had she heard Lydia say in the kitchen just yesterday? *I don't watch pornography, I do it.* Right. Chicks and cats. Free Love. He was so full of shit it was coming out his ears. She took his hand and squeezed it. "Star and Pan," she said.

"You know, I thought you were coming over here to ask do I have any more of those downs left, because I know you right through to the bone and I was figuring you were going to want to sleep tonight, isn't that right?"

She gave him a blossoming smile. "Mind reader."

"You're going to have to come with me," he said, reflexively patting the pockets of his jeans. "I got a little paranoid and went and stashed everything under this rock up in the woods. It's like three minutes from here."

And then they were walking off into the deep pit of the night that pulled all the light down into it like a black hole, and she was feeling her barefoot way, Ronnie's hand locked on hers like a magnet. Across the field and into the trees, and now her eyes began to adjust and she could see that there was a moon, a softness of light poured softly over every blade and leaf, pale stripes limning the dark trunks and a ghost-lit carpet spread uniformly over the ground from one corner of the night to the other. An owl hooted in the distance. The air had a taste to it, clean and cool, like a draught of water. "So where're you taking me, anyway?"

Ronnie worked his fingers between hers, gave her hand a squeeze. "Just up here, by that rock – see that rock?"

Up ahead was a big knuckle of extruded sandstone, glowing faintly in the moonlight, a landmark you could see from the kitchen window. In daylight, it was the haunt of lizards – and Jiminy, who liked to use it as a backrest when he was reading or meditating or whatever he did off by himself. The sight of the rock – the knowledge of it, its *familiarity* – saddened her. She was going to miss this place.

Ronnie let go of her hand and ducked into the shadows, and she heard him shifting things around in the dark, a rustle of twigs and then the sigh of plastic. "I got reds," he said. "What do you want, two?"

She felt the touch of his hand, the faintest tactile apprehension of the two smooth weightless capsules. She chased them down with a gulp of sweet wine. In the distance, the glow of the fire painted the sky and she could hear the music starting up with a thump of tambourines and the rudimentary chord progressions of Sky Dog's guitar, or maybe it was Dale Murray's. They were dancing back there, dancing for joy, for wisdom, for peace. Star didn't feel like dancing anymore. She didn't feel like anything – she was numb, neutral, and all she wanted now was sleep. But then Ronnie ran a hand up her leg and rose from the shadows to press his mouth to hers, and she wanted to tell him no, wanted to tell him to go back to Lydia, wanted to tell him it was over between them except in the purest brotherly and sisterly sense and that being from home didn't mean anything anymore – that was what she wanted to tell him. But she didn't.

15

It never rained in June, not in California, because California had a monsoon climate and the climate dictated its own terms – rain in winter, drought in summer. That was the way it was. That was the way it had always been. "You can make book on it," Norm would crow to the new arrivals from the east coast, "not a drop's going to fall between April and November. You want to live outdoors? You want to throw away your clothes? You want to party like the Chumash? Go right ahead, be my guest, because this isn't New Jersey or Buffalo or Pittsburgh, P.A. – this is *California*." Marco had spent the driest summer and wettest winter of his life in San Francisco, trying to make a go of it in a big rambling old Victorian with a leaky roof and thirteen bickering communards, and he thought he'd got a grasp on the weather at least. Still, when he woke the morning after the solstice celebration, he woke to rain.

He hadn't slept well. Or much. Star had drifted away from him when the bonfire was at its height, and she hadn't come back. At the time, he'd hardly noticed. He'd had a couple of beers, and he was batting Alaska around like a shuttlecock with Norm and Alfredo, up over the net and back again, reach low for the implausible shot, leap high, *whack!* Everything was up in the air at that point, people gathering in stunned and angry groups *(The Nazi sons of bitches, this is still America, isn't it?)*, trying to feed on this new dream, this dream of starting over, of building something from the ground up like the pioneers they all secretly believed they were, and so what if they suffered? So what if it was cold? Did Roger Williams worry about physical comfort when he went off to found Rhode Island? Or Captain John Smith when he set sail for the swamps of Virginia? One by one they stripped off some garment or charm or totem and flung it into the fire, all the while pledging allegiance to the new ideal, to freedom absolute, to Alaska. It was an adolescent fantasy — the fantasy of owning your own island, your own country, making up the rules as you went along — but it was irresistible too. Marco could see it on every face, a look of transformation, of *mutation,* and he was caught up in it himself.

He was there, with Norm, sitting kneecap to kneecap over the embers of the fire, drinking Red Zinger tea out of a chipped ceramic mug and trying to read every nuance and foresee every impediment, when the sky began to lighten in the east. Everybody else had gone to bed, even Mendocino Bill, who'd spent the better part of a dimly lit hour rasping away over the need — no, the *duty* — to hire a lawyer and fight this thing, but Norm said he was done paying lawyers, done paying taxes, done with the straight world once and for all. "Look at that," Norm said, waving his mug at the sky, "like God's big rheostat, huh?" And then he was on his feet, brushing at the seat of his overalls. "Time to file it away for tonight. We've got six days maybe, if we're lucky. Logistics, man, I'm talking logistics here. A lot to do."

But now it was raining, a steady, gray, vertical assault of water in its natural state, unexpected, unheralded, wet. Marco woke to the sound and smell of it, and discovered that the roof was leaking. He'd never bothered to test it with a hose — it kept the dew off, and that was enough, and who would have thought it would be raining in June? He'd split the shakes himself, but he'd had no tar paper — or tar, for that matter — and the plywood he used had been left to the elements so long it was honeycombed with rot. Lying there in his sodden sleeping bag, he felt angry with himself at first, and then just foolish, until finally he realized how futile the whole business was: this was a treehouse, that was all, the sort of thing a twelve-year-old might have thrown together as a lark. He'd just been playing around here. He could do better. Of course he could.

He breathed in and out, watched his expelled breath hang in the air like its own little meteorological event, listened to the incessant drip of the rain.

At least Star was dry. He tried to picture her curled up on one of the couches in the big house, listening to records and gossiping with Merry and Lydia and whoever else had come in out of the wet, or maybe in the kitchen, whipping up a little dish of veggie rice or pasta for forty. She was a good cook, good with spices. She could do Indian, and he loved Indian. And she must have been in the big house, because she wasn't here. Clearly. Nothing here but an abandoned longhair in a wet sleeping bag.

She'd complained of a headache the night before, and he assumed she'd gone back to the treehouse to crash, but when he climbed up the ladder in the stone soup of dawn, the sleeping bag was empty. And so he further assumed she'd spent the night in the big house, as she sometimes did, in the room Merry and Maya had partitioned with a pair of faded Navajo blankets strung across a length of clothesline. Marco had been in there once or twice – this was an open society, after all, and theoretically there was no private space – but it made him uncomfortable. The room smelled of women, tasted of them, of their perfumes and balms, their scented candles and incense and the things they wore close to their bodies, and it was orderly when the rest of the house was in disarray. And dark, dark and candlelit, even in the middle of the day, with sheets of cardboard and posters nailed up over the windows. Norm called it the seraglio. The big orange tom, no fool, liked to nest there among the bedclothes and have his ears rubbed.

Did he miss her after one night? Did he resent the fact that she hadn't slept beside him? Was he worried? Jealous? Possessive? He didn't know. But he peeled himself out of the clammy sleeping bag, stepped into his jeans and climbed barefoot down the ladder to cross the muddy yard to the big house and find out.

He went round back so as not to track mud through the house, and came up the rear steps thinking about boots – he was going to need a new pair, a pair of work boots from the Army and Navy store, if he expected to survive a winter up north – and he paused a moment to rinse his muddy feet in the fan of water shearing off the eaves. Inside, the teapot was going and the windows were steamed over. It wasn't cold, not really, but he found he was shivering as he pushed open the door on a wall of cooked air and a complex admixture of scents: fresh-baked bread, coffee, basil, vegetable stock simmering in a bright scoured pot on the stove.

Star was there, leaning over the pot, her child's hands cupped beneath a load of chopped celery. She gave him a smile, dropped the celery into the pot and crossed the room to hold him briefly and give him the briefest of kisses. "Where were you?" he breathed. "I missed you." And she said, under her breath, "With the girls."

Verbie was there too, with her sister, a long-faced girl with a bulge of jaw and eyes set too close together, and Merry, Maya and Lydia, all of them hovering around the stove with coffee mugs cradled in their hands. The two yellow dogs lay on the floor at their feet. "You eat yet?" Star wanted to know, and then she was back at the chopping board, scooping up vegetables for the pot.

"I feel like I'm in a Turkish bath or something," he said, and found himself a seat at the table, smoothing his wet hair back with the palm of his right hand. He parted it in the middle, like everybody else, but the parting always seemed ragged, as if his head wasn't centered on his body, and unless he made a conscious effort with comb and brush there wasn't much hope for it. "No," he said, in answer to Star's question, "not yet – but what time is it, anyway, you think?"

Merry answered for her. "I don't know – two? Two-thirty?" She poured a cup of coffee, two teaspoons of sugar, a float of goat's milk, and brought it to him. "What time did you turn in last night?"

He made a vague gesture. "Norm," he began, "I was with Norm," and they all – even Verbie's long-faced sister – burst out laughing. He liked that. Liked looking at them, at their small even teeth, brilliant gums, eyes squeezed down to slits. The laughter trailed off into giggles. "Say no more," Star said.

And then he was dipping warm bread into his coffee, wrapped up in the cocoon of the moment, not quite ready to start anything yet. The conversation flowed round him, soft voices, the rhythmic heel-and-toe dance of the knife on the chopping block.

"The goats are going, right?"

"I don't know. Yeah. I guess."

"Do they need like a special, what do you call it – a wagon? Like horses, I mean?"

"Oh, you mean a goat wagon." More giggles. "We can just go out to the goat wagon store and get one."

"I'm serious."

"Okay, so am I. What are we going to feed them?"

"The goats?"

"Yeah."

"I don't know – grass?"

"In the winter."

"Hay?"

"Where're we going to get hay in the middle of Alaska?"

"Buy it."

"With what?"

"Barter for it, then. Like we do here. You know, dip candles, string beads, pottery, honey, that kind of thing."

"Who's going to want beads up there?"

"The Eskimos."

"There aren't any Eskimos where we're going. It's more like woods and rolling hills. Like Minnesota or something. That's what Norm said, anyway."

"So Indians. They've got Indians up there, haven't they?"

"Indians make their own beads."

"Teenagers, then. Teenagers dying to escape the grind. We'll start a revolution. Flower power on the tundra!"

"Yeah, right."

Star was the one concerned with the goats. They were her domain now – nobody else seemed to bother with them. She even smelled of goat, and he didn't mind that, not at all, because it was a natural smell, and that was what they were getting here: nature. And if they could keep it together long enough to get to Alaska, they were going to get a whole lot more of it.

"I wouldn't be worried about goats, I'd be worried about long underwear – I mean, what are we supposed to wear up there? Mink coats? Mukluks?" Pause. "What *are* mukluks, anyway?"

"We'll just go to Goodwill or something. Get a bunch of sweaters and overcoats. And knit. We could knit, no problem – "

"Layers, that's how you do it."

"I hear if you get overheated the sweat like freezes on your body and you wind up like dying of hypothermia or something."

"I don't sweat."

"You will, once we get you your mink panties and ermine bra."

They were laughing. They were happy. They'd go to Siberia, Tierra del Fuego, Devil's Island – it was all the same to them. It was an adventure, that was all. A lark. They were the women. They were the soul and foundation of the enterprise. And sitting there in the kitchen with the rain tapping at the windows and the stock simmering on the stove and the women's voices casting a net in the air around him, Marco couldn't help but feel that everything was going to work out after all.

It was late afternoon and raining still when the dogs lifted their heads from the floor and cocked their ears – a vehicle was coming up the drive, something big, preceded by a rumble of wheels or maybe treads and the stuttering alien wheeze of a diesel engine. Marco was still in the kitchen, sitting at the window with a book, feeling confined and constrained, but in no mood to go back and crouch over a wet sleeping bag in a leaky treehouse for the rest of the day. He was bored. Anxious to get started, to do something, see to details, arrange things, get this show on the road – Alaska, Alaska or Bust, and all he could see was a log cabin in a glade overlooking a broad flat river so full of salmon you could walk across their backs to the other side, and moose, moose standing in shallow pools with long strips of vegetation decorating their antlers. But it was raining, and he had a book, and he was going nowhere. As for the rest, the cast of characters had changed somewhat – Reba was at the stove now, making a casserole to go with the soup, and Alfredo was hunkered over a game of solitaire at the kitchen table while Che and Sunshine hurtled in and out of the room in a sustained frenzy that might have been called tag or hide-and-go-seek or gestalt therapy. Star and Merry were making piles of things in the corner – *Six teapots, do we really need six teapots?* – and Maya was sliding jars of preserves into a cardboard box with the grudging slow imponderability of a prisoner. The light was a gray slab. Things were slow.

But the dogs were on their feet now, clicking across the floor on stiff black nails. Freak began to bark suddenly, and then Frodo joined in, and everybody was thinking the same thing – the bulldozers. "Oh, shit," Alfredo said, his head jerking up as if it were on a string. Reba gave him a stricken look. "It couldn't be," she said, "not yet. Norm said Friday, didn't he?" Marco flung down the book without marking his place – *Trout Fishing in America,* one of the titles Star had mysteriously interred beneath the leaves yesterday, and he still couldn't fathom what she'd been thinking – and then he was out the door, down the steps and into the battleground of the yard.

At first there was only the noise, a grinding mechanical assault tearing at his heart and his brain till he didn't know whether to stand his ground or run – and what would he tell them, what would he do when they started battering it all to pieces? He clenched his toes in the mud, heard the others gathering on the porch. "They can't just come in here like this" – Reba's voice, wound tight, spinning out behind him – "can they?" There was a flash of yellow – bright as Heinz mustard – and the shape of something moving through the trees along the road, and it was no bulldozer, it was too big for that, too *yellow* . . .

It was a bus. A school bus. And Norm, sleepless Norm, fueled on amphetamine and black coffee, was at the wheel, the suede cowboy hat pulled down to the level of the black broken frames of his glasses and Premstar perched in his lap like a ventriloquist's dummy. The gears ground with a shriek, the massive face of the thing swung into the yard and beat the mud into submission and the rain sculpted the two long streaming banks of windows in a smooth wrap. There was the wheeze of the air brakes, a heavy dependable sloshing, and then the bus was idling there before them, as if all they had to do was pick up their schoolbags and lunchboxes and climb aboard.

The door folded in on itself with a sigh, and Premstar, the former Miss Watsonville, with her high tight breasts and perfect legs, was stepping down from the platform, an uncertain smile puckering her lips. She was wearing white lipstick, blue eye-shadow and a pair of big blunt high-heeled boots that crept up over her knees. Marco watched, riveted, as she stepped daintily into the mud, brushed the hair out of her face, and glanced up at him. "We got a school bus," she said in a breathy little puff of a voice, and she might have been describing a trip to the grocery for toilet paper, " – me and Norm."

Norm pulled the hand brake and came down the steps behind her, the bus idling with a stuttering grab and release, the smell of diesel infesting the air. The rain spattered his hat and his fringed jacket, the drops dark as blood against the honey-colored suede. His eyes were tired. The rain made him wince. "Go ahead," he said, waving an arm, "take a look. It's a ninety-one-passenger

1963 Crown, is what it is, the kind of thing you could get if you were real lucky and real smart on a straight-up trade for a slightly dented, almost-like-new 1970 VW van, if you know what I mean."

Alfredo was standing there in the rain now too, and Reba beside him; Star came up and slipped an arm round Marco's waist. They were all grinning, even as Premstar ascended the back steps and Norm slouched on by them, his shoulders slumped and his head dropped down between them like a bowling ball. "But I don't want to shut it off, that's the thing," he said, "because it was a real hassle getting it started – the cat that sold it to me said it was a little quirky, especially on cold mornings."

"Cold mornings?" Alfredo said. "This is the *afternoon,* and if it's anything less than maybe sixty-five out right now, then we need a new weatherman."

"Yeah, well, this is a good machine, heavy duty, no more than like a hundred twenty thousand miles on it and it could go three times that, easy, so what I'm saying is I haven't slept in two days and I've done my part, more than done my part, and I think somebody – like Bill, for instance – should be looking to the tune-up or whatever, and the rest of you people should be loading your shit aboard, because time and the river and the county board of supervisors wait for no man." He mounted the back steps and put an arm round Premstar. "Or chick, for that matter. But I've had it, I'm wiped, and somebody's going to have to build a rack or something all around the roof, for storage, and we're going to need rope and bungee cords and like that. And food, I mean, bins of just the basic stuff, dried beans and flour and whatnot, from the coop down in Guerneville."

He paused, patted down his overalls and dug a money clip from the inside pocket. "Here," he said, peeling off a hundred-dollar bill and holding it out over the steps so that the rain darkened it till it was like a piece of wet cardboard, like play money, "you take it, Reba, okay? For food?" And then he pulled open the screen door and edged his way in, Premstar tucked neatly under one arm.

The next five days were gypsy days, that's what Marco and Star were calling them, their little joke, no time for sweet wine or beer or dope or meditating with your back up against the big yellow knuckle of rock in the middle of the field, no time for sleep even – the caravan was moving on, fold up your tents, untether the goats and snatch the legs right out from under the chickens. If anyone had entertained any doubts about Norm Sender's seriousness of purpose, the bus erased them. There it was, massive and incontrovertible, dominating the mud-slick yard like some dream of mechanical ascendancy, and all day, every day, from dawn till the last declining stretched-out hours, people were swarming all over it with tools, bedding, food, records, supplies.

The previous owner – one of Norm's old high school buddies who'd evolved into a ponytailed psychologist in Mill Valley – had installed a potbellied stove, an unfinished counter and sink, and eight fold-down slabs of plywood that served as bunks. He'd had a dream, the psychologist, of outfitting the thing as a camper so he could take some of his patients from the state mental hospital on overnight outings, but the dream had never been realized for the reason that so many dreams have to die: lack of funds. He'd left the first half dozen rows of seats intact, and they'd each seat three adults abreast and sleep at least one, and all the way in the back, across from the stove, there was a crude plywood compartment with a stainless steel toilet in it. According to Premstar, who gave up the information in a sidelong whisper when Norm was out of earshot, the psychologist had got the bus cheap after a collision with a heating oil truck in which three kindergartners had been burned to death. The accident had left the frame knocked out of alignment, though the psychologist had tried to set it right with the help of another old high school buddy who owned a welding shop, and that was something they were just going to have to live with – the thing always felt as if it were veering sideways when it was bearing straight down the middle of the road. And no matter what anybody did by way of sprays and lacquers and air fresheners, a smell of incinerated vinyl – and maybe worse – haunted the interior.

When Jiminy saw the bus that first night, even as the rain was folding itself back into the mist and a derelict moon crept up over the trees, he drifted barefoot through the mud and embraced the cold metal of the hood as if it were living tissue. "Magic bus," he murmured, and then he began chanting it under his breath,

"Magic bus, magic bus, hey, hey, magic bus." Marco was holding a flashlight for Mendocino Bill, who was peering into the engine compartment with a wrench in one hand and a screwdriver in the other, and Alfredo, for lack of anything better to do, was supervising. Reba had hung a Coleman lantern from one of the hooks inside, and the women were in there, five or six of them – Star included – adjusting things, running a sponge over the seats and a mop over the floor, already seeing to the division of space.

"You know what we can do?" Jiminy said, his cheek pressed to the front fender. "We can paint it. Like Kesey, like the Pranksters. Mandalas, peace signs, weird faces, and fish – fish all over it, like Peter Max fish, blowing bubbles. And porpoises. That kind of thing. We'll freak them out from here to fucking Nome."

Mendocino Bill made an affirmative noise in the back of his throat, but it wasn't particularly enthusiastic – here was another adolescent fantasy, and what was wrong with washo unified skirting both sides of the bus in black bold adamantine letters?

"I don't want to tell you what to do," Alfredo put in, "but we have to cross the Canadian border here – like twice – and the last thing you want is a freak parade, you know what I mean?" He jumped down from the bench Bill had propped himself up on and gave Jiminy a look. "Like you, for instance, *Jiminy* – that's how we know you, but what's your real name? I mean, like on your draft card?"

Jiminy looked down at his feet. "Paul Atkins."

"Paul Atkins? Yeah, well, that's what they're going to want to know at the border, and you better have a draft card to show them too. And maybe a birth certificate on top of it. What are you, 4-F?"

Jiminy looked hurt, put-upon, and Marco wanted to say something, but he didn't. "They don't ask that shit at the border," Jiminy said. "Just are you a citizen, right? And how long'll you be in Canada?"

"Look, man," Alfredo was saying, "you were probably still in junior high the first time I went up to Canada – in Ontario, this was – and maybe they might have been cool about it back in those days, but believe me, with the war on and all these draft dodgers –

187

who I support, by the way, so don't get me wrong – it's going to be a trip and we are really going to have to play it right. Get it through your head, man – this is no game, no three-day rock festival where you can just go on home when it's over. This is survival we're talking about here – they're driving us off the *ranch,* for Christ's sake. What do you think that says?"

Marco wasn't listening anymore, because he was seeing that border, a vague scrim of trees, a checkpoint dropped down on the highway in a pool of darkness, and what was he going to do if they questioned him? Work up a fake ID? Get out three miles down the road and sneak across through the scrub? Was there a wire? Was it electrified?

"Keep the light steady, will you?" Bill said. "I can barely see what I'm doing here."

"So what are we supposed to be then," Jiminy wanted to know. "The Washo Unified Lacrosse Team? With our cheerleaders and band along for our triumphant tour of British Columbia?" He pushed himself away from the bus and hovered over the twin craters his feet made in the mud. "Easy for you to say, but you don't have to worry – you're too old for the draft."

The rain was nothing more now than the faintest drizzle, and the flanks of the bus shone with it as if they'd been polished. The moon glistened in the mud. From inside the bus, the sound of giggling.

Alfredo didn't answer right away. "That's right," he said finally, "I'm too old by four years and three months. But that doesn't mean I'm not looking out for you and Marco and Mendocino Bill and all the other cats here. This is a war, man, and we are going to win it. Drop City North, right? Am I right?"

"It's still America," Marco said. "The forty-ninth state. They've got the selective service up there too."

"Yeah, but we're going to be so far out there nobody's even going to know we exist."

In the morning, while Marco was up atop the bus with Star, trying to fashion scavenged two-by-fours into the world's biggest luggage rack, he reached over the side for another stick and found himself peering into the upturned faces of Lester and Franklin. "So what's this I hear?" Lester wanted to know, his voice padded with cotton wool as if he were afraid he might bruise it. He tugged at the brim of his oversized porkpie hat to shield his eyes from the sun. "You all are really going to up and desert Franklin and me? To go where – to fucking Alaska?" And then he began to chuckle, a low soft breathless push of air that might have been the first two bars of a song. "You people," he said, and he was still chuckling, "you are seriously deranged."

Marco had a hammer in his hand, so he didn't have to say anything in reply. He just banged a couple of nails into the corner at the front of the box, and yes, the humped steel roof of the bus was going to be a problem, but he was thinking if he built the rack up high enough and they strapped everything down as tightly as possible, it ought to get them where they were going – as long as the roof didn't crumple under all that weight. Star said, "Maybe so," and she was smiling so wide you would have thought her cheeks would split. "But in case you haven't heard, Alaska's the real thing, the last truly free place on this whole continent."

"Shit," Lester said, grinning now himself, "that's what I thought about California – till my ass wound up in Oakland. And the Fillmore's worse than Oakland, even, and the Haight's worse than that."

"What about us?" Franklin asked, and he was staring up at them out of a pair of yellow-tinted shades that looked like the top half of a gas mask. "They going to take down the back house too?"

"That's what I want to know," Lester put in. "And Sky Dog. And Dale. Because it's going to be kind of unfriendly around here when they come in with those bulldozers, you know what I mean?" He dropped his head, kicked a stone in the trammeled mud that was already baked to texture. Then he looked up again, one hand shielding his eyes from the sun. "But what I really want to know is are we invited? Because we got the Lincoln and there's no way you're going to fit everybody in that bus, and Pan's car, and whatever – that beat-to-shit Bug Harmony's got."

Marco looked down from on high. He didn't like Lester and he liked Sky Dog even less, and he hadn't forgotten that day in the ditch either, or what they'd done to the treehouse, but this, this really strained credulity. Lester was serious. He really thought he was part of all this, really believed in the credo of the tribe, in peace and love and brotherhood. Or he wanted to. Desperately wanted to. It was a hard moment, and Marco felt like Noah perched atop the ark and looking down his nose on all the bad seed toiling across the sodden dark plains below. He looked at Star and she looked away.

"Or maybe I'm talking to the wrong person, maybe I ought to talk to Alfredo. Or Norm."

"I hear they got gold up there," Franklin said, and he was straining to look up too. "Is that what you're going to do, pan for gold?"

"Hey, come on, man," Lester said, "let bygones be bygones, right? Brothers, right?"

A long moment ticked by. No one said a word. Marco could feel the bus shift beneath him as Reba and Merry climbed aboard with two more boxes of dishes, pots and pans, tools, cutlery, preserves. They were going to mount the big KLH speakers from two racks in the back of the bus and run the record player off a car battery, so they could have music at night when they pulled the bus off by the side of the road or into a public campground. Maya was fixing up curtains for the windows and Verbie and her sister were cutting up a roll of discarded carpet and fitting it to the floor. Even Pan was contributing, doing up a fish fry with chips and coleslaw so the women could be free of the kitchen and concentrate on the business at hand. Marco could hear the soft thrum of the voices below him, the sound of something growing, taking shape in a unity of effort that made all the pimples and warts of Drop City fade away to nothing. He felt good. Felt omnipotent. Felt like one of the elect.

"So what do you say?" Lester's voice floated up to him, soft as a feather. "We invited or not?"

Marco plucked a nail from his shirt pocket, set it in place and drove it home with two strokes of the hammer. The sound exploded out of the morning like two gunshots, one after the other, true-aimed and fatal. He shrugged. "Hey," he said, and he could hear the finality in his own voice, "it's a free country."

part four

the drunken forest

Life is here equally in sunlight and frost, in the thriving
blood and sap of things, in their decay and sudden death.
– John Haines, *The Stars, the Snow, the Fire*

16

The honeymoon was over before it began, and that was a shame, worse than a shame – it was a crime. A crime committed by a man with a gun, a Remington semi-automatic .22-caliber Nylon 66, judging from the flattened pieces of lead Cecil Harder dug out of the corpses of Bobo, Hippie, Girl, Loon and Saucy. Of course, the slugs could have come from any .22 rifle, but Joe Bosky had a Nylon 66 – he favored it, as many did, for the lightness of its plastic stock – and Joe Bosky was the only man on this green earth who would even so much as think of shooting somebody's dogs. You didn't shoot dogs, and you didn't burn down people's cabins or rape their wives or put a bullet between their shoulder blades as they were gliding past in their canoe. Sess Harder was trying to live off the land, and everybody knew that. The better part of his income came from furs, and without dogs to run the looping forty-odd miles of trapline he'd inherited from Roy Sender – and improved and extended on his own – he was out of luck. Everybody knew that. A child knew that.

So instead of a homecoming, instead of lifting his bride in his arms and carrying her through the dogtrot and across the threshold, instead of sorting out the wedding gifts and stocking the larder and maybe lying out nude with her on a blanket in the sun – one of his enduring sexual fantasies – he had to dig five holes while his heart clenched with hate and regret and his head rang with the bloody whoop of revenge. Pamela tried to comfort him, but it did no good. She was in shock herself, and that was the worst of it – that just compounded the crime right there. Bad enough that the psychopathic son of a bitch of a sneaking gutless leatherneck reject had done the deed, but to expose Pamela to this kind of thing, and on the day after her wedding, no less? He was going to kill Joe Bosky, as soon as he could, and there were no two ways about it. Joe Bosky had made his declaration. Joe Bosky was asking to be killed. He was begging for it.

"You can't, Sess, so don't even think about it. You'll go to jail – it's murder. There are laws up here too, you know – "

He was down in a hole, breaking through permafrost, flinging dirt. He'd been back an hour, with his bride, and he hadn't unloaded the canoe, looked to the garden, settled her in the house or even so much as pecked a kiss to her cheek. "What do you know about it?" he said, and he didn't just say the words, he snarled them.

She was right there beside him, in her shorts, with her magnificent legs on display, her hands on her hips. Her mouth was set. This was their first argument, one day married, a night in heaven, and now this. "I'm not going to talk to you like you're a child, Sess, and I'm not going to remind you that I'm part of this now too . . . We'll go to the law, like civilized people, put the law on him – "

"The law doesn't come for dogs."

"For murder? Does the law come for murder? You think I married you so I could visit you three hours a week in some prison someplace?"

He drove his pick at the frozen earth, all his rage concentrated in his shoulders and arms and the iron-clad muscles of his chest. "I see him," he grunted, and the pick dropped again, "I'll kill him."

"All right. Fine. I can see you're upset, so I'll leave you to do what you have to do here and I'll start bringing the things in. Does that sound like a plan?"

Upset? he was going to say. *You think this is upset? Wait till I get my hands on a gun, then you'll see upset – wait till I pin that son of a bitch to the wall and make him cry like a woman.* He didn't have the opportunity, though, because she'd already turned on her heels and headed down the slope, through the sun-bright glitter of bluebells and lupines and avens and saxifrage, to where the canoe shone against the everlasting gleam of the water.

She made supper that night, things left over from the wedding feast, salads and cold cuts and whatnot that wouldn't keep, and they ate at the picnic table in seventy-five-degree sunshine while the silence of the world closed in around them. He was in a

T-shirt and patched jeans; she wore a top that bared her midriff and she'd combed her hair out so it draped her shoulders like a golden flag, and that was something, really something. The sight of her there in his yard, at his table, living and vibrant under the stretched-away sky, moved him and humbled him and made him forget his rage for whole minutes at a time. She was his wife. He was married. Married for the first and last time in his life.

Down the rise, two hundred feet away, the river played a soft tinkling accompaniment to the shrugs and whispers of their conversation, and it could have been the silken rustle of a piano in a dark lounge. Even the mosquitoes, their whys and wherefores beyond any man's capacity to guess, seemed to have taken the night off. He ate cold ham and three-bean salad and listened to his wife, hungering after each inflection, watching her lips, her eyes. A bottle of wedding wine stood open on the table, Inglenook Pinot Noir, 1969, Product of the Napa Valley, and beside it, a pitcher of Sess's own dark bitter beer. He'd become a brewer when he moved out here and built the cabin because the nearest convenience store wasn't all that convenient, and when he wasn't off getting married or spying on Howard Walpole he produced a six-pack or so a day in the big plastic trash can just inside the door. So drink up, that was his motto, because he only had thirteen quart bottles and what didn't get bottled or consumed turned to swill in a heartbeat. He reached for the pitcher, poured himself another, then toasted her with a soft metallic clink of tin cups that echoed as sweetly as the finest crystal.

An hour ago, when he was done with the dogs, he'd come into the cabin and saw that she'd already packed everything in and found a place for it, rearranging his own squirreled-away bachelor lode in the process, and he'd felt a flash of irritation. The canned food was on the wrong shelves, a dress was hanging like a curtain from a cord in the middle of the room and there was a tumble of boxes full of clothes and books and even an alarm clock – an alarm clock, for Christ's sake! – crawling up the wall where the bed had to come down every night. And posters. She'd hung posters of some musician with a pageboy haircut – Neil Diamond, that's who it was – on the back wall. What was she thinking? This was a cabin, a wildwoods cabin, not some dorm room.

He didn't say anything. This was her first day, their first day, and he was crazy with rage over what Joe Bosky had done, and he had to tell himself that, tell himself not to let Bosky in, not to let him spoil this, and he went over to her where she stood arranging flowers in a coffee can and hugged her from behind. And that led to kissing and stroking and her softest whispered words of melioration and surcease. "If it's a question of money," she said, pulling back from him to look into his eyes, "I've got money."

His irritation flashed up again. "What are you talking about?"

"The dogs. We can buy dogs. Go back to Boynton. Fairbanks. Wherever."

"What, and put an ad in the paper? 'Wanted, trained sled dogs for trapline'? I'd be the joke of the town. I'd never live it down, never. Besides, nobody traps anymore, nobody hardly even mushes."

She gave him a look he hadn't seen before, hard lips, a dual crease come to rest between her perfect eyes. "Everybody has dogs," she insisted, "and everybody has litters. You ever been to Kiana or Noorvik or any of the Eskimo villages? Because there's five dogs to every man, woman and child up there."

"Okay, so let me get this straight – we're supposed to fly to some Eskimo village and buy dogs and fly them back in a four-seater Cessna?"

"I'm not saying that. I'm saying we could ask around Boynton. Or Fairbanks."

Every sort of emotion was at war inside him, love, hate, sorrow, grief. "Look," he said, "look, let's just drop it."

And so what did he do? He drank too much. On her first night as his wife in his hand-hewn cabin in the middle of nowhere, when she must have been as confused and disoriented and as full of second-guesses and doubts as any bride who'd ever leapt without looking and found herself in a strange place with a man who was revealing himself to be stranger and stranger by the minute, he finished off the bottle of wedding wine and two pitchers of beer and insisted on digging out his quart bottle of Hudson Bay rum, 150 proof, and throwing back flaming shots till the sun fell down in back of the hills. At first she matched him, cup for cup, shot for shot – she was a good drinker, Pamela, with real endurance, strong in every way – but finally her eyes lost their focus and he was the only one talking.

"You want to know about trapping?" he was saying, lecturing now, whether she wanted to hear it or not. "I'll tell you about trapping."

And he told her. Told her about the work Roy Sender had put into clearing forty-some-odd miles of paths through the trackless waste, all the way up one side of the Thirtymile and each of its attendant tributaries, and then down the other, a nine-day loop tramped in weather so bitter it would have killed anybody who was less than superhuman, and Roy Sender working the line till he was seventy-one years old. Roy had taken him under his wing, taught him how to make his sets for every kind of animal, to build a sled of birch eight feet long and no wider than his own shoulders, to skin out lynx and fox and ermine and make baits that were little atom bombs of stink designed to prick the nose and perk the ears of every predator in the country. He was a bachelor – a coot – cranky as a Ford with two cylinders missing, chewing him out and cursing him every step of the way, a man no woman had ever wanted to waste her time on, and he lived like a coot, denned up all winter in his cabin where he spent his time rearranging his things and making his living space as comfortable and squared-away as the picture of some low-slung and wood-gleaming saloon in a sailing ship. Sess sat at the feet of the coot of all coots, glad to be in his crusty company, and after the months sailed off over the horizon and they began to talk in seasons, seasons stretching to years, the old man warmed to him.

"Why don't you build down at the mouth of the river there?" he said one spring night with the snow coming down like ticker tape and Sess camped in a canvas tent out back of the cabin. "Plenty of country for you here and the snowshoes coming up on their ten-year boom so there'll be plenty of fur for everybody, if anybody even wants it anymore. Hell, I don't have to tell you I'm not the man I used to be, you follow me? I got my knee, my back, my lungs for shitsake that make me feel like I'm drowning all the time – all of that, the price of getting old. And I get thinking about all the hard work I've put into this country and thinking it's all going to waste."

That was Roy Sender, that was his blessing. And to think of it now, out here in the cabin that had materialized out of the hopeful solicitation of that night – out here with his wife, with Pamela – was enough to stop him up with an emotion so transcendent he could barely draw his next breath. Suddenly he was sentimental, the glass of him half-filled with sorrow and half with joy. Suddenly, he was drunk.

Pamela was two feet from him, sitting there at the table with her chin propped up on two fists, and her eyes were slipping south. Something rustled in the bush out back of the garden, and it wasn't the dogs – the dogs wouldn't be rustling anymore. He poured another shot of rum, struck a match and watched the blue flame flicker atop it before throwing it back. The night was mild, still mild, and the mosquitoes hadn't come on yet. Maybe they were observing a nuptial truce, maybe that was it, he thought. Damn decent of them too. He'd have to remember that next time he crushed half a dozen of them on his forearm or temple – live and let live, right? "Pamela," he said, and her eyes flashed open.

"I'm drunk, Sess," she said. "I'm afraid I've gone and got drunk here." And she smiled, a slow, weary, sanctified smile. "It's all your fault. Bringing a girl out here, getting her drunk. I'll bet you think I'm easy, don't you, huh?"

He gave her the smile back, reached out for her hand and closed it in his own. He didn't want to talk anymore, all that fuel was gone from him now, didn't want to tell her how it felt the first time he walked the trapline and found a wolf like a big dog caught by one half-gnawed foot in a double-spring Newhouse trap intended for fox and how it just sat there staring at him out of its yellow eyes as if it couldn't comprehend the way the country had turned on it in this cold evil unnatural way and how he'd felt when he shot it and missed killing it and shot it again and again till the pelt was ruined and a hundred and ten pounds of raw wilderness lay spouting arterial blood at his feet, or how Roy Sender had taught him to rap a trapped fisher or ermine across the snout with a stick and then jerk at its heartstrings till the heart came loose from its moorings and the animal went limp without spoiling the fur. He didn't tell her he was just one more predator, one more killer, as useless as the wind through the trees, taking life to feed his own. He didn't tell her any of that. "You want to go to bed now," is what he said, "I can see that. You want your man in your arms. You want to be naked."

She moved in close, threw an arm over his shoulder and pressed her forehead to his so that he couldn't see anything of her but her eyes, huge eyes, pale as water. "I'll tell you a secret," she whispered, and the *s*-sound went slushy on her. "I am easy. For you. Only for you, Sess Harder."

He was very drunk. Profoundly drunk, but what did that mean, anyway? Profoundly drunk? That he was ready to go deep, get deep, be deep? Her breath, fecund with wine, with smoked and processed ham, with his beer and what lay at the very essence of her, was a thing that stirred him. He was instantly hard. His breath mingled with hers. "What do you want me to do?"

"Everything," she said.

In the morning it was all right. He hadn't got this far without adversity, hadn't felled the trees for his own cabin and trapped two winters and sold the furs and refused unemployment and food stamps and any kind of institutional handout or government tit without things going radically wrong at one time or another. Adversity hardened him, annealed him. It made him rise to the challenge and beat it back till he knew in his own mind that there was no man like him in all the country, nobody tougher, more resourceful, more independent. The dogs were dead. He would get new ones. And when the time came, when he had the leisure and the inclination, he would settle his scores.

But now it was morning and the cabin was lit by a thick wedge of sun that held the window over the bed in its grip and set fire to the jars of honey on the shelf behind the stove. He lay there a minute, a long minute, Pamela's sweet palpable form pressed to his till they were like two spoons in a drawer, and watched the sun on the wall as if he'd been locked in a closet all his life and never seen anything like it before. They'd slept late, but that was the way it was in summer – you stayed up half the night with the sun looping overhead and then slept in till the next day took hold of you. He had a hangover – and the half-formed feeling of shame and unworthiness that goes with it – but he wasn't going to let it affect him, not one iota. Today was going to be Pamela's day, all day, a day that would make up for yesterday, and if she wanted to just sit naked in the sun and weave slips of forget-me-nots or bluebells into her pubic hair like Lady Chatterley (another of his enduring fantasies), then that was all right with him. Of course, just thinking about it got him hard and he woke her to the slow gentle propulsion of his lovemaking.

And what did she want to do after he served her a plate of eggs, bacon and potatoes fried in four tablespoons of semi-rancid lard whose origins even he suspected? She wanted to do, to make, to get going on the rest of their lives, setting one brick atop another – or log, as the case may be. "Show me where the add-on goes," she said, and she was already out the door, in the knee-high weed, pacing off a room she could see in her mind, a cleaner, airier space that would more than double what they had and give them a proper bedroom with a real and actual freestanding bed in it. And shelves, miles of shelves, and built-in drawers maybe. Bentwood rockers. Little tables. She had that little-table look in her eye, he could see it, could see the way she was calculating.

"You want to catch the sun," he said.

She shaded her eyes with the slab of her hand and grinned at him. Wildflowers rose to her shins. Her skin glistened like buttered toast. He thought he'd never seen a picture so ready for framing. "So we build out to the east, then?"

"Depends on whether you like morning sun or afternoon. Of course, in the winter, we're talking moonlight. You ever been out here in winter – away from town, I mean?" He was thinking of Jill now, *Jill wants out*. Everybody wanted out when the night set in, the night that never let up, when the cabin walls seemed to shrink till you felt like you were in one of those Flash Gordon serials where the walls came together like a vise to squeeze the pulp out of you. Flash always managed to escape, though. So did the better part of the women who came into the country, which was why there were three bush-crazy bachelors for every female in Boynton. The night took inner resources, and most people, women especially, didn't have anything more than outer resources to keep them going – shopping, gossip and restaurants with sconces on the walls, to be specific.

"I've been to Boynton," she said. "I'm *from* Anchorage."

He wanted to explain to her that that wasn't enough, that was nothing, because in a town or a city you could always go to the bar or to a movie or watch TV, and sure, you wanted to see some sunshine, and maybe you flew to Hawaii, if you had the wherewithal, but the fact that it was dark day and night outside your gas-heated apartment's double-paned windows was no more than an afterthought. He wanted to tell her about the couple Jill had known who thought they'd try pioneering in an old miner's cabin up along the Porcupine River drainage and nearly fucked themselves to death out of sheer boredom, four, five, six times a day, till they were both rubbed to the consistency of flank steak and came out of there in spring looking like survivors of a concentration camp. After which they got divorced and probably went off to work in the doughnut industry. He held his peace, though, because she was too pretty and too pleased with herself and this wasn't the time or the place. This was the time for optimism, for love – for beginnings, not endings.

"I don't know," she said, "I guess morning sun. What about you?"

"Afternoon sun's my ticket, which is why I put that little window to the west over there, but then your weather's coming down out of the northwest, and you can never get the window caulked up tight enough, not when the wind starts blowing."

She wasn't listening. She'd balanced herself on one sylphine leg, a bare foot braced against her knee in the pose of a wading bird. She was looking off to the south, where a stand of black spruce clawed at the sky a hundred soggy yards off. "Is that what we're going to cut, that stand over there?" she said.

He came up to her then, took hold of her, rocked her in his arms. The trees were two hundred years old, at least, though they were no taller and no bigger around than fifteen-year plantation pines in the lower forty-eight. "I don't know," he said, "those trees are awful pretty to look at. I thought we'd go upriver, maybe float some logs down like they did in the lumberjack days."

"You've done that?"

No, he hadn't. He'd taken the wood for the present cabin from what was at hand, but he justified that to himself on the grounds that a cabin needed a clearing to stand in, and there were the stumps out there in the circumvallate yard, buried in fireweed, monkshood and yarrow. But it seemed like an idea, and he could see the two of them working side by side across the river from Roy's old place, maybe, he felling the trees and she knocking back the branches, and then just rolling them into the river and guiding them down with the canoe and some rope and maybe the gaff or a notched pole. It would be more work, especially down at this end, because the logs would take on water weight and they'd be a bitch to drag uphill, but then they'd need to dry out and season anyway. "Sure," he said, "sure. It's no big deal. Especially now I have a royally tough bushwoman to do it all for me."

For the next two weeks, he forgot all about his dead dogs, or at least he tried to. He and Pamela went up the Thirtymile each day and took white spruce off the riverbank for the roof poles, and black spruce that was maybe ten inches in diameter (and growing from seed when George Washington wasn't even born yet) from the hills stacked up in back of it. They packed a lunch and sometimes a supper too, and twice they camped under the stars in a steady drizzle of mosquitoes. The trees went down like cardboard and Pamela hacked tirelessly at the branches with a hatchet, the little-table look in her eyes day and night. They both felt the work, in their arms and shoulders and the rawness of their hands that pussed up, blistered over and toughened, and though they were exhausted by the time they quit for the night – sometimes as late as eight or nine – they found time to make love, in a sleeping bag or right out there on the sandy bank of the river, as if they'd invented the whole idea of sex and had to keep trying it out to make sure they'd got it right.

At the end of those two weeks they had a pretty fair collection of logs hauled up on the bar that fronted the cabin, and they were feeling pretty good about themselves, or at least that was the way Sess saw it. Pamela seemed to be enjoying herself, and never mind that she was a city girl and had her degree and could have been tanning herself at some resort on the Côte d'Or. She worked like a man, like two men, and she never stinted and never said quit until he did. And when the logs hung up on rocks or sleepers, as they invariably did, she was as likely as he to plunge chest-deep into the scour of forty-five-degree water to free them.

They were sitting there atop their log pile at the end of the last evening's run, forking up squares of the cold macaroni, tuna and cheese she'd made in the glare of morning, and looking up to the cabin where these logs would fit right into place, the worst part of the work behind them, when Pamela, in her khaki shorts and too-tight T-shirt, with her lumberman's hands and her hair pulled back tight, paused between bites and said it was time to go into town.

He gave her a look. The logs had to be peeled with an adze, hauled up the hill and stacked to dry, then notched and set in place. Then chinked. Then the roof had to go up and they'd both of them bust a double hernia working the center pole into place, if women got hernias, that is. "What for?" he said.

"And I don't just mean Boynton."

"You want to go all the way into Fairbanks?"

She just nodded.

"Okay," he said, and he would have driven her to Topeka and back if that was what she wanted, "I'll give it another try. What for? Shopping?"

"Oh, that's part of it," she said, setting her plate aside. She perched atop the pile of river-run logs like a genie, as if all she'd had to do was snap her fingers to make them appear. "I do want some things to feminize that coot's den of yours, and stock up on groceries too – we might be eating moose all winter, but I see nothing wrong with some stewed vegetables, rice, condiments, pickles and all the rest to go with it. Lasagna. Spaghetti. Hershey bars. Saltwater taffy. Marshmallows."

He pushed himself up, stretched his legs – he'd been sitting in one place too long and he felt the stiffness radiate from his backside and down both his thighs. "So that's it, marshmallows. The cat's out of the bag. Me and my wife are going to the big city for marshmallows."

She gave him a grin that made him feel all over again what he already suspected – that he was no longer in charge of his own life and never again would be. "That's right," she said, and paused to watch a cloud shaped like a wedding ring – or maybe a noose – blow over. "We're going to town for marshmallows." Then her voice dropped and the grin disappeared. "And dogs. Don't you think it's time?"

They left for Boynton at six the next morning, and by eight-thirty they were beaching the canoe and striding hand in hand up the hill to the shack. And that was an odd feeling for both of them – a sentimental feeling, nostalgic already. The vegetation was trampled in a wide oval where the dancing had gone on, and the odd bottle or spangle of confetti caught the sun from clumps of fireweed along the margins, artifacts of the ritual they'd enacted there two weeks ago. You could see where the birds had been at the flung rice, filling their crops to bursting, and there was a crescent-shaped depression where the barbecue pit had been. It was filled with cold white ash, through which scraps of charred bone protruded like the trunks of miniature trees in a burned-over forest, and the ash was crisscrossed with the tracks of weasel and ground squirrel. All the rest was gone, like a gypsy circus, like a magic act. "It was one hell of a party," Sess said, "and I bet nobody's going to forget it."

"Right," she said, giving him a sidelong look. "Till the next one."

They poked aimlessly around the shack for a few minutes, silently taking inventory and setting aside things – tools, mainly – they might want to haul back up to the cabin, and then they leaned into the screen door at Richard Schrader's place and chorused his name until it became apparent that he was either dead and stuffed or out somewhere on business. His pickup stood in the front yard – the pickup that was essential to the expedition under way since Pamela's Gremlin now belonged to the short-order cook at the Northern Lights Diner on C Street in downtown Anchorage and Sess hadn't owned a car in three years – and so they reasoned he hadn't gone far. They further reasoned that they deserved a drink after a beerless run down the river under a spitting sky, and Pamela wanted to call her mother to make sure she'd got home safe and to reassure her that all the tricky business of love had worked out to her satisfaction. And Sess was fine with that. He was fine with everything. The rain would be good for the garden, they'd just put in two weeks' work that was like no honeymoon anybody ever spent, there were some faces at the Three Pup and the Nougat he wouldn't mind reacquainting himself with in the afterglow of the wedding, and though he wouldn't breathe a word of it to anybody, he was going to need to acquire some dogs, and Fairbanks was the place to do it, where nobody would be asking any questions.

He dropped Pamela at the general store, where Wetzel Setzler had a ham radio set up to patch into the phone lines Bell Telephone so generously provided for everybody but the renegades, anarchists, xenophobes and wild hairs who chose to live at the dead and final end of the last road in the country, and then he ambled over to the Nougat, just to stick his head in the door. He had no expectation of running into Joe Bosky, because Joe Bosky was a coward and a backstabber and he wouldn't show his face after what he'd done, but Sess wouldn't mind scaring up Richard to see what the chances of borrowing the pickup were.

The Nougat featured the same setup as the Three Pup, only it was half the size, didn't have a kitchen and limited its offerings to booze and potato chips out of the eight-ounce bag, with cellophane-wrapped beer nuts and stale pretzels for the connoisseurs. A pair of mounted caribou heads stood watch over the bar and a moose with soot-blackened jowls presided over the woodstove. Clarence Ford, who owned the establishment, had meant to call it "The Nugget," but orthography wasn't his strong suit.

When Sess stepped into the early-morning gloom of the place, there was nobody there but Iron Steve and an Indian he didn't recognize, both of them passed out at the bar. Wetzel Setzler's youngest, Solly, was in the back room, rattling bottles around in their slit-top cardboard boxes and making notations on a steno pad. Six hundred billion flies – at least – rumbled against the windowpanes and made a collective noise like a cello at midrange. Iron Steve's breathing was slow and stertorous, every second breath catching on the horns of a snore. The whole place smelled of extinguished cigarettes – old extinguished cigarettes – and it was a sad smell, a reminder of all the traffic that had gone down here, the elbows propped, the glasses drained, the arguments, the bullshit, the women won and women lost. At quarter past nine in the morning, to a dogless man with his lungs full of sweet river air, it was almost depressing.

"Hey, Solly," Sess called in an exaggerated whisper, lest he should wake anybody prematurely, "can a man get a beer out here? Or is this the place people come to die of thirst?"

Solly Setzler was twenty-four years old, with his father's ski-slope shoulders, milky eyes and colorless eyebrows, and nobody really thought it odd that he worked for the competition because it was a kind of miracle that anybody at all would want to stand behind the bar of a roadhouse this time of year. His hair was a miracle in itself, the exact color of fiberglass insulation, and his eyes lacked a human sheen. He'd been home-schooled, and he was as misinformed, brooding and ignorant as anybody Sess had ever met, especially anybody that young. Now he looked up with a wrung-out neck, like a bird in the nest craning for a grub in the parental beak. "Sess," he said, looking lost in the bar he'd been working for three years, as if he'd awakened there out of a dream, "I thought you went upriver."

He didn't know where Richard Schrader was, but he located an Oly and cracked it and never thought to offer up a celebratory shot for the newlywed, which Sess would have declined in any case because it was early yet and he had a drive ahead of him and all the responsibilities of a married man who couldn't just come into town and go on a bender like some talk-starved bush crazy with ingrown toenails and hair coming out his ears and nostrils.

At the Three Pup, he ran into Skid Denton, who seemed to have changed his allegiance from the Nougat, at least since Lynette had come to town. Skid Denton was having a breakfast of steak and eggs drowned in Tabasco and chopped onion, along with home fries, toast and a mug of beer with a shot of tomato juice in it – "Bloody beer," he called it, whenever anybody bothered to ask, " – it's how I get my vitamin C." He looked up from his plate to inform Sess that Richard Schrader had gone downriver to his fish camp in the expectation that the kings would be running any day now. Lynette, slouching over the bar so that her sidearm rode up her skinny hip, confirmed the intelligence. "Some tourist," she said, as if she'd lived here fifty years, "caught a thirty-two pounder right off the gravel bar out there not two days ago. Or was it three?"

He had another Oly, just to balance out the one he'd thrown down at the Nougat – spread the trade around, that was his motto – and nobody offered to buy him a celebratory shot here either, and that was just fine, as per his resolution, so he went back up the road into town to check on Pamela at the general store. He wanted to tell her the bad news – no truck available – and let her stock up on what she would, because if they weren't going to Fairbanks where there was free and open competition, they'd have to pay Wetzel Setzler's captive prices, at least for now. Of course, in the winter they wouldn't have any choice, and if they didn't have dogs they wouldn't be sledding down the river to Boynton in any case, so there would be no picking up the odd forty-ounce can of Greek olives that you could expire for the want of or socializing at the roadhouse or at Richard's or anyplace else.

But then, two beers sitting pleasantly on his stomach, a light breeze off the river ruffling his hair as he put one foot in front of the other and the near shacks of the paint-blistered town rose up to greet him like so many old friends and boon companions, he had a thought involving a prime 1965 fastback Mustang he just happened to know about. It was a criminal thought, but then one good criminal act deserved another, didn't it?

17

To Pamela's mind, the inside of the general store was a perfect example of order in chaos. She'd always believed in the kind of probity that comes of sparseness and the ascetic lifestyle, and she'd kept her Anchorage apartment free of the clutter and kitsch that dominated her friends' places – the soapstone and walrus tusk carvings, the polished caribou racks, taxidermy displays and native scenes in birchbark frames, not to mention the stereos and crockpots and closets full of shoes, handbags, cableknit sweaters and beaded mukluks. Things oppressed her. Man-made things, trinkets and gizmos and the newest and the latest, all the incalculable piles of junk every good red-blooded American needed to survive. She wasn't buying into it, and she never had. What she admired was the kind of self-sufficiency of the early prospectors who thought nothing of going out for a month at a time with little more than a gun, a length of fishing line, a sack of rice, six ounces of salt and some loose tea in a tin. Strip it down to the basics. Live off what the land gives you.

Still, she had to admire what Wetzel Setzler had done with the two low-slung rooms of the big blackened overblown log structure that dominated the main street – the only street, really – of Boynton. Sess had told her the place was a remnant from the time at the turn of the century when Boynton boasted twelve hundred people, an opera house and twenty-eight saloons and the sourdoughs' pans were still showing color along the Kandik and the Charley, a time when the Northern Navigation Company ran thirty-two stern-wheel steamboats up and down the river to accommodate the traffic, and that made her wonder all the more what these hordes of people were thinking when they came swarming into a territory they didn't know the first thing about. But then she already knew the answer: rape and plunder, that was what they were thinking, and nothing beyond. Take the gold out of the country, take the meat, take the furs, and then fold up your tents and vanish to Cleveland, to Sacramento, to Montpelier and Miami Beach.

Wetzel Setzler probably had three thousand items on display, from spark plugs, cartridges, fishing lures, beaver traps and crescent wrenches to maraschino cherries, insulated socks, overalls, canned wax beans, hard liquor and sixteen different varieties of candy and gum, and every one of them in its separate bin and clearly marked with a price in hand-printed block letters so uniform they might have been stamped on by the manufacturer. There was a stove in the middle of the place with a couple of chairs set round it, a dangle of things trailing from hooks nailed into the overhead beams and a glass-front cooler with soft drinks, canned beer and even milk, butter and whipping cream brought in once a week from a supermarket in Fairbanks and sold at three times the price. If it weren't for the cooler the place could have jumped right out of the pages of a book of old-time photos or maybe even daguerreotypes, the kind of thing her mother always had out on the coffee table for guests to thumb through, *How Our Forefathers Lived* or *Country Stores of the Old West*.

When Pamela stepped in the door, there was nobody in the place, though it was ten o'clock in the morning and people were moving up and down the street outside like bloodclots working their slow way through the veins of the town. A bell over the door announced her presence, but no one – not Wetzel Setzler or a shopboy, if the breed existed this far out – appeared from the back room to acknowledge her. It was preternaturally still, as if the place existed outside of time; the only light was what spilled in through the windows. The thought came into her head that she could rob them blind, take anything she wanted, take all she could carry and set up a rival store across the street, and they wouldn't be any the wiser. "Hello?" she called. "Anybody here?"

She found herself staring into the jaws of what must have been a bear trap dangling from a chain overhead, a huge dark wedge of blue-black steel, faintly glistening in the morning light. Here was a trap that meant business, lethal and unyielding, and she imagined it artfully buried next to a carcass or along a game trail like the discharge of a bad dream, and for just a moment, looking into its teeth, she felt the cruelty of it, and was this what Sess had been trying to tell her the night they'd got drunk? It was a trap. A necessary accoutrement to the wild life. You trapped things and then you killed them, skinned them and fed them to the dogs, and the money from the skins bought you sugar, coffee, cartridges, more traps. That was what she was buying into, and it was a matter of choice, of her own pleasure and inclination, as much as it was about survival – all those little lives would feed her own, as if she were some god on high demanding sacrifice.

Next to the trap, nailed to the swell of the shellacked beam as if to make light of the whole business, was an old-fashioned bicycle horn with its tarnished brass tube and black rubber bulb. Before she could think, she was reaching up to squeeze the bulb and a low flatulent wheeze of a sound announced her presence. "Hello?" she called again.

No response.

But maybe they weren't open yet, maybe that was it. Maybe they were all so trusting they just left their doors unlocked up and down the street and people could come and go as they pleased, pick out what they wanted and pay on the honor system. There was a door at the rear of the place marked office in the same meticulous block letters that set out the prices on the bins, and she went to it and tried the handle. She rapped formally with the knuckles of her left hand even as she pushed the door open and found herself on the threshold of a windowless den with a desk, a filing cabinet and cardboard boxes of liquor stacked floor to ceiling against the walls. There was a smell of burnt wax or lantern oil, something chemical, at any rate, mingled with the scents of Pine-Sol and the mold it was meant to defeat.

As she leaned into the doorway, the floorboards groaned beneath her feet and she stopped where she was, embarrassed suddenly. She had no business in the lair of a man she barely knew, his socks and yellowed T-shirt laid over the back of the chair to dry as if he'd done his washing one piece at a time, his tooth-worried pipes laid out in a row atop the filing cabinet beside a framed photo of his younger self and a woman twice his size in a print dress, both of them glaring into the sun as if they'd just emerged from a cave. There was a pair of boots in the corner, pipe cleaners in a jar, a dismantled fishing reel laid out on a piece of newspaper. She saw the radio then, right there on the desk with a set of headphones and a mike attached to it, and that impressed her in the way of the bear trap – this was a different world out here, a different life, and it was going to take some getting used to. Of course it was. And her mother could wait, she decided, thinking it would be cheaper to call from a real phone in Fairbanks, anyway – *if* they could dig up Richard Schrader, and *if* his truck was available – and she backed out of the office and eased the door shut behind her.

She called out once more – "Hello? Is anybody here?" – and then she drifted down the aisles, lost amidst the galvanized buckets and Blazo cans, the deck screws, pickaxes, fishing lures and cellophane-wrapped loaves of six-day-old bread. Just for an instant, she felt a pang. She did want to talk to her mother – it was vital – and not so much to reassure her as to let her know that she could succeed where her mother had failed, that she knew what she was doing and it was all turning out right, better than right. She was happy. Ecstatic. And her mother ought to know that.

Her mother had seemed to approve of Sess in a general way, but she'd been leery from the start about the whole idea of living in the bush. "I had enough of that when your father was prospecting all those summers when you were little," she said, and it was like a litany, like a catechism Pamela could have repeated word for word. "Oh, it might have been a lark for you two girls, but for me it was just another cross to bear, trying to cook for four over an open fire, staying up half the night swatting mosquitoes and wondering if he was ever going to come back, if he'd broken a leg or been attacked by a bear or drowned fording a creek, and that was the worst of it, to think of him floating out there like some waterlogged piece of yesterday's meat, food for the ravens, for the ants – "

Pamela had been young then, just eight the first year they went into the backcountry, and her only memories of that time were happy ones. She remembered the three of them – she and her mother and Pris – sprawled in the big canvas tent while the rain made a whole Latin rhythm section out of the walls, her mother dealing out the cards for pinochle, poker, hearts or euchre while the smell of ginger-marinated rabbit or squirrel stew ruminated in the corners. There were oatmeal cookies baked to sweet density in a camp oven, brownies, even cakes. She read all of Nancy Drew, the Brontë sisters, Sherlock Holmes. They swam, fished, canoed, and for the month of June and half of September, her mother led her and Pris through their arithmetic, their spelling, their essays on Andrew "Stonewall" Jackson and Thomas Paine. It was a kind of dream. And, as in a dream, the memories came back to her in fragments of color and emotion, one moment blurred into the next in a montage that spanned all those six summers till her father wandered off and never came back again.

She didn't know how long she drifted through the store in a fog, fingering one object after another as if she'd never before in her life seen hinges or threepenny nails, but the soft, almost apologetic toot of a horn from beyond the front window brought her out of it. There was a car out on the street – white, with blue stripes, some sort of racing car that was totally out of place in a town where vehicles were worked like dogs and if you didn't have a pickup you had a wagon. At first she thought the man behind the wheel must have been a tourist come up from Anchorage or even the lower forty-eight, but he seemed to be gesturing to her through the intervening lens of the windshield and there was that toot again, insinuating, persistent, familiar even. It took her a moment, and then she had to laugh to think she didn't even recognize her own husband, because there he was, leaning out the window now and calling her to him with an urgent rippling curl of the fingers of both hands. All right. But here she was in front of the precisely labeled bin of Hershey bars, no shopkeeper in sight and a long ride ahead of her. She took two without thinking and had almost made it to the door when she caught herself. And though Sess tapped twice more at the horn, she turned away, tripped down the aisle to where the cash register sat untended on the back counter and laid two quarters beside it.

Outside, in the light of day, the car looked even stranger, as if it had been set down here in the heart of the country by some demented pit crew with access to one of those big Huey transport helicopters you saw in the TV coverage of the war. It just did not compute – a race car in Boynton, one hundred and sixty miles from the nearest paved road? She slid into the seat beside Sess and handed him a Hershey bar, even as he put the thing in gear and tore a patch of gravel out of the road. "Nice car," she said, her shoulders pinned to the seat. "Where'd you get it?"

He was tearing open the candy with his teeth, racing the engine in first gear and using his left hand and right elbow to steer the car through a series of ruts and bottomless puddles and out onto the Fairbanks Road. He hit second gear then and the chassis shivered over a stretch of washboard ridges, mud flying, stones beating at the fenders like machine-gun fire, and they shot past the Three Pup before she could even begin to think he might be evading the question. "Make your phone call?" he shouted over the roar.

"There was nobody there," she said, and the tension of the springs over the unforgiving surface keyed her words to a shaky vibrato. He hadn't slowed down yet, the speedometer jumping at eighty on a road that was barely safe at half that, and what was he up to, her husband with the big hands and pelt of hair and the grin etched in profile as he gnawed at the chocolate out of one corner of his mouth? Was he trying to impress her like some teenager out on a date in his father's souped-up street machine? Was he turning adolescent on her, was that it, or was he just shot full of high spirits? Whatever the cause, he was going to tear the car apart if he didn't slow down – or maybe kill them both. She took his arm. "Sess," she said, "Sess, slow down, will you?"

Immediately the speedometer jerked down to forty and he turned to her with a grin. "Like it?" he asked, a froth of chocolate and saliva obliterating his front teeth so that he looked like some mugging comedian on TV, like Red Skelton or she didn't know who. There was something wild in his eyes, some bubbling up of emotion she hadn't seen before, and she reminded herself that she was still learning to read him – this was her honeymoon, after all. He was her husband and she loved him, but how well did she really know him after two weeks?

She gave him the grin back, gave his wrist a squeeze where it rested on the gearshift as the wheels beat at the road and the road beat back. "Sure, it's nice. But there's no backseat or anything, so how are we going to – "

"Dogs, you mean? Hell, we'll strap them to the roof." He goosed the accelerator and the car shot forward with a jerk and then fell back again as he let up. He hadn't stopped grinning yet, and she was going to repeat her question – *Where'd you get the car?* – when she noticed that there was no key in the ignition, just a shining empty slot staring at her like a blind eye. And below it, below the steering column, there was some sort of plug hanging loose in a bundle of dangling wires.

A moment slipped by, scrub on either side of them, trees flapping like banners in a stiff breeze. Then he was fishing under the seat for something, his head cocked to keep one eye on the road. "Here," he said, straightening up and handing her a can of Oly, "I already got a head start on you and didn't we say we'd reward ourselves with a couple beers this morning?" He stuck a second can between his thighs and worked the punch top while the car fishtailed across the road and righted itself again.

She accepted the beer, popped it open, took a sip. "You're drunk, is that it? Is that why you're acting like this?"

The grin had faded while he was rummaging under the seat, but now it came back, tighter than ever. "Hell, no, Pamela – I mean, two beers and a chocolate bar on a mostly empty stomach? Just feeling good, that's all. Super. On top of the world."

She cradled her beer, studying him. "Where'd you get the car, Sess?"

He looked straight ahead, the grin frozen on his lips. He shrugged, but didn't shift his eyes to her. "Around."

"Oh, yeah?" she said, and this wasn't cute, not anymore. This was criminal, that was what it was. Irresponsible. Wrong. "Then why are there no keys in it? And what's that mess of wires down there?"

Another shrug. He put the beer to his lips and gunned the engine again. "I borrowed it."

"Borrowed it? From who?"

"You want to see if we can scare up anything on the radio?"

"From who, Sess?"

Now he looked at her and the grin was gone. Something – a tawny streak – darted across the roadway in front of them. "Joe Bosky."

"Joe Bosky?" she repeated, as if she hadn't heard him right, and maybe she hadn't – maybe the roar of the engine and the wind through the open window was playing tricks with her ears.

He didn't say anything, just stared at the broad brown tongue of the road before them.

"You mean Joe Bosky who you were ready to kill a couple weeks ago? That Joe Bosky?"

She studied him in profile a moment and there was no give in him at all. "You're talking grand theft auto here, Sess. You're talking jail time. Is it worth it? Is it really worth it just to, to what – show off? Be the big man? Is that what you're doing? Showing off for me?"

"Tit for tat. You hurt me, I hurt you. It's the law of the jungle out here, Pamela, and you better get used to it."

"Don't give me that crap," she said, "don't even think about it," but they drove on, going too fast, and the stones flew up to nick the paint and corrupt the body of Joe Bosky's 1965 Shelby Mustang GT350, which he'd bought the day he set foot in San Diego after his second tour in Vietnam with the money his dead mother left him, and which he'd shipped up to Anchorage and driven at twenty-five miles an hour out the Fairbanks Road to store in the only garage in Boynton, courtesy of Wetzel Setzler and a ten-dollar-a-month rental fee. She didn't know what to say. She was furious. All this was so childish, two overgrown boys bullying each other, and what did Sess hope to gain? His dogs were dead and he was taking it out on Joe Bosky's car. But what if Joe Bosky got wind of it because Sess had been right out there in the main street honking the horn for all the world to see? What if he got Wetzel Setzler to call the sheriff on his ham radio? Then what?

"Stop the car, Sess," she said. "Stop the car. I'm not going to be party to this."

His hands choked the wheel. He stared straight ahead. "You already are."

There was a patrol car sitting alongside the Steese Highway when they came into Fairbanks, a long, low, ominous-looking sedan with the sun glancing off the windshield so you couldn't see inside. Just the sight of it made her heart skip, but Sess eased off the accelerator, stuck an arm out the window and gave the invisible cop a hearty wave. She didn't dare turn her head, but she watched the patrol car in the side mirror as if she could fix it there by force of will, all the while expecting it to spring to life in a fierce tumult of light and noise. Nothing happened. The police car receded in the mirror, lifeless as a pile of stone. A pickup truck passed them. They went round a bend. Sess put both hands on the wheel and drove like an egg farmer on his way to market.

They had lunch out on the deck at the Pumphouse, her favorite place in Fairbanks, and the sun on her face and the breeze and the two beers she tipped back went a long way toward calming her. She got a copy of the paper and they scanned the classifieds under "Pets," but none of the dogs sounded promising to Sess – he was being difficult now, all the gaiety gone out of him – and they could both see that the day was going to be a waste. He kept saying they ought to be back at home, setting out their gill nets, but then he'd tip back his beer and drain his shot glass and rumble that there was no point in worrying about salmon or anything else if you didn't have dogs because if you didn't have dogs you were doomed to failure anyway and the whole idea of living in the wild was just a pipe dream, a joke. It depressed her to see him like this – worse, it scared her. He was her rock and foundation, the dominant male she'd chosen out of a whole pack of lesser males, the man she'd been waiting for all her life to lead her into the wilderness, and if he was defeated, she was defeated too. The waitress was hovering, and she could see in his eyes that he was about to order another round, so she said, "Listen, what about the pound?"

"I don't even know where it is," he said, throwing up obstacles.

"Oh, you mean the *dog* pound?" the waitress put in, reaching for the bottles on the table and giving each an exploratory shake. "I can tell you where that is, because my boyfriend and me just found the cutest little toy poodle there – Mitzi. That's what we call her. Wait. You want to see a picture?"

The pound was behind some sort of factory or warehouse on a piece of flat foot-worn ground devoid of trees or even shrubs, a squat prefabricated building in front of which a single battered panel truck was parked at a skewed angle, as if the driver had run off and abandoned it. The railroad tracks ran within a hundred feet of the back end of the place and the boxcars sat there humped up to the horizon like dominoes. Sess didn't even want to get out of the car, but she prodded him, and a moment later they were standing there in the lot, gravel crunching under their feet, and she was thinking this was about as far from the Thirtymile as you could get and still be in the state of Alaska. An ammoniac smell hit them then, carried on a light breeze with a handful of mosquitoes in it. There was a feeble anguished sound of yipping and whining, and it seemed to be coming from everywhere and nowhere at once. "What can we lose?" she said, trying to mollify him as he gave her a glum look over the roof of the ridiculous car.

Inside, the smell was concentrated, and she thought of the only big-city zoo she'd ever been to, in San Francisco, where the ratty animals lay festering in concrete troughs and the multiplied stink of them – a stink so intense it made her panicky – was the only lasting impression she had of the place, of the whole city, in fact. The floor was concrete, the light inadequate. A blocky woman with pouffed-up hair and teardrop glasses grinned at them from behind a plywood counter with a Formica top. "You here for an adoption?" she asked over the racket of the dogs, which had gone up a notch since they'd stepped in the door. "Or just thinking about it maybe?"

Then they were walking down a cement corridor between rows of mesh cages, dogs of every size and description leaping at the wire, yodeling, yapping, whining, their paws like windmills, their eyes alive with eagerness and hope. The woman stooped to one or another of them, cooing, and they poked their shining noses through the mesh to worship her fingers and the back of her hand. There was a terrific scrabbling of nails as the dogs fought for purchase on the wet concrete. One of them, a beagle mix with flapping ears and deep, liquid eyes, clambered up on the backs of three others to stick its snout through the gap where the cage door had pulled back from its hinges, and Pamela slid her hand in against the wall to feel the dog's appreciation, its pink tongue extracting every molecule of flavor from her skin. She wanted to adopt them all.

"Now, Buster," the woman was saying, pressing her hand to

the mesh where a white-faced retriever crouched over its bad hips, "Buster's the sweetest thing you'd ever want to see. He'd make a perfect house dog. And he loves kids. You two have kids?"

Sess was right there with her, but he didn't seem to hear her. He was focused on a dog in the back of the cage, a lean big-headed thing with paws like griddles that couldn't have been more than eight or ten months old. "That one," he said, "can I see that one?"

The woman looked dubious. "You mean Peaches? That's Peaches," she said, glancing over her shoulder at Pamela. "He's not a house dog, but if you live in the country and you've got some space, well, I guess he'd be fine. He's shy, that's all."

"That's because he's got wolf in him," Sess said, and his mood had lifted – she could hear it in his voice. "You see the angularity of those back legs, Pamela? And the snout? The pointy snout means he's got longer vertebrae so his chest muscles fan out and he can really cover ground. That's a fast dog there. And he'll pull too." And then he was in the cage, three or four dogs swarming at his hands, tails whacking. The wolf dog shrank back in the corner and Sess went down into a crouch, squatting over his knees and extending his right hand. "Peaches," he said, his voice burnished and low, "what kind of a name is that for a dog? Come here, boy, come on." It took a minute, Pamela and the woman watching from outside the cage, and then the dog came to him, five feet across the cement floor, in the submissive posture of a wolf, creeping on its elbows and dragging its belly. Sess smoothed back its ears, ran a hand over its snout. "I'll take this one," he said.

At the grocery he wouldn't let her get more than they could carry on their backs, and he didn't offer any explanations and he didn't bother coming in with her to push the stainless steel cart up and down the aisles of plenty like every other husband and wife in creation. He stayed out in the dirt lot with the dog – at the very end of it where it trailed off into knee-high weed – and though he'd brought a homemade leather leash and collar along, he didn't use it, not yet. He controlled the dog with his voice alone, and when she went in the store he was just squatting there, watching it, the soft soothing flow of his words working on the animal like an incantation. She could have bought the store out, but she had to settle for some cosmetics, toothpaste, fresh fruit and vegetables – which she was already starved for – and as much pasta and stewed tomatoes and tomato sauce as she reasonably thought they could carry. When she came out of the store wheeling a cart, Sess rose to his feet and crossed the lot to her, never even glancing back at the dog, but the dog put its head down and followed him.

On the way back, he was nothing short of exuberant, chattering away at her as if he'd just won the lottery. The groceries were stuffed down behind the seat, and the dog – he wouldn't demean it by calling it "Peaches" – sat like a tensed coil in her lap, its head out the window. He drove slower now, but still shot ahead in bursts and cranked through the gears as if he wanted to rip them out of the transmission, slamming into potholes and flinging up sheets of coffee-colored water as if the car were a skiff shearing across a muddy inlet. Every other minute he'd reach out a hand to stroke her arm or pat the dog. Before long, he was whistling.

"Trotter," he said, "what about Trotter? That's a good name. Descriptive, you know? Or Lucius. I've always liked Lucius. As a name, I mean – "

She'd almost forgotten they were in a stolen car, playing a dangerous game with a man who put bullets in the skulls of another man's dogs and that there was retribution to come, because she was in this moment, now, and they were both working on fresh beers to celebrate the fact of this sterling dog in her lap and the two others Sess had paid five dollars each for against the day he'd be back with Richard Schrader's pickup. "How about Yukon King?" she said.

He let out a laugh and reached again to stroke the dog, which reeled its head in to give him a look of subjection and fealty. "Never thought of that one. But sure, I mean, what could be more fitting than to name a real dog after some actor dog that probably couldn't get out of the way of a sled if it ran him over, and by the way, did you know that Lassie is really three different dogs and they're all male?"

She didn't know. But she did know the origin of the feud

between him and the black-haired man, because he'd told her over his second morose shot of Wild Turkey at the Pumphouse while she read off the descriptions of the dogs for sale or trade or "free to good home," and he rejected them one after another before she could get to the end of the first line. Two winters ago Joe Bosky had appeared in Boynton dressed up like something out of the pages of *National Geographic* in a caribou-skin parka lined with wolf and a rifle slung over one shoulder. The plane that delivered him hadn't even refueled yet for the return trip to Fairbanks, and he was already hip-deep in bullshit at the Nougat, with the deed to Tilda Runyon's cabin spread out on the bar – the cabin she'd left to her half-breed son, who was a drunk and a gambler, a thief and liar, and who'd apparently been in the Corps with Bosky. What was he doing in the country in the middle of February? He was going to live wild, that was what. And he moved into Tilda Runyon's cabin, chopped wood, drank to excess and lived off what the mail plane brought him two days a week. By the first summer he was building himself a cabin on Woodchopper Creek and making money hand over fist flying tourists and fishermen into the backcountry in the Cessna 180 he floated in on one fine day, and by the fall he was wandering the hills and watercourses, scouting out the country for signs of fur. He settled finally on Roy Sender's trapline, the trapline Roy Sender had cleared and maintained and expanded over the course of forty-odd years and ceded to Sess when he left the country. The first winter, it was stolen bait and sprung traps and no evidence of a man's footprints in the snow, as if the perpetrator could fly, because Joe Bosky was clever and a quick study and the country grew out of his skin. By the second winter, he was running his own traps and poaching from Sess's.

"You didn't know that about Lassie? You really didn't?"

She shook her head. "You read it someplace?"

"I read it someplace. *TV Guide*, most likely."

"*TV Guide?* Why in god's name would you read *TV Guide* when you've never had a TV in your adult life and never will?"

He gave her a look. Shrugged. "I was flat broke one winter when I was still in Fairbanks – remember, I told you? Drinking too much, and out of money for drink. This bookstore had a box of old *TV Guides* they were giving away. I must have read every one cover to cover. Twice. At least twice. You know *Citizen Kane?*"

A black-and-white image came into her head, the darkened room, the roll and flicker of the tube and her mother with her feet up, doing her nails, the jowly glow of Orson Welles's face, the stark rectilinear halls of a mansion whole armies could camp in. "I've seen it. Or parts of it, anyway."

"Nineteen forty-one. Orson Welles, Joseph Cotten. Directed by Welles. Four stars. *The Mummy's Ghost?* Nineteen forty-four. Lon Chaney Jr. Two stars. *The Savage Innocents,* Anthony Quinn, 1960 – and they must have played that one six times a week – three stars. I could tell you the ratings for every movie ever made, but I doubt if I've seen more than maybe fifty of them in my whole life – and that was when I was a kid at home with my parents."

The dog shifted in her lap. "You miss it – TV, movies?"

She expected him to say no, to give her the usual bush crazy's party line – too busy out there, too beautiful, the whole natural world better than anything you could ever hope to see on a little screen and the aurora borealis blooming overhead in living color too – but he surprised her. "On a moonless January night with the stove so hot the iron glows and the floor so cold you don't want to get out of bed to save your life, you miss just about everything."

Then they were silent and the dog hung his head out the window and the sun defeated the clouds to light the road ahead of them like an expressway and Joe Bosky's Mustang lurched into the ruts and sought out the puddles. Traffic wasn't a problem. They overtook two cars going their way – probably heading for Boynton Hot Springs, where there was an old tumbledown resort for summer people – and six or seven vehicles came at them headed for Fairbanks, all of which Sess recognized. He whistled his way through four quavering versions of "My Favorite Things," something from Dvor?ák, she wasn't sure what, and, maddeningly, "I Saw Mommy Kissing Santa Claus (Underneath the Mistletoe Last Night)," and then it was evening and they were three miles outside of Boynton and he was pulling over on the side of the road in a place where Birch Creek meandered along the shoulder and the odd fisherman had worn a blistered dirt hump in the bank. "Time to get out, Pamela," he said, and before she could find the door handle he was around her side of the car and pulling open the door for her. "Time to stretch your legs. Come on, Lucius, that's a good dog. You want to stretch too?"

The creek was a river actually, slow and deep here, with water the color of steeped tea. The dog lifted his leg, sniffed. Sess took her in his arms and gave her a kiss full of passion and hunger, and then he let her go and started fitting the groceries into the two backpacks they'd brought along. The mosquitoes were over-joyed. "What are you up to, Sess?" she asked, standing over him. "You're going to leave the car here, is that it?"

He didn't answer. The tendons stood out in his neck as he stuffed cans, jars and plastic bags of pasta and marshmallows into the packs with an eye to balancing out the load.

"I don't see that it matters, Sess," she heard herself say, and she didn't mean to nag – tried to catch herself, in fact, but couldn't. "Because you were right out there on the main street of town this morning where everybody could see you, beeping the horn even, and if anybody wanted to know our fingerprints are all over the thing. Dog hair too." She tried to inject something light into it, though she was fuming all over again: "What would Perry Mason make of that?"

He looked up from the squat of his knees, genuinely puzzled. "Who's Perry Mason?" Then he rose to his feet, lifted both backpacks by their straps and set them to one side in the tall weed. "Pamela," he said, "I need you to do me a favor here for just a minute, would you?" He didn't wait for a reply. "Just take hold of Lucius so he doesn't get spooked, okay?"

"Spooked? What are you talking about?"

"Just do it, will you?"

And then the grand finale that made her heart dwindle down to nothing, because he was out of control, this husband of hers, out of his mind, and there was no going back from this, this was final and irrevocable and you might just as well hope for peace between the Brits and the Irish, the Israelis and the Palestinians. He slid back into the car, fired up the engine with a roar and left the driver's side door swinging wide on its hinges. "You know, there's probably not five hundred of these Shelby Mustangs in all of the United States of America," he said, raising his voice to be heard over the engine, and then he gunned it up over the dirt hump and on into the creek, jumping wide as the water took hold of it and the tail end bobbed up for just an instant and then settled back down again, the slow steady seep of the current washing it clean.

18

Ronnie was loving this, absolutely and truly loving it. He was on the road again, his wrist draped casually over the wheel of the Studebaker, Star and Marco wedged in beside him, the roof piled high with roped-down boxes and Lydia stretched out across the backseat in a see-through blouse. He was dogging the bus, Merry and Maya making faces out the back window and the goats bleating away at sixty miles an hour from their ramshackle pen atop the thing, and that was a trip too – the bus was such a top-heavy, loaded-down piece of swaying and reeling spring-sprung shit even the Joads would have run screaming from it. Washo Unified, yes indeed. It gave him pleasure just to look at it, because it was a kind of in-joke, and he was in on it. And behind him – all he had to do was glance in the rearview mirror for the comfort of it – was Harmony's liver-spotted Bug, rattling along just beyond the nose of Lester's Lincoln.

And that was a whole other trip: Lester and Franklin. They showed up at the last minute, shuffling around in the dirt, hands going in and out of their pockets and their eyes locking on every face as if they were equipped with built-in lasers, and announced they were coming along for the ride even if they didn't think they'd make it all the way up to the frozen hinterlands, because it was a free country, wasn't it? Pan didn't really care one way or the other – they were all right, he'd hang with anybody, though he had his doubts about how much good they'd be trapping a lynx or shooting a moose or peeling logs for a cabin. And Sky Dog. He was in the backseat of the Lincoln amidst a heap of sleeping bags, cooking gear and a bleached-out tent that looked as if Eisenhower had used it in the Normandy Invasion, and his buddy Dale Murray was bringing up the rear on his bike. What was it Alfredo kept saying all week – the last thing we need is a freak parade? Well, here it was, and the sun was steady on the horizon, the gas tank topped up and the radio spewing rock and roll, and Pan, for his part, was proud and pleased to be part of it.

Not that it was all fun and games. Some real residual *nastiness* had come out when everybody was deciding whether they were going to sign up or drift on back to San Francisco or try to hook up with one of the other communes, and a whole raft of people just packed up and left. And then there was the question of space – who was going to ride where and when and with whom? For a few days there, brotherliness and sisterliness just broke down like an old junker with a thrown rod and refused to budge. It was a mess. Totally disorganized. Reba tried to crack the whip, and of course Alfredo had his nose in everything, and the Krishna cat (Tom Krishna, everybody was calling him now) came out of his Krishna funk long enough to show some real skill with a hammer and saw, and the chicks, all of them, kept putting things in boxes like a disaster-relief crew – but still, it looked as if Drop City was going nowhere right up until the minute the county dicks came up the drive in their county dick cars with the little gumball machines whirring on top and the bulldozers swung in off the highway.

At least they brought the bulldozers in the night before and left them out on the main road so everybody could get a good long look at them in case they needed their memories jogged – two Cats the size of houses, one on either side of the dirt drive. Mendocino Bill wanted to pour sand down the gas tanks, and to Pan's mind that wasn't a half-bad idea at all – he'd done plenty of that sort of thing out back of the development when he was a kid just for the pure uncomplicated destructive *rush* of it – but Norm said no, let them be. And that was no joy either, strung out across the hill in back holding hands and singing some lame Joan Baez song as the first of the Cats came clanking up the drive and took down the back house as if it were made of pasteboard and toothpicks, Jiminy shaking his fist and cursing, Star with tears burning down her cheeks and Norm all the while looking over his shoulder for the county sheriff with his arrest warrant. Dust rocketed up into the air. Walls fell. Harmony's yurt went down without so much as a whimper, and all Ronnie could think of was those World War II documentaries his father was always so obsessed with, the Battle of Britain, the Siege of Stalingrad, one wall down and a whole cozy little tea parlor exposed. And then *whump, whump,* the bombs hit again and the dust just rose and rose.

"So where do you think Norm's planning to stop tonight?" Star said over the decelerating thump of Canned Heat – a miracle of a little college station out of Portland, and Pan was the one with the nimble fingers to find it. "I mean, *if* he's going to stop, and with him there're no guarantees, right?"

"Right," Marco said, "but the more miles we make, the better."

"That's the theory," Ronnie said, and before the caravan left Drop City he'd hunted and gathered one hundred pharmaceutical-grade Dexedrine tablets from a cat he knew in the River Run bar in Guerneville and handed them out like candy – *at cost* – to anybody who was even thinking about getting behind the wheel.

Star's legs were bare, and her feet – perched up on the dashboard like two fluttering white birds – were bare too. She was wearing a white midriff blouse and a pair of cutoffs and probably nothing else beyond her own natural essence, though she sometimes dabbed a little extract of vanilla behind each ear and in the crease between her breasts. Ronnie leaned into her and took a furtive sniff. She smelled of sweat, of the natural oils and artificial emollients she used on her hair, and there it was – just the faintest hint of vanilla, like the residue at the bottom of the glass after you've finished your shake and let it sit on the counter half an hour. She'd wanted to ride in the bus. But what had he done? He'd begged and pleaded and made her feed on her own guilt through all its thousands of layers and permutations because they'd come all the way across the country in this very same car, with this very same radio and her very same feet perched up on the very same dash, and didn't that count for anything? All right, she'd said finally, all right, sure, yeah, of course. Of course I'll ride with you. But only if Marco comes too.

Now she said: "It takes all the fun out of it that way. I want to see the country – especially like when we get into Canada. I want to feel it between my toes and stretch out in the sun if only for like ten minutes, smell the air, you know, and I wonder if that's too much to ask?"

No one said anything. The scenery streamed by in a wash of gray, green, brown.

"And all these creeks and rivers – it's like they don't even exist, as if I'm imagining them – like there, right there, see that? – and I just want to get out and swim, swim all the way to Alaska, like in that Burt Lancaster movie where he swims home from one pool to another. Don't you want to do that? Don't you want to get out and swim? Or just splash around even?"

"Burt Lancaster?" Ronnie said. "What planet are you coming from?"

Marco snaked his arm up over the back of the seat and put it around her and pulled her close, a little act of intimacy Pan didn't pay even a lick of attention to. "Yeah, but don't you want to get there? Don't you want to see the place, all of those millions of acres for the taking, the lakes there, the rivers? See the cabin? Walk off the site where we're going to build? Plus," and he was smiling now, "I'll bet that water's just a wee bit chilly, wouldn't you think?"

Lydia's voice rose up out of the void of the backseat. "I'm hungry. And I have to pee."

Ronnie glanced over his shoulder to where Lydia lay sprawled beneath her breasts, then exchanged a look with Star. "Lydia's got a point," he said.

From the backseat: "What point? That I have to pee?"

Lydia was sitting up now, and he studied her a moment in the rearview mirror before he responded. She was looking good – if the light hit her just right, she could look very good, sultry, like one of those big-shouldered women in the Italian movies, her black hair windswept, her makeup smeared, and that randy, let's-lick-the-sauce-off-the-spoon-together look on her face.

"What I mean is, maybe it's time to pull over for the night. We've got to find a place to crash, right? And cook something up?"

"I don't know," Star said, "yeah, sure, I could stop."

So Ronnie calculated and took his chance and swung out into the fast lane till he came up abreast of the bus, the air roaring at the windows, insects giving themselves up to the superior force in a quickening series of thumps and splats – and why, he wondered, were they all uniformly yellow inside, was that their blood, was that it? And there was Norm, sitting up high in the driver's seat with his arms wrapped round the wheel as if it were the head of some seabeast he was wrestling, a fixed, no-nonsense, I-am-driving-the-bus look in his Dexedrine-tranced eyes, and Ronnie was flapping his left arm up over the roof of the car and laying on the horn. Marco rolled down the window and shouted to Norm to pull over at the next stop because Lydia had to pee and everybody was tired and hungry and wrung-out from driving straight through the first night and day and on into the evening that was even now spreading its wings out over the hills ahead of them like a big celestial bat.

Norm jerked his head back and gave them a faraway look, as if they were just anybody burning down the highway in a rusted-out Studebaker with New York plates, but then the shining white-hot gleam of recognition came into his eyes and he started fumbling with the little window at his elbow, all the while cupping a hand to his ear and pantomiming his bewilderment. What could they possibly want? Had he dropped a wheel? Run down a passel of Vietnamese orphans? Did the road ahead end in the sheer drop-off of a Roadrunner cartoon?

And this was fun, this was hilarious – anything for a little diversion. Side by side, hurtling down the road, Marco shouting and laughing, and Star and Lydia getting into the act now too, people in the bus – Premstar, Reba – making faces and sticking out their tongues like six-year-olds, *Casey Jones, you better watch your speed!* But then, gradually, Ronnie became aware of another sound altogether – a horn, sharp and insistent – and people on the bus were pointing behind him, like *look out,* and he brought his eyes up to the rearview mirror. It was only a heartbeat between awareness and recognition, but his first thought had been *the man,* what else? But it wasn't the man, it was three crewcut young Oregonian shit-flingers in a Ford pickup the color of arterial blood. They wouldn't have liked hippies, anyway, and Ronnie had seen *Easy Rider* – three times now and counting – but that didn't figure into the calculus of the moment. They were giving him the finger, riding his bumper, laying on the horn. Assholes. Redneck assholes. Red-faced redneck assholes.

Ronnie feathered the brakes, then feathered them again – and again, till the rednecks had to ride their own brakes and the bus slid ahead of them like a big yellow wall, Harmony's Bug, Lester's Lincoln and Dale Murray's ratcheting bike pulled along in its wake like the twisted little things it had given birth to. When Dale Murray cleared the Studebaker, Ronnie was going about twenty-five and the middle finger of his right hand was fixed just over the reflection of his eyes in the rearview mirror. He expected the rednecks to pass on his right in a flurry of hoots and catcalls, but they just held there in the passing lane, right on his tail, and so he eased in behind Dale Murray and hit the accelerator.

But the occupants of the pickup surprised him. They swung in behind the Studebaker and put on a sudden burst of speed, looming up on his rear bumper as if they meant to hook on to it. "Son of a bitch," Ronnie said, and it came out of him in a stunned and wounded gasp, as if he'd been punched in the stomach – he wasn't even driving anymore, just floating. And now Lydia made herself known, kneeling on the backseat so they could get a good look at her and alternately flashing the peace sign and blowing them kisses. Which enraged them even more. Twice they tapped the bumper – at something like fifty or fifty-five miles an hour, and what were they, not simple rednecks but redneck frat boys, because there were all the frat boy decals, delta upsilon, u. of oregon, go ducks, plastered across the windshield as if they meant something. Ronnie braced himself for the next thump.

"Are they crazy or what?" Marco said. He leaned out the window and showed them his fist.

The wind was wild, everybody's hair whipping, and it seemed to snatch the breath right out of Ronnie's lungs. "Stop the car," Marco shouted, whirling on him. "Just fucking pull over!"

Star said no. "Just forget it," she said. "Ignore them."

"Forget it?" Marco's face was like a bad dream, and Ronnie saw that and registered it, because there was a violent divide here, and he wouldn't want to find himself on the wrong side of it. Ever. "I'm going to fucking kill them, all three of them! You with me, Ronnie – Pan? You with me?"

Ronnie's hands were frozen on the wheel, his eyes pasted to

the rearview mirror. "Peace," Star kept saying, "peace and love, remember?" Ronnie looked at the three faces ranged across the hood of the car behind him, looked at Lydia's shoulders, the mad flying tangle of her hair, and his heart was looping back on itself. "I hear you, man," he said.

But then the whole procession was slowing, chain reaction – bus, Bug, Lincoln, motorcycle, Studebaker, pickup – and Norm had the big amber blinker going on the bus and the yellow wall was sliding into a turn, a side road, and there was the sign that spelled relief in foot-high letters: public campground, all cars welcome, 2$ per nite. Now, surely now, Ronnie was thinking, the pickup would peel away from them and vanish on down the highway, but no, it came on still, the faces behind the windshield taut and pale and vengeful.

The pavement gave out beneath him, and the Studebaker was thumping into a big rutted dirt lot interspersed with trees, barbecue smoke snatching at the air, cars and Winnebagos pulled up around tents and picnic tables, kids chasing each other in a flash of motion while white-legged old stick-people sucked bourbon out of paper cups and dogs yapped in a territorial frenzy, and this was it, America the beautiful, home of the brave, all cars welcome. Lydia had to pee. She was hungry. They were all hungry. But before Ronnie could twist the key off and set the brake, the three frat boys were at the driver's side window, and a hand, a meaty red outraged hand, was snatching at his hair, even as he flung his head back and away and Star let out with a screech that just about stopped his heart.

"Fucking longhair!"

"Get out of the car, asshole!"

All in a flash, it came to him that his antagonists weren't simply the frat boy rednecks he'd taken them to be, but frat boy redneck football players, or maybe weight lifters, all puffed up like toads in their Oregon Ducks T-shirts. One of them, the guy who'd been driving, was like a monument ripped from its pedestal with two livid eyes and a blond crewcut drilled into his skull. *Son of a bitch.* A bitter taste of impotence and rage clotted in Pan's throat, because he'd been here before and he knew what was coming. He was afraid, and then he wasn't, because all at once he was beyond fear, beyond anything, and he leaned back into the door and snatched at the handle at the very moment the meaty red hand converted itself into a fist that exploded in his left ear with a sound of wind rushing down a tunnel.

The sequel was mostly a blur, because he was dazed, that was it, though the speed was churning through him like a thousand little engines whizzing round the tracks of his veins, and he was in the car still, Star cradling his head. But Marco came round the hood of the Studebaker and slashed into the knot of them, that much he was sure of, and then Dale Murray and Sky Dog were there, and it was a scrimmage, everybody everywhere, down in the dirt and out across the lot, cursing and thumping at one another. Franklin stepped into it next, in one silent gliding motion, and put one of the frat boys down with a single blow, and now the whole bus was emptying out in a spangle of white-faced hippies and the old stick-people were sucking at their bourbon and all the flying kids gathering round and shouting in their piping attenuated half-grown voices.

Norm was the one who put an end to it. Two of the frat boys were on the ground and a whole flotilla of blunt-toed hippie boots was going at them at ramming speed, even while the third one – the driver – was engaged with Dale Murray, *slam, bam-bam,* as if this were a heavyweight bout, when Norm stepped between them and it stopped right there, just like that. "Enough!" he said. "Peace!" and he barked it out as if he were shouting "Maim!" or "Kill!"

They were bleeding in mosaic, all three of them, shuffling their feet in the dirt and huffing like fat men going up an endless flight of stairs. They were outnumbered. They had nothing to say. But Pan did, oh, yes, his head hanging out the window of the Studebaker now, and his life in this moment as sweet as anything on this planet. "Next time you want to beat up on a bunch of hippies, you better think twice, you sorry-ass mother-fuckers – "

They'd already edged back to their pickup, jeans, boots, T-shirts, muscles, and one of them, heaving still – the one with the blond crewcut and the scalp that shone through it like boiled ham – said, "Yeah, and fuck you too, all of you." That was what he said, but it was just bravado, and everybody knew it. The three of them slammed back into the pickup, wiping grit and blood out of their eyes, licking at split lips and wondering what that ringing in their ears was, and as they put it in gear Ronnie just sauntered up to them with a shit-eating grin and flashed the peace sign. They didn't even bother to spin the tires.

Later, when the jug of wine was going round and the chicks were spreading out loaves of bread and jars of peanut butter and jelly and mixing up pitchers of Kool-Aid and everybody was congratulating themselves on the way they'd handled things there in the naked dirt of the lot, Pan sprang his surprise. On the morning before they'd left, he'd taken the Studebaker down through Guerneville and the cut-over hills of the Russian River valley to Marshall, where the Pacific beat against the rocks and gave up a mist that hung in the sunlight like the smoke of a fire that never went out. The air was cold, the water colder. He waded right in in his cutoffs with Marco's hunting knife in one hand and two burlap sacks in the other.

There were gulls overhead, cormorants and pelicans scissoring the rolling green flats beyond the breakers. It was low tide, and the rocks were fortresses half-buried in the sand, every one of them glistening black with a breastwork of mussels. Pan worked under a pale sun, shivering in the wind that blew up out of nowhere and dodging the spray as best he could, and in the course of an hour he cut a hundred mussels from the rocks, two hundred, three, four, maybe even five, but who was counting? Back at the ranch, he rinsed and de-bearded them himself, and everybody was so preoccupied with the bus, with moving and packing and getting clear of the bulldozers, nobody even so much as glanced at him. He'd sneaked the two big sacks of mussels into the trunk of the Studebaker and set aside a pound of salted butter and half a dozen lemons from the tree out back of the pool. Now it was time to steam them. Now especially, because who wanted peanut butter and jelly on tasteless crumbling two-day-old home-baked bread, when they could glut themselves on the bounty of the sea?

Nobody said a word as he built a fire in one of the blackened cast-iron barbecue grills that grew up out of the dirt in the lee of each picnic table, but Merry – looking like two scoops of ice cream in a macramé top – drifted over when he set the five-gallon pot atop it. She handed him the nub of a joint she'd just removed from her lips, and nobody worried about that, about where the sacramental dope was going to come from through a long hard winter before they could have a chance to get a crop in the ground – nobody worried about anything, because this was the adventure, right here and now. He drew on the roach and she smiled. "What you got cooking?"

He shrugged, gave her back the smile. "Nothing. A little surprise. Something even a vegetarian could get behind."

She poked one of the sacks with a bare toe. "What?" She smiled wider. "Clams? Lobster?"

"You'll see. In about five minutes. But you wouldn't eat anything with a face on it, would you? You wouldn't even slap a mosquito or breathe in a gnat, right?" The roach had gone out. He handed it back to her for form's sake.

"I don't know. Depends, I suppose."

"On what?"

"On how hungry I am, and what's going in that pot. It's not meat, right?"

People had begun to set up tents in a cluster round the bus. Sky Dog, Dale Murray, Lester and Franklin were off by themselves, sitting on a picnic table in the near distance, their legs propped up on the buckled slats of the seats, and Sky Dog and Dale were strumming their guitars. A bunch of people were on the far side of the bus, visible only as lower legs and feet, and Che and Sunshine were at the center of a flying wedge of straight people's children, pale limbs, shouts, a kickball chasing itself from one end of the lot to the other.

"Would I do that to you?" Pan took a step back from the fire and glanced at the bus. The windows were down all along the near side and an invisible presence had just dropped the needle on "God Bless the Child," a tune he loved, and for a moment he just looked out across the lot and listened to the horns feed off the vocals. Then he turned back to Merry. "Where you sleeping tonight? The bus?"

"I guess."

"Want to sleep with me? Big seat in the back of that Studebaker. Or I might just do a sleeping bag on one of the picnic tables, like if there's no dew or rain or anything – "

"What about Lydia?"

"What about her?"

She settled into the corner of the picnic table with a shrug, one haunch balanced there, the dead roach pinched between her fingers. "I don't know," she said. "Where's she sleeping?"

He didn't answer her, just upended the first of the burlap sacks into the big gleaming pot. It was like shifting rocks. There was a clatter and a hiss, and then he dumped the other bag in. "That's a Billie Holiday song," he said, "you know that?"

"No," she said, "I didn't know. I thought it was like Blood, Sweat and Tears?"

"Originally, I mean. Like in the thirties or whenever."

"Oh, really? So it's like really old, huh?"

"Yeah," he said, and he looked off into the trees that weren't all that different from the trees at Drop City, or not that he could tell, anyway.

"What are those, mussels?"

"Yep. Pure protein, bounty of the sea. And wait'll you taste them with Pan's special lemon and butter sauce. You ever have mussels just steamed like clams or maybe dropped in a marinara sauce at the very last minute?"

She didn't know. And she was a vegetarian. But he watched her as the steam rose and butter melted in a pan and he sliced and squeezed the lemons, and she looked interested, definitely interested. "What about Jiminy," he said, "where's he sleeping?"

When she shrugged, her breasts lifted and fell. "In the bus, I guess."

He was thinking about Lydia, thinking about Star, about Marco and the way he'd put his arm around her and drawn her to him in the Studebaker. He'd gone to high school with her. They'd come all the way across the country together. "Sleep with me," he said. "What's it been, like weeks?"

That was when Reba came out of the trees with an armload of firewood and a hermetically sealed face, Alfredo trailing in her wake. He had a hatchet in one hand, a half-rotted length of pine in the other. Reba's eyes locked on the pot. "What's that?" she said. "You cooking something, Ronnie?" Oh, and now she smiled, oh yes indeed. "For everybody?"

She was wearing moccasins she'd stitched and sewed herself and she'd stuck an iridescent blue-black raven's feather in her beaded headband – give her a couple of slashes of war paint and she could have been a squaw in a John Ford movie, and that was funny because Star kept saying that all the way across country, that the whole hip style was just like playing cowboys and Indians, from the boots and bell-bottoms that were like chaps right on up to the serapes and headbands and wide-brimmed hats. He'd denied it at the time, simply because he hadn't thought about it and the notion scuffed at his idea of himself, but she was right, and he saw it in that moment. Reba was playing at cowboys and Indians, and so was he, and everybody else.

"It's mussels," he said. "Enough to feed the whole camp-ground, heads and straights alike."

Alfredo was standing there in his boots and denim shirt with a wondering look on his face, as if he'd just been cut down from the gibbet by his amigos in that very same western. "Mussels?" he echoed. "Where'd you get them?"

Pan was feeling good. Pan was feeling expansive and generous, feeling brotherly and sisterly. He gave them an elaborated version of his struggle against the sea two mornings ago.

And what was Alfredo's reaction? The reaction of the least-together, most tight-assed member of this whole peripatetic circus? How did he respond to Pan's selfless gesture and all the pride he took in it? He said, "You must be fucking crazy, man. Don't you realize they're quarantined this time of year?"

"Quarantined? What are you talking about?" If he was onto fishing licenses and seasons and all the rest of it, he might as well be talking to his shoes. "June doesn't have an *R* in it – "

Alfredo set down the hatchet and lifted the top from the pot. The mussels roiled blackly in the churning water. "Jesus," he said. "You could have poisoned all of us."

Ronnie peered into the pot, then looked to Merry and Reba before settling on Alfredo. "Bullshit," he said.

By now, some of the others had begun to gather round – Maya, Angela, Jiminy – and Ronnie had no choice but to hold his ground. "Bullshit," he repeated. "So what if they're quarantined?"

"Toxic shellfish poisoning," Alfredo said. "Something like four hundred people died of it one year in San Francisco at the turn of the century, I think it was. There's this dinoflagellate that will concentrate in huge numbers, like a red tide, when the water temperature gets above a certain level – in summer, only in summer – and the mussels, and clams and whatever, concentrate the toxin from them, and it doesn't bother the mussels at all, only us."

"You know the CIA?" Jiminy put in. His face was a sunlit wedge of nose, cheekbone and bright burning eye chopped out of the frame of his hair. He was thrilled, overjoyed, never happier. "Their assassins use it on a needle and they just prick you in a crowd, a little stab you can barely feel, and then you're dead."

"Paralyzed," Reba said. "First your extremities go, then your limbs, until you're a vegetable and you can't move anything or feel anything – "

"Right," Alfredo said, " – and then it shuts down the vital organs."

There was an aroma on the air now, a sweet scintillating smell of mussels steamed in their own juices with butter and lemon, salt and pepper and maybe a hint of tarragon. Ronnie wasn't hovering over a picnic table at a two–dollar–a–night campground in Oregon, he was inside a cage at the zoo, and all these people – his friends, his compatriots, his brothers and sisters – were poking at him through the bars with sharpened sticks. "Bullshit," he said for the third time. "I don't believe it."

"Believe it," Alfredo said, already turning to leave, and he was taking a whole raft of faces with him. Merry looked as if she'd been shoved over a cliff, and Jiminy was just waiting for the signal to get down on all fours and start barking like a dog.

Alfredo. Dinoflagellates. Quarantine. Ronnie was having none of it – it was nonsense was what it was, just another stab at him, as if it would kill Alfredo if he ever got any credit for anything. He stirred the pot, fished out a specimen and set it on the wooden plank of the table. It was perfect, tender – you can't cook them a heartbeat too long or you'll be chewing leather – the slick black shell peeking open to reveal the pink-orange meat within, and he was going to hold it up for Merry and run through his mussel routine, about how the lips and the flesh looked like a certain part of the female anatomy and how at medical schools the gynecology students had to study steamed mussels because the real thing was so hard to come by, but Merry was gone, her arm slipped through Jiminy's, bare feet in the dust, off to consume her ration of stale bread and peanut butter.

Only Angela, Verbie's narrow-eyed, lantern-jawed sister, stayed behind to watch as Ronnie forced open the two leaves of the shell – *bivalves,* the term came hurtling back to him from Mr. Boscovich's Biology class, that's what they were, *bivalves,* and all the tastier for it – removed the glistening pink morsel and tentatively laid it on his tongue. "You're not really going to eat that, are you?" she said, and he might as well have been the geek in the circus with his incisors bared over the trembling neck of the squirming chicken while the crowd held its collective breath. Of course he was going to eat it, of course he was.

It took him a long moment, his tongue rolling the bit of flesh round his mouth, before he brought his teeth into play. And what was wrong with that? The juices were released, butter, tarragon, the sea, and the taste was fine, great even – this was the best and freshest mussel he'd ever had, wasn't it? He chewed thoughtfully, lingeringly. And then he spat the discolored lump into his hand and flung it into the bushes.

19

Star had never stolen a thing in her life, even when she was twelve or thirteen and pushing the limits and there was a compact or tube of eyeliner she could have died for and nobody was looking because her friends had distracted the old lady at the counter and they'd all got something in their turn – a comb, a package of gum, M&M's – as if it were a badge of honor. It wasn't that she didn't have the nerve – it was just that she'd been brought up to respect private property, to do right and think right and be a moral upstanding good little Catholic girl. But here she was in a supermarket just outside Seattle, smoking a cigarette in front of the cheese display in the dairy section, the pockets she'd sewn into the lining of her coat heavy with fancy imported cheeses, with Gouda and smoked cheddar and Jarlsberg, and never mind that it was eighty-two degrees outside and nobody else in the world was wearing a coat or even a sweater.

Reba and Verbie were pushing a cart down the aisle across from her, moving slowly, prepared to trade food stamps for fresh produce, whole wheat bread and family-sized sacks of rice and pinto beans, all the while secreting cans of tuna, crabmeat and artichoke hearts in the purses that dangled so insouciantly from their shoulders. "It's a family thing," Reba explained as they were coming across the macadam lot, " – feed the family, that's all that matters. This place, this whole chain, is just part of the establishment, them against us, a bunch of millionaires in some corporate headquarters somewhere, devoting their lives to screwing people over the price of lettuce. Don't shed any tears for them." Ronnie, who'd driven the three of them over in the Studebaker, couldn't have agreed more. "Fucking fascists," was his take on it.

Still, her heart was going as she drew on her cigarette and

pretended to deliberate over the cardboard canister of Quaker Oats in her hand, her brow furrowed and her eyes drawn down to slits over the essential question of 100% Natural Rolled Oats versus one dollar and sixty-nine cents. She didn't see the man in the pressed white shirt and regulation bow tie until he was on top of her. "Finding everything all right?" he asked.

She met his eyes — a washed-out gray in a pink face surmounted by Brylcreemed hair with the dead-white precision part that was as perfect as the ones you saw in the pictures in the barbers' windows. He was twenty-five, he'd knocked up his girlfriend and dropped out of high school, and he'd been working in this place since he was sixteen. Or something like that. He was a member of the straight world, and that was all that counted. He was the enemy. Star never flinched, though her heart was going like a drum solo. "No," she said, "not really," and she could see Reba and Verbie draw in their antennae at the far end of the aisle — she was in this on her own now. "I was just looking for like a really nutritious cereal for my daughter? I don't want her eating all that junk we had as kids, Sugar Pops and Frosted Flakes and whatnot. So I was thinking oats, maybe. Just plain oats. With milk."

"How old?" He was smiling like all the world, the assiduous employee coming to grips with the discerning shopper.

"What?"

"Your daughter — how old is she?"

"Oh, her . . ." And to cover herself, she made up a name on the spot. "Jasmine? I named her Jasmine, isn't that a pretty name?"

"Oh, yeah," he said. "Very pretty." He paused. "It does get cold in here, doesn't it?"

For a moment, she was at a loss. Cold? What was he talking about? She looked down at her coat, and then back up again, and her heart was in her mouth. "I'm very sensitive to it," she said finally, trying to keep her voice under control. "I'm from down south, this little town in Arizona? Yuma? You ever hear of it?" He hadn't. "*Johnny* Yuma?" she tried. Nothing. She shrugged. "It's just that you've got all these refrigerators going in here, the meat, the dairy — "

He just nodded, and she realized he could see right through

her, knew damned well what she was doing, saw it ten times a day. Especially from the likes of her, from heads, hippies, bikers, renegades of every stripe, *chicks*. "You know, I have three kids myself. The oldest one, Robert Jr. – Bobby – he's in the second grade already. And they all eat nothing but junk, the sugariest cereal, candy, pop – "

"Oh, well, Jasmine," and it came to her that he wasn't going to say a thing, just so long as she played out the game with him, "she's only like one and a half or something, you know, and she's, uh, well, I don't want to get her into any bad habits, if you know what I mean."

Oh, yes, he knew – she didn't have to tell him. And could he help with cereals? Cream of Wheat was good, if you cooked it with milk instead of water, and farina, of course. By the way, was she from around here, because he didn't remember – ?

So that was it. He was hitting on her, just like any other *cat*. Just in case. Just on the off chance.

"We just moved in," she said. "My husband's in Aerospace." And then she thanked him and found herself stuck at the checkout across from Reba and Verbie with the Quaker Oats still in hand. Her heart was doing paradiddles, but she laid a wrinkled bill on the counter and prised the change out of her pocket, and then she was out in the parking lot and heading for the Studebaker, the very Queen of Cheese.

They got a late start out of Seattle that night, because Norm had taken Harmony's Bug and gone to see his uncle and stayed through the afternoon and on into the evening while everybody else sat on the bus and wondered if they'd been deserted. Norm had pulled the bus off at the first exit he came to and found a spot to park in a patch of weed at the side of a two-lane blacktop road. It was an ugly spot, the trees nothing more than scrub, some sort of factory putting out smoke in the near distance and the ubiquitous ranch houses of suburban America clustered all round them. Some of the men gathered up twigs and refuse and got a fire going, and the best the women could do was throw together a kind of paella, thick with appropriated tuna and greens and whatever spices they could find that weren't already packed away.

Cars shot by like jet planes. The shouts of kids at play came to them as ambient noise. People ate hurriedly, guiltily even, because this wasn't what anybody expected. Even Che and Sunshine seemed lethargic, disoriented, and they barely touched their plates. Around eight, right in the middle of the meal, two men in sport shirts made their way across the street from a white ranch house with cream-colored trim and a new red car sitting in the driveway. "There's no camping here," Star heard one of the men say to no one in particular, and heard the other one say, "And no fires." After that, everybody climbed back on the bus and circled the block a couple of times, Lester and Ronnie in tow, till they wound up back where they'd started and just sat in the vehicles with nowhere to go and nothing to do, waiting for Norm as the darkness settled in. When he finally did appear and the caravan moved off again, they felt as if they'd all been rescued.

It was past midnight when Reba broke out the crabmeat and the smoked oysters and all the rest of it, and Star delivered up the cheeses. The bus was moving through the wall of the night. There was the green glow of the dash, a soft lateral rocking as if they were all inside a giant cradle. Norm was up front, his hands clenched round the wheel, Premstar squeezed into the cracked vinyl seat along with him. Ronnie was a pair of headlights somewhere behind them, Mendocino Bill and Verbie and her sister keeping him company, taking their turn, share and share alike. Marco, who'd gone along with Norm to visit the uncle – "To keep him company, and find out exactly where that mountain of gold is located, just in case we need some spare change" – was in the back of the bus with Alfredo and some of the others, playing cards under a light Bill had rigged up. The kids were asleep. So was practically everybody else.

And so it was Reba, Merry, Maya, Lydia and Star, the women, spread out across three seats, gossiping and feasting as the bus jostled down the road and the vague lights of single homes, gas stations and farmhouses flashed at the windows in an unreadable code. "You get tired of just plain fare all the time, you know?" Reba said. "Tofu paste. Tahini. Brown rice. Even though it's healthy. Even though I'm committed to it. But this" – and she laid a sardine across a thin slice of wheat bread, licking the oil from her fingers – "this isn't just a luxury, this is a *necessity,* know what I mean?"

Appropriated crackers went round, more bread, a bottle of Liebfraumilch Reba had liberated from the liquor department. They all knew what she meant. And Star ate wedges of cheese and licked the oil from her own fingers – smoked oysters, that was her weakness – savoring the moment. In the inner fold of her backpack, the pouch between the frame and the main compartment, way down at the bottom and wrapped in a sock, were three one-hundred-dollar bills nobody knew about, not Marco, not Ronnie, not Merry or Maya. This was what she had left of her nest egg, the money she'd accumulated before she quit teaching, living dirt cheap at her parents' house when her only expenses were for records and clothes and maybe a Brandy Alexander or Black Russian at the Surf 'N' Turf, the nearest thing to a club Peterskill could offer; the rest had gone for gas and food coming across country, and everything since – food stamps, unemployment, whatever her mother managed to send c/o Drop City – had vanished into the communal pot. There was no way she was breaking those three bills, whether for luxury or necessity, and besides, Norm had guaranteed he'd float everybody through the first winter, at least as far as the basics were concerned.

Lydia, lounging in the seat across from Star, said "Paté," as if she'd been thinking about it for weeks. "That's what turns me on. And those celery sticks with blue cheese inside. Swedish meatballs on a toothpick. Canapés and champagne. They used to have these parties at the place I used to work, and I'd just camp in front of the hors d'oeuvres tray and pig out."

"Will this do?" Reba said, and she leaned forward in the flicker of passing headlights and handed Lydia a box of Ritz crackers and two cans of deviled ham.

"Lobster," Merry said. "With drawn butter."

"You haven't lived till you've had the Crab Louis at this place called Metzger's on Tomales Bay," Maya put in. "I went there once, just after high school, with – "

"I know," Reba said, " – this guy named Jack. With hair down to his ass and a Fu Manchu mustache."

Star laughed. They all laughed.

Maya's voice went soft. "Actually, it was with my parents. They took me and my brother out west on a vacation. For my graduation present."

No one had anything to say to that, and they were all silent a moment as the bus lurched through a series of broad sweeping turns, heading for the Canadian border. The engine propelled them forward with a steady *whoosh,* as if there were a big vacuum cleaner under the hood. Wind beat at the windows, a spatter of rain. They could hear Norm's voice from up front, an unceasing buzz of fancy, opinion and incontestable fact fueled by Ronnie's speed and Premstar's lady-lotion skin, and who liked Premstar, who could even stand her? Nobody. On that, they were all in silent accord.

"Shrimp cocktail," Reba said, feeding another sardine into her mouth. "For my money," and she was chewing round her words, "a good shrimp cocktail, with big shrimp now, shrimp as long as your middle finger, with a spicy cocktail sauce and served on a little bed of ice, that's what I'd go for every time."

Star said, "Pistachios. In the shell. And your fingers get all red. Has anybody in this world *ever* had enough of those?"

"You know," Merry said, and her voice was so drawn down and muted you could barely hear her, "I haven't seen my parents since I was sixteen. That's like five years. I can't believe it. And I don't hate them or anything either. It's just the way things worked out."

"Where you from again?" Reba wanted to know.

Softly, as if it were a prayer, or the name of a prayer: "Cedar Rapids."

"Cedar Rapids? Where's that?"

"It's in Iowa," Lydia answered for her.

"Oh, *Iowa,*" Reba said, and she made it sound as unhip and lame as Peoria or New Jersey, and Star felt the mood start to slip away.

"There was this guy," Merry began, her face lit suddenly by a pair of headlights, then sinking into shadow, "this cat, and he was twenty-three and he had his own car and money like I'd never seen before, like rolls of twenties and whatever. But that's not what did it – I wasn't like that. I'm not like that now. Money didn't mean anything to me, except that it could buy you freedom – and my parents, *Jesus,* and my school. You know the story. Everybody does, right?"

No one rose to the bait. Star shifted in her seat. She could hear Lydia forcing her hand down into the box of crackers.

"His name was Tommy Derwin and he was from down south, Mobile, and his accent just killed me. The way he would say things, like 'Ahm just honahed that you would con-sent to be mah date tonight, Miss Merra Voight,' and then he'd take me to a bar in Iowa City where nobody ever got carded and then a motel, as man and wife, on the way back to Cedar Rapids. I never thought twice. He said let's go to San Francisco, that's where the scene is, and I went."

Lydia was passing out crackers smeared with deviled ham, and Star took one, and so did Reba, but Maya and Merry passed – ham was meat, after all, pig, dead pig, no matter how you disguised it. "So what then?" Lydia said, and she wiped her lips with the back of her hand.

"We stayed a couple places. People he knew. We did drugs. I worked checkout at a Walgreens for a while, and when nobody was looking I'd shake pills out of bottles, you know, that sort of thing." The cheese came round, and they all watched as Merry cut herself two thick slices and fitted them to crackers. "I don't know," she said. "And then we joined this commune – Harrad House? It wasn't like this, not at all. More into sex. A group marriage kind of thing."

"And how was that?" This was Lydia, the resident expert. "Did you have to sleep with everybody?"

"I'd hate that," Star said. "I'd really hate that."

"Sounds groovy to me," Lydia said. "The more the merrier."

Reba laughed out loud. She took a long swallow of the wine and passed the bottle to Lydia. "That's what you say now, but believe me – I mean, before I met Alfredo, I was pretty wild, like I was in heat all the time, like the only way I could relate to men was in bed, but that got old fast. Real fast. Right, Merry? You agree?"

"It stunk. There were way more guys than girls and Tommy was like a ghost or something – I hardly ever even saw him. I was on my back half the time, and if I refused some guy, one of the family members, I was the one who was uptight, I was the one spreading the bad vibes and poisoning the atmosphere, because that was the way it was. The bedroom down the hall. Take off your clothes. Five a.m., five p.m. Let's ball." She paused, and her voice sank right down through the floorboards. "Everybody had jobs, like mop the floor, cook the pasta, go out and bring in a paycheck. My job was to fuck. Like a machine. Like a goat."

"Where's Verbie when we need her – Women's Lib, right?" Reba said, missing the point. As usual.

Star could feel her heart going, and it was as if she were back in the supermarket again with fifteen dollars' worth of cheese shoved down her coat. "It's the Keristan Society all over again."

"The who?"

But she was staring out the window now on a scene from another century, the sharp-edged pines and a farmhouse framed in its own pale glow and the shadow of the barn beyond. They were asleep in there, the farmer and his wife, the kids, the dog. There would be an old oak table in the kitchen, heavy pink Fiesta ware set out for breakfast, a calendar on the wall. The refrigerator would clank on, it would hum, and then shut down, and no one would even notice, not even the dog.

"I don't know," she said. "It's not important."

They reached the border sometime after two. Star was asleep, curled up awkwardly in one of the bunks, and she felt the bus shift beneath her as if the whole world were in motion, then it shuddered and came to a halt, and she was awake. They were off on the side of the road, parked beneath a sign that said international boundary 2 miles. Norm was coming down the aisle, rousing people from sleep. "It's the border, people, come on, wake up," he was saying, his face a pale bulb hanging in the gloom, his shoulders hunched and arms dangling as if he'd lost the use of them. This was it. This was the big moment. If they couldn't get into Canada, then they couldn't get to Alaska, and Drop City was dead.

Marco was in the bunk beneath her, and he woke with a start. She reached a hand down to him, her hair trailing, and edged over the side of the bunk so she could see him. He was staring at nothing, the moistness of his eyes just catching enough light to show her they were open. "Hey," she said, as gently as she could, "we're here. Time to wake up."

"Shit," he said, and he brushed her hand aside. "Already?" He pushed himself up and slid out of the bunk all in one motion, and then he was running his fingers through his hair and tucking in the tail of his shirt. People were shuffling around like zombies, bumping into one another, cursing softly. The dogs began to whine. Somebody sneezed. "Where's Ronnie?" he said, and there was an edge to his voice she didn't recognize. "Where's Pan? Is he here?"

For the past two days all he could talk about was the border, the border this and the border that, and how he ought to sneak across in the trunk of the Studebaker or find someplace out in the middle of nowhere where he could just step from one country to the other as easily as moving from the front of the bus to the back. Star had tried to talk him out of it, because if they opened the trunk – and why wouldn't they? – they'd nail him on the spot, but there were thirty people on the bus, not to mention two dogs and a cat, and the chances of their checking on everybody were slim. Especially in the middle of the night.

"You don't need Ronnie," she said. "Just sit tight, that's all. Everything's going to be fine," she said, and then she said it again, as if the words could make it so.

"All right," Norm was saying, and his voice was up to its usual volume now, somewhere between a shout and a roar, "all right, everybody just listen. The border's two miles ahead, and we are just going to breeze right on through it, no hassles, no worries. You know what we are? All of us? We're a rock band."

Weird George let out a groan.

"No, we are. And we've got big dates in Fairbanks and Anchorage, and where else? I don't know, Sitka. You people with guitars get 'em out, and a little strumming or even a group sing here would be nice, you know what I mean? Know what I'm saying?"

It was two-thirty in the morning. They were at the Canadian border. Nobody felt like singing.

"All right. Just let me do the talking. And you chicks – come on, you chicks, you Drop City Miracles – try to look sexy, right? You're the backup singers."

That got a laugh, and you could feel the tension lift. People started chattering, the guy – *cat* – everybody called Deuce pulled out his harmonica and started a slow blues, and pretty soon Geoffrey joined him on guitar and two of the back-of-the-bus girls, Erika and Dunphy, let loose with a few random verses of "Love in Vain." Norm took his hunched shoulders back up to the front of the bus, where Premstar was perched on the driver's seat like a present he'd forgotten to unwrap. Marco gave Star a look, and then followed him. "Norm," he was saying, "listen, Norm – I need to talk to you a second." She slid down from the bunk, afraid suddenly, and went after him.

Then the door of the bus wheezed open and the three of them – Norm, Marco and Star – were standing by the roadside with Ronnie and Mendocino Bill while the Studebaker idled behind its headlights in a pall of exhaust. A light rain spat down out of the sky and made the pavement glisten. Someone had broken a bottle here, and Star had to be careful where she put her feet. "So what do you want to do, then," Norm said, "walk across? That wouldn't draw any attention or anything, would it?"

"If they catch me I go to jail."

"Relax, man, nobody's going to catch you. It's Canada, that's all. Bunch of hicks, right, Pan? Am I right? Star?"

The Studebaker's headlights threw a cold lunar glare on Marco's face. He ducked his head as if the Mounties were already on him, snapping whips. "What about Pan's car? The trunk, I mean?"

Norm shook his head very slowly. His eyes jumped behind the lenses of his patched-up glasses. "We used to sneak into the drive-in like that. I think we got two cats and a chick in there one night, and then I couldn't get the trunk open." He laughed. "That was pretty wild. That was one wild night, let me tell you."

Ronnie said, "I don't think so. If they like open the trunk, then I'm the one in deep shit, right? I'm a smuggler, right?"

Nobody said anything. Star took hold of Marco's arm. "Come on," she said. "Let's get back on the bus. Let's get it over with."

"Plus, I've got all my dope back there – *our* dope. Inside the spare tire. And that would be a major fuckup. I mean, if they found that."

Lester's Lincoln pulled up then, and a moment later Dale Murray ratcheted in on his bike. Suddenly there was a whole lot of engine noise. And fumes. Lester rolled down the window. "So what now?" he said. "We go across, or what?"

"Fuck, I'm freezing," Dale Murray said. He was wet through, his hair painted to both sides of his face. "We got to stop and camp or something or I think I'm going to fucking die."

"We go across separately," Norm said, "because we don't want to give them a whole hippie freak show all at once. Ronnie, you're first. Then you, Lester. And, Dale, you go through anytime you want, just make like you don't know us – nobody knows anybody, dig? – and when we're on the other side we'll see if maybe we can't get the bike aboard the bus somehow. How does that sound? Is it a plan?"

Star was the only one who said anything, and she could barely hear herself over the ratcheting of the bike. "Yeah," she said. "It's a plan."

Up ahead, the night bloomed with artificial light, trucks braking amidst the fading ghosts of cars, the Peace Arch aglow like an alien spaceship set down in a field of darkened wheat. There were gray metal booths bright with windows, figures in some kind of uniform moving like skaters across the shimmer of pavement. Ronnie's car swung out ahead of the bus, out in the left lane, and everybody pressed their faces to the windows. They watched as the Studebaker's taillights flashed red in a shroud of smoldering exhaust and a figure emerged from the near booth. The rain had quickened, beating with real authority now at the roof of the bus and driving pewter spikes into the roadway and the soft shrouded chassis of the cars. The figure leaned into Ronnie's window – fifteen seconds, that was all it took – then straightened up and waved him on. Star watched the Studebaker ease forward and fold itself back into the night.

Norm had pulled in behind a truck and the truck was taking its time. Nobody could see what the delay was because the back end of the truck was blocking their view, but the guitars kept strumming and half a dozen people were singing Beatles songs now – first "Rocky Raccoon," and then "Everybody's Got Something to Hide Except Me and My Monkey," the choice of which would have struck Star as nothing short of hilarious if it weren't for Marco. Poor Marco. He was huddled against the window in the seat beside her, sunk into the upturned collar of his denim jacket. His hair was like tarnished gold, like winter-killed weeds in a vacant lot. His eyes were drawn down to nothing. "I'm doing this for you," he said. "I hope you know that."

Then it was Lester's car, pulling up into the space vacated by

Ronnie's. The same figure emerged from the booth, only the figure was wearing a rain slicker now and it – he – produced a flashlight and shined it in Lester's face. In the next moment, the truck was creeping forward, its blinkers flashing, and Norm was moving up to the booth even as the man with the flashlight waved Lester into the farthest lane over – the lane reserved for searches and seizures – and Lester, Franklin and Sky Dog all climbed out of the car and into the rain.

But before anybody could even think to worry about that, the bus lurched to a stop, the door folded back with a wheeze, and a man in a yellow rain slicker came up the steps. "Greetings," Norm shouted. "It's a bear out there, huh?"

The man nodded and said something in a low voice to Norm and Premstar. From where she was sitting, Star could see him only as a dull yellow glow, like something growing in the dirt of a cellar. Behind her, all the way in the back, people were singing "I Want to Hold Your Hand."

"American," Norm said, and then Premstar, her voice floating back to Star like a fluff of dander on a sterile breeze, pulled her chin down and concurred: "American," she said.

The man in the slicker said something else, and Star couldn't catch it.

"Just passing through," Norm said in a ringing voice. "We're a rock band. Big dates in Alaska, they're just dying for us up there – not that we wouldn't want to perform for you Canadians too, but that'll have to wait till next time. We're booked, know what I mean?"

One by one, the people in the back stopped singing, aware now that something was going on up front. Star leaned forward. Marco shrank into the seat.

"What *band*?" Norm called out in disbelief. "You mean you don't recognize us?"

The man in the slicker shook his head from side to side. Star could see his face now – he was grinning. She saw the flash of his teeth in a face so red he might have been holding his breath all this time for all anyone knew.

"Oh, man, you're hurtin' me," Norm said, and he shot a look down the length of the aisle, mugging now, "you're really hurtin' me. Give you a hint," he said. " 'Sugar Magnolia'?

'Truckin' '? 'Friend of the Devil'? No? Oh, man, you're killin'
me. All right, Premstar, you tell him – "

The tiny wisp of her voice: "The Grateful Dead."

The man in the yellow slicker was grinning still, and so was
Norm, as if it were some kind of contest. "You've heard of us,
right?"

"Oh, yeah," the man said, his voice muffled by the floppy
yellow rain hat, "sure, yeah, I've heard of you."

"I'll be happy to give you an autograph if you want, no
problem, man," Norm said, and he held out his hand and the
man took it.

Then the man said something Star missed, and Norm swiveled
around in the seat and looked down the length of the bus. "All
right, people, just give this gentleman your attention a minute
here now, because he just wants to ask everybody if they're a
citizen, okay? Okay, now?"

Down the aisle the man in the slicker came, red-faced and
grinning, and Star saw that he was older – gray hair in his
sideburns – older even than Norm. He didn't want any trouble.
He didn't want anything, except to be out of the bus and back
in his booth. "American citizen?" he asked. "American citizen?"
And everybody said yes, and then, just for variety, he asked,
"Where were you born?" and people said Buffalo, San Diego,
Charleston, Staten Island, Kansas City, Hornell. They watched
his face as he came down the aisle, and they watched his
shoulders as he made his way back up it. Che and Sunshine
slept on. The dogs never even lifted their heads.

There was a smattering of nervous laughter when he descended the steps, and the laughter boiled up into a wild
irrepressible storm of hoots and catcalls and whinnying shrieks
as the door pulled shut and Norm put the bus in gear and headed
off toward the lights of Canada. Star alone looked back. The last
thing she saw was Lester, up against the rain-washed Lincoln, and
a man in a yellow slicker patting him down.

20

Though they hammered it twenty-four hours a day up through Canada and over the infinite roaring dirt incline that was the Alaska Highway, stopping only for gas and the bodily needs of thirty-one tight-lipped claustrophobes, the bus held up. By Marco's count, it broke down three times, once just outside of Prince George, the second time at the crest of Muncho Pass, and then in a place that was no place at all, but Mendocino Bill and Tom Krishna were equal to the task and they were never stranded more than an hour or two. People played cards, read, slouched, strummed guitars. They made love under blankets, passed mugs of coffee, Coke and herbal tea from hand to hand and row to row, got stoned, dozed and woke and dozed again. Norm barely slept. And when he did sleep, crumpled across one of the seats as if he'd been deboned, Marco or Alfredo took over at the wheel, humping through country that made your eyes ache with the emptiness of it. Even Pan pitched in, turning the Studebaker over to Star and propelling the bus on through the dwindling hours of the night when nobody else could keep their eyes open. There were no Mounties, no speed traps, no cops of any kind anywhere. The scenery bared its claws. All anybody wanted was to get there, just that.

Vanderhoof, Smithers, Cranberry Junction, Johnson's Crossing, Whitehorse, Marsh Lake, Destruction Bay, Burwash Landing, so many ticks on a map, hello and goodbye. They saw a big rig folded up on itself in Wonowon, a dead moose stretched out in the dirt beside it and a calf the size of a quarter horse running wild with grief. There was a fire burning along the banks of the Donjek River, flames peeling off the tops of the trees and riding up into the night sky and not a human being in sight. They made a pit stop at Haines Junction and inadvertently left Jiminy behind, looping back nearly a hundred miles to find him standing in the rain by the gas pumps, his thumb outstretched and a look of cosmic incapacity bleeding out of his eyes. Out the window the rivers fled in gray streaks, the Takini, the Goodpaster, the Tetsa, the Sikanni Chief, the Prophet, the Rabbit and the Blue.

When they reached Alaska intact, as improbable as that might have seemed when they set out, the bus still rolling over its ten wheels and the Studebaker and Bug flagging on behind, everybody singing, sandwich-fed and hopeful, they pulled off to the side of the road and sat in a circle, hands clasped, while Reba and Tom Krishna led them in a chant. This was in a place called Northway Junction, forty-two miles from the border and the customs agents who wore flannel shirts, sipped coffee out of styrofoam cups and waved everybody on through, good morning and welcome to the U.S. of A. Reba's kids strung up God's eyes they'd made of yarn and strips of wood and Alfredo drew a big mandala in the dirt with a crooked stick, working back and forth over the pattern like a dowser looking for water until it showed dark against the pale duff of the forest floor. People lit candles and incense and circulated one of Harmony's big ceramic bongs.

The air was heavy with the smell of rain-soaked vegetation, of berries run riot and a sun that soaked up the moisture and gave it back again, day after day. It was a smell that brought Marco back to his childhood on the east coast, and he realized that this wasn't the west anymore, this wasn't California or Oregon – this was the same sort of environment he'd grown up in, the rolling boreal forest of the northeast extended all the way out here as the globe narrowed toward the pole. He remembered reading Thoreau's *The Maine Woods* in college and marveling over the fact that there had been caribou in Maine no more than a century ago, right out there amongst the spruce and hardwoods – and now here he was in a place where there were caribou still, the chain yet unbroken. Staggered by the thought, he wandered up the road a hundred yards, half-expecting to see a herd of them just off the shoulder, but there was nothing to see but the dust of the road flung up into the trees and ladled a quarter inch thick over the weeds. He ambled back to the sound of a truck straining up the grade and took his place in the circle.

He'd been there no more than a minute or two, accepting the bong from Maya, taking a dutiful hit and passing it on, when Star came out of the clearing behind them with an armful of wild-flowers, flushed and smiling; he watched her dance round the group, dispensing flowers, and then she settled in beside him, a lavender spray of fireweed tucked behind each ear, and what was that song that made him grit his teeth every time he heard it – something about going to San Francisco with flowers in your hair? Whatever hack was responsible for that drivel should have seen Star in that moment and he might have learned something about flowers and hair.

She was in a blue-and-white granny dress that brought out the color of her eyes, and the material strained against her knees and the long smooth slope of her thighs as she eased herself down. He put his arm around her to pull her in close, and as he did – in that exact moment – there was a flurry overhead and a quick-beating outsized bird that might have been an emperor goose or maybe an eagle, shot low through the trees and vanished so quickly nobody could be sure they'd seen it, and maybe none of them had, since just about everybody had their eyes closed. He let out a low exclamation. "Did you see that?" he said.

She turned to him as if for a kiss, her hair soft against his face. "Yes!" she said. "Yes! Wasn't it amazing? What was it – a hawk?"

"I don't know, but it's a good omen, don't you think?"

Tom Krishna was leading a chant. Everybody clasped hands and she leaned away a moment to take hold of the person on her left – it was Weird George, with chicken bones knotted in his hair and a string of garlic cloves slung round his neck to ward off vampires – and then came back to him and intertwined her fingers with his. "I'm so happy," she said. "I never knew I could be this happy, never even suspected it. Aren't you happy too? Couldn't you just die for it?"

He told her he was. And he could.

In Fairbanks, Norm pulled the bus up in front of a diner, and they all filed out, everybody, the whole family, including the dogs, while the goats bleated from their ramshackle pen and Che and Sunshine shot up and down the sidewalk like guided missiles. Nobody had ever seen anything like it. Cars stopped dead in the middle of the street. People came out of stores, the barber shop, town hall. And Drop City, arrayed in all its finery, went into the diner in shifts and ate them out of milk shakes, ice cream, grilled cheese, hamburgers, tuna salad, lettuce, lemon meringue pie and soup of the day, and all of it at triple the price they would have paid in California because every mouthful had to be shipped up from the lower forty-eight. Marco counted out his share and he paid for Star, too, but he sank into his denim jacket and pulled the collar up as if he could lose himself in it – he hadn't seen a salmon yet. Or a caribou. A bear. Even a rabbit.

"Don't worry about the money," Star told him, tucking the shining ropes of her hair behind her ears. She hadn't washed it in a week. Nobody had washed, but for the odd splash under the faucet at a truck stop or gas station, and Norm refused to stop for a communal scrub-down or swim or anything else though they passed a thousand glittering streams and rivers and lakes so clear they weren't even lakes but a kind of subset of the air. Keep it rolling, twenty-four hours a day, that was Norm's motto.

"I'm not worried," Marco said, but he was.

Star leaned across the table and took hold of his wrists. "This is America up here, that's the beauty of it. We can get food stamps, unemployment, welfare, just like anyplace else." Behind her, outside on the street where the sun raked at their sloping brows and kinked their hair and brought the angles of their cheekbones and noses into unblunted relief, three squared-up middle-aged women in flower-print dresses gaped through the window as if they were at the zoo. If he were in a lighter mood, Marco would have waved to them or maybe skewed his tongue in the corner of his mouth and scratched at his armpits, er-er-er. As it was, he just dropped his eyes. "Besides," she said, lowering her voice, "I have a few bucks put away. For emergencies. And you're definitely an emergency, you know that?"

He didn't know what to say to this, and he was irritated, impatient, tired of the whole dog and pony show. Where were the trees to cut and peel and notch, where was the river, where were the postcard vistas, the fish, the game, nature red in tooth and claw and just crying out to be manipulated and subdued – and enjoyed? What about enjoyment? Where was that on the schedule? He was wrung-out. Depressed. His throat was sore. In his pocket there were sixteen dollars and eighty-seven cents, and when that was gone, there'd be a long precious wait for food stamps and welfare and whatever else the all–giving and Great Society wanted to dole out – and how would the checks even get to them out in the bush? Was there mail delivery up the Yukon? Parcel post? Carrier pigeon? "I'm not worried," he repeated.

Across the room, too wrought up even to sit, Norm swayed over the Formica–topped tables, forking up the macaroni and cheese special with a side of Waldorf salad, his eyes sucked back into his head with fatigue, exhorting them to eat up, get with it, *mobilize*. "A hundred sixty more miles," he rasped, too depleted to shout. "An inch and a half on the map. That's all, people – we're already home. Can you smell it? Smell that river?"

Nobody could smell anything. Their jaws worked, their smiles glistened. It was a festive moment, presided over by a shell-shocked cook and a dazed waitress in a pleated skirt and a blouse with rodeo figures embroidered on the collar. And so what if Fairbanks was exactly like a half-mile strip torn out of any industrial city anywhere in America, like Detroit or Albany or Akron, like the very burgs they'd all escaped from in the first place? They were here. They were in Alaska. The end was in sight.

Norm handed his plate to the waitress and people began to move reluctantly from the counter, the tables, the oversubscribed rest room in back. "Drop City North, man," he said, spreading his arms to address the room at large, which included an Indian woman of indeterminate age frozen behind a paperback book in the far corner and two red–eared locals hunkered over coffee mugs and staring fixedly at the wall behind the counter as if the secrets of the universe were written there in infinitesimally small letters. "Land of the Midnight Sun!" From where he was sitting with Star, Marco felt detached from the whole scene. There was Norm, the reluctant guru, waving his arms in exhortation, pale and flaccid Norm who never wanted to lead anybody, at the end of his tether in a greasy spoon diner in a place that made nowhere sound like a legitimate destination. Marco felt embarrassed for him, embarrassed for them all, and the flare of optimism that had lit him up at Northway Junction was just a cinder now. This was crazy, he was thinking, the whole quixotic business. If they lasted a month it would be a miracle.

Outside on the street he shared a cigarette with Star, everybody milling around as if this was what they'd come for, to squat in the sun on the dirty sidewalks of a flat-topped frontier town that managed to look both pre- and postindustrial at the same time, sagging log cabins giving way to Quonset huts and abused brick and the rusted-out prefab warehouses that were elbowing their way across the flats like wounded soldiers. Pan and Lydia sat perched on the hood of the Studebaker, the same Top 40 hits you could have heard in Tuscaloosa or Sioux City whining out of the radio in thin threads of recognition, while Verbie and her sister fought over something in a hissing whisper. People kept trooping in and out of the bathroom at the rear of the diner, going back for toothpicks, breath mints, gum – anything to delay getting back on the bus – and then Norm just took Premstar by the hand and mounted the worn steel steps and everybody followed suit. He did a quick head count, the engine turned over with a grating blast of spent diesel, and the bus jerked away from the curb in a black pall of exhaust.

They cranked through the bleak downtown streets, across the Chena River and out the Steese Highway, replete with overpriced diner food, with grease and sugar and phosphoric acid slithering through their veins like slow death. Cigarettes circulated from hand to hand, the odd joint, a bota bag of wine. Maya and Merry blew kisses and flashed the peace sign to the slumped Indians and stave-eyed drunks who seemed to be the only inhabitants of the place, pavement gave way to potholes and potholes to dirt, and then they were folded up in the country again, the world gone green on them and the final stretch of road lapping at the wheels like a gentle brown sea.

Up front, behind the wheel, Norm came back to life. It was amazing. One minute he was dead and buried and the next he couldn't stop bobbing his head, couldn't stop talking, and Marco wondered about that, about how much of the holy and rejuvenating pharmacopoeia Drop City had brought along in their private and communal stashes – ounces, pounds, bales? Norm drummed at the wheel, rotated his shoulders, tapped his feet. He was a tour guide now, leaning into the windshield and crowing out the names of every creek and culvert they passed, lecturing anybody within earshot on the history, geology and botany of the sub-Yukon and the lore of the skin-hunters and prospectors, or what passed for it. "See that?" he said, pointing to an expanse of bleached-out scrub crowded with the thin dark slashes of spruce trees tipped and scattered as if they'd been bulldozed.

Marco was tasting wine in the back of his throat. He passed the bota bag to Star and pressed his face to the window. Across from them, Premstar, her hair lank and unwashed, had a seat to herself. She was wearing shorts and her legs were tented on the cracked vinyl seat so you could see the crease between them, her knees knocking rhythmically, her bare ankles scalloped and white. She was reading a magazine with the picture of a glossy woman on the cover. Norm might as well have been talking to himself.

"See the way the trees are leaning all over the place – see those two right there, like crossed swords? That's what they call the drunken forest, as if the trees were all whacked out of their minds and couldn't stand up straight." He swung round in the seat, squeezing the words out of the corner of his mouth. "Marco, you listening?"

Star answered for him. "We're listening," she said. "What else have we got to listen to?"

"Premstar?"

Premstar didn't look up from the magazine.

Norm's head swung back round and he addressed his words to the windshield as the engine churned and the bus heaved over the ruts. "Permafrost, that's what does that. Two feet down it's like rock, frozen since the Ice Age, *before* the Ice Age, like back in the time of the woolly mammoths and all that. Saber-toothed tigers. The dire wolf. Remember those mammoths, Prem, what a bitch they used to be? *Premstar*. I'm talking to you. I said you remember what a bitch it used to be saddling up those mammoths?"

Her voice leaked out from behind the magazine, barely a whisper: "Yes, *Norm*. A real bitch."

"So what happens is the trees can't put down their roots more than maybe twenty-four inches or whatever and then the wind comes along and gives them a shove. And don't think there's anything wrong with them – it's not that at all. They're alive and thriving. It's just that they're never going to grow straight. Or much."

Permafrost. The drunken forest. Now here was something, the kind of revelation that made all this concrete, that made these scrubby hills and swamps and miniature forests seem exotic, and they *were* exotic, Marco kept reminding himself, because this was Alaska, appearances to the contrary. He'd begun to have his doubts. Where were the glaciers, the waterfalls, the snow-capped mountains and untrammeled forests? Not here, not in the interior, anyway. This looked more like Ohio, like Michigan or Wisconsin or a hundred other places. He strained his eyes looking for eagles, looking for wolves, but there was nothing out there but scrub and more scrub.

Norm was onto something else now, his mind peeling back memories layer by layer – he'd expected a wolf behind every bush the first time he'd come up here, salmon hanging from the trees, gold dust in his coffee grains – but Marco wasn't listening. He wasn't feeling all that steady. Everybody on the bus had been trading round the same cold for a week, one of the hazards of communal living, especially when you were cooped up like this, and now he had it too. His head ached. He was sniffling. And the wine scoured the back of his throat and sat hard on his stomach, a mistake, and he knew it was a mistake even before he'd passed the bag to Star and she'd passed it to Premstar and Premstar took a delicate white-throated sip and passed it to Mendocino Bill. The bus lurched, righted itself, lurched again, and he looked down at Star's hand entwined in his own as if he didn't know what it was. The next moment he was making his way down the aisle to the bathroom.

Though the sun was high and it couldn't have been past seven or so, most people were asleep, Reba with her head back and snoring, Jiminy and Merry camped under one of the faded Navajo blankets that had hung in the back room at Drop City in a time that seemed so distant now he could barely remember it. Mendocino Bill and Deuce were playing chess on a magnetic board, the dogs were curled up beneath the seats and Che and Sunshine, snot glistening on their upper lips, stared numbly up the aisle as if they were watching a home movie, of which Marco, suddenly sick to his stomach, was the star. The bus lurched again and he staggered against one of the seats, then he was through the kitchen and into the rear of the bus, rattling at the door of the makeshift bathroom. The smell didn't help. The whole bus reeked of unwashed bodies and festering feet, of the tribe that dabbed powdered hand soap under their arms and rinsed their hair in grimy truck stop rest rooms, but the chemical toilet was something else altogether – this was where the thin gruel of the road poured out of them, brothers and sisters alike. Marco forced himself inside and flipped the latch.

He was sweating, the hair pasted to his forehead under the red bandanna he hadn't unknotted since they'd left California. It was dark and close, the only light a peep-show flicker through the grate in the door. He needed to vomit, because if he vomited he'd feel better – or that was the theory, anyway – and so he crouched over the stainless steel seat and thrust two pinched fingers down his throat. He gagged, but nothing came up. The contents of the bowl sloshed and rotated and gave off an evil smell. He braced himself against the ringing metal wall and was about to try again, two wet fingers poised at his lips, when the floor suddenly skewed away from him and then came bucking back up to pitch him face-first into the door. Then they weren't moving anymore and everybody seemed to be shouting at once.

His nose wasn't broken, or at least he didn't think it was, but the blood had darkened his T-shirt and pretty well ruined the gold-and-black brocade vest Star had picked out for him at a thrift shop in Ukiah, and that was a shame – a drag, a real drag – because it had become part of his identity, his signature article of clothing, the essential garment that announced to the world who he was and what he intended to do about it. It was hip, quintessentially hip, and now it was ruined. But that was all right, he told himself. In six months he'd be wearing caribou hide, wearing wolf, bear, ermine – and what was an ermine, anyway? A kind of weasel, wasn't it?

The excess blood had dried in his mustache and at the corners of his mouth, and he sat by the side of the road alternately rubbing the flecks of it loose and swatting at mosquitoes while the rest of the tribe milled around watching Mendocino Bill and Tom Krishna trying to work the wheel with the shredded tire off the axle, and of course it had to be an inner wheel – what else would you expect? Truly, at this point he didn't care whether his nose was broken or not, didn't care about the blood or the throbbing dull pain in his sinuses and couldn't remember what he'd been doing in the steel cage of the bathroom in the first place, but like everyone else he was so frustrated he could cry. By Norm's calculation, they weren't more than three or four miles from Boynton, *walking* distance, no less – and here was one more delay, one last impediment to keep the tents from going up and the trees from coming down. Just to sleep on the ground for a change, that was all anybody was asking. To get there. To arrive. To sit around an open fire and be a family again instead of a traveling circus.

Star had been sitting with him, the mosquitoes coming fast and furious, but she'd climbed back into the bus to change into a pair of long pants and a jacket, and he'd asked her to dig a bottle of bug repellant out of his backpack so he could get some relief himself. It was a wet country, boggy, the top two feet of the ground defrosting in summer but holding the water like a sink because it couldn't permeate the frozen layer beneath, and that was ideal for *Culex pipiens* and their wriggling waterborne larvae. They'd swarmed through the summer nights in Connecticut when he was growing up, and he'd been south too, to Florida and Louisiana, but the mosquitoes here – his first introduction to Alaskan wildlife, how about that? – were something else alto-gether. He slapped at his arms and clapped a hand to the back of his neck, and when he sneezed a wad of disjointed insects blew out of his nostrils in bits and pieces. His nose pulsated like a freshly rung bell, and he was drinking Spañada out of the bota bag to compensate – Alfredo had gotten a deal on a case of half-gallon bottles in some outpost somewhere along the way – and with each sip he told himself to stay calm, be patient, go with the flow. At least he wasn't queasy anymore, at least he had that.

He watched Star climb down out of the bus with Merry, Maya and Jiminy in tow, all four of them looking conspiratorial. She'd changed into a pair of red corduroy bells and her denim shirt with the signs of the zodiac embroidered up and down the arms and across the plane of her shoulders – the archer, Sagittarius, flexing his bow back there as if to ward off any harm that might come to her. The four of them trooped across the road to him, their faces shining and triumphant under the high slant of the sun, and he could see from the way she cupped her right hand and held it close to her body that it was more than just insect repellent she was carrying. He watched her hips slice back and forth, watched her sandals compact the dust of the road. Her features were regular, her eyes luminous. She gave him a smile so serene she could have been a Renaissance Madonna – or maybe she was just stoned. Maybe that was it.

"Let me guess," he said, "nobody could wait, right?"

They eased down in the weeds beside him, the homey familiar scent of marijuana clinging to their hair and clothing. There was a rustle of vegetation, wildflowers crushed and displaced – lupine, fireweed, what looked to be some sort of poppy – and Jiminy's knees cracking as he dropped down and inserted half a dozen joss sticks into the friable dirt at their feet. "That's right," he said, leaning forward to touch a lighter to the tapering ends one by one, "and we're mosquito-proofing this holy shrine that surrounds you too, my good man. Be gone, bothersome insects. And for the rest, be merry and of good cheer."

"Some of us were thinking of walking it," Maya said, "just to see what the town's like – I mean, we're so close. But Norm didn't think so. He didn't think it would be cool."

People were out in the road throwing Frisbees and shouting while the dogs irrigated the bushes and Norm rasped and gesticulated and tugged at his beard, and Pan – the back of his head with its thin wisps of hair visible just below the line of vegetation clinging to the far shoulder – flung a lure at the dark surface of the river that slid along the road here like the lining of a jacket. There was no traffic. There'd never been any traffic. They might as well have had a flat out on the Serengeti or the Kirghiz steppe.

"I'd walk it in a heartbeat," Marco said.

"Me too," Jiminy said without conviction. Smoke had begun to rise from the joss sticks, and the clear cool unalloyed air carried a freight of burnt punk.

"Just to see it, you know what I'm saying?" Marco persisted – he couldn't help himself. "I've seen it in my head to the point where I know I'm going to be disappointed. Or maybe not. Maybe I'll be pleasantly surprised. That happens, doesn't it? Don't you get pleasantly surprised once out of a hundred times?"

"Nothing's the way you picture it," Star said. "The mind creates its own reality, and how could the real and actual thing ever match that? It's like a movie compared to a cartoon." She was right there beside him, and in her palm the veined and speckled pill that looked like one of the color tablets you'd use to dye Easter eggs.

"Or a book," Maya said. "A book compared to a movie."

"I don't know, I think I'd listen to Norm," Merry said, leaning back on the twin props of her elbows and stretching her legs out into the roadway as if she were sinking into an easy chair. Her pupils were dilated to the size of a cat's. She was wearing a serape over her jeans and a flop-brimmed vaquero's hat and her feet were bare and dirty and fringed with mosquitoes. Marco saw that she'd painted each of her toenails a different color, and though he wasn't stoned – not yet, anyway – he thought he'd never seen anything so beautiful, and why didn't all women paint their toenails like that? All men, for that matter? "I mean, what's the hurry?" she said. "Can't we just groove on this sky, the wildflowers, the river? I mean, look at it. Just look."

Marco took it as an injunction and looked off down the sunstruck tunnel of the road, and there was the Studebaker and there the Bug, pulled up on the shoulder, but there was no Dale Murray on his motorcycle, and where was he when you needed him? It would be nothing to horse the thing into Boynton and back, see the river, ride right into it, snuff the breeze, all hail and hallelujah, Boynton or Bust. But Dale Murray had turned back the day after they'd crossed into Canada to see what had become of Lester and Franklin and Sky Dog, and he'd never reappeared. Marco didn't feel one way or the other about it, because when you came right down to it he hardly knew the guy and he certainly couldn't write any recommendations for the people he associated with. But Dale Murray had two legs and two arms and a pair of hands and they were going to need every pair of hands they could muster to put this thing together – it would be a long dark age before any runaways or weekend hippies found their way up here to swell their ranks, that was for sure.

There was some noise from the direction of the bus, a lively debate between Mendocino Bill and Norm as to the viability of the spare – "There's no doubt in my mind," Norm was saying, "no doubt whatsoever, so go ahead, put it on" – and then Star was pressing the pill into his hand. He accepted it, accepted it in the way he'd been conditioned to – if somebody gave you drugs, you took them, no questions asked – and he even went so far as to bring his hand to his mouth and make the motions of swallowing. Burnt punk rose to his nostrils. The sun cupped a hand at the back of his neck. No one was watching him – their gazes were fixed across the road, on the bus, on Norm, on the black wheel laid out like a corpse in the dirt. They weren't there yet, that was what he was thinking, and he wasn't going to celebrate until they were. He slipped the pill into the blood-stained pocket of his ruined vest.

Star let out a laugh in response to something Jiminy had said, and then they were all laughing – even him, even Marco, though he had no idea what he was laughing about or for or whether laughing was the appropriate response to the situation. No matter. The smoke rose from the joss sticks, the Frisbee hung in the air like a brick in a wall and they were stretched out on the side of the road and laughing, just laughing, and you would have thought the cabins had already been built, the wood split for the stove, the gold panned, the furs stretched and the larder stocked, because nobody here had a care in the world. Merry handed a roach to Star and she held it to her lips till the stub of it glowed red and then she handed it to Marco, who pinched it from her fingers and held it to his own lips a moment, sucking in the sweet seep of smoke as he'd done a thousand times before. Everything seemed to slow down, as if the earth were transfixed on its axis and the fragment of sky overhead was all they would ever need. And then, out of the corner of his eye, the laziest, slowest movement in the world: the dogs were emerging from the strip of blue shadow beneath the bus and stirring themselves with a dainty flex and release of their rear paws. They both gazed intently up the road, and Freak, his hackles rising, let out a low woof of inquiry.

A dog had appeared round the far bend – or no, it was a wolf, with the rawboned legs that seemed to veer away from its body as if they'd been put on backward, a wolf trotting down a road in Alaska. Marco was on his feet. "Look," he said, "look, it's a – " He caught himself. There were two figures coming round the bend now, a man and a woman striding along easily under the weight of their backpacks, and this was no wolf, or no wild wolf anyway. The Frisbee slid back down its arc, people eased to their feet. "Norm," somebody said, "hey, Norm."

The man was tall, hard-muscled, lean. He was wearing a weather-bleached flannel shirt with the sleeves rolled up and a pair of jeans so knee-sprung and tattered they made Marco's look new. His hair was short, thick, and it stood up straight from his head. He was walking as if walking were a competitive event, the steady pump of his legs and the clip of his boots reeling in the road before him, a man moving in silhouette against the bright splash of the day, and Marco couldn't tell what he was, a bum, a gas station attendant, the Scholar Gypsy himself. The woman – she was in her twenties, her blond hair tied back in a ponytail like a cheerleader's, her shorts showing off the muscles of her calves and the clean working lines of her buttocks and thighs – raised a hand to shade her eyes as if she couldn't quite decide whether the bus was a mirage or not. Up the road shot a yellow blur, paws gathering, muscles straining, and Freak and Frodo were on them, but the man never broke stride and his dog never wavered either – it just ducked its head and followed at his heels. For a moment the yellow dogs bobbed round them, dust rose, and then the gap closed to nothing and the man and woman were standing right there amongst them on the deserted road.

Tom Krishna had been busy with the axle, with the big ridged tire and the stubborn wheel that just that moment slid forward to kiss the spare. He looked up into the silence and saw the hikers standing there with their swollen backpacks and the dogs moiling around and the road dust rising. "Hey," he said, coming up out of his crouch, "what's happening, brother," and he reached out a greasy hand for the soul shake that never came.

The man just looked at them with an amused grin, looked at them all, while the sun glanced off Norm's glasses and Marco stood suspended at the side of the road and Merry and Maya exchanged a giggle. "You people aren't – " the man began, and then caught himself. There was flat incredulity in his tone. "You aren't *hippies,* are you?"

Norm came forward, boxy in his overalls, rings glittering on his fingers. The bell tinkled at his neck. From the goats atop the bus, a forlorn bleat of disenchantment: they wanted down, they wanted out, they wanted to graze their way to Boynton. Norm bellowed out his name – "Norm Sender!" – and pumped the man's hand in a conventional handshake before turning to the woman and showing the gold in his rotting teeth. "We're Drop City, is what we are, avatars of peace, love and the *higher* consciousness, come all the way up from California to reclaim my uncle Roy's place – Roy Sender's? – on the sweet, giving and ever-clear Thirtymile. And we're all of us pleased to meet you."

The man scratched the back of his head and tossed his gaze like a beanbag from face to face. "I'll be damned," he said. "You *are* hippies."

The girls giggled. The dogs danced. Mendocino Bill said, "That's right. And we're proud of it."

And then the man in the worn flannel shirt seemed to think of something else altogether, some new concern that disarmed him totally, and Marco watched him shift his feet in the pale tan dirt of the road. Watched the brow furrow and the grin vanish. The man's gaze flitted around again and finally came back to Norm. "Did you say *Roy Sender*?"

21

That was what he'd said, *Roy Sender – Roy Sender's place* – and Sess tried to control his facial muscles, but his body betrayed him. He took a step back to disengage himself, ran a hand through his hair. This was crazy, purely crazy, a page torn out of one of the newsmagazines – "The Woodstock Nation," "Sex, Drugs and Rock and Roll" or some such – torn out and given three dimensions and flesh, acres of flesh, because these hippie women sitting on the side of the road were the stuff of the wild hair's winter fantasies, and two of them, the little blonde and the brunette in the cowgirl hat with her legs stretched out in the road, could have made the pages of another kind of magazine altogether. He was thinking *Playboy,* thinking *Dude,* thinking *The Thirtymile? Did he say the Thirtymile?* when the big greasy character with the gold-plated teeth – the nephew – loomed up on him with a whole string of questions: Who were they? Where were they headed? Had they ever been to Boynton? Did they know if the salmon were running yet, and what about the berries? Were the berries ripe out there?

Sess gave Pamela a glance. She'd stiffened up like some neophyte anthropologist set down amongst the wrong tribe – headhunters when she'd been expecting basket-weavers – and she wasn't giving them anything, not even a half a smile. And Lucius, Lucius wasn't giving in either – he just backed himself up against Sess's legs while the two yellow dogs pawed the dirt and poked their snouts at him. People were coming down off the bus now, a whole weird Halloween procession in mismatching colors, bells, beads, headbands, pants so wide you couldn't see their feet and hair like a river so you couldn't tell the men from the – oh, but you could, unless you were blind, and he guessed they must have all gone ahead and burned their brassieres.

Sess took hold of the nephew's hand for the second time, but this time on his own initiative, and of course he was half-lit, drinking all day and full of the hellfire exuberance of dunking Joe Bosky's car for him, and so he worked up a smile and introduced himself. "Sess Harder," he heard himself say, and wasn't this a riot, wasn't it? "And this is my wife, Pamela. And my new dog, Lucius." To this point he'd just answered with a grunt or a nod to the questions thrown at him, but he felt expansive suddenly and he told them that the kings were running and the berries ripening and that he'd been with Roy Sender the day he left the country. Helped him move, in fact.

"Really? Like no shit? You knew my uncle?"

He didn't tell him that Roy Sender was a father to him when he had no father of his own left breathing on this planet or that Roy Sender had taught him everything he knew or that Roy Sender was no hippie and never could be because he believed in making it on his own, in his own way, no matter how poor the odds, and that he was the kind of man who'd lie down and rot in his own skin before he'd take a government handout. He didn't tell him about the solace of the Thirtymile, the clarity of the air, the eternal breathless silence of forty below and the snow spread like a strangler's hand across the throat of the river. All he said was, "Yeah," and Pamela, silent to this point, said, "Washo Unified? You're some kind of school group, is that what it is?"

A woman had got off the bus, dark hair in pigtails, a sharp decisive face, eyes that took you in and spat you back out again. She was thirty, thirty at least, wearing a faded denim shirt and some sort of improvised leggings that weren't exactly pants and weren't exactly a skirt either. Her feet were bare. And dirty. "We're a family," she said, coming right up to Pamela and holding out both her hands. "Just a family, that's all."

Pamela – and this made him smile because she was so good-natured and sweet, not a malicious bone in her body – took the woman's hands in her own a moment and held them till etiquette dictated she let go.

"See that man over there?" the woman said, and they all turned their heads to where a skinny shirtless dark-skinned man with a full oily patriarch's beard stood on the bank of the river skipping stones. "That's my husband. And over there" – she indicated a pair of half-naked children bobbing and weaving along the water's edge in two matching squalls of mosquitoes – "those are my kids. And these others, everybody else here? These are my brothers and sisters."

The nephew could barely keep still during all this, jerking his head back and forth and doing a little dance in his sandaled feet. "Listen," he said, "I don't know what your trip is or where you're going to camp tonight or like any of that, but what I mean is a friend of Uncle Roy's is a friend of mine, and you people are welcome, I mean more than welcome, to ride into town with us, and let me *extend* an invitation right now to the first annual celebratory communal feast of the Drop City North pilgrims and fellow travelers, to be prepared on the banks of the mighty Yukon this very evening while the sun shines and the birds twitter and the hip and joyful music rides right on up into the *trees*."

Pamela said she didn't think so. "We've got things to do," she said. "And the walk's nothing, really, just a couple of miles."

It was then that one of the hippie men, a guy in a bandanna with what looked to be blood on his shirt, handed Sess a wineskin and Sess threw back his head and took a long arcing swallow before passing it to Pamela. He looked round him. All the hippies were grinning. The nephew looked as if he'd been dipped in cream, the wildflowers jerked at their leashes, the river sang. Joe Bosky's car was flotsam now – or was it jetsam? Pamela's lips shone with sweet wine.

"Sure," Sess said. "Sure, we'll take a ride with you."

The Three Pup featured the usual human backdrop – Skid Denton mumbling French poetry into a shot glass, Lynette propped behind the bar with her arms locked across her breasts and no key in sight, Richie Oliver and his consolation prize drinking themselves into another dimension and grinding beer nuts between their teeth in a slow sure cud-like way. Iron Steve was bent over the pool table with a heavyset, sharp-beaked man who must have been a tourist because Sess didn't recognize him, and Tim Yule, the tip of his nose still bright with a dab of fresh mucus and the paper carnation he'd worn at the wedding still tucked into his button hole, stood there beside them, clinging to his cue stick as if it were bolted to the floor. The place smelled the way it always did, like an old boot stuffed with ground beef, fried onions and stove ash and left out in the sun to fester for a couple of days. The usual drone of mid-Appalachian self-pity spewed out of the jukebox and the usual embattled mosquitoes hung in the air.

Sess blew through the door like a hurricane, all clatter and gusto, and he had Pamela by one hand and the hippie wineskin by the other, feeling dense and lighter than air at the same time, and so what if the big greasy sack of a nephew was right on his heels and all the rest of them too? They were people, weren't they, just like anybody else? Dirtier, maybe. Lazier. They smoked drugs and screwed like dogs. But the world was changing – men had hair like women, women wore pants like men and let their tits hang loose, and who was going to argue with that? Wake up, Boynton, that was what he was thinking, wake up and join the modern world. But he wasn't really thinking too clearly and Pamela would never nag – one beer, that was all, one beer and they'd stay in the shack tonight and go upriver first thing in the morning and let Wetzel Setzler and the rest of the town fathers scratch their heads over a busload of hippies who wouldn't know a moose from a caribou. Or a hare from a parky squirrel, for that matter.

Tammy Wynette gave way to Roger Miller on the jukebox – "King of the Road," a song Sess hated so utterly and intensely it made him want to punch things every time it came on and it came on perpetually – and in the brief hissing caesura between records everybody in the room, even Tim Yule, turned to the door. In came the nephew, roaring, and then the one with the blood on his shirt and the little blonde and then a bleached-out monster in a greasy pair of overalls and a whole spangled chittering parade that filled the room before Roger Miller could limp from one mind-numbing verse to the next. "Drinks for everybody in the house!" the nephew boomed, laying a bill on the bar. "The first round's on Roy Sender – the *legendary* Roy Sender! Anybody here know Roy Sender?"

Nobody said a word. Nobody moved. They all concentrated on Roger Miller as if they were at Carnegie Hall listening to Oistrakh. Tim Yule cleared his throat. "These people friends of yours, Sess?"

In answer, Sess crossed the room to the jukebox and gave it a kick that sent the needle skidding across the record with a long protracted hiss of static. Then he dug out a quarter, inserted it, and hit B-9, "Mystic Eyes," three times running. Lynette, who'd seen everything, or at least pretended she had, began cracking beers and lining them up on the bar, and by the time Van Morrison came in after the mouth harp with his black-hearted vocal everybody was talking at once.

It was a short song, no more than two minutes or so, but by the second run-through a couple of the hippies had begun to sway their shoulders and shuffle their feet; by the third time around they were dancing, throwing out their elbows and letting their arms writhe over their heads. The nephew had got hold of a thin blond girl in stacked-up shoes who looked like Twiggy's American twin, and a little five-foot girl with a missing tooth and a tie-dyed shirt grabbed Iron Steve by the hand and started pogoing around the room with him. Sess put another quarter in, hit the tune three more times. Skid Denton let out a groan, Richie Oliver put a finger to his temple and pulled an imaginary trigger, and still more hippies poured through the door and spilled back out into the parking lot where somebody cranked up the big speakers in the bus and a whole shimmering spangle of weird hippie guitar music drifted out into the muskeg. There'd been nothing like this here since the last alien visitation, and Sess was too young to remember that.

"Sess!" Skid Denton was shouting over the uproar, waving a full shot glass as if he were proposing a toast. "Where'd you find these freaks, anyway – the Ringling Brothers' circus?"

"And Barnum and Bailey," Sess shouted back. He snaked his arm between a chinless character with a beard so sparse it was barely there and a big-shouldered girl – woman, Pamela's age at least – whose breasts were on full display in some sort of leotard thing, and said, "Excuse me," as he reached for his second beer. But the woman reached for it simultaneously and got there first. She let the neck of the bottle sprout between her thumb and forefinger before bringing it to her lips for a long calculated swallow and then handing it to him. "Hi," she said, and he could see the mascara caked on her eyelashes, definitely a downtown sort of girl and what was she doing in the Three Pup? "I'm Lydia," she said. "And you're Norm's friend, right?"

Norm? Who the hell was Norm? He just smiled, and the guy with the nonexistent beard smiled, and she smiled too. "Yeah," he heard himself say, "that's right."

And now her face really lit up. "Well, I just wanted to thank you, that's all, on behalf of all of us, I mean, because we really didn't know how our whole trip was going to go down up here – I mean, we didn't know if it was going to be like *Easy Rider* or *Joe* or what."

"Trepidatious, that's what we were," the guy said, but he was a kid, really, twenty, twenty-one maybe, with a head that was too big and shoulders that were too narrow and a pair of eyes that were a vast delta of broken veins. He slipped his wrist inside Sess's and attempted some sort of secret hippie handshake, but the beer bottle got in his way, so he leaned back and made the victory sign with two fingers. "Peace, man," he said, and then he started off on a monologue about how he'd always wanted to shoot a moose and skin it and a bear too and have a bear rug on the floor and maybe catch a king salmon and have it stuffed at the taxidermist's – for over the fireplace, you know what I mean? – and did he, Sess, have any idea where the moose were this time of year, like up in the hills or down by the river or what?

The thump of the bass was like friction: the floor was moving one way and Sess was going the other, even though he was standing stock still. He looked across the room to where Pamela sat at a table with the pigtailed woman, waving a beer and declaiming about something, and then the woman chimed in – it was all in pantomime over the intervening roar – and Pamela chattered right back at her. The hippies had caught on and kept feeding the jukebox quarters and the only song they played – the song of the night, the anthem – was "Mystic Eyes." It was a joke. Hilarious. Fifteen times, twenty, twenty-five. They danced and pounded and threw back beers and shots of peppermint schnapps and whatever else they could lay their hands on. All was movement and noise and the swirling interleaved colors of the dancers' shirts and jackets and the flapping wind-propelled cuffs of their pants. *We went walkin' / Down by / The old graveyard / I looked at you –*

Sess was going to answer the kid – he was going to tell him that the season was fish, not meat, and that the average moose stood taller than any of the cabins along the river and just might be a tiny bit too much for a chinless, slack-armed, eye-bleeding, California hippie to take on before he got his feet wet and pulled his head up out of his ass – but he never got the chance, and Lynette was the deciding factor. She came out from behind the bar like the shadow of something swift-moving and vast and jerked the electric cord out of the socket beside the jukebox. The music died. Everybody froze.

"I want you out!" Lynette cried in a wild strained falsetto that made it sound as if she were trying to take the song to the next level and beyond. "All of you – out! Now! If you think I'm going to listen to that shitty rock and roll crap one more time you're out of your mind. Now get out! Everybody! This place is *closed*."

From outside, in the mosquito-hung lot, there came the sound of the hippie guitars, more noticeable now in the absence of the jukebox. It was a mournful, contemplative music, each note plied out of a crevice to be held up and viewed from all angles before the next one allowed itself to be dug out and the next one after that. Sess stood immobilized amidst the throng, and then he felt himself moving toward the door and the sad sparkling wrung-out promise of the music. He drained his beer. He felt Pamela at his side. Then they were outside in the air that had a sweet riparian smell to it, the smell of the river recharging itself with meltwater, and the hippies were dancing like moonwalkers to the drugged-down testiduneous beat. Lucius was there, nosing at his cupped hand, and he realized he hadn't fed him since he'd claimed him from the pound, and that was remiss, it was. "Come on, Sess," Pamela was saying, tugging him toward the corner of the porch where they'd dropped their packs full of marshmallows and dill pickles and cheese graters and all the rest of the claptrap they just couldn't seem to live without. "Time to go. We've got a big day tomorrow. The garden, remember? All those logs that need to be peeled? The salmon?"

That was when he locked eyes with the woman who'd put her lips to his beer – Lydia – and she gave him a long slow re-evaluative look out of eyes the color of the lupines sprouting along the road, one thin slant of sun catching her face, and whoever made her, whoever pulled the genes up out of the parental hat, sure didn't stint, that was what he was thinking. But then the brunette in the cowgirl getup looped her arm through Lydia's and she turned her back and began a weaving in–and–out snakedance that was like dripping hot oil right down the front of his pants.

"Hello, Sess. Remember me, your wife?"

He blinked twice, grinned.

"Enjoying the scenery?"

"They sure don't waste a lot of money on underwear, do they?"

She slipped an arm round his waist. The notes fractured and burst like bubbles, bubbles of aluminum, of pewter, hard metallic bubbles made by a machine somewhere in hippie land and bursting through the hippie speakers secreted in the back of the hippie bus. What was it? What would they say? Mind-blowing. It was mind-blowing. Skid Denton came through the door then with a soft-faced girl on either side of him, talking French a mile a minute. "No," Pamela said, leaning into him, and she was feeling pretty good herself, no offense taken and the night was young, still young, "no, I don't guess they do."

And then it was Iron Steve, his shoulders hunched and head bowed low so as to better breathe in what the little gap-toothed girl was all about – "Oh, yeah," he was saying, "yeah, it gets cold, *shit, yeah*" – and Sess discovered another beer in his hand even as he was helping Pamela duck into the straps of her pack.

The nephew was the agent of the beer, standing there with his crack-frame glasses and the color showing in his teeth, two more beers bunched between his knuckles, one of which he handed to Pamela; the other he kept to himself, giving it a good long suck till the foam flecked his beard. "You know something?" he said, pulling away from the bottle and grinning wide. "I like your taste in music."

Sess gave him his grin back, then bent at the knee so Pamela could help him on with his pack. "Yeah, but Lynette – you've got to forgive her. She's new here. She's from Seattle. I guess she's just got a hair up her ass."

"It was a gas," the nephew said, rooting in his beard as if he'd lost something there. "What'd we play it – like fifty times? But listen, I was serious about the invitation – the chicks'll have something cooked up inside the hour, I guarantee it, and well, you know, it's been a long hard road and all that and we have just *got* to get down and raise some pure celebratory hell tonight. Nothing fancy – lentil soup, rice and vegetables. And wine. Sweet red wine." He took another pull at his beer and looked out into the backlit trees.

"You're camping out tonight?"

The nephew shrugged. His shoulders were bare under the straps of the coveralls, hairy, furred with mosquitoes. "Sure. Why not?"

"But Roy's place – " He faltered. How could he begin to convey the complexity of the arrangement, the untenanted cabin that might sleep five or six at most, the treachery of the Yukon with its load of silt that would pack your clothes and drag you down in a heartbeat should you give it a chance, the lack of basic comforts? What were all these people planning to eat? Where were they going to get their pink lipstick and face paint and their jugs of sweet wine and their uppers and their downers and their pot and all the rest of it? And did he really want neighbors, thirty and more of them set down on his river within shouting distance of his trapline?

"It's pretty far," Pamela put in. "Three hours, at least, by canoe."

The nephew lifted his beard and let it drop. His hand was like a big soft fluttering moth as he brought the beer to his lips. "Oh, I'm apprised, I'm apprised," he said. "I know the place, though it's been something like – *Jesus* – twenty years? Oh, man, *twenty* years, can you believe it?" He began to laugh to himself, the pale shoulders bunching and heaving beneath a layer of fat, and the strap of the coveralls slipped down his right shoulder to reveal a tattoo in three colors – a cartoon character, and which one was it? Disney. A cross-legged fawn with outsized eyes. An image rushed up out of Sess's childhood, his mother in a pink dress and his sister with her fist sunk deep in a box of extra-buttered popcorn: Bambi. The man had *Bambi* tattooed on his shoulder. Sess had never seen anything like it. He'd seen anchors, daggers, death's heads, seen hearts transfixed with arrows and dripping

274

blood, the cheap blue fading appellations of wives, sweethearts and ex-lovers, an eagle with a fish in its claws – but *Bambi?*

"I'm no greenhorn," the nephew was saying, "and I can tell you I know at least a modicum of what I'm talking about when it comes to this country, because I lived three summers and the better part of two winters up here with my uncle when I was a kid – which is not to say I haven't got a lot to learn, man, you know? Because I do. But we got three canoes up on top of that bus" – Sess turned his head to contemplate the big yellow box on wheels and found himself staring into the boneheaded, slit-eyed faces of a pair of goats that could have been the templates for cartoon figures themselves – "and I made a deal with this bush pilot – Joe Bosky, you know him? – to ferry three loads of people and supplies upriver, including like tools and the *basics* because all these people, all my brothers and sisters, need to like get their *heads* together, you know what I mean? I mean, they think it's all going to be milk and honey, but I know better – "

The nephew went on for a while with his speech, and Sess and Pamela stood there as if they were in a lecture hall, except that they were swatting at mosquitoes and pulling at their beers while the shattered, tinkling music rained down on them and the skinny blonde with the pink lipstick came up and draped her arms over the nephew's back and held on as if he were a buoy in a swirl of darkening waters. "So what I was thinking," the nephew said, in what seemed a valedictory sort of way, "was we'd just pull up someplace by the river and camp for tonight and the next couple of days maybe – "

Pull up where? Sess was going to ask, because there wasn't a square foot of property anywhere along the riverfront that wasn't already spoken for. You couldn't buy, beg or steal a lot in Boynton since the Feds started in with the Native Claims Settlement business, and if you set foot outside the town line you were on government property – and Wetzel Setzler, the local shill for the Forest Service, could get pretty squirrelly about that. Plus, a bus full of longhairs in mufti wasn't likely to provoke a warm response from whoever they chose to trespass on, and they were already tied up with Joe Bosky, the worst kind of river scum, and that was another strike against them – no matter how you sketched it, it wasn't a pretty picture.

The nephew sucked beer and grinned at him. He wore a halo of insects round the crown of thorns that was his greasy unbarbered hair and he looked so helpless he might have been newly hatched from the egg. "What do you say, brother?" he wanted to know. "You with us?"

Sess looked to Pamela. She was giving him the let's-go-home-and-pack-the-canoe look, and she was right: they had to get upriver, had to split and dry salmon if they were going to have fish come winter, had to tend the vegetables, haul wood, erect the new room and fit it out with a stove – and little tables, don't forget the little tables. Still, Sess reminded himself, this was Roy Sender's flesh and blood standing here in his sandals and beard like one of the lost prophets, and that had to mean something, if only for Roy's sake. Before he could think, and with his voice lubricated with all that beer and the sweet hippie wine that rode its own currents and seemed to settle flush in his ringing ears, Sess heard himself say, "Why don't you just camp at my place?"

part five

drop city north

Hey, Bungalow Bill,
What did you kill?
— John Lennon Paul McCartney,
"The Continuing Story of Bungalow Bill"

22

Jiminy was limping around with his arm in a dirty sling, looking as if a tree had fallen on him, but a tree hadn't fallen on him and the sling consisted of two strips of frayed cotton that used to be the sleeves of somebody's college sweatshirt, because who needed sleeves when the sun was shining twenty-four hours a day? Was it broken? No. You sure? Oh, yeah, man, yeah – I'd *know* if it was broken. So what's the problem, then? A sprain, that's all, man. Just a sprain.

Not that Pan would accuse him of *shirking,* what with every able-bodied cat within shouting distance taking down six thousand trees a day and Alfredo all over the place barking out orders like the ass-faced little prick of an assistant principal they'd all had to sweat in junior high, and Norm, laid-back Norm, erupting like a volcano every thirty-seven seconds. If he'd sprained his arm or shoulder or elbow or whatever it was and sported a purple bruise that was like a birthmark creeping out from under the ragged hem of his cutoff jeans, that was understandable. Especially since Ronnie had been there when it happened.

Everybody had just got done with the evening mush (brown rice with canned peas and the odd greasy chunk of Thirtymile salmon, and praise the lord for Spiracha hot sauce in the economy-sized bottle), and a bunch of people were fooling around with the aluminum boat Norm's uncle had left behind when he decamped for Seattle. (And that was strange beyond comprehension: he'd left *everything* behind, from his boots and folded-up piss-stained old man's underwear to his pornography collection to the .30-30 Winchester lever-action rifle and Smith & Wesson pistol with the worn black leather leg holster hanging from a hook on the wall, though Norm swore he was an old man with cancer of the prostate and had no intention of coming back.

Ever. He'd even left the stove all primed to go, with paper, kindling and matches ready to hand. Why would he do that? Why would he leave all this good and valuable stuff behind, including the two bowie knives that made Marco's Sears Roebuck version look like something the Boy Scouts handed out for whittling exercise? It was the way of the country, that was why – or so Norm claimed. "You leave the cabin stocked and ready to go for the next man through, not so much as a matter of courtesy, you understand, but as a matter of *survival*. Plus, what does he need with a bowie knife in a nursing home anyway?" Okay. Yeah. Sure. Point taken.)

Jiminy wanted in the boat. So did Merry. Mendocino Bill, the whole big mush-warmed sack of him, sat in the stern, revving the outboard engine, Verbie, Angela and Maya were squeezed into the middle seat, and Weird George was in the bow. "Room for one more," Bill announced, sucking back the thin blue exhaust of the engine. Everybody had humped it all day, taking down trees and whacking off the branches, kicking and stumbling through the brush in a blitzkrieg of mosquitoes and hard-earned sweat, and now they'd passed round the smokes and the pot and the last of the sticky red wine, the pale green half-gallon jugs already filled back up with Tom Krishna's gaseous home-brewed beer that looked like motor oil drippings and didn't taste a whole lot better. The dogs were yapping, the goats were bleating, people were perched on stumps with guitars and books and strings of electric blue beads that froze and shattered the light as they threaded them in a dance of sunlit fingers. Merry said, "Fuck you, Jiminy, I was here first," and Jiminy said, "No, you go next – it's my turn," and things just escalated from there.

For his part, Pan didn't much care who went for a boat ride and who didn't. He was feeling good, feeling beyond compare, with his head primed on a sliver of the chunk of blond Lebanese hash he'd sold to Alfredo for three times what he'd paid for it and the wine working its sweet slippery magic on the wad of mush in his gut. He was tanned like a macaroon. His muscles were hard from paddling, chopping, lifting, from hauling the net full of salmon out of the current and flinging the three-inch silver lure with the wire leader out into the deep cuts under the bank for pike – *great northerns*. He couldn't believe it. Great northern pike.

He'd caught something like twelve or thirteen of them in his spare time, no effort at all, just like in the *Field and Stream* and *Outdoor Life* articles he'd feasted on as a kid, and so what if they were ninety percent bone? The chicks made fish soup, fish stew, fish porridge and pike à la meunière. And for the meat eaters – and their party was growing by the day – he'd brought back ducks, geese, ptarmigans, even two lean black dripping muskrats, which nobody would eat but him and Norm, the meat dark and greasy, with a subtle aftertaste of dead insects and rotting twigs. As for the boat, he had priority there anytime he wanted it – *Dibs, Pan has dibs on it,* that's what Alfredo said at one of the eternal meetings they seemed to have every other day now – because he was the designated fisher and hunter while Marco and Bill and Norm and the rest had become full-time architects and structural engineers, at least for the time being.

"Just give me this," Merry's voice rose up, and she was ready to sob, the grief congesting her diction and dulling her consonants like a head cold, "that's all I ask, and you are one selfish little prick, you know that? Huh, Jiminy? You are. You don't care about me. You only care about yourself."

Ronnie was sitting on the bank in a spray of brittle wildflowers and coarse-grained sand that held the heat of the sun and gave it back to his flanks and the hard bare work-worn soles of his feet. He was feeling very calm, feeling the peace that comes of getting stoned after a hard day's work outdoors and a double helping of salmon mush, and he watched Jiminy dance round Merry as if he were Zeus looking down from Olympus. The boat bobbed in the water. The current thrummed. The two of them jockeyed for position on the vagrant log the camp used as a kind of all-purpose pier and canoe-minder. Mendocino Bill's voice rose up over the suck and sputter of the engine: "Come on, already, for Christ's sake – you'd think you were six-year-olds, both of you."

Then Jiminy shoved her and she shoved him back and suddenly he was waving his arms and looking small-faced and embarrassed and in the next moment he lost his footing and landed awkwardly in the bottom of the boat, spilling everybody into the Thirtymile. The chicks shot up out of the current as if they'd been launched – because it was *cold* beyond anything anybody in California had ever even dreamed of – and Mendocino Bill choked and sputtered and came up cursing with his beard rinsed and his hair showing bald on top while Weird George churned up water like a human eggbeater and fought for purchase on the slick and whirling stones of the riverbed. Merry ducked away from the splash, her bare toes digging in like fingers as the log rose and fell, and then she turned her back, made a delicate little leap ashore and stalked away through the weeds. She didn't offer any apologies.

But Jiminy. He came out of the water dragging his arm, and after the initial shock he had to go find Reba and have her bind it up and tell him it probably wasn't broken. And that was a trial, because Reba didn't know her humerus from her femur, but she was Drop City's resident medical authority by virtue of the fact that she'd dropped out of nursing school midway through her first year and could toss around terms like *speculum* and *tongue depressor* with the best of them. She always broke out her little black leather medical kit when anybody came down with anything, a kit Pan had taken it upon himself to look into one day when she was downriver, in the hope of turning up something interesting that she might not miss – morphine, maybe. Or Demerol. But it was just the basics: a needle and thread for suturing, Mercurochrome, gauze, the handy rectal thermometer. So Jiminy wasn't shirking, not a bit. In fact, it wouldn't surprise anybody if his arm *was* broken in about eighteen places after Reba had got done with it.

Actually, Ronnie was more concerned with the outboard engine, whether it would start with saturated spark plugs and water in the fuel line and what to do about it if it wouldn't. Jiminy would heal, but that Johnson outboard was the key to Drop City's existence, the mechanical mule that carried every little thing upriver on its back. Still, he didn't actually get up out of the sand till the boat was righted and everybody had cursed out the principals as thoroughly as they could under the circumstances, and when he did push himself up it wasn't to fuss over a bundle of wet wiring and a starter cord that produced nothing but a nagging cough while Bill bored him into an upright grave with reminiscences of other outboard motors he'd known and loved and Tom Krishna quoted something apposite from *The Bhagavad Gita*. No, he found himself sauntering after Merry, with the idea of calming her down and maybe just *insinuating* himself a little because Star was off on her own trip with Marco, living in a dome tent out on the slope beyond the half-finished cabin that was going to be Drop City's new meeting hall, and Lydia was back in Boynton with a couple of the others, sleeping in the bus and taking care of things on that end, and beyond that the pickings got pretty slim. Maya, no beauty to begin with, had bloated up on a steady diet of mush, and some sort of acne or scale was eating her face up (dishwater face, that was the clinical term for it, as if she'd been scrubbing the pots and pans with her cheekbones instead of her hands), Premstar was property of Norm, at least for the time being, and Verbie and her sister were strictly for emergencies only as far as Pan was concerned. And what was that song – "Make an Ugly Woman Your Wife"? Uh-uh. No way. Not in Pan's scheme of things.

(As for the other surviving Drop City chicks – Louise, Dunphy, Erika and Rain – they just weren't his type in any way, shape or form, members of the long-faced chant-before-breakfast-lunch-and-dinner school, hairy-legged, sour-smelling, secret as thieves unless the subject of women's lib came up, and then they were onto it like Verbie. Plus, they were all spoken for, and the only passable-looking one of the group – Erika – lived in a tent with two guys, Weird George and Geoffrey, and they all three balled one another in combinations Pan might have found fascinating in the abstract, but you could forget about getting up close with anything like that.)

He found Merry out behind the original cabin, the one Norm's uncle had built all on his own with an axe, a crosscut saw and two hard-knuckled hands. She was sitting in the dirt, her legs splayed, hair curtaining her face. The furor had died down, nothing lost, nobody hurt but Jiminy – and he had it coming anyway. The peeled yellow logs of the meeting hall shone in the sun, the goats bleated and strained at their tethers. He eased down beside her and put an arm round her shoulders. "Hey," he murmured.

Fine hairs glistened on her shins. She smelled of woodsmoke, of mush, of the river. "Jiminy can be such a prick sometimes," she said.

He wanted to agree – as in, *Yeah, he is a prick, so why not get it on with me instead?* – but held his peace. He pulled her in tighter, began to stroke her hair. "Come on," he said, "it's no big deal – everybody's a little tense, that's all. Once we get the buildings up, once we get things together, I mean, and have time to catch our breath – " He was talking horseshit and he knew it, but horseshit was what was called for under the circumstances – what was he going to use, logic?

She swept the hair away from her face and gave him a sidelong look. "You don't seem so tense. In fact, I'd say just the opposite."

And now the grin, aw shucks, and yep, you got me. "Blond Lebanese," he said, "but I haven't got enough for the whole crew and you know how they're onto the *smell* of it like hounds – Jiminy, in particular, and Tom Krishna . . ." He paused to let that sink in, incontrovertible reasoning, and then tucked the most copacetic suggestion in the world under the lid of the moment: "You want to maybe just slip into my tent a minute?"

The tent was Creamsicle orange, a one-man affair somebody had left in one of the overstuffed closets at Drop City. Pan had taken possession of it when they unloaded the bus because at the moment he didn't need anything more by way of space since he wasn't really sleeping with anybody – plus, it gave him a little privacy and a place to stash his own things. He'd pitched it two hundred yards away from the main cabin, on a sandbar upriver, and no, he wasn't worried about bears, grizzly or otherwise, because he slept with the Springfield rifle he'd shot the deer with back in California and the Winchester Norm's uncle had left behind, not to mention the .44 magnum pistol he kept strapped at his side at all times. Just let a bear poke his head in the tent. Just let him.

It was warm. Merry's hand was clamped in his. Half the tribe was mewed up in the cabin now, sitting around and picking their toes as people read chapters of *Slaughterhouse Five* aloud, smoke drifting up and away from the stovepipe and the big pan heating water for the dishes. He and Merry caught a view of them as they drifted by the open door – heads and shoulders, slumped backs, cradled arms, splayed feet – and he saw that Marco was in there. And Star. Of course, that was nothing to him, and he'd already read the book twice – and he'd rather be fishing anyway. Or fucking. Ideally, that is.

He stole a glance at Merry. Her face was neutral, chin set, eyes squinted against the sun. Her hair swayed with each step, billowing and settling and billowing again. She kept her fingers entwined in his. He saw the dogs, two streaks of liquid fire wrestling over a bone in a spray of sun on the porch, and heard Reba's kids shrieking somewhere downriver while Mendocino Bill and Tom Krishna tried to make sense of the engine that whirred and shuddered but refused to come back to life. Nobody even glanced up as he led Merry along the bank to where the tent stood slack against the ragged line of the trees.

Inside, it was so close they had to sit yoga-style, their knees touching and their hands gone idle in their laps. But Pan, Pan got right to it, turning from the waist to dig out the pipe, the matches, the tinfoil, the hash and the razor blade, all of it kept close in a plastic baggie in the front pouch of his backpack. Merry said, "I love the sound of the river," just to make conversation because conversation filled the void when people were preparing drugs for you, and Ronnie said something expected like, "Yeah, it's cool," and he held the pipe out for her and lit a match. He watched her lips purse as she took in the smoke, watched the light settle in the rings on her fingers. They were in a cocoon, hidden away from the world, the skin of the tent lit up like the lens of a flashlight. Or a sausage. That's what it was. "I feel like we're inside a big orange Italian sausage, the hot kind," he said, taking a hit and immediately feeding the pipe back to her because she was the one who needed to catch up –

Her eyes watered. They swelled and fractured, and her cheeks distended with the effort to hold in the smoke that was always precious but never more so than out here under the bleached white sky of nowhere. Then she was coughing, hacking till her lungs were blistered and her lips flecked with spittle, and he was coughing too. "It never fails," she gasped in a faltering little squeak of a voice that could have belonged to Maya, "because I think – it's my theory, anyway – that you get just as high from coughing as from the dope itself."

Pan smiled. He agreed. Couldn't have agreed more. He hacked into his fist. After a moment he laid his hands on her thighs and began to work them back and forth with a soft tentative friction. "Music would be cool right now," he said, just to say something, just to keep it going, and he thought of Lydia, back in the bus, cranking any record she felt like, and then he shook that thought right out of his head. "But you know, in some ways it's just as well that we don't have it, because we've got to *resensitize* our ears to the environment, like the moose, the caribou, the wolves – you hear the *wolves* last night?"

Her eyes were closed. She murmured something – yes, no, maybe – and then her eyes flashed open and she laid her hands atop his and guided them up her thighs. For a long moment they both looked down at their two pairs of hands working there against the hard lateral stitching of her jeans, pushing and kneading in concert, and then she leaned into him and kissed him. He heard the hiss of the river with his resensitized ears, felt the blood beating in his temples. And then he was pulling the T-shirt up over his head and fumbling with his belt and the black heavy load of the gun he kept strapped to his thigh like some TV gunslinger, like Matt Dillon or Johnny Yuma – he was a cowboy, how about that? – and she eased out her legs with an awkward rustle of the Creamsicle orange fabric of the tent and jerked her jeans and underpants down to her knees in a single motion. His hand went right to her and their mouths met again, and then –

And then Jiminy was calling her name – "Merry! Merry?" – and his sodden Dingo boots were crunching in the gravel along the bank. "You out here? Merry?"

Pan froze. So did she. Jiminy couldn't see them, nobody could. The tent wasn't made of ultralightweight semitransparent Creamsicle-colored nylon – it was made of steel, steel lined with lead and with six inches of concrete on top of that. Pan was exploding. The buckle wouldn't give. He didn't dare move.

"Merry?"

The front flaps parted suddenly and the odd mosquito drifted in on the unfiltered glare of the night just as Jiminy's face hove into view, suspended there like a second sun. That was a moment, Pan caught with his fingers in the cookie jar, Merry's eyes anything but merry and Jiminy's face working itself through a whole catalogue of conflicting emotions, beginning with slap-faced shock and progressing through enlightenment to lust, grief and hate. The river coiled and uncoiled itself. The birds said nothing. And then, with the sound of a pebble dropped from on high into the deepest pool in the broad running length of the Yukon, Jiminy gave it one more try: "Merry?"

In the morning, Ronnie volunteered to take the boat downriver to pick up two of the bus people (they were working on the furlough system) and the eight hundred sixty-seven absolutely indispensable items of manufacture and trade without which Drop City North would cease to exist in short order – and that included building supplies, tools, candy, cigarettes, shampoo, sun lotion, potato chips and cheap paperbacks of any quality and on any subject, so long as they were in English. And the mail, don't forget the mail. Everybody gave him a list – Marco, Star, Reba, Bill and Premstar, even Jiminy (and that took some balls after what had come down last night). But that was all right. They were all brothers and sisters, no hard feelings, no grudges, Free Love in a free society. Pan collected money and wadded-up slips of paper and gave back assurances and disclaimers – "Sure, sure, if I can find it, sure, yeah." He was the man of the hour and they all came to him, even Norm ("Hard candy!" Norm roared, wading out into the river as he was about to shove off, and there wasn't a thing wrong with the engine a couple of dry spark plugs couldn't rectify, putt-putt-putt, *varoom*. "The old-fashioned kind, with like butterscotch and cinnamon and whatnot. Get a big tin of it, ten pounds of it. Twenty. A hundred!")

The only problem was Verbie. She was going with him, and no, he didn't need the company, didn't need anybody except maybe Lydia on the other end of the line with her legs spread wide, but Verbie's mother was in the hospital with some harrowing nightmare of a female cancer that was turning her insides to soup and Verbie had to phone home and lighten the load though she'd walked out the door three years ago and hadn't spoken to her mother since. There was no arguing with that. *Angela* was staying. *Angela* was going to give herself over to the needs of Drop City and stay behind to scrub pans, peel logs and whip up big cauldrons full of rice pap and mush three times a day, and she shared the same mother as Verbie – wasn't that sacrifice enough?

So at nine a.m., with the sound of sifting sand in his ears and the sun like a hot poker stabbed first in one eye and then the other – too much hash, too much of Tom Krishna's poisonous homebrew – Pan swung the bow of the skiff out into the current of the Thirtymile and headed downriver, Verbie perched in the middle of the seat in front of him for ballast. Unfortunately, she was *talking* ballast, and before they even made Sess Harder's place she'd managed to change the subject six or eight times, moving without transition from the health benefits of ginseng to carpet bombing along the Ho Chi Minh Trail to mercury in tuna and the plight of the farm workers because the lettuce boycott just didn't go *far enough*. Ronnie stared off past the sidewall of her face, the too-small eye, the sickle nose, the dark gap where the tooth was missing in front. She was talking over her shoulder like some sort of cockatoo, like a trained parrot that could twist its head round twice and never miss a beat. He wasn't listening. He was trying to focus on the country, on the joy of being here, the sun warm on his back and the breeze cool on his face, his eyes scanning the near shore for something to put a bullet through. Because that was his job, that was what he was doing here, no different from Sess Harder or Joe Bosky or any of the rest of them. And who was he? He was Pan, Pan of the North, and you could forget about Nanook.

Riding with the current, it was no more than fifteen minutes to Harder's place at the junction of the Thirtymile and the Yukon, and Ronnie spotted Sess and his old lady working a log into place where they were extending the cabin out along the flank of the river. He pulled the tiller-arm hard right and swung the boat in along the bank with the intention of asking Sess if he needed anything from town, common courtesy out here, the sort of thing anybody would do, but the fact was Ronnie used every excuse he could just to *talk* to the man, to sit at his feet and pump him for information about pike holes and drift nets and the best way to smoke and press a duck.

"What do you think you're *doing?*" Verbie leaned into the turn, the breeze kicking up tufts of her chopped red hair. She tried to swing round to confront him, but the centrifugal force was too much for her.

Pan snuffed the breeze, exulting in the river smell and the speed that drove it to him. The skiff planed over the surface. He didn't bother to answer.

"We've got no time for this, Pan. *Ronnie.* Come on. You know we've got to grub everything out of that little shitbird of a store owner, who like threw a fit over the food stamps last time, and get the mail and all that and be back by tomorrow night – and that's *if* Lydia and Harmony ever went into Fairbanks for the window glass and the batteries and I don't know what else."

"Hey, this is *Alaska,* Verbs," he said, and he cut the throttle and let the skiff coast into shore on its own steam. "These people are our neighbors. I mean, I just want to ask them if they need anything – don't you think they'd do the same for us?"

"No," she said, "no they wouldn't. Not if their mother was dying and they had twenty-four people depending on them and three cabins and a meeting hall to put up before winter – "

So she was a pain in the ass. She was born a pain in the ass. Like Alfredo. Like Reba. Such were the joys of communal living. "Five minutes," Pan said. "I swear."

Sess hardly glanced up as the boat swung into shore. He and Pamela had just set the log in place, chest-high, and he was smoothing the upper surface of it with a drag knife, slivers of wood leaping away from his hands like insects in a field. He was wearing an old thermal shirt with the sleeves ripped out and his patched jeans and work boots and he'd sweated through the shirt so many times it looked as if it had been tie-dyed in eight progressively paler – and *ranker* – shades of yellow. The hair hung in his eyes, trailed down his neck and over his ears, almost long enough to qualify as hip. And from the look of him he wasn't exactly wearing out his razor either.

Ronnie tied up the boat and leapt ashore, Verbie clambering over the gunwale behind him and getting her feet wet in the process, and now the wife looked up and waved, and she was wearing dirty jeans and a plaid shirt three sizes too big for her, her hair tied back in a ponytail and her arms bare and smudged with what might have been grease or maybe mud. If Sess was the original dropout – *Sess Harder, mountain man* – then she was already halfway there, the prom queen shading to pioneer, to helpmeet, to fish skinner and plucker of goose and duck. And wasn't life beautiful?

The dogs were racketing, jerking at their chains and nosing at the sky, elevating dust. Behind them was the garden, probably a quarter acre of squash and peas and whatnot, tomatoes in a greenhouse made out of Visquine thrown over a willow frame, and to the right of that was the cache, a miniature cabin set up on timbers eight feet off the ground, where the meat was stored in winter. Sess had nailed flattened Blazo cans round each of the four posts, to discourage weasels and wolverines and anything else that might want to scramble up there and make off with tender frozen morsels of moose, duck and fish, and there was a crude ladder set to one side of the cache so humans could get at it. Then there were the drying racks. They were set out along the bank in the full blaze of the sun, and they were so congested with salmon split down the middle they were like walls of flesh – they *were* walls of flesh – and all of it free from the river. And what did you do in the summer? You collected food for winter. You hunted, farmed and fished and sat up all night under the sun that never set with a beer in one hand and a smoke in the other. And they called this work.

Ronnie came up through the brittle weed and clinging wildflowers, grinning with the thought of it – Sess Harder was the *man,* and didn't he have the world snowed? "Sess," he was saying, "what's happening, man? And, Pamela. Hey, what's happening?"

"Nothing much," was all Sess said. He went right on working, smoothing the log, blowing away the debris, even laying his head flat on the planed surface to sight along the length of it. The dogs took it up a notch as Verbie sloshed up the bank, and Pamela, holding her end of the log fast, gave her a smile with nothing but welcome in it. "You two want some tea?" she called. "I can put on the kettle."

"Oh, don't bother about us," Verbie said, kicking at the heels of her hiking boots as if that could even begin to dry them out. "We were just – "

"Sure," Ronnie said. "That would be cool. You need a hand there, Sess? And by the way, we just stopped to ask if you might need anything from town because we've got a load of stuff to pick up and we were just wondering – I mean, it would be no problem, no problem at all . . ."

They drank the tea out of shiny new ceramic cups that looked as if they'd just been unpacked from the box, and this was no herbal *rinsewater* but the real and actual stuff, brewed so strong it made your jaws ache, and they sat at the picnic table in the yard and took a break while Verbie chattered at Pamela and Pamela chattered right back and the dogs settled down around their chains. Pan was feeling uncluttered and *clean,* just soaring on the wings of the day and the glimpse he was getting into Sess Harder's intimate life. He had a thousand questions for him, but Sess wasn't quite as lively as he'd been the last time Pan had run into him (at the Bastille Day Wildflower Festival and Salmon Feast Norm had proclaimed a week back), and the only answers he got came in the form of grunts and semaphore. Sess was looking from his woodpile to his garden to his dogs, purely distracted, and after ten minutes of tea-sipping, he pushed himself up from the table and said, "Okay, Pamela, let's get back to it."

Verbie fell all over herself assuring them that it was no problem – she and Pan really had to get going, because of *x, y* and *z* – and she thanked Pamela for the tea and Sess for the company and *blah-blah-blah.* But Pan was soaring and he just had to do something for them, to express his awe and gratitude, and he kept saying, "It's no hassle at all, man, really, we'll be back like tomorrow night, I mean, store-bought bread, hamburger buns, a pint of scotch, whatever you want," until finally Pamela reached into the pocket of her jeans and extracted a bleached-out five-dollar bill that looked as if it had been printed during the Roosevelt administration and said, "Some cigarettes, maybe – Marlboro's – and we could use, I don't know, some of those Hershey bars with almonds, maybe five or six, and that good coffee Wetzel has on special – the Maxwell House? In the five-gallon can?"

Then they were back on the river, skating out of the Thirtymile and into the roiling big freightyard of the Yukon, Verbie as entranced with talking to herself as she might have been delivering up her wit and wisdom to an audience of thousands, a sweet mist of spray in their faces, clouds whipping by overhead and Pan scanning both shores for movement. The only time he responded to anything she was saying was when she lit on the subject of Jiminy and Merry and how right for each other they were and then locked her pincers into what had gone down last night. Somebody said he'd been involved. Was that true? No, he said, shouting over the motor, it was just bullshit, that was all. And he wasn't lying, necessarily, or even fudging the truth. The way it turned out, he *wasn't* involved, if involved meant getting his dick wet, because Merry snapped her legs shut, jerked her pants back up over her hips and crawled out of the tent to get all weepy and forgiving and apologetic with Jiminy, and up the river they went, his right arm in a sling and hers wrapped like a field dressing round his waist.

Half an hour slid by, the throttle open wide and the current pulling them by the nose, and he turned the volume all the way down on Verbie and listened to the way the outboard engine broadcast its news to the world. He'd just about given up on seeing anything substantial – like a moose up to its nose in a willow thicket or maybe an eagle with a fish in its claws – when something moving in the water up ahead caught his attention. It looked like a pillow off one of the sofas in his grandmother's den – or no, an ottoman, the whole ottoman, bobbing in the foam as if this were the East River instead of the Yukon. Still too far to make it out . . . but now, closing fast, he could see that it was moving against the current, and wait, wasn't that a pair of ears – and a snout?

Verbie shut down her monologue long enough to shout, "Hey, are you crazy or what?" even as the skiff veered sharply to the left and the ottoman was transformed into the head of a bear, a grizzly, with its scooped-out face and the silver hump of its back spiking out of the glacial milk of the river like a paradigm of power. Pan was electrified. *A grizzly. His first grizzly.* And here it was, all but helpless, caught out in the middle of the river, swimming. He wasn't thinking of the meat or even the hide as he eased back on the throttle and reached for the rifle. It was the claws he wanted. He'd seen an Indian shooting pool one night at the Three Pup and when the guy leaned over to line up a shot you could see the necklace dangling free of his shirt, five grizzly claws strung out on a piece of rawhide, each of them as long and thick and wickedly curved as a man's fingers – a big man's fingers. Ronnie had wanted that necklace badly enough to ask the Indian to name his price, but the Indian just gave him a blunt-eyed look and bent forward to line up his next shot. And he'd understood: you didn't buy a necklace like that; you went out to where the bear dictated the terms and you tracked him down and took it.

He cut the throttle with his left hand and shoved back the tiller so the boat looped in on the big floating head and the rippling shadow of the hulk that trailed behind it, all the while clicking off the safety on the rifle and trying to keep his hands from trembling with the sheer *excitement* of it all, and this had to be the ultimate trip, right here and now – nobody was going to believe this, least of all his Hush-Puppied, slope-shouldered, lame-ass father entombed in his Barcalounger with a gin and tonic clenched in one hand and a cigarette in the other. The rifle was at his shoulder, the boat was pitching, the big head swiveled to take him in, and there were eyes in that head, eyes that locked on his with a look of mortal surprise and maybe terror, because what was this floating piece of jetsam *bearing* down on him with people in it, people and *guns* –

"Ron*nie*!" Verbie was shouting. "Don't, don't, *Ronnie* – Pan, no!" And before he could register this new threat on the horizon she'd swung round in the seat and swiped at the gun, and that threw off his aim because he flinched at the crucial moment and felt the stock kick back at his shoulder as if the bullet were coming out the wrong end and simultaneously saw the bear's head shy away in a pink puff of spray. He'd hit it – or no, he'd grazed it, and the thing only had one ear now and there was blood, grizzly blood, streaking the water in long raking fingers of color.

Verbie was on him, her balled-up fists exploding on his forearms and her still-wet hiking boots lashing out at his knees, his thighs, his crotch, the boat pitching and yawing and the engine caught in the waking dream of neutral even as the stern dipped to the right and the first bucket of water sloshed in. "You asshole! You fucking asshole! What do you think you're doing? Did that animal ever do anything to you, huh? What is it with you? Big man, right? You've got to be the big man all the time!"

That was when the engine died. That was when, fighting her for the gun, Pan realized that the bear's big humped ottoman head had a mouth full of teeth in it and that the bear wasn't heading for shore anymore. No, the bear was coming for *them* now, plowing through the weave of the current like a torpedo in one of those grainy old *Victory at Sea* reruns his father couldn't get enough of. He snatched a look at Verbie and saw that she'd reconsidered her position – *Verbie,* the den mother, the Buddha, the hack-haired chick who was never wrong. Who never faltered. Who knew it all and was ready to tell you about it twenty-four hours a day. That was her thing, that was her trip, that was why she'd been christened *Verbie* in the first place. But now a look came over her face that fomented as much real terror in him as he'd ever known, a look that said she'd miscalculated, she'd interfered, she'd opened her big downer mouth at the wrong time and was going to pay for it with her life. And his.

Ronnie shoved her down, hard. The big head was surging across the water, no more than twenty yards away. This was a crisis. The first real crisis of his life. Nothing like this had ever happened to him, nothing, and his heart clenched and un-clenched even as he tugged at the starter cord and heard the engine cough and die, cough and die. He never even thought of the gun. It was lying in the bottom of the boat where he'd dropped it, lying there inert in three inches of water. Nor did he think of the .44 strapped to his right thigh or the bowie knife strapped to his left. *The oars,* that's what he thought. And in a pure rocketing frenzy of panic he snatched them up, jammed them into the oarlocks and began digging for all he was worth. Which, admittedly, wasn't much, because he hadn't actually had a pair of oars in his hands – hadn't actually *rowed* a boat – since he was twelve or thirteen. The oars slipped and missed, chopping at the water. Back they came, and missed again. But then they caught and held and the boat swung its nose into the current and the seething monumental toothy head of the bear – which had been so close, ten feet away, ten feet or less – began to fall back, inch by inch, foot by foot, till he couldn't hear the roar of its breathing anymore, till he couldn't hear anything but the creak of the oarlocks and the deep punishing hiss of the river.

Boynton wasn't much – a collection of unpainted shacks and log cabins the color of dirt, explosions of weed, clots of trash, stumps, rusted-out pickups, eight or ten powerboats pulled up on the gravel bar or drifting back from their painters like streamers on a kid's bike – and it would have been easy to miss if it wasn't for the bus. The bus was right there, fifty feet from the gliding dark surface of the river, planted amidst the debris outside Sess

Harder's shack – or his pied-à-terre, as Skid Denton liked to call it. Pan focused on the bus as he swung the skiff round the final bend east of town – and yes, the engine was working just fine, thank you, after he'd got done performing fellatio on the fuel line and pulling the starter cord so many times it felt as if his arm was coming out of the socket – but the bus wasn't yellow anymore, or not strictly yellow. He saw that Lydia and the other truants had been at it with their paints, an exercise in boredom at base camp, playtime, free time – *recess,* for Christ's sake – while everybody else had been humping logs and eating mush out of the ten-gallon pot. But how could he complain? This was *art,* the fruit and expression of civilization, and the strictly functional schoolbus yellow had given way to fluorescent purple and cherry-apple red, to doppelgänger green, Day-Glo orange and shattered pink. Freaks should be freaky, shouldn't they?

"Wow," Verbie said, and it was the first syllable out of her mouth since the bear incident, "wow, do you dig that?"

"What?"

"The bus. It's all done up in faces, in what do you call them – caricatures. Cartoons, I mean. Look, that's Norm, right there by the door? And Reba. And look, it's you, *Pan,* down there by the tailpipe, with a fish in your hand – "

He skated the boat in, watching for obstructions, but when it was safe, when he'd tipped the propeller up out of the water and let the thing ride, he took a closer look, and there he was, at the far end of the bus, with a head like a lightbulb and a tiny dwindling little anemic body and two fish – two *minnows* – dangling from the stringer in his hand.

"Pan," she said, "the mighty hunter."

"Verbie the yapper," he said.

He was climbing out of the boat now and he'd just about had it with her shit – they'd almost died out there, didn't she realize that? "I don't see *you* up there," he added, just to stick it to her.

Her face was clenched like a fist. She stepped out into six inches of water, and she was devastated, he could see that – imagine Verbie excluded from the Drop City pantheon – but then she recovered herself and shot him a look of pure and vibrant hatred. "I'm on the other side," she said, "you want to bet on it? Or the back, look on the back."

He wasn't looking anywhere. He really didn't give a rat's ass whether her portrait was plastered all over the bus inside and out or whether they'd raised a statue in honor of her or burned her in effigy – this was childish, that's what it was – and he crossed the yard to the bus and stuck his head in the open door.

It was deserted – you could see that at a glance. But he stepped up on the milk crate somebody had set there in the dirt to ease the transition to that first elevated step and gave a look down the aisle. Sun leaked through the curtains in thin regular bands and illuminated the dust motes hanging in the stagnant air. There was the usual clutter of clothes, books, record jackets and dirty plates, the odd smear of crushed flies and mosquitoes rubbed into the cracked vinyl seats, and a smell he couldn't quite place, some- thing promiscuous, something *communal*. "Anybody here?" he called.

No answer. And that was odd: Where could they all be in the middle of the day? In the shack? Up the bank of the river tossing daisies in the water? Tooling around in the Studebaker? But no, he could see the car out the window, sitting idle on the verge of the dirt road, and Harmony's Beetle humped there beside it under half a ton of dust. Verbie's voice came to him then, a little whoop of triumph from the far side of the bus: "Here I am! Look, I told you – I'm right here next to Angela and, and – this must be Jiminy!"

Pan backed out of the bus, his head as clear as it was ever going to be, since he hadn't had so much as a beer or a toke since he'd rolled out this morning, and no food either (breakfast, in its entirety, consisted of the honey-sweetened tea at Sess Harder's place and the handful of stale crackers Pamela had fanned out on the table like a deck of cards). Clear-headed? Light-headed was more like it. He was starving, that's what it was, wasting away like a mystic in the desert, and if he didn't get a burger and a couple beers in him pretty soon he was going to start speaking in tongues and spouting fire from his ears. For a long moment he stood there puzzling over the deserted bus, contemplating the pattern of footprints in the dust at his feet – the impress of bootheels, the elaborate punctuation of bare soles and the little necklaces of toeprints strung across the path that ran through the trampled weed to the road – and then he knew: they were at the bar, the saloon, the roadhouse, whatever they called it. The Three Pup. They were at the Three Pup, tipping back beers and maybe the odd shot of Everclear, getting a buzz on, salting fries, listening to the sizzle of burgers on the grill and the rattle of the jukebox as the record dropped and the stylus maneuvered into place. Pan was already making it up the road when Verbie came out from behind the bus. "Hey," she said, her voice trailing away till it became no more noteworthy or troublesome than the routine buzz of the mosquitoes in his ears, "where is everybody?"

The clouds had closed out the sun by the time he turned the corner onto the Fairbanks Road. Somebody's dogs rose up from their chains and howled at him and somebody else's dogs took it up at the other end of town. The breeze had shifted to the north all of a sudden, as chilly as the air leaching out of the mouth of a cave, and you didn't have to be a meteorologist to know it was going to be raining like holy hell in about three minutes. He could hear Verbie panting behind him, but he never looked back. If her legs were shorter than his, that was her problem – an accident of birth, that was all, an evolutionary dead end, *survival of the fittest, baby,* and get used to it. A faded blue pickup rolled by and he flashed the peace sign at the driver (nobody he recognized, unless maybe it was that scrawny chicken-necked old loser they called Herbert, or was it Howard?), and he ducked his head against the wind, thinking he really ought to go back to the boat for his denim jacket, but he dismissed the thought as soon as it crept into his head – going back would delay the cracking of the first beer and the sweet redolent slap of the first burger on the grill.

There was a handful of vehicles in the dirt lot out front of the Three Pup, including a tow truck with a Fairbanks logo painted on the driver's side door and what looked to be a Shelby Mustang jacked up behind it. Something was dripping from the back end of the Mustang and puddling in the dirt – water, it looked like, dirty water flecked with leaves and stripes of pond weed – and the wheels were packed like ball bearings in something that might have been grease, but wasn't. It was mud. Mud the color of shit, oozing out of the chassis and caking on the ground. Pan saw it, registered it, ignored it. In swung the screen door of the Three Pup and up rose the smell of the grill, of bourbon and scotch whiskey and beer spilled and wiped up and spilled again.

It was dark inside – why waste energy lighting up a sixty-watt bulb when you're running off a generator that runs off of gasoline hauled out the Fairbanks Road and it's light out day and night, anyway? – and at first he couldn't see whose shoulders and half-turned heads were crowded in at the bar. "Hey, Pan, what's happening?" somebody called out, and it was Harmony, Harmony there in the far corner with his rust-colored Fu Manchu and beaded headband and an arm round Alice, and then somebody else called out his name and the jukebox started up with a maddening skreel of country fiddles and where was Lydia, anyway?

But wait a minute – and this was something that really challenged his newly resensitized powers of perception – who was this looming like an apparition out of the cigarette haze with his wide-brimmed outlaw's hat cocked down over one eye and his high-heeled Beatle boots rapping at the worn floorboards like a medium's knuckles? It was Lester, that was who, Lester standing there grinning at him as if he'd just stepped out on the porch of the back house with a jug of wine in his hand and Marvin Gaye going at it on the stereo through the flung-wide door. Lester was holding a tumbler of whiskey in one hand and a joint in the other, Franklin's big head and Sky Dog's mustache framed behind him against a backdrop of astonished faces and Lynette's furiously compressed lips and bugging eyes. Dale Murray was at the end of the bar, his rings flashing, yellow-tooth necklace dangling, working on a burger and a beer and running Skid Denton as solid a line of bullshit as Denton was running him, the big tall ramrod of a guy they called Iron Steve perched up on a stool between them like a referee. "Pan, my *man*," Lester puffed in his softest imitation of a human voice, shifting the joint to his lips so he could take Ronnie's awakening hand in his own for the soul shake that reaffirmed the identity of the tribe and plumbed the deepest pockets of brotherhood. And then he was turning to crow over his shoulder: "Hey, look who's here, the bad cat himself, Pan the child-raper, the hippest baddest cat north of what? – Fairbanks. Fairbanks, yeah."

The sequel involved a whole riotous tornado of soul-shaking and back-thumping, and Pan was dazed, he had to admit it, because he'd forgotten these people even existed and it was a real adjustment in context to create them anew in the lost world of the Three Pup – and what had it been, a month? But the joint helped and the beer and a shot that went down on an empty stomach like flaming gasoline and pretty soon he was in close conference with all four of them, absorbing their tale of potholes, Nazis in the guise of the Canadian Mounted Police, blown tires and moose dancing down the highway like chorus girls.

"Shit, they busted Sky in some no-horse town in B.C.," Dale Murray said, up from his stool now and waving his beer like a conductor's baton to a sudden crescendo of hilarity, Lester so far gone with it he had to set down his whiskey and brace himself against the bar.

"For what?" Ronnie wanted to know, even as the light went leaden and Verbie stumped through the door with a dumbstruck face and the first few random drops began to thump against the windows.

"He showed his big wicked thing – " Lester began, but he couldn't go on – it was too much.

"Scared them girls up there," Franklin said, showing his teeth in a grin, and what did Pan feel? Left out. A pang of jealousy shot through him: they'd had the adventures and he'd been eating mush.

Sky Dog leaned back into the bar, lit a cigarette and managed to look rueful and put-upon at the same time. The country-inflected strains of one song faded away and another started up in its place. Everybody at the bar was looking at him, waiting for clarification. "Public indecency," he said. "I was just – "

"He was pissing against a tree, that's what he was doing," Lester said, panting between hoots of laughter. "Put a real fear into them girls, isn't that right, Franklin?"

"Whole town was terrified."

A new round of laughter. Dale Murray joined in too, whinnying along with the rest of them. Sky Dog looked abashed. He ducked his head and shrugged. "It wasn't all that funny, man – it cost me a night in jail."

"Right," Lester said, "and this spade's twenty-five bucks,

American. Which you still owe me, by the way." Then he turned to Ronnie, took a long slow sip of the whiskey, and let his eyes drop to his boots and rise again. "And you, my friend," he puffed, his voice so soft it was barely audible, "what are you dressed up to be – Wild Bill Hickok? Or maybe it's Buffalo Bill? One of them honky *Bills* anyway, right?"

Lester was enjoying this. He had center stage now, as exotic in the Three Pup as a panther on a leash. They'd seen Indians up here, they'd seen Eskimos, Finns, Swedes and Frenchmen, but a *spade* was something else altogether, and Pan could appreciate that, appreciate the strain it must have been on Lester to delve ever deeper into the redneck fastness of the last outpost of the forty-ninth state, but there were limits to what he could take. He'd let the child-raper comment pass, but now the man was mounting the balls to stand here and mock him for the way he was dressed? Well, fuck that. "I don't know what the fuck you're talking about," he said.

"The heat," Lester said, pointing to the holster. "And this – what's this?" and he had the knife out of its sheath before Pan could react, twisting the blade in the dull wash of light for the amusement of everyone at the bar. "Don't tell me you're a mule skinner now – or do you just use this thing for cleaning your nails?"

"Mule skinners don't skin anything," Dale Murray put in. "Least of all mules."

Verbie was there at his elbow, the pale muffin of her face, looking for someone to buy her a beer. "Twenty-Mule Team Borax," was her comment.

Pan couldn't have said where the anger came from or how it rose up so quickly and luminously, but he took hold of Lester's upraised wrist – the wrist attached to the hand with the knife in it – and in the same instant snatched off his hat and sailed it across the room. Lester's eyes went cold. The hair was flattened to his head, linty, dirty, twisted into something like cornrows with a couple of sky blue rubber bands, and nobody had ever seen anything like that, not since Farina anyway. "And what are you dressed up to be? You're the one in the cowboy hat."

Soft, so soft: "That's my Hendrix hat, man." And Lester let him take the knife and fit it back into the sheath while Franklin crossed the room and bent to retrieve the hat. "Touchy, Pan, touchy," Lester chided. "Don't you know I'm just goofin'? Don't you know that? Huh?"

That was when Lynette turned away from the grill, one hand at her hip, and informed them if they wanted to roughhouse they were going to have to do it over at the Nougat because any more of this sort of thing and they were out the door, all of them. "And I don't tolerate cussing in here either – you ought to know that, mister, and I'm talking to you, Ronnie. And you better inform your friends too."

"Come on, man," Sky Dog was saying, "come on, have a beer and forget it – you know Lester. He's just fucking with your head is all. It's a joke, man – can't you take a joke?"

And then it was all right and somebody found the only two rock and roll sides on the jukebox and the beers went round for everybody, even Verbie, who wound up sitting in Iron Steve's lap and drinking on his tab while he kneaded her breasts and licked the side of her face like a deer at a salt lick. Sky Dog produced another joint – "We brought a ton of the shit, man, and they almost nailed us at the border too if they were only smart enough to like look *inside* the spare tire" – and the sky darkened another degree till it was like twilight. Pan didn't hold any grudges. He was glad to see them, glad to see them all, new faces, new stories – some *life,* for shitsake – and he drank first to Lester, to put that to rest, and then to Franklin, Sky Dog and Dale. And Harmony, don't forget Harmony. And Alice too.

He had a wad of money in his pocket, and he hardly knew where it came from. It seemed to him he was a long way from home, any home, and as he contemplated his own sun-enlivened features in the mirror behind the bar he felt his life was only just beginning. Already it had taken him to strange destinations and there were stranger yet still to come. Tom Krishna was always talking about karma, and so was Norm, Verbie, Star – all of them were. What if it was true, what if he'd been a saint in some previous life and now he was set to reap the rewards? That was a thought. He smiled at his image in the mirror and tuned out what Sky Dog was saying to him about the Lincoln – they'd parked it around the corner, up in town, and hadn't he seen it? Great car. Tended to overheat and it burned oil like a hog, but

. . . he liked the way his beard was filling in, and his hair – it was long enough to eat up the collar of his shirt. He was looking hip, absolutely, indubitably, but who was going to know about it up here? Who even cared?

The rain started to pick up and the tapping at the windows became more insistent. He lit one cigarette off another and lost count of how many shots, let alone beers, he'd had. The day seemed to concentrate itself. Verbie went off on a laughing jag, Lester sniggered, somebody slapped him on the back. And when the door swung open and Lydia walked in with her hair hanging wet and full of chaff and twigs and flecks of seed because she'd been on her back in a field somewhere, her soaked-through top layered over her tits and her hand clenched like a sixth grader's in Joe Bosky's, he hardly glanced up. It was nothing to him, nothing at all. He was liquid to the bones, he was deep down and pressurized through and through, every square inch of him, a whole new medium to swim through here, and look at the *colors* of those fish. He fumbled in his pockets – "No, no, Joe, I do, I want to buy you a beer, I insist" – until he came up with a velvety worn five-dollar bill that looked as if it had been scooped out of the river and hung up to dry on a salmon rack. He held it a moment, working it in his fingers, and then laid it on the bar.

23

She was singing to herself, softly, tunelessly, a song she used to like by the Doors, the lyrics as elusive as the melody – *Break on through,* she kept repeating – *break on through to the other side.* That was it. That was all she could remember, and if she missed one thing, if there was one thing she could rub a magic lantern and wish for, it would be music. Alfredo and Geoffrey weren't half bad on the guitar, and the communal sing-alongs were great – *righteous,* as Ronnie would say – but there was no comparison to flipping on the radio or putting a record on the turntable any time you felt like it and just letting yourself drift away into some other place altogether. She used to do that at her parents' house, shut up alone in her room while the TV droned in the vacuum below and her father shouted himself hoarse over some seven-foot basketball player and a tiny little hoop, or in the car with her mother nattering on about drapes or the price of veal and a single guitar suddenly emerging from the buzz of static on the radio in a moment of shimmering triumph. Music was like food, like water, like air – that necessary, that essential – and here she was in a break-on-through mood and nothing for it but her own stumbling version caught like lint on her tongue.

You couldn't have everything, she told herself. Nobody could.

Reba and Merry were working alongside her, in the garden they'd fertilized with goat pellets and fish heads, the garden Norm had told them to forget about because the growing season up here was maybe a hundred days max and thirty of those days were in June, already dead and gone. But what they thought – the women, all the women together – was why not give it a try? Maybe they'd get lucky. Maybe there'd be a late frost this year, maybe the round-the-clock sunlight would magically accelerate the whole process of sprouting, maturing, fruiting. They worked like lunatics to get a patch of ground cleared and planted by the tenth of July, concentrating on cool season vegetables – turnips, cauliflower, Brussels sprouts – but also laying in potatoes, sugar snap peas, zucchini and pumpkin. And pot, of course. The pot plants were already two feet high and rising up so fast you could almost see them growing, and even if they didn't have a chance to bud there'd at least be the leaves and stems.

What they were doing at the moment was unrolling the big sheets of black plastic Lydia and Harmony had gone into Fairbanks for and Ronnie had brought upriver in the speedboat. The stuff came in rolls a foot in diameter and two and a half feet long, and it was perforated every couple of feet so you could rip off a sheet and use it to line your trash can out in the garage of your split-level home on your quarter-acre plot in a tree-lined suburb. But they didn't have trash cans out here – or they did, but they were strictly for storing things like lentils, rice and oats out of reach of the mice that seemed to be everywhere – and they were using long carpets of the plastic to insulate the ground around their plants, a trick they'd picked up from Pamela Harder.

And that was something totally unexpected – Pamela. She and Star couldn't have been more different – she was older, born and raised in Alaska, she didn't do drugs, or not yet, anyway, and she'd never heard of The Band or Crosby, Stills and Nash, let alone Abbie Hoffman or Gloria Steinem, the Fillmore East, roach clips, mellow yellow, Keith Richards or Mick Jagger even – and yet when Star took a canoe downriver for a visit, she felt as if she were sitting with one of her own sisters, it was that relaxed. They settled in with a pot of tea at the picnic table out by the river while Sess split wood or fed the dogs or went off someplace with his gun, and they just talked, and that was nice, because Pamela was starved for the company, and for Star it was a break from the routine, from the same faces and the same little tics and grievances and the gossip and rumors she'd heard a hundred times already.

"I don't want you to get the impression that I'm not happy here," Pamela told her the first time she'd taken the canoe out just to get a little breathing space and then seen the smoke and heard the dogs and thought she might just stop in and say hello, because why not, they were both women, weren't they? They'd already finished a cup of tea each, and Pamela, nudging a plate of homemade chocolate chip cookies across the table, paused to measure out two cups more. "Because I am. I'm the happiest woman in the world. It's just that Sess – well, he's used to being alone out here and sometimes he gets into a yes and no mode, and no matter what I say he just nods his head and gauges whether yes or no or sometimes maybe is what I want to hear. You know what I'm saying?"

The tea was like fuel, so sweet and strong it made your teeth ache. Star gazed off across the river to where the sun illuminated the trunks of the trees like slats in a fence, the dark shapes of birds swarming there like insects, everything placid but for the sharp intermittent rap of Sess's hammer from somewhere behind the cabin. "Sure," Star said, coming back to her, to her tanned face and chipped nails and big work-hardened hands stroking the cup, to her eyes that were like rooms you could live in, "and that's what I mean about Drop City, about having your own brothers and sisters around all the time – especially sisters."

"Never a dull moment, huh?"

Star opened up her million-kilowatt smile. "Oh, no, never."

"You don't get on each other's nerves?"

"We do, of course we do. That's part of it. Norm says the biggest lesson is in just learning to think alike, to anticipate, to *give,* you know what I mean? And the flow. That's important too. To feel the flow and know you're not just a me anymore."

"Is that it, then? Is that what you're trying to accomplish – kill off your ego?"

The question had taken her by surprise. She'd never really thought in terms of a clear-cut goal you could reduce to a single phrase or really even explain to anybody – she was drifting, like anybody else, hoping to break on through if she was lucky. She set down the cup and spun a globe out of her hands. "It's the earth, I guess," she said. "Nature. You know, rejecting material things and living close to nature so you can feel the heartbeat of God – or whatever you want to call that force, Gaia, the oneness of being, nirvana. And my brothers and sisters are part of it – they're my support group and I'm theirs. I mean, just look at me – I'm sitting here by this out-of-sight river in this amazing place

305

having a cup of tea with you, and that's something I never would have been able to do on my own."

"But the hair," Pamela said. "What about the hair and the weird clothes and all that? And the drugs? What does that have to do with getting back to nature?" She paused to light a cigarette, store-bought, out of the shiny cardboard box. Star watched her shake out the match and drop it to the dirt under the table. "You know what getting back to nature to me is? Just this, living day to day, working hard and taking what the land gives you, and that has nothing to do with face paint or LSD or bell-bottom pants . . ."

Star shrugged. "I don't know, it's hard to explain. It's just hip, that's all."

Pamela worked the cup between her hands, and it was her turn to gaze out over the river. She sighed. "It takes all kinds, I guess."

Star was going to agree, but she wasn't sure if the comment was a not-so-subtle dig, as in *It takes all kinds and you people are a bunch of greasy freaks and dopeheads who ought to pack up your beads and your sandals and head back to California before the going gets rough.* And then she was going to say, *And what kind are you?* but in that moment it dawned on her that Pamela was just like them. She wasn't buying into the plastic society, she wasn't going to live the nine-to-five life in a little pink house in the suburbs and find her meat all wrapped up in plastic for her at the supermarket. She'd done that – worked in an office in downtown Anchorage – and she'd dropped out just as surely as anybody at Drop City had. She was pretty, she was smart, she knew what she wanted – she was confident, that's what she was, confident in a way Star had never been, and that was something to aim for. The thought came to her: What if there were no Marco, no Norm, no Drop City? Would she be able to go out into the world and survive? Or was she just another *chick* newly hatched from the egg, all fluffy and warm and helpless?

But here she was out under the open sky nailing down strips of black plastic to feed the heat of the sun to the garden, working just as hard as any *cat* on the place, and you could hardly call that helpless. And when she was done with that she was going to haul buckets of water up from the river and dump them at the base of each plant, and when that was finished she was going to milk the goats, whip up a batch of fried rice and teriyaki salmon for lunch and pick a bucket of highbush cranberries and put them up in wax-sealed jars with a scoop of white cane sugar out of the ten-pound bag and two jiggers of brandy each, and when *that* was done, well, she'd see what the rest of the day would bring.

Merry was saying, "No way. Uh-uh."

Reba drove a sliver of wood through the plastic to hold it in place. "Jiminy said you pushed him. Everybody said so – Bill, Verbie, even Weird George. And Pan. I hear Pan was involved too."

"Well, if I did, I didn't mean to. I really like him, you know that. But sometimes he gets so fucking, I don't know, *stubborn,* like he's six instead of nineteen, and as far as Ronnie's concerned, yes, I did go up to his tent. And we got high. That's all. Not that it's anybody's business."

"What about Jiminy's? Isn't it his business? Didn't I hear you say you were going to try to make that work, no more sleeping around and da-da-da?"

Merry looked up from the other end of the sheet, disrupting the flow of it, and Star could see the light pooling like oil in the dark folds of plastic. At the far end of the garden was the original cabin, the one Norm's uncle had left behind, the logs gone gray with age, trees growing out of the sod of the roof. Beyond that was the new meeting hall, square all around and roofless still, the logs yellow as an animal's teeth where the bark had been stripped away, and a dozen people clambering all over it with saws, axes, hammers. Star could hear the muffled thump of metal on wood, the shriek of the chainsaw, the occasional curse. "I don't know, " Merry said, "I may be mistaken, but wasn't that you I saw coming out of the bushes with Deuce two nights ago? Upriver? Late? With a smile on your face?"

"We were looking for blueberries, that's all. Because if you think – "

Star could see she was lying, not that it made any difference. If Reba wanted to be a hypocrite, that was her business. And Alfredo's. She smoothed plastic. Hammered in a stake. She had a view of the hacked-over field behind them, stumps bleeding all the way down to the river, and she saw Che coming before she heard him, and they all three heard him at once, his voice raised in an unholy shriek. "Uh, Reba, I think Che needs you," she was saying, and there he was, livid protoplasm, upright and outraged, coming across the field from the river holding one limp hand out before him and wailing, Sunshine trailing behind.

Between gasps he shouted out her name – "Reba! Reba!" – because even in his extremity, whatever it was, he knew enough not to call her *Mom* like some mind-controlled zombie kid out of a suburban development. He was a brat, undernourished, unschooled, stoned before his time, but at least he knew that much. Reba got to her feet, her face gone stiff. She was wearing a beige-and-yellow western shirt with embroidered pockets, and she took a minute to dig her cigarettes out of one pocket and a lighter from the other, and even as Che came running to her to bury his screaming face in the *V* of her conjoined thighs she was exhaling the first blue puff of smoke. "What is it now?" she demanded.

He couldn't tell her. He just stamped his feet till the plastic sagged and the stakes came up and she reached down and took him in her arms while Sunshine looked on with her hands on her hips and rehearsed her own version of events. Naked, browned, pocked with the angry red eruptions of a hundred bug bites, she was the original wild child, suckled by wolves, fed on honey-dew and the milk of paradise. Her hair was kinked, tangled, sun-bleached. Her eyes were watchful. "I did not," she insisted as her brother whined his accusations into their mother's crotch. "He did. He was the one."

There was a shout in the distance. Star ignored it. They were busy here, couldn't people see that? There was work to be done and she had no patience for screaming children or the catastrophe of the hour – and they were regular as clockwork, one per hour, on the hour – and couldn't somebody find the time to sit down and read these kids a *book?* Was that too much to ask?

But the shouts were furious now, mounting – "Star!" they were calling, "Star!" – and she jerked her head round to see a knot of people running toward the goat pen with the two yellow dogs out front in a surge of kneading yellow muscle. Reba threw down her cigarette. Che's sobs died in his throat, an ache, a quiver, then nothing. Star rose to her feet at the same time Merry did, the black plastic rippling like a dark sea beneath them.

The goats were in a rudimentary pen made of eight-foot lengths of birch and cottonwood lashed to posts five feet high, a pen they planned to roof and convert to a barn for winter – and there'd been a whole storm of debate about that, because nobody really featured the goats stinking and bleating and dropping their pellets *inside* the cabins, yet they didn't really want to put the work in when there were infinitely more important things to do, like erect cabins, install stoves and split a hundred cords of wood so they wouldn't *freeze their fucking asses off* come winter. Star understood what the priorities were, but she didn't care. She'd gone ahead and built the pen herself, with a hatchet and a coil of old clothesline, and the tent she and Marco shared was pitched up against it so she could keep track of her charges in the gray wash of night.

The dogs were barking now, panting breathless gasps of assertion and rage that rang out over the river and rebounded again, and one of them – it was Frodo – was trying to clamber up into the pen. She dropped the hammer at her feet and took off running.

Everybody was shouting, crowding in against the rail as if they were at a rodeo, Frodo's hind end perched there statue-like for an instant and then disappearing even as Freak scrabbled at the crossbars and fell back. What it was, she couldn't see, the goats bleating – screaming, screaming in a key she'd never before heard or imagined – and a blur of motion visible through the gaps, now here, now there, torn from one side of the pen to the other. And when she was there, everything in an uproar, Jiminy bolting for Pan's tent to get a gun and Marco and Alfredo straddling the rail with clubs in their hands, she still couldn't apprehend what she was seeing, as if there were some essential gap between her eyes and the part of her brain that processed visual information. "It's a bear!" somebody shouted.

The white of the goats, the yellow of the dog, the wild shifting raging *brownness* of this thing that didn't belong there in the pen, that didn't compute, that was no bear at all but something else entirely, claws, teeth and fur in a fury of grinding perpetual motion and a keening sharp-edged growl that never faltered, and by the time Marco and Alfredo waded in on it with their clubs the goats were dead and gutted and Frodo was lying there in the dirt with his throat torn out and this thing, this emanation of the deepest hole in the blackest part of the last and wildest stronghold of the hills that bristled round her like breastworks, faced them down and in one leap was gone, a dark rumor in the high weed out beyond the silent pen. And later, even when she knew what it was – *Gulo luscus,* the glutton, the wolverine, the big buffed-up weasel that was so blood-crazed it had been known to drive grizzlies off their kills, she still didn't understand. All she knew was that Ronnie had the guns downriver – all three of them – and that there would be no goats to tend, not anymore, and no milk, no yogurt, no cheese. There was a party, led by Weird George, Mendocino Bill and Norm himself, that wanted to butcher the goats and make use of the meat – the whole business regrettable, sure, a real bummer, but why let the meat go to waste, that was their thinking – but she came at them like that thing itself, raging, absolutely raging, and "Why not skin Frodo, then," she said. "Why not eat him?"

She dug the holes herself. Marco stood off at a distance with a solemn face and two empty dangling hands, but she wouldn't let him help. The ground was like rock. The mosquitoes drained her. Sweating till her eyes stung and the ends of her hair clung like tentacles at her throat, she dragged the carcasses of the goats – of Amanda and Dewlap, and yes, she could tell them apart now, even at this late hour when it no longer mattered and their eyes were closed on the world – dragged them across the yard and buried them.

In the morning, when she went out there in the tall weed amidst the stumps to lay a few flowers on the raw earth and gather her strength and maybe think some consoling thoughts and tell herself it was all for the best, all part of the plan, the *flow,* there was nothing to see but two empty holes and the naked long gashes that claws make in the dug-up dirt.

Ronnie and Verbie didn't come back on Thursday night as planned, and they didn't show up on Friday either. People began to wonder, and then they began to worry. This was a slippery place, wild, unbridled, full of surprises – and if they hadn't fully appreciated that because they were so wrapped up in themselves, so focused on their hands and feet and the planing of logs and scooping salmon from the river and berries from the hills, then that thing out of the woods had served them notice. This wasn't California. This wasn't Indiana or Texas or New Jersey. They were here in this country and they were going to stick it out, no question about it, and it was beautiful here, paradise almost, but it was a whole lot *dicier* than any of them could have dreamed in their infancy back in California when there was nothing more to fret over than is there gas in the car and do they have cassava and artichokes down at the supermarket yet? They'd been lulled by the sun, by the breath of the river and the scent of the trees and the syrupy warm days that went on forever. But now there was an edge. Now they knew.

Star went out on Friday night and stared down the length of the river till her eyes felt the strain. She was worried for him, of course she was. Ronnie was the closest person in the world to her besides Marco, and she didn't know what she'd do if anything happened to him. He was her link – her only link – to all that past history, to Mr. Boscovich and the yearbook and her parents even, and though she'd never go back to that, though she'd hated it all then and hated it now, the farther she got from it the more important it became – it was as much a part of who she was as the atoms that composed her cells and the *blood material* that flowed through her veins and she needed that. Everybody did. She talked about it with Marco all the time, and with Merry and Maya. To come here, to be part of this, to do what they were trying to do at Drop City, you had to sever the ties no matter how painful that might be – but that didn't mean you had to give up the past, erase it as if it had never existed. She'd been Paulette once. She'd gone to Catholic school. She'd baked cookies with her mother, piloted her bike through the blazing blacktop streets of the development and listened to the tires peel back the tar anew with each whirring revolution, developed crushes on boys and wrote in her diary and stayed up all night talking on the phone to Nancy Trowbridge and Linda Sloniker about the most important things in the world. That mattered. It did. And Ronnie was part of it.

But Friday came and went and he was nowhere to be found. It

rained all day Saturday and people hunkered down in their tents and crowded into the one workable cabin, the original one, which was really just a single tiny room no bigger than the paneled den where Star's father and her brother Sam used to sink into the couch and watch football on Saturday afternoons. There was a chill in the air – it couldn't have been more than fifty degrees out – but still it was too hot in the cabin, too hot by far, what with the stove going in order to cook in shifts all day and the press of bodies strewn all over like human baggage, people playing cards, grousing about the weather, getting high and generally making a shithole of the place while Star and Merry tried to find room to conjure up a pot of beans and eight loaves of bread that were destined to be doughy and raw on the inside and burned black on the bottom, and what they wouldn't give for a couple of packages of La Estrella tortillas from the grocery back in Guerneville. Norm had taken possession of the only bunk in the place – the cabin *had* belonged to his uncle, after all, and the communal spirit only went so far in a pinch – and he was in it now, propped up on one elbow beside Premstar. They were playing hearts, the only game she knew, and when she slipped the black queen to him she squealed as if she'd been named Miss Watsonville all over again.

Outside in the rain, Marco and Alfredo and some of the others – it looked like Deuce, Tom Krishna, Creamola and Foster – were setting the big support beams in place for the roof of the meeting house, and wouldn't that be nice, to have some space when the weather turned really nasty? Or just space in general. Because she might have been smiling – always smiling, two sweet chick lips pressed together in beatific hippie chick bliss – but what she really felt was that she was a heartbeat and a half from going out of her mind, and if she had to step over one more stinking sockless foot or scrub one more caked-on plate because some idiot had just flung it down in the yard without rinsing it first, she was going to start screaming and only a gag and a straitjacket were going to stop her.

She glanced up and saw them there in the intermediate distance, huddled scurrying figures in drab-colored ponchos, struggling against the mud, the pelt of the rain and the shifting uncontainable weight of the timbers, and she wanted to go out and pin medals to their chests. Everybody else had given up for the day – the ones who'd even bothered to crawl out of their sleeping bags in the first place, that is. Reba had certainly made herself scarce, but maybe that was a blessing in itself because at least the kids weren't howling in and out the door every thirty seconds. Mendocino Bill had been working with Marco and the others all afternoon, but nobody had a poncho big enough to fit him and now he was huddled under the eaves of the cabin, paging through a finger-worn copy of *Rolling Stone* and shivering so hard you could hear the glass rattle in the windowframe, his overalls soaked through, his bare splayed feet like two deep corings of hard clay mud pulled up out of a drill shaft. Of course, he was *blocking the light,* that was the important thing, but Star didn't have the heart to stick her head out the door and ask him to move. She swung round, two steps to the stove, and plunged a handful of dishes into the dishpan. Jiminy was right there underfoot, nursing his arm in a filthy sling and whittling little figurines out of alder – his voodoo dolls, he called them, and he had a whole collection already, one for each sister and brother in Drop City, though they were so crude only he could tell them apart. The hair curtained his face as he worked.

Star had a vision of the future then, of the winter, music-less, dull as paste, everybody crowded into a couple of half-finished cabins with no running water and no toilets and getting on each other's nerves while the snow fell and the ice thickened and the wind came in over the treetops like the end of everything. She held it a moment and then shook it out of her head.

"You know," Norm said, raising his voice to be heard generally above the crackling of the stove and the steady drone of the rain, "somebody really ought to take a canoe on down to Boynton. I mean, to see what the deal is with Pan and Verbie, because I am hip to the fact that Verbs, at least, wouldn't want to cause anybody any hassles up here by *delaying* delivery of the window glass and the new blades for the saws and the two-stroke oil and the drag knife and timber chisels and all the rest of the wares and objects we are all crying out with need for here . . . unless maybe her mother's thing might have been, I don't know, maybe *heavier* than she thought" – and here he looked to Angela, who was wedged into the corner beside Jiminy, working a crossword puzzle in a book of crosswords that had already been deliberated over, filled in and erased by a dozen different hands. Angela never even lifted her head and you would have thought he was talking about somebody else's mother altogether. But then what could she do short of hopping in a canoe herself? Or sprouting wings?

Jiminy said, "They'll be all right. It's the weather, that's what it is."

"But what about yesterday," Star said. "And the day before." She was at the table now, trying to make salsa from canned tomatoes and a cluster of yellow onions that had lost their texture and given up their skin to a film of black mold, and even to think of chilies or cilantro was a joke. They could have drowned. Easily. In fact it was a miracle that everybody had made it upriver in one piece the first time, even with the help of Joe Bosky, who must have made five or six round-trips with gear and people and supplies while the canoes crept up against the current and Norm peeled off the hundred-dollar bills to keep the propellers whirring and the floats skidding across the water through one long frantic afternoon and a night that never came.

Premstar was concentrating on her cards and the others were just staring out the open door, mesmerized by the rain. Norm folded his hand, then looked up at Star and gave his beard a meditative scratch. "I guess I better call a meeting," he said finally, and Star followed his gaze out the door and into the dwindling perspective offered by the rain.

The next morning was clear, the sun already high and irradiating the thin blue nylon of the tent when she woke beside Marco, her mouth dry and sour and her shoulder stiff where the bedding – spruce cuttings, no longer fresh – had poked at her through the unpadded hide of the sleeping bag. Everything was damp and rank. She was glutinous with sweat because the sleeping bag was good for twenty below zero and she'd zipped it all the way up the night before, shivering so hard she could barely stand to shake her clothes off. It had been raining still when she went to bed nearly an hour after Marco had turned in, and it couldn't have been any colder than maybe forty-five degrees, but the tent felt like a meat locker, and that, more than anything, made her appreciate the concerted seven-days-a-week effort they were all putting in to get those cabins up. Teamwork. Brothers and sisters. Everybody pulling together, one for all and all for one.

Marco had told her there were old-timers up here who'd overwintered in a canvas tent with nothing more than a sheet-metal stove and some flattened cardboard boxes to keep the wind out, but she couldn't even begin to imagine it. A tent? In the snow? At fifty and sixty below? That was when you crossed the boundary from self-sufficiency to asceticism — to martyrdom — and she had no intention of suffering just for the sake of it. There was nothing wrong with comfort, with twelve-inch-thick walls and an extravagant fire and a pile of sleeping bags to wrap yourself up in and dream away the hours while the snow accumulated and the wind sang in the treetops. And why not sketch a cup of hot chocolate into the picture — and a good book too?

They'd already sited the cabins, walked them off in the dirt and sat there to admire the prospect of the river each of them would have, a little semicircle of neat foursquare peeled-log cabins like something out of a picture book, and as soon as the meeting hall was finished, they were going to start in on them. And the big question was how would they divide up the space? Who was going to live with who and would they switch midwinter if somebody really freaked out? She was thinking she and Marco would go in with Merry and Jiminy, for sure, and maybe Maya and one of the unattached guys — *cats* — but four would be nice and two even nicer.

She stretched, careful not to wake Marco. He was hunched away from her, wrapped up like a corpse in his battered Army surplus bag, exhausted from working nonstop all day in the rain. He'd been so burned out the previous night he'd skipped the meeting altogether, and at dinner he could barely lift a fork to his mouth, all the jokes and debates and crack-brained theories that made dinner so lively and communitarian every evening just flying right by him. She was thinking she'd slip down to the cabin and see what Dunphy and Erika were cooking up for breakfast (today it was their drill, and nine'd get you ten it was going to be flapjacks, with hand-carved slices of bacon on the side for the carnivores) and bring a plate of it to him here in the tent, breakfast in bed and hello and good morning and how are you this fine day, my love?

Sometime in the night she must have flung off the T-shirt she normally slept in, though she had no recollection of it, nor of having unzipped the bag either, and her thoughts were moving slowly, as if her brain were an unfilled kettle and each thought the thinnest reluctant drip of a leaky faucet. She'd smoked the night before – pot and a couple hits of the hash Alfredo was circulating after the meeting – and as she lay there now staring at the intense unearthly blue dome of the tent's roof, she felt dragged out and sluggish, as if one of Weird George's vampires had slipped in in the middle of the night, drained her blood and pumped sand into her veins in its place.

It seemed to take her forever just to sit up – was that coffee she smelled, drifting up the slope from the cabin? – and then it hit her that there would be no milk in the coffee today, unless it was powdered, unless it was canned and tasted of tin and some Elsie Borden factory tucked away somewhere in the very rusted-out epicenter of the military-industrial complex they'd all come up here to escape. The goats were dead, that was the fact of the matter. One minute they'd been pulling up brush and tender sprouts of this and that with those dainty little jerks of their heads and staring off into the slit-eyed distance in some sort of deep-dwelling goat trance, and the next they were lying there torn inside out like a pair of bloody socks. And Frodo. Everybody loved that dog. You could throw a Frisbee a hundred feet, two hundred, and he'd be there to catch it every time, magically, as if he rode on air – he'd even learned to smile, as some dogs do, the really special ones, wagging his head and lifting his upper lip to show his front teeth in a weird canine parody of the master species' favorite greeting. He was dead too. And Ronnie – what about Ronnie? And Verbie?

They'd all decided that if the two of them weren't back by noon today somebody would have to go downriver in a canoe and see what the deal was, whether it was just a delay in getting the windows and the building supplies because maybe the Studebaker had broken down or they were having a problem with the outboard engine, a leak in the bottom of the boat, choppy conditions on the river, whatever – or whether it was something darker, something nobody really wanted to think about. And who was going to go? They couldn't spare anybody, actually, because they were racing against time here and everybody, even one-armed Jiminy, was vital to the cause, but finally Angela had volunteered – it was her sister, her mother – and Bill said he'd go with her to make sure she didn't get lost, because after all she was just recently released from the penitentiary of a whole life lived in Pasadena and her notion of wilderness to this point hadn't extended much beyond the bounds of Griffith Park.

It *was* coffee. No smell on earth like it. Star kicked her feet free of the sleeping bag and pulled on her underwear and a pair of shorts, both so damp you could have used them to wipe up the linoleum floor back at home, then she slipped a very grungy tie-dyed T-shirt that might have been Marco's – two sniffs; it *was* – over her head and bent forward to lace up her hiking boots. It was then that the nothing sounds – wind in the alders, the willows, the cottonwoods and spruce, the erratic complaints of the birds, the rustle of the river – began to feature something else, something *un*natural, man-made, the drilling, straight-ahead monotone of an internal combustion engine.

She stepped out of the tent in time to see the shot-silver streak of Joe Bosky's floatplane dip behind the curtain of trees along the river and then emerge to skate out across the water on two flashing parabolas of light. The engine revved and then died as the plane faced around and its forward motion carried it up on the gravel beach in front of the cabin. By the time she got there Ronnie was already out on shore, securing the plane with a line looped around the big minder log. There was a dead moment, and then the sun grabbed the door of the plane and let it go again, and Joe Bosky was there beside him, in camouflage fatigues and a black beret, the two of them bent close, laughing over something.

It was early yet – no later than seven or so – but other people had heard the engine too and were poking their heads out of their tents or just standing there looking dazed in their bare feet and underwear. Star was the first one down to the water, and she was still half asleep herself, the tall grass tickling at her calves, insects springing away from the tread of her feet in revolving cartwheels of color. From somewhere in the depths of the cabin,

Freak let out a sharp introductory bark. "Ronnie," she called, coming across the strip of gravel and reaching out her arms for him, and all at once she was lit up with joy, just beaming, she couldn't help herself, "we were worried about you."

Ronnie didn't smile, didn't say anything. He just took hold of her – *Pan* – and he wasn't settling for any brotherly and sisterly squeeze either, not this time, wrapping her in his arms and pulling her tight to his body as if he wanted to break her down right there. And then, before she could react, he threw her head back and kissed her hard on the mouth, too hard, and held it too long, so that she wound up having to push away from him while Joe Bosky stood there grinning as if he were at a peep show or something. "Don't I rate a kiss too?" he said, and the taste of Ronnie was the taste of alcohol and cigarettes and how many nights without sleep? "Jesus," Ronnie said, "you look like shit."

She let a hand go to her temple and she shook her hair back and away from her face, vulnerable, always vulnerable. "What do you think? – I just got up. I haven't even brushed my hair yet or washed my face or anything – "

"She looks good to me," Joe Bosky said. "Like something I could spread with butter and just eat all day long." His grin was even, loopily steady, his eyes poked back in his head as if an internal whip were lashing out at them. He wore a pistol at his waist, strapped down like Ronnie's, and he'd rolled up the sleeves of his shirt to show off the cut meat of his biceps. He leered at her a moment, then clapped on a pair of silver reflective glasses that gave back nothing. He was stoned, that's what he was, up there in the air stoned out of his mind, and Ronnie was stoned too. She saw it all in a flash, the money on the bar, the dirty jokes and backslapping and the cigars and joints and one more round and hey, man, let's fly upriver and drop in on Drop City.

"So where's the boat?" she asked. "Where's Verbie?"

Ronnie gave her a look she knew from Kansas, from Denver, from Tucumcari, New Mexico, poor Ronnie, put-upon Ronnie, Ronnie the crucified and ever-suffering. "She's such a *cunt*," he said. "And I'm sorry, but I just couldn't take it anymore."

"Yes? And?"

Bosky shuffled from one foot to the other. His face was

petrified, his arms rigid at his sides. She had the sense that he wasn't with them anymore, at least not in that moment. Ronnie started to say something, and then swallowed it. His eyes were hard little pins stuck to the corkboard of his face, *too much fuel, too much*. He glanced away from her to where people were ambling down from their tents now, scratching at their morning heads and hiking up their jeans like farmers on the way to a dance. He shrugged. "I told her to go ahead and take the boat without me. She's on her way up now, with Harmony and Alice and some of the – with the windows, at least. We passed over them on our way up. Or at least I think that was them."

The cabin door flew open on this last bit of clarification and Freak came tearing across the yard, trailing a string of high, mournful barks – and yes, animals can mourn, she believed that to her soul – and Norm's voice rose up in a bellow from behind the screen: "Well, knock me down with a Cannabis bud, here he is, folks, the prodigal son returned in time for breakfast!" And then Norm was out on the porch in his unstrung overalls, all chest hair and fat puckered nipples.

Ronnie gave him a wave and Joe Bosky lifted a dead hand in the air too, after which they both turned back to the plane and began to unload what little Ronnie had thought to bring back with him. First it was his rucksack, bulging seductively. Then the guns – the rifles that belonged to Norm and Norm's uncle respectively, and why did he have to take both of them when a single bullet could have stopped that thing that had got at the goats? – and then a laminated white box with two handle grips that said u.s. postal service on the side of it, and at least he hadn't forgotten the mail, at least you had to give him credit for that. People were milling around now, eager looks, everybody waiting for the orders they'd put in, for the magazines and candy bars and eyeshadow and honey-herbal shampoo and all the rest of it, but Pan was done, Pan was turning away from the plane empty-handed, sorry, folks, come back tomorrow, all sold out. She watched him standing there fussing over his pack, the pistol strapped to one thigh, the big sheathed knife to the other, his genuine cowhide go-to-town blunt-nosed boots with the stacked-up heels dark with river water, his workshirt open to the fourth button and his three strings of beads swaying loose –

two of which she'd personally strung for him in the long, glassed-in hours coming through the dead zone of the high plains – and she thought, It's over. He's done.

But he surprised her. Because he hefted his backpack, slung a rifle over each shoulder and turned to the nearest of his brothers and sisters – it was Tom Krishna, Tom with his head bowed out of shyness and his handcrafted aluminum foil mandala catching the light at his throat – and told him, so everybody could hear, that all the rest of the stuff was in the boat, no worries, and the plane could only hold so much, dig? "We brought the mail, though," he said, and he gave the cardboard box a nudge with the wet toe of his boot.

The morning stretched and settled. Star brought a plate and a mug of coffee up to the tent and watched Marco eat in greedy gulps, the long spill of his naked torso plunging into the folds of the sleeping bag as if that was all that was left of him, and he cleaned the plate and lit a cigarette without shifting position. "That my shirt you're wearing?" he said, and she said, "Yeah," and went down to get him seconds. Everybody was awake by now, pushing flapjacks around their plates, tanking up on creamless coffee and sorting through the box of mail Tom Krishna had set out on the picnic table. There was nothing for her – she'd already checked – and nothing for Marco, because they'd fallen off the edge of the world here and nobody, least of all their parents, knew where they were. She loaded up the plate, drowned the flapjacks in syrup, and told herself she was going to have to find the time to write people – her mother, Sam, JoJo, Suzie – because it would be nice to get a letter once in a while, to correspond, to reaffirm that there was a world out there beyond the cool drift of the river. As she went back up the hill with the laden plate the polar sun reached out and pinned her shadow to the ground.

By ten o'clock it was eighty-seven degrees, according to the communal thermometer Norm had nailed up outside the door of the cabin, and the whole community, even Jiminy in his sling, even Premstar, was gathered in the yard out under the sun, focused on the task at hand: roofing and chinking the meeting house. "Finishing touches!" Norm sang out, slathering mud.

"The first and most significant building of Drop City North rising here before your unbelieving eyes, and what do you think of that, people?"

He didn't really expect an answer – Norm was talking just to hear himself, and that was his job, as guru and cheerleader – but people were feeling good, playful, celebratory even. The mud – heavy clay dug out of the bog behind the goat pen and mixed with water to consistency in a trough fashioned of old boards – was all over everybody, and there'd been at least two breaks for mud fights, but still the trowels kept going and the dead black slits between the logs gave way to handsome long horizontal stripes of ochre mud, hardening in the sun, and yes, Virginia, this was going to keep the *wind* out all winter. The roof poles – a whole forest of them, white spruce stripped and glistening and as straight as nature and a little planing could make them – were handed up brigade-style to Marco and Tom Krishna and then set in place against the roof beams, no nails, no ligatures or sheet metal couplings needed, thank you very much, because the weight of the sod – big peaty chunks of it two feet thick and with every sort of grass, flower and weed sprouting like hair from the surface of it – would hold them in place. Or that was the theory, anyway.

Star helped Dunphy and Erika make up sixty peanut butter and jelly sandwiches, a fruit salad – two kinds of berries, Del Monte peaches fresh from the can and apple wedges with the bruised skin still intact – and five gallons of cherry Kool-Aid, mildly laced with acid, just to give the occasion the right sort of send-off, and Tom Krishna saw to the music situation, setting up a little portable Sears Roebuck stereo to run off a car battery that had to be used *sparingly,* people, because there was no way to charge it up again. The music – so unexpected, so disorienting, so immediate and all-absorbing – put them over the top. People broke free to link elbows and do-si-do a step or two and then went right back to slinging mud, and then they had a sandwich and a cup of Kool-Aid, and through it all the steady wet thump of the Grateful Dead slinging drumbeats and converting steel strings to a rain of broken glass, *A friend of the devil is a friend of mine.* Star found herself hugging everybody, and she'd forgotten all about the goats, about Ronnie, who'd crawled off to crash in his tent, and she would have forgotten about Joe Bosky too – creep extraordinaire – if he wasn't right there in her face every time she turned around, helping himself to the Kool-Aid and sandwiches, rocking back and forth on the balls of his feet as if he were balancing on a pole, blowing her kisses, juggling a hatchet and a pair of kitchen knives in a dumb show that just went on and on.

But nothing could dampen her spirit. This was like a barn raising, was what it was, like something out of the history books, and here they were living it, doing it, making it happen in modern times because it was never so modern you couldn't take a step back. "This is like an old-fashioned barn raising," Star said aloud, to no one in particular, and she liked the notion of it so much she said it again, and then again, but nobody really paid any attention to her because by then they were all into their own trips, the chinking trip, the roofing trip, the take-two-steps-and-swing-your-partner trip, and the only one who responded was Joe Bosky, right there at her elbow, tossing his hatchet and his knives, and what he said was, "It sure is, sweetheart, and I'd raise a barn with you anytime."

It was late in the afternoon, the meeting house chinked inside and out, the roof in place and buried in sod so that it looked as if a whole meadow had been transposed from the earth to the air, just floating there like a magic carpet strewn with flowers – and that was a trip, it was, everybody agreed – before anybody gave a thought to Verbie. Dinner was cooking – salmon fillets rubbed with dill and roasted over the open fire, with brown rice, stewed cranberries and a pot of communal mustard on the side – and all of Drop City was feeling relaxed and confident. They'd done it. They'd come all the way up here and built a place from scratch, with the materials at hand – free materials, provided by nature – and if they could do that they could build the cabins too, and why stop at three? Why not four or five or six of them? Why not make a whole camp of the place, like Camp Minewa, where there were four girls to a cabin, bunk beds up against the wall and plenty of space for everybody? Marco was talking about a smokehouse and Norm was pushing for a sauna and maybe even a hot tub, and at lunch he went into a long, acid-fueled oration on the Swedes and hot rocks and hotter water, on

Chippewa sweathouses and purification rites, until he talked himself hoarse. Sure, people said. Yeah, sure, why not? Because there wasn't anything they couldn't do, and if anybody still doubted it, all they had to do was take a look at the meeting hall standing there tall and proud where before there'd been nothing but scrub and trees and a pile of dead gray rock. And so everybody was smiling, and it wasn't just the mellowing influence of the acid either. This was genuine. This was real. And Verbie? She was on her way upriver, wasn't she?

Star was outside, setting the big split-log picnic table for dinner, when the high sharp whine of an outboard engine broke free of the trees. Verbie, she thought. And Harmony and Alice and the shampoo, magazines and flashlight batteries she'd put in an order for, and chocolate – she could die for chocolate. She dropped what she was doing and let her feet carry her down to the river.

Half a dozen people were already there, the water giving back sheets of light as it paged through its boils and riffles, the sky striped with cloud till it looked like one of the paint-by-numbers scenes she'd never had the patience to finish as a child. Weird George was perched barefooted atop a rock out in the middle of the current, wet hair trailing down his back like a tangle of dark weed, Erika waist-deep in the water beside him. The dog was there too, Freak, in up to his chest and wagging the hacked-off stump of his tail, and it was warm still, very warm, no different from high summer on the Jersey Shore. And that was what she was flashing on – the Jersey Shore, she and Ronnie and Mike and JoJo and some of the others from the stone cottages and the weekend they'd spent camped on the beach there, all sunlight and the tug of the salt drying on your skin, bonfires at night, clams steamed in their own juice – as the boat drew closer and she began to realize that this wasn't Harmony at the tiller-arm, or Verbie or Alice either. That was Verbie, there, in the bow, the pale mask of her face riding up and jolting down again, but who was that in the middle seat, and who in the rear?

The engine droned. The boat came on. Star turned her head and gave an anxious look over her shoulder to where Marco and Alfredo were kneeling atop the roof of the meeting house, inspecting their work, and she wanted to call out to them –

"Look, look who's coming!" – but she checked herself. A few of the others glanced up now, curious, because two arrivals in a single day was unprecedented, and she could see their faces lighting up – Jiminy and Merry at the door of the cabin, Mendocino Bill and Creamola pausing dumbstruck over a game of horseshoes, Premstar with her hair piled up on her head and a magazine in her hand lurching out of the hammock Norm had strung for her. A breeze came down the riverbed, rattling the willows along the shore. Freak began to bark.

She turned back round just as the boat slid behind the rock where Weird George was waving his arms and shouting something unintelligible over the noise of the engine, and for an instant he blocked her view. Then the boat shot forward and she saw who it was standing up now in the middle seat, and she couldn't have been more surprised if it was Richard M. Nixon himself. "Dale!" somebody shouted. "Hey, Dale!" And then, before she could think or even react, Sky Dog was gliding by, one hand on the tiller, the other flashing her the peace sign.

24

They were talking nonstop, really spinning it out, and if he didn't know better he would have thought they'd just been released from separate cages, one tap on the steel bars for yes, two for no. It was a kind of verbal diarrhea – a tag-team match – Sky Dog rushing in to fill the void when Dale Murray paused for breath, and vice versa. And the thing was, people wanted to hear it, every word of it, because this was the diversion, this was the entertainment for the evening. Nobody had left the table. A bottle of homebrew made the rounds, hand to hand and mouth to mouth. Norm produced a fresh pack of cigarettes, shook one out, and passed the pack on. Bones and salmon skin stuck fast to the plates, the leftover rice went hard in the pot, flies buzzed, mosquitoes hung like ornaments on the air. People's eyes were on fire. They laughed, chatted, laid communal hands on one another's shoulders, and it was just like Leonardo's reprise of the Last Supper, except the Christ figure was two Christs, Dale Murray and Sky Dog.

"And that was a trip, the whole bike thing, because in – where was it at, Dale?"

"Dawson."

"In Dawson, they'd never even *seen* a Honda before, especially a beast like that, seven hundred fifty cc's, Windjammer fairing, I mean, *chrome* everything, and the first guy out the door of the saloon offered him twenty-two hundred for it – *Canadian* – and Dale, I'll tell you, Dale never looked back."

"That's right, man. Bet your ass."

Marco shifted his weight from one buttock to the other on the hard split plank of the seat, thinking he could do without the heroic exploits and the thick paste of smirks, nods and asides that seemed to have everybody glued to their seats, thinking the two of them should have stayed in Dawson or Whitehorse or wherever they'd blown in from, anywhere but here. They'd shown up like conquering heroes when the worst part of the work was already finished, that was what he was thinking, and what had Dale Murray – or Sky Dog, for that matter – ever done for Drop City? He exchanged a look with Alfredo, elbow-propped across the table and two places up, but Alfredo was keeping his own counsel. And hadn't they banished Sky Dog once already? Or was he dreaming?

Up at the head of the table, seated at the right hand of Norm, Premstar was giggling, and the pot – Sky Dog's pot, Dale Murray's pot, Lester's and Franklin's pot – kept circulating. When the communal joint came Marco's way he took it like anybody else, a pinch of the thumb and index fingers, Joe Bosky's compressed fingertips giving way to Star's and Star's to his own. The Kool-Aid was gone, and he thought he felt a mild residual buzz from it – it hadn't been intended as anything intense, but just something to focus behind, and he'd had maybe two cups of it hours ago – and now Reba and Merry were hovering over the table with a big blackened pot of hot chocolate and people were dipping their cups into it and the steam lifted off the pot in a transparent crown. Freak had stopped begging – glutted finally – and he lay at Star's feet, grunting softly as he plumbed his balls and nosed under his tail for fleas. Jiminy got up and held his lighter to the pile of brush and lopped-off pine branches he'd raked together for a fire, and before long the smoke was chasing round the table at the whim of the breeze, a nuisance surely, but at least it discouraged the mosquitoes.

Dale Murray said, "Kicked his ass for him, what do you think?"

Norm said, "Public *what*? Indecency? You got to be kidding."

Marco exhaled and passed the joint on to Dunphy, her fingers cold, spidery, bitten, thin, the briefest fleeting touch of skin to skin, and she gave him a blank-eyed look and half a smile and put the roach to her lips and sucked. He glanced down at his own fingers, at his hands laid out on the chewed plank of the table. The fingernails were chipped, the cuticles torn, dirt worked into every crack and abrasion in a tracery of dead black seams. These were the hands of a working man, a man putting in twelve- and thirteen-hour days, the hands of a man who was building something permanent. Pride came up in him in a sudden flush. And joy. That too.

"Tired?" Star murmured, leaning into him.

For answer, he pressed his palms together in prayer, then tilted them and made a pillow to lay his head on.

"And Lester," Sky Dog was saying, "you should have seen Lester – man, they wanted to lock him up so bad, just on general principles, you know? But he gave them the old shuck and jive and smiled so hard at this one guy – I don't know what he was, a Mountie, a sheriff, something – I thought he was going to melt right down into his boots like a big stick of rancid butter. Oh, and, shit, the moose – did I tell you about the moose?"

Alfredo cut in. He wanted to know where Lester was – was he planning on coming upriver? Because if he was, it was going to be sticky, real sticky, after what went down in California, and he didn't want to sound prejudiced or anything, because prejudice had nothing to do with it –

"He stayed behind at the bus," Verbie said, picking at a crescent of white bone. "With Franklin. They're panning for gold."

Joe Bosky let out a hoot. "Fucking greenhorns," he said. "Cheechakos."

"All's I know," Sky Dog put in, "is they got this vial half-filled with gold flakes already, and all they been doing is just catching what comes out of that creek up north of town – "

"Last Chance Creek," Bosky said, folding his arms. The pale white ridge of a scar crept out of his aviator's mustache and curled into the flesh of his upper lip. You could see where every hair of his head was rooted. "They should've called it No Chance Creek. Nothing in there but sewage leaching out of people's septic tanks."

"Sorry, man, but I saw it, I'm telling you – that was *gold* in there."

"Iron pyrites," Verbie said, and then Norm weighed in. "Could be gold, who knows? You want to talk gold country, this is it, and I fully intend to get out there and rinse a couple pans myself, me and Premstar. Once the cabins are up. Because why not? It's *money* in the bank, people, and it's out there for the picking, just like the berries and the fat silver salmon coming up the river, and do I have to *remind* anybody what we're doing up here in the first place?"

Jiminy said he could feature some gold – maybe Harmony could figure out a way to melt it down and make ornaments and figurines and the like – or maybe they could just sell it and use the money for things like a new generator so they could have a little music more than once a week. And lights, what about lights. Wouldn't lights be nice?

People ran that around the table a while, the gold flecks that would invariably prove to be iron pyrites growing exponentially in each Drop City head till the creek across the river ran yellow and the trees on the hills gave up their roots and toppled because it wasn't earth they were growing in, but solid gold nuggets. Marco tuned them out. He'd never been so tired in his life. And if it wasn't for the elation he was riding on – the meeting house was up, the walls chinked and the roof in place, and who would have believed it a month ago? – he'd have crawled into his sleeping bag by now. But he held on, stroking Star's bare arm with the tip of one very relaxed finger and letting the marijuana turn the blood to syrup in his veins.

They'd made the meeting house two stories, with the beams laid inside for a loft where people could sleep if the need arose, and that was good thinking, a happy result of sitting down with a sheet of paper and a pencil and talking it all out beforehand with Tom, Alfredo and Norm. Norm knew what he was doing, for the most part, at least, and Sess Harder, fifteen minutes down the river, was like an encyclopedia – he was the one who told them to lay flattened cardboard over the roof poles so none of the loose sod would leach through the cracks – and the uncle had left behind a pristine copy of *The Complete Log Home,* copyright, 1910, which they could consult as needed, but really, Marco couldn't help marveling over how *basic* it all was. You cut and peeled the timber, notched the ends of the logs till they were no different, except in scale maybe, from the Lincoln Logs every ten-year-old in America constructed his forts and stockades with, dug down two feet to permafrost at the four corners and stacked up rock to lay the first square across and built on up from there. Then you laid the floor – with planks carved out of spruce with a chainsaw ripper – cut holes for the windows and a six-inch slot for the stovepipe, and you had it. Basically, that was it. And if they could all pitch in and build something like this – two stories high, twenty feet long and eighteen across – then the cabins would be nothing more than a reflex.

"What about Harmony and Alice?" This was Norm, leaning into the table and giving Sky Dog and Dale Murray a look over the top of his glasses. "And Lydia, what about her?"

"You know Harmony," Sky Dog said. "He's got a kiln set up outside the bus and he says he's experimenting with some things and he's not ready to come upriver yet, at least that's what he told me and Dale. Plus the Bug is broken down."

"He ordered a new fuel pump for it," Verbie put in. "From this place in Anchorage."

Norm dug his fingers into his beard, slid the glasses back up his nose. "And Lydia?"

To this point, Joe Bosky had been subdued, his dig at the gold situation the only thing out of his mouth all evening. He'd been locked behind the wrap of his silver shades since morning, stoned on a whole variety of things. When the hot chocolate went round he'd shuffled unsteadily to the plane and came back with a bottle of Hudson Bay rum and set it on the table, and a couple of people followed his example and spiked their chocolate with it. He cleared his throat in response to Norm's question and leaned over to spit in the dirt before bringing the solidity of his face back to the table. "She's in Fairbanks," he said.

"Fairbanks?"

A murmur went round the table. If it was true, this was disturbing news, evidence of their first defection, the first betrayal of the ideal. People eyed one another up and down the table – who was next? Where would it end? Was the whole thing going to come tumbling down now? Was that what this meant? Marco slouched over his plate. For the moment, at least, he was too tired to care.

"What do you mean, Fairbanks?"

Joe Bosky's voice was thick in his throat. "I got her a job at this place I know. A saloon. She's going to be a dancer."

And now Verbie: "Only till winter, though, is what she told me. To get some money together, for all of us – she's doing it for

329

all of us – and then she's going to come back to the fold. That's a promise, she said – tell them that's a promise."

"And if any of you other girls are interested," Bosky said, and here he turned to Star and fixed his null gaze on her, "I can arrange it, because Christ knows they are starved for women up here. And Lydia. I mean, she's a natural, with that body she's got on her – "

"You mean topless, right?" Maya said.

"Right down to her G-string, honey, because full frontal nudity is still against the law in this state, but I tell you she's going to take in more tips a night than you people'll get in a month out of welfare or food stamps or whatever it is you're on."

Everyone looked to Norm, whether they were conscious of it or not. And Norm, at the head of the table, hair dangling from the cincture of his headband, the cowbell like a cheese grater hung round his neck, set down his cup of chocolate and licked his mustache till all the sweet residuum was gone. "All right," he said finally. "Cool. I mean, we can live with that, right, people? Lydia's going to show off what she was born with and make a little cash for Drop City in the bargain, and where's the problem with that?"

Verbie's voice came back at him like a whipcrack. "It's exploitation."

"Exploitation of what?"

"Of the female body. It's sexist. I mean, I don't see any of you men up there dancing in your jockstraps or whatever – "

"Only because they didn't ask," Norm said, and people were laughing now, avowals going up and down the table, and then Sky Dog said he'd do it in a heartbeat.

"Oh, yeah," Verbie shot back. "Then why don't you do it now? Why not get up on the table and give us something to look at, come on, let's see what you got, big boy, come on – "

Sky Dog rose unsteadily from his seat and began undoing the buttons of his shirt while the catcalls rang out, but once he got his shirt off, he seemed to lose track of what he was doing – gone into the wild blue yonder – and he sat back down again.

"Chicken," Merry said.

"See, what'd I tell you?" Verbie said.

And then Premstar, propped up beside Norm like a painted

mannequin, Premstar the beauty queen who was more worried about her nails and her lipstick and her eyeliner than about anything that could possibly go down at Drop City, past or present, entered the conversation for the first time all night. "What about our treats?" she demanded. "All the things we ordered from Pan, I mean. Did everybody forget, or what?"

That was the unfortunate moment Ronnie chose to come bobbing across the field from his tent, the sun firing the threads of his hair, his torso riding over his hips as if he were walking a treadmill, and the table fell momentarily silent to watch his progress. Everyone was thinking the same thing. Pan had been crashed in his tent all this time, out of sight, out of mind, but the boat had come in with Verbie and Sky Dog and Dale, strange cargo indeed, and the windows for the meeting house and the three prospective cabins were there, uncracked and true, and the cans of kerosene and the bar oil and blades for the saws, but nothing else. No candy bars. No underarm deodorant. No books or magazines or tubes of suntan lotion. And if they weren't in the plane and they weren't in the boat, then where were they?

"Hey, Dale," Sky Dog said, trying to get it going again, "remember that shit they tried to palm off on us in, where was it, Carmacks, in that roadhouse? *Moose*burger they called it?" But nobody was listening. All eyes were on Pan as he shuffled up to the table, tucking in his shirt and swatting absently at mosquitoes. Even Freak lifted his head from the dirt to give him a look of appraisal. The smoke drifted. The moment held.

"Hey, what's happening," Ronnie said, leaning over Marco's shoulder to peer into the depths of the nearest pot. "Am I too late for dinner?"

At first, he tried to deny everything, squeezing himself in on the bench between Star and Joe Bosky and scraping what he could out of the bottom of the pot, all the while mounding it up on the first plate that came to hand, and never mind that it had already been used, he wasn't fussy. He was wearing his glad-to-be-here look, all smiles and dancing eyes, and he'd put a little effort into his clothes too, his denim shirt clean and maybe even pressed and what looked to be a new bandanna wrapped round his head. He found a fork, wiped it on his jeans, and began to feed the hardened dregs of rice into his mouth, too busy eating to address the issue of Drop City's trust and the two-column shopping list he'd wrapped round the wad of bills everybody had thrust on him five days ago. Marco studied the side of his head, the sparse thread of his sideburns tapering down into the sparser beard, the wad of muscle working in his jaw, but Ronnie was making eye contact with no one, least of all Premstar, who'd just looked directly at him and said, "So where's our stuff?"

Now she repeated herself, and Reba, the hunt in her eyes, said, "Yeah, *Pan,* what's the deal? Are you going tell me you forgot, or what?"

If Ronnie was hoping it would blow by him, he was going to be disappointed, Marco could see that. He hadn't given him any money himself – he'd been too busy to think of needing or wanting anything – but Star had, and that was enough to involve him right there, more than enough. To this point, Pan had been fairly innocuous, shying away from the construction or anything that smacked of real work, maybe, but taking charge of the boat and the drift net Norm's uncle had left behind and assiduously drilling holes in anything that moved out along the river, and that was meat nobody else was going to go and get, at least not till the cabins were up anyway. He's doing his own thing, that's what Star said whenever his name came up in relation to the work details Alfredo was forever trying to organize – the latrine crew, the bark-stripping crew, the wood-splitters and sod-cutters – and the way she defended him was an irritant, certainly, but Marco wasn't jealous of him, or not that he would admit. *Of course I love him,* Star had insisted, *but like a brother, like my brother Sam, and no, we never really slept together, or not in any way that really meant anything –*

"Is that booze I see here on the table? Distilled spirits? *Al*-co-holic beverage?" Ronnie lifted his head and darted a glance at the sun-drenched bottle of rum rising up out of the wooden slab at Bosky's elbow. "What are we mixing it with?"

"The stuff, Ronnie, the stuff," Reba said. "We were talking about the stuff we all gave you money for – where is it? Huh?"

He reached for the bottle, found a cup, poured. Everybody at the table watched him as if they'd never before seen a man lift a cup to his lips, and they watched him sip and swallow and make a face. "I thought it was – didn't we bring it in the plane, Joe? I mean, this morning?"

But Joe Bosky was no help. He sat there frozen behind his glazed lenses, not even bothering to swat at the mosquitoes clustered on the back of his neck. A dense spew of smoke raked across the table and then dissipated. No one said a word.

"Jesus," Ronnie said, slapping at his forehead. "Don't tell me I left all that shit back at the bus – "

"Oh, cut the crap, already. You didn't leave anything anywhere, did you, man?" Mendocino Bill rose massively at the far end of the table. He'd put in an order for Dr. Scholl's medicated foot powder, because he had a semipermanent case of athlete's foot and the itching was driving him up a wall. "You fucked up, didn't you?"

Ronnie looked wildly round the table, his mouth set, eyes jumping from one face to another. He was calculating, Marco could see that, dipping deep in the well, way down in the deepest hole, fishing for a lie plausible enough to save his neck. Marco had no sympathy for him, none at all, and in that moment he realized how expendable he was, whether Star needed him as confessor or not – or no, especially because she needed him. Or thought she did. The shadows deepened. A hawk screeched from a tree at the edge of the woods. "What about it, Pan?" he heard himself say.

"Talk about the third degree," Ronnie said, and he was looking down at the table now, toying with his fork. Suddenly he let out a laugh – a high sharp bark of a laugh that startled the dog out of his digestive trance – and he raised his head and gave Marco a sidelong look. "All right," he said, "all right, you got me. I fucked up. Had one too many drinks, you know, and I just . . . I don't know, I just, I guess it slipped my mind – "

He must not have found much comfort in the look Marco was giving him, because he ducked his head again and murmured, to no one in particular, "So go ahead and hang me."

A moment ticked by, everybody staring at the spool of his bowed head, the rings flashing on the fingers of his right hand – a ring on every finger, even the thumb – as he fed congealed rice pap into his mouth with the slow, trembling incertitude of a penitent. Freak got up from under the table, stretched, yawned and stared off at something across the field and into the line of the trees. Star sat there rigid. Her face was white, bloodless, drawn down to nothing. She was giving Ronnie a look Marco couldn't fathom – was she afraid for him, was that it? Or was she ashamed? Ashamed and disgusted? He was almost surprised when her voice broke the silence: "So you'll be giving everybody their money back now, right?"

Ronnie took another pull at the mug, again made a face. He looked like a cat scratching around in a litter box. "Christ, has anybody got a Coke? Or a Pepsi? I'd settle for Royal Crown, even – this shit is *harsh*." He shot a glance at Star, then looked down at his plate. "Well, not exactly," he said, and an angry murmur burned from one end of the table to the other. "Because, you've got to understand, I saw this opportunity – pot, I mean, the pot Lester and Franklin smuggled in, because where else do you expect to find weed in Alaska? Beyond what we brought, I mean. So I figured what do we need most of all, the single biggest thing? And what are we going to need to get us through those long dark nights that are going to be coming before you know it? Right? Weed. So I made an investment for all of us."

"You're a real altruist, Pan," Reba said.

Bill hadn't sat down yet. He was still hovering there at the far end of the table, the fat firming to muscle in his shoulders and arms, the long slant of the sun crystallizing the strands of grease in his river-washed hair. He looked pained. Looked as if someone had just poked him with a sharp stick. "Yeah, right," he said, and he growled it, his voice hoarse and raw with suppressed rage, "you mean the pot you tried to sell me this morning for thirty bucks a lid?"

"Fuck you," Ronnie said, and he was on his feet now too, trying to untangle his legs from the table, trying to get serious, get angry. "I mean, fuck you, you fat sack of shit."

And of course Bill rose to the bait, coming round the end of the table in the swelled-up shell of himself, coming at Ronnie like a moving mountain, and Marco thinking two or three punches and they're separated and Ronnie can go off in a huff to his tent, put-upon and abused, after which there would be an offering of pot, not all of it, maybe, and certainly not anywhere near the value of it, and by the end of the night the blame would be meliorated and the sinner redeemed. But he was wrong. Because before any of it could play out, Joe Bosky entered the mix. Somehow he managed to lurch up and kick himself free of the bench in time to intercept Bill before he could get to Ronnie, who was only then bracing himself to meet the first rush. Everybody else sprang up simultaneously from the table, Reba cursing, Che and Sunshine looking lost and bewildered, Alfredo shouting, "No, no, no!"

Bosky never hesitated. He dropped his shoulder and slammed into Bill as if they were out on a football field, helmet to breastbone, and Bill's feet got tangled and he went down heavily in the dirt. Almost immediately he pushed himself up, his face transfigured with rage, but before anyone could intervene, Bosky hit him with two quick white fists – two uppercuts delivered as he was blundering to his feet – and Bill went down again. That was when Alfredo and Deuce made a move to wrap Bosky up in their arms, but Bosky swatted them away as if they were nothing and swung round to face off the whole camp. "Nobody fucks with Pan like that," he snapped. "You understand? It's not right, because I want to tell you" – and here his voice got sluggish and he staggered back and caught himself – "I want tell you Pan is Joe Bosky's buddy and nobody fucks with Joe Bosky."

Marco was just standing there with the rest of them, hands at his sides. It wasn't his fight. Then he saw Bill scrabbling in the dirt with a split lip and a film of blood enlivening his teeth and Bosky standing over him in his paramilitary getup, and began to grope toward the realization that maybe it was his fight after all. What was Bosky doing here, even? And what was this business with Star – he'd been coming on to her all day and Marco had let it pass. Maybe, he was thinking now, he shouldn't have.

But here was Jiminy, all hundred and thirty-five pounds of him, pushing his way through the crowd. "Who the hell are you?" he said, throwing it back at Bosky. "You're not part of this – you don't even belong here."

"That's right," somebody said, and then Reba was there, her face a mask of war, doing what nobody had yet thought to do – namely, help Bill up out of the dirt.

Bill was heaving. There was blood on his coveralls. Reba

stood there beside him with her honed eyes, propping him up. She looked first to Ronnie, then to Bosky. "We don't need this kind of shit here," she hissed. "You want to have your drunken brawls, take it someplace else. We've got kids here."

And there they were, Che and Sunshine, backed up against the slashed crossbars of the cabin porch, hair in their faces, their eyes reduced to twin nubs of malleable black rubber, and anybody could mold those eyes, Marco thought, make them laugh, make them cry. He felt nothing but sad. "I'm with Reba," he said.

"All right," Joe Bosky spat, "I know when I'm not wanted, don't let the door hit you on the way out, right?" and he started off toward the plane, unsteady on his feet. He hadn't gone five yards before he turned round and focused the glare of his silver shades on Pan, on Ronnie. "You coming," he said, "or what?"

Ten minutes later, while people milled and debated and groused and Bill pressed a cold wet towel to his face, they heard the plane's engine start up with a sucking roar, as if someone were out there vacuuming off the surface of the river. Then the accelerating whine of the propeller came to them and they looked up to see Joe Bosky's floatplane glide out from shore, catch the current and taxi into the mouth of the trees only to rise a moment later and flare off into the night sky with a single reflective flash of the declining sun. Marco stood there watching it a moment, then took Star by the hand and walked her down through the field of foot-worn flowers and trampled weed to a place where they could look out over the ripples and braids of the current. He eased himself down, and she sat in the gravel beside him. "There goes Ronnie," he said.

Star drew her knees up and knotted her arms round them. For a moment she said nothing, just seesawed back and forth, her white compact feet beating time to the motion of her body. "He'll be back," she said.

"You really think so?"

She looked off across the river. It was late, midnight or thereabout. The colors went up in layers, from the scoured tin of the river to the dense black-green of the trees to the pink band of the sun-brushed hills. A sickle moon, pale as ice, sketched itself in over the trees. She cursed and slapped a mosquito on her ankle, then another on the back of her arm. "Really?" she said finally, turning to hold his eyes. "Truly?"

He shrugged, as if it didn't matter one way or the other.

"No," she said. "I don't think so. I think he's – " There was a catch in her voice and he wanted to rock her in his arms but that catch made him hesitate, made him angry and hateful and jealous. "I think he's gone," she said. "For good."

That was when they heard the motor out on the river and they looked up unbelieving, because this had been a day of arrivals and departures, an unprecedented day, nothing like it yet in the brief history of Drop City North – first Bosky and Ronnie, then Verbie, Sky Dog and Dale Murray – and now who was this slashing up against the dark run of the current? They watched as the boat – it was a skiff, flat-bottomed, snub-nosed, like any dozen of them up and down the river – took on color and shape and finally emerged from the dark screen of the littoral and swung into shore fifty feet from them. A stooping, raw-boned figure clambered over the seat from stern to bow, flinging something ashore, a sleek bundle that fell formless to the gravel, and then a pair of scissoring legs splashed ashore and there he was. "Hey, hello there," he said, stooping to the bundle and pulling himself up out of the fade of light. "Isn't that – ?" Star began, and they were both on their feet now, but she couldn't supply the name.

Marco gave back the greeting and the man came toward them, the stripped bones of his face under the long-billed cap, the awkward challenging height of him, and then he knew: it was the one from the bar, from the Three Pup, the one they called Iron Steve.

Iron Steve was in gum boots and a plaid flannel shirt and his hair was slicked tight to his head, and his every step was like a leap, as if the ground were cratered beneath his feet. "Hey, I sure hope I'm not bothering you people this late, but I was, uh, well – I was looking for Verbie. She around?"

Star said sure, she thought so, if she hadn't gone to bed yet, and there was an unspoken question tagged on to the end of it.

Iron Steve raised his right arm and the bundle came with it, stiffened feet and limp naked ears, the sleek jackets of fur –

rabbits, he was holding up a string of rabbits on a twisted coil of wire, and all Marco could think of was fish, dark dangling strips of flesh strung through the gills. "I brought these for her," Iron Steve was saying. "I thought I might surprise her. You know which tent is hers?"

Star gave Marco a look and they were both thinking the same thing, thinking dead meat for a vegetarian? And rabbits – *bunnies* – no less? But then Marco saw the beauty of the equation: Ronnie was gone, gone no more than half an hour, and here was his successor. Subtract one Pan, add one Iron Steve.

"I also brought her this," Steve said, and he held out his palm to show them a coil of wire and a medicine bottle with what looked to be matches packed inside.

"What is it?" Star asked. It was twilight now, the sun edged down beyond the ridge, the sickle moon brightening. She stood with her legs apart, hands on her hips, and the mosquitoes meant nothing to her though they danced and swarmed and played their thin music over the backbeat of the river.

"This? Oh, this is just a little something I thought she ought to have – in case she gets lost."

"Gets lost?" Star said.

Iron Steve pulled back his hand, ducked his head. "Oh, yeah," he said, "everybody gets lost up here, whether it's your plane going down or your tracks getting obliterated in a whiteout or you're just out there chasing after something and you turn around and can't tell one tree from the other."

"So what is it," Marco said, "some kind of compass?"

"Oh, hell, no," Steve said, grinning, and out came the hand again, the palm supinated to display the wire and the thick brown glass of the medicine bottle. "Long's you have wire, you can snare rabbits," he explained, "and the matches, I dipped them in paraffin myself and sealed them up tight. Because if you keep your matches dry you got yourself a fire to kick back the cold and roast your rabbits – "

Star gave him a blank look. Marco couldn't help but smile.

"You know," Steve said, "for emergencies." He kicked a foot in the fan of gravel and studied the slow rotation of the toe of his boot as if it were a divining rod. Then he looked up, grinning still. "Up here we call it living off the land."

25

It was the first really brisk day, August tapering off into September, high summer giving way to low fall, and Pamela was alone in the cabin, baking bread in the woodstove in the front room. The recipe was her mother's – 3 cups white flour; 1 cup whole wheat flour; 3 tablespoons sugar; 1 teaspoon salt; 2 cups sourdough sponge; 2 to 3 tablespoons melted bear fat (she was using canned butter because as far as she knew the bears were all still alive and well and judiciously carrying their own fat around with them) – and she'd modified it a bit through the ten or twelve times she'd baked here on the Thirtymile, but still, if the stove was hot enough and she had the patience to let the dough rise for two hours or more, she usually got a rich heavy glistening loaf that had Sess pulling the superlatives out of his slow-grinding jaws. Outside, a sky the color of soapstone hung low over the hills. The wind was blowing down out of the northwest, tearing leaves from the trees along the river, fanning the cabbage and lashing at the stiff canes of the Brussels sprouts in the garden. Every once in a while a gust would rattle the windows.

Sess was out in the yard with Iron Steve, who'd stopped by on his way down from the hippie camp. The two of them were splitting wood (Steve as a down payment on the dinner he knew to expect), drinking beer out of Mason jars and keeping an eye on the weather. It looked like rain – or sleet – and if the wind settled there would be frost for sure. Sess had his woodpiles heaped up at the four corners of the garden, ready to generate some heat through the night, because like every tiller of the earth he wanted to extend the growing season as long as possible, and you never knew, you could have a killing frost tonight and then a week or two of Indian summer to follow. He'd grown some champion tomatoes in the greenhouse, Early Girls and Beefsteaks both, and the cherries had run riot till he had to lift a panel off and let them creep out into the world. They'd had butternut squash till it was coming out their ears, and there was plenty more of it ballooning on the vine, and pumpkins too. She'd been canning day and night, stewing beans and tomatoes and zucchini in the big pot on the stove, peas, broccoli, anything that came up out of the ground in the crazy abundance of light. Her herb garden was a jungle in itself, and the root cellar was stacked high with carrots, onions, potatoes, turnips.

She'd just put the bread in the oven when there was a tap at the door and Iron Steve shifted into the room. He was bent nearly double to avoid cracking his head on the doorframe, which he'd already managed to do twice in the course of the afternoon and too many times to count in the past. Pamela didn't know how tall he was exactly – six-six, six-seven – but he towered over every-body in Boynton like an old-growth tree, and with his long-billed cap cocked at an angle on his head he grazed the ceiling of the cabin and had to work his way through a gauntlet of lanterns, kettles, tools, spatulas and fry pans hanging from the rafters just to get to the table to sit down. Pamela had no problem with that. She liked him. He might have been tight-lipped and more than his share of odd, not yet thirty and already a proto-coot, drunk more often than he was sober, but for all the raw-boned mass of him and the hard Slavic architecture of his face, he was gentle and good at heart. Before he'd got his hat and gloves off she handed him a cup of coffee, a can of evaporated milk and the sugar bowl.

"Bakin', huh?" he said, blowing steam off the cup.

"That's right," she said. "What else is a young housewife to do – especially on a day like this. Think it'll snow?"

"Uh-uh."

"Frost?"

"Oh, yeah. No doubt."

There was a pause. She laid a few more sticks on the fire – the trick was to keep a consistent temperature for the hour or so till the bread was done. "Those hippies ever get anything out of their garden?"

"Not much. Rabbits got most of it."

"Plus they started late."

Steve just nodded. He drank off an inch of coffee, poured half the sugar jar into the cup and then filled it back up with evaporated milk.

"They know enough to light smudge fires tonight?" She couldn't help worrying for them – for Star, especially, and Merry, she liked Merry too and wanted to see her make it through all this without suffering, or suffering more than she could bear. It was amazing – they were all so naive, so starry-eyed and simplistic, filled right up to the eyeballs with crack-brained notions about everything from the origins of the universe to the brotherhood of man and how to live the vegetarian ideal. They were like children, utterly confident and utterly ignorant – even Norm Sender, and he must have been forty years on this planet. They should have known better. All of them.

"I already told them, but they're mostly just sitting around the stove in that big clubhouse they built, you know, playing cards and board games and that sort of thing."

"What about Verbie, you tell her?" She poured herself a cup of coffee and eased in at the table across from him, the space so tight their elbows clashed every time they lifted the cups to their mouths. "If anybody'll get it done, she will. She's a pretty dynamic girl."

Steve ducked his head and looked away. "Oh, yeah," he said. "I told her."

Another pause. A gust ran across the roof like a jet plane coming in for a landing. She glanced up at the window and saw the first white driven flakes in horizontal motion. "How's that coming," she said, "you and her?"

He caught her eye for an instant, then glanced up at the window. "Guess I was wrong," he said. "But it won't amount to anything. Won't even whiten the ground."

"You and Verbie," she said, and she felt her lips forming into a smile. "It's a romance, isn't it? Come on, Steve, we all know you like her – Star says you two have been going at it pretty hot and heavy – "

Now his eyes came back to her, two settled green eyes with a hazel clock in one of them. "It's more than that, Pamela – I love her. I do. To me, she's the greatest thing that ever happened – I've been helping them with those half-built cabins, you know that, right? Because they're a little short on manpower since Pan and Sky Dog and what's his name – that one that looks like a horse going backwards – "

"Dale."

"Right, Dale – since they left."

"What did they, go back to California?"

"No, hell, no – they all moved in with Joe Bosky in that place he's got down on Woodchopper. The bachelor hole. Four skunks in a burrow." He looked beyond her, into the intermediate space of the cabin that was like any other cabin, cramped and cluttered and hung with all the accoutrements of life lived in a place without a garage or a basement or a convenient three-bedroom, two-bath, kitchen/dining, liv/fam floor plan. "I don't want her sleeping in a tent all winter, but I tell you, they haven't even got roofs on those cabins, or stoves either. You know, I was thinking, I've got my place in town and all, and I know it isn't much, but – "

There was a thump at the door, and Sess was there, his hair dusted with snow, a look of high excitement in his eyes. "Better sharpen up your *ulu,* Pamela," he was saying, the words jerked out of him as if he could barely stand to waste breath on them, and then he was snatching the rifle down from the crossbeam above her head and spinning back out the door, checking the action. "The garden," he said, "look at your garden," and the door pulled shut behind him.

The startle came into Steve's eyes and he jumped up from the table and cracked his head on the crossbeam, heading for the door behind Sess even as she dashed into the new room to look out the window above the bed, where she could get a view of the garden and this strange white element beating against the green of the leaves and the black nullity of the plastic. She had a moment, only that – seconds – to register the hulking dark form grazing there in the midst of the windblown vegetable garden like an overfed cow, and then there was the report of the rifle and the thing went down without a fuss, without a whimper, three hundred fifty pounds of meat, fur and fat delivered right up to them, right in their own garden, and she hardly had time to register the joy and triumph of it when she spotted the cub. It was a yearling, with its big bottom and narrow shoulders and pale stricken face, and it hurtled through the Brussels sprouts like a cannonball, going so fast Sess's second shot didn't have a chance of catching up to it.

The snow didn't last – a few handfuls of white pellets flung at the windows and lost in the gray-green weave of the tundra – but there was a hard frost that night and the next morning dawned cold. Sess was up at first light, out in the yard fooling with the dogs. He had five of them now, enough to pull a sled over his forty miles of trapline, but he kept saying he'd like two more, for speed, so he could mush his wife down the river to Boynton in style on a Saturday night and have a few shots and a burger and maybe dance to the jukebox into the bargain. Pamela had felt the bed give when he slipped out of it and she'd smelled the rich expiatory aroma of coffee wafting in from the other room, but she'd stayed in bed, wrapped in furs, listening to the cabin tick to life around her. Sess had done a pretty good job of banging things about in the next room, metal clanking on metal, the thump of the big black cast-iron pan hitting the stove, and then the crackle of meat sizzling – bear, fried in the fat it was no longer wearing out there in the watercourses and swamps of the world. The smell was something new to her, or reminiscent, anyway – she hadn't eaten bear since she was a girl out there in a summer tent with her mother and Pris and the man with the gray-seamed beard and cracked blue eyes she called Daddy – and her olfactory memory triggered a hundred other memories until she drifted back to sleep over the image of her father stumping into camp with the hindquarter of a black bear slung over one bloody shoulder and a grin as wide as the Koyukuk River.

She woke to the sound of Sess's voice rising high and strained over the clamor of the dogs and the bludgeoning thump and screech of a resistant object jerked by main force through the high grass and willow. "Gee!" he shouted, "gee, you fuckers!" And "Haw! Haw! I said. *Haw!*" She raised her head, peered out the window. Sun slammed at the yard, at the garden, at the still-smoldering smudge fires. Most of the plants were standing and green still, but she could see where the frost had blackened some of the leaves of the snap beans and the cherry tomatoes. It was something that registered with her in the moment of waking – frost, smudge fires, minimal damage, new sun, more sun – but which she hardly had time to reflect on before a blur of man, dog and sled interposed itself between the window and the garden and then was gone. "Haw!" Sess cried. *"Haw!"*

Then she was out in the yard in a pair of shorts and a sweatshirt, seven forty-eight by the clock she insisted on over Sess's objections, and the morning warming toward the low forties. She watched him make a turn at the edge of the woods, then tear up along the bank of the river, turn again and come straight for her with the dogs digging at their harnesses and a whole world of dust and threshed weed gone up into the air. He did manage to stop them more or less in the yard, throwing the brake (a sort of anchor that flailed and leapt and finally dug a furrow a hundred feet long), and wearing out the heels of his boots while he roared commands and the two wheel dogs went for each other's throats in one of those ill-tempered canine disputes that seemed to erupt every five minutes throughout the day. He let go the handles and got in between the dogs, kicking and cursing, until they finally got over whatever it was and sat panting in their traces. Sess was powdered with dust and weed, his shirt was torn and both his forearms were drooling blood where the dogs had bitten him. "Hey, baby," he smiled, "want to go for a ride? I'll take you round the world – you know what that means?"

"Don't get dirty on me, Sess."

Then he was holding on to her, rocking her gently back and forth. "You know I wouldn't do that," he said, breathing into her ear.

The dogs turned to look at them, ten wolfish eyes fixated on Sess's back, Lucius, in the lead, looking as if he could go out and run a hundred miles without even breathing hard. Sess had them hooked up to his training rig, a heavy narrow box of dense wet wood with three-inch aspen poles for runners and two pairs of wheels he must have scavenged from defunct wheelbarrows – or maybe children's tricycles – at the four corners. The wheels were useless. The rig weighed a ton. He just wanted to work the dogs, he told her, train them to work as a team, and to pull weight.

"I've been thinking I might take them up the trapline today," he said, "just a little ways, to give them the sight and smell of it and to maybe cut back some of the brush and branches and whatnot. I'll be back tonight. Late, though. Real late."

She was amazed. "With that? The whole thing'll fall apart before you go two miles."

He didn't try to deny it. "The wheels'll have to come off, I guess – when we get into the muskeg, anyway. I'm just going to let them skid the thing till they poop out. And by the way, really boil the hell out of that piece of bear for the stew – they're worse for trichina than pigs even."

She knew that, knew it from twenty years ago, but she didn't say anything. The bear was quartered and hanging from the poles at the bottom of the cache, they'd had the liver fried with onions for last night's dinner, and the big yellow-white chunks of its summer-laid fat were already rendered and put up in coffee cans to cool and harden.

"And you might," he added, and it was the last thing he said to her, "you might want to keep after that hide, scrape it good and then stretch it and hang it out where it can dry."

Later, after she'd made herself a sandwich with the leftover bread and drunk enough coffee to get her nerve ends firing, she dragged the bear's hide out to the picnic table and sat in the sun working the flesh off it with the *ulu* Sess had given her for a birthday present. The *ulu* was an Inuit tool, a bone handle attached to a crescent-shaped blade, and it was ideal for scraping hides, a task she guessed she would be performing pretty regularly as the winter months came on and her husband brought her the stiffened corpses of whatever he'd managed to kill out there in the secret recesses of the country. And how did she feel about that – how did she feel about this, about this stinking, flea-and-tick-ridden hide under the knife right here and now in a hurricane of flies and the blood and grease worked up under her nails and into every least crease and line of her hands so that she'd never get the smell out? She felt content. Or no: she felt irritated. This was the first time he'd left her since they'd been married, the first of a hundred times to come and a hundred times beyond that, and all he expected of her was to sit and wait for him and be damned sure the stew was simmering and the hide was scraped clean. She slapped a mosquito on her upper arm and the imprint of her hand was painted there in bear's blood. She flicked flies out of her face. Was this really what she wanted?

The *ulu* scraped, the flies rose and settled. There wasn't a sound in the world. She worked the hide out of inertia, for lack of anything better to do, worked it in a trance, and only when the canoe appeared on the horizon did she snap out of it. She watched it coming from half a mile away, because she could only study the stippled red meat and white sinew of the hide for so long before staring off into the immensity and just dreaming, and here was this slab of aluminum riding the current in a bolt of light, two people – two women – digging at the paddles. She stood, wiped her hands on a scrap of filthy rag, tried to do something with her hair. It was Star – she could see that now – Star and Merry, dressed alike in serapes and big-brimmed rawhide hats, maneuvering the battered silver canoe as if they'd been doing it all their lives. She watched them angle toward shore and then she waved and went down to meet them.

Star sang out her name as the canoe crunched gravel and Merry sprang out to secure it. "We thought we'd come over and make your day – how does that sound?" Star called, clambering out of the canoe and hefting a half gallon of red wine like a trophy. "Girls' day out!"

Sess was gone. The bear hide was a stinking collapsed filthy welter of raw meat and insects and the cabin reeked like a slaughter-house. Winter was waiting in the wings – it was fifty-five degrees in the sun – and already she'd begun to feel sorry for herself, begun to feel resentful and left out, and here were her friends come to rescue her. She took the jug from Star's hand, screwed off the cap and held it to her lips and let the taste of it sweeten her mouth and scour her veins. Up the hill they went, arm-in-arm-in-arm. "I can't tell you how glad I am to see you," Pamela said.

When they got to the picnic table, Merry pulled up short. "God, what is that?" she said. "Is that a bear? A grizzly bear?" Merry was the spacey one, more than a little Gracie Allen in her – Say goodnight, Gracie – as lost and out of place in the country as anybody Pamela could conceive of. Every coot, sourdough and weekend nimrod in the Three Pup had fed her the usual horror stories about grizzlies – the way they smelled out sexual lubricants and menstruation, their power and fearlessness and the trail of dismembered corpses they left in their wake – and she backed away from the table as if the hide could come back to life and wrap her in its killing arms.

346

"It's a black bear. A sow. Sess shot it in the garden last night."

"Wow. Far out. So what are you going to do, make a bear rug?"

"Of course, what do you think?" Star said, and she tipped back the jug of wine now herself, and both Pamela and Merry watched her drink, the excess running down her arm in blood-red braids. She wiped her mouth with the back of her hand and held the jug out to Pamela. "Maybe we should get some cups and try to be a little more ladylike," she said, and they all three burst into laughter.

"A bear rug," Merry said, after the laughter had trailed off. "That's cool, I guess, I mean, especially up here – but what about the rest of it, the whole animal that was living out there in the woods yesterday and doing nobody any harm. What about that?"

"They eat it," Star said.

"Don't," Merry said, and her eyes jumped from Star to Pamela and back again.

"Right, Pamela?"

She just nodded, because she was trying to maneuver the big jug of wine up to her lips again, and to hell with it, to hell with everything, really, that was the way she was feeling.

The flies had settled thick on the raw meat of the hide, but they'd be dead soon too, winter-killed any day now, and the mosquitoes that went for blood every minute of every day and night, they'd be gone along with them. Merry rocked back on her heels, reached up to pull down the brim of her hat and remove the oversized pink discs of her sunglasses, the better to focus her blunted brown eyes on Pamela. "You mean it's true? You actually – I mean, people – actually eat *bear?* Bear as in Winnie-the-Pooh? Yogi Bear? Smokey Bear? Only you can prevent forest fires?" She giggled. "You're goofing on me. Come on, tell me you're goofing."

She could feel the wine singing in her veins. She didn't want this, didn't need it – she just wanted to let go. She shrugged. "Listen," she said, "let me get some cups," but she didn't move. The two girls stood transfixed, looking at her. "All right, yes," she sighed. "We eat bear and anything else we can get our hands on up here, moose, rabbit, duck, fish, lynx – better than veal, Sess tells me – even porcupine and muskrat, and I can testify to that, because you wouldn't think it but muskrat can be as sweet and tender as any meat you can name – "

347

Merry was giving her a look of undistilled horror. "But to kill another creature, another living soul, a soul progressing through all the karmic stages to nirvana" – she paused to slap a mosquito on the back of her wrist with a neat slash of her hand – "that's something I just couldn't do."

"You just did."

"What? Oh, that. All right, I agree with you, I shouldn't have, and I wish I didn't have to – I can't wait till it's winter and the earth mother lays them all to rest, really – but a bug is one thing – and I know, I know, the Jains wouldn't think so – and like a *bear* is something else. They're almost human, aren't they?"

Pamela had to think about that for a minute, standing there in the yard with the flies thrumming, the meat hanging in the shade and the thick yellow-white fat hardening in the cans on the shelves. She had to think about the traps and the foxes and brush wolves that chewed through their own flesh and bone and tendons to escape the steel teeth and about the cub Sess had orphaned, the cub that was too young to dig a den and destined to die of inanition and cold when the long night came down. "Yes," she said finally, "yes, they are."

And then it was all right. She bundled up the half-flensed hide and flung it over the salmon rack like a beach towel gone stiff with crud, scooted the flies from the table and brought out three cups and a bottle of Sess's rum. "Iron Steve," she said, setting the bottle down and easing in beside Star. "He was here last night for dinner, and guess who he talked about nonstop?" And *there* was a topic. The wine sank in the bottle, shots went round, and the hounds of gossip went barking up every tree.

It was late afternoon by the time Merry and Star stumbled down to the river, bouncing off trees like pinballs caroming from one cushion to another in a pinball game as big as the world, and Pamela said, "It's a good thing you don't have to drive anywhere," and they all laughed about that, all three of them, until their heads began to ache and they felt they'd laughed enough, at least for one day. She watched them shove off, the canoe uncertain in the current until they balanced out their weight and the paddles caught them and the bow swung upstream. "Be careful!" she called, and she wouldn't let herself think about the canoe overturning and the cold swift rush of that water. She waved, and Star, backpaddling to keep the nose straight, lifted a hurried hand from her grip on the paddle, and then they moved off and got smaller and kept dwindling till the country ate them up.

Then there was the silence again. She stood there on the bank for a long while, staring at nothing, at the trees that were all alike, at the water that jumped and settled and sought the same channels over and over, and she felt something she'd never felt before. An immanence. A force that took her mind away and drew her down to nothing. She wasn't Pamela Harder standing on the banks of the Thirtymile. She wasn't a newlywed newly deserted. She wasn't anything. The sky rose up out of the hills and shot over her head with a whoosh that was like the closing of an air lock and then the clouds came up and blotted the sun and still she stood there. She'd never used drugs in her life, had believed everything she'd heard and read about the evils of addiction, about people taking LSD and staring into the sun until their retinas burned out, mutilating themselves, jumping off buildings because they thought they could fly, but when Star had laid out the two thin white sticks of rolled-up marijuana on the picnic table, she said to herself, Why not? If Star could do it, if Merry could, then why not? There is no knowledge worth the name that doesn't come from experience.

She might have stayed there forever, stock-still and feeling the way the loose ends of things came together in one mighty bundle, might have turned to stone like in the folk tales, but a pair of gulls, yellow beak, steady eye, brought her out of it. They swooped in low to investigate her, to smell the death on her and see it ground into the lines of her hands and worked up under her fingernails, then reeled off screeching in alarm. She looked down at her hands hanging out of the frayed sleeves of her sweatshirt. They were cold. Simply that: cold. A wind rustled the leaves and she shivered and looked over her shoulder to where the cabin sat the hillside. It seemed to take her forever to make her way up the slope, stepping through invisible hoops and trapezoids that kept appearing and vanishing, moving in slow motion past the table with its litter of bread crusts and cups and the empty wine bottle and the ashtray with the inch-long stub of a marijuana cigarette laid across it like a sentence of doom, but then she was at the door of the cabin and the sky snapped back again and the clouds began to rumble.

Inside, everything was familiar, and it was all right. There was a routine here, a routine to follow, and it had nothing to do with scraping hides or hippie drugs or the sky coming unhinged. She stoked the fire. Lit a cigarette. Added water to the cooked-down meat and chopped vegetables at the cutting board. Outside, the thunder detonated over the hills, lightning lit the room and the rain came with a hiss, sweeping out of the woods and stabbing at the dirt of the yard in swift violent pinpricks of motion. Star had lit the marijuana as casually as she might have lit a cigarette and passed it to Merry, who drew in the thin pale smoke that smelled of incense, of myrrh, and what was it? – frankincense – and then Merry passed it to her. She put it to her lips, inhaled, and it was no different from a Marlboro, except there was no taste to it. "You want to know something?" Star said. "You don't know what making love is till you've done it with this. Really. It's like every neuron is firing at once, and your skin, your skin just *burns* for the touch of a man."

At some point she went out in the rain and brought in the rum and the cups and the ashtray with the wet stick of marijuana in it, and at some point she laid the marijuana on the stove to dry and dipped herself a bowl of bear stew. She was hungry, hungrier than she'd ever been before. She had a second bowl. A third. She wiped up the gravy with bread, poured herself a cup of coffee. The rain held steady and she put wood on the fire and let the faintest hint of worry over Sess run in and out of her head – he could take care of himself; this was nothing, nothing but rain. Later, she stared at a magazine for what seemed hours, and still later, she went to the stove, picked up the dried-out stub of the marijuana cigarette and smoked it down to nothing, to two thin strips of saliva-yellowed paper which she tossed into the fire by way of hiding the evidence. It was dark when Sess came in, and though he stank of dog and the wet of the woods, though the cabin reeked of boiled bear and bear fat and the first death of a multitude to come, she stripped his clothes off him, piece by piece, and pulled him down and let herself melt beneath the living weight of him.

26

He would never admit it, least of all to himself, but Sess Harder's hands were cold, and if his hands were cold, Pamela's must have been freezing. They were both wearing thermals, sweaters and the matching flannel shirts with the red and black checkerboard pattern Pamela's sister had given them as a wedding present, but their gloves were tucked away in their breast pockets, high and dry. He didn't know what time it was – never did – but he figured it couldn't have been much later than nine a.m., the temperature stuck in the high teens despite the early influence of the sun, and with every dip of the paddle the river took a nip out of his hand. He'd stroke twenty times, then switch sides, but now the rising hand, still wet, was exposed to the wind raking upriver from the southwest, and that went numb on him. Patches of ice floated the water like gray scabs and both shores were crusted with it. Each breath came in a cloud. Up front, Pamela leaned into her paddle, switched sides with a quick flick of her wrists, and never uttered a word of complaint.

Mid–October, the alder, willow and birch gone into a blaze of dead red and streaky yellow, a hard freeze every night, and the swing of the season felt good, as if the whole country were undergoing a blood transfusion, and Sess Harder himself had never felt better. He'd got his meat – the lucky bear and an even luckier moose, a big bull in rut that had drunk so much water Sess had heard the sloshing of it in his gut from a hundred yards away – and he'd netted maybe a hundred washtubs full of whitefish and suckers on their annual migration to the deep holes of the river where freeze-up wouldn't affect them. And rabbits. The newborn of the year, crazy for anything green to put on winter fat, and as easy to snare as the air itself. The cache was full, the berries picked and the vegetables canned, and this was his wife, his sweet-cream wife, sitting the seat in front of him with the long arch of her athlete's back rising up out of the anchor of her hips and flank, working the paddle with her squared-up shoulders and tailored arms, and not so much as a peep out of her.

They were on their way to Boynton and thence to Fairbanks in Richard Schrader's truck, if Richard Schrader's truck was available, and he had no doubt it would be, unless maybe the rear end had fallen out of it, which, come to think of it, it was threatening to do last time he'd driven the thing. Pamela had wanted a break for a few days, and so had he, bright lights, big city, one more dose before winter set in. They were both of them hankering to spend a little of the money that had come their way in the form of much-handled bills wrinkled up in plain envelopes or stuffed inside wedding cards, and there were things they needed, obviously, to fill up the new room of the cabin and top off their store of dried beans, rice, tea, coffee, cigarettes, pasta and the like. And toothpaste, never forget toothpaste. He'd spent one whole winter brushing his teeth with his forefinger and another using a mixture of baking soda and salt that ate the bristles out of the brush. Soon the river would be impassable, and then they'd have to wait till freeze-up to come downriver with the dogs, and their destination would have to be Boynton, unless they wanted to mortgage the farm and fly to a place where the sun was more than just a rumor.

So here they were, out on the river. With cold hands. But there would be warmth in spades at the Nougat and the Three Pup, and by the time they hit the Fairbanks Road the sun would be well up and the temperature peaking in the forties or maybe even fifties. A wedge of noisy scoters shot past overhead, moving south, intelligent birds, get out while the going is good. His paddle shifted ice. "How you doing up there, Pamela?" he asked. "Hands cold?"

She looked over her shoulder, smiling wide, the dimple bored into her near cheek and those neat white teeth and little girl's gums on display. "Super," she said, in answer to the first question. And, "A little, I guess," in answer to the second.

He loved her. Loved her more than anything he could ever conceive of. "Hang in there," he said, proud of her toughness, glowing with it. "When we get to the Three Pup," he said, digging at the paddle, "the first shot's on me."

"Big spender," she said, and her laugh trailed out over the river, hit the bank and came rebounding back again.

They'd both removed their sweaters and their hands were fully recharged by the time the big sweeping bend that gave onto Boynton came into view. It had warmed more than he'd expected – into the sixties, he guessed – and with both shores lit with fall color the last few miles were nothing but pleasure. His eyes were roving ahead – always roving, a hunter's eyes – when something moving in the shallows at the head of Last Chance Creek caught his attention. He held the paddle down on the last stroke and angled them in on a line for the creek, puzzled, because this was no moose or bear or congress of beaver, no half-submerged sweeper bobbing in the current and no boat either – it was something unexpected, out of place, one of those aberrations of nature that made life so damned interesting out here in the wastelands, because just when you thought you'd seen it all –

"Who is that out there wading in the creek?" Pamela said, and her eyes were keener than his, how about that? And then it – they – came into focus for him. He saw the two figures grow together and then separate like shards of glass in a kaleidoscope, the canoe slicing closer now, the two of them bending to the water and coming back up again, standard-issue hip waders, glossy shirts, the flash of light from the linked silver band that looped the crown of a flat-brimmed hat. He was dumbfounded, absolutely dumbfounded. There were two black men – two Negroes, *hippie* Negroes – out in the sun-spangled wash of Last Chance Creek, panning for gold.

"Hello," he called as the canoe drifted up on them, "how you doing?"

Neither man said a word. They gave him looks, though, fixed dark eyes bristling with distrust and hostility. The current surged at their thighs, at the sagging skin of their waders. They regarded the canoe for a long solemn moment, as if it had appeared there spontaneously as some sort of compound of the water and air, and they looked first to Pamela, and then Sess, before turning back to their work, rinsing scoop after scoop of sand in the dull gleam of their pans till all the false clinging grains of silica were washed free.

"Showing any color?" Sess asked, because he had to say something.

The smaller one looked up out of a face like a tobacco pouch worn smooth with secret indulgence. His voice was soft, a whisper. "Naw, ain't nothin' here, isn't that right, Franklin?"

The other one glanced up now, one wild eye and a look that invited nothing. "Naw," he seconded, "nothin'."

Then the first one: "Place isn't worth shit. Right, Franklin?"

"Right."

Sess said he guessed he'd be seeing them later, then, and Pamela said good luck, and they both dug at their paddles, eager to work their way out of earshot and run this episode through the grinder. They'd gone three or four hundred yards, when Pamela lifted her paddle on the glide and turned her head to him. "What was that all about?"

"Beats me," he said. "But they wouldn't find half an ounce of gold in that creek if they panned it for a hundred years."

"They sure don't act that way. They act like those wild hairs in *The Treasure of the Sierra Madre,* like Humphrey Bogart and I don't who – "

"Walter Huston," he said.

"Right, Walter Huston."

The canoe drifted. The sun cut diamonds out of the water. "They were black men, Pamela. Negroes. Where in god's name do you find Negroes up here?"

Boynton had come into view now and she arched her back and dipped her paddle. "Jesus, Sess," she said, throwing the words over her shoulder, "black men, red men, Chinese, what difference does it make? You sound like you've never seen a black man before."

He was going to say, "I haven't," but just then a new feature, as strange in its way as the two figures in the creek, leapt out of the shoreline at him in an explosion of color. It wasn't a house exactly, more like a Quonset hut, wedged in between Richard Schrader's weathered gray clapboard box and the shack, and the presence of it there stymied him a minute, but then he knew what it was and knew the answer to his question all in a single flash of intuition: Where do you find Negroes up here? In a hippie bus, that's where.

If he expected warmth and conviviality at the Three Pup, he was mistaken. Lynette was laying for him, and so was Skid Denton. The minute he ushered Pamela in the door, Lynette backed away from the bar and said, "Whoa, here he is, the hippie king himself. Or should I say, hippie landlord?"

Skid Denton was welded to his seat at the end of the bar, as usual, a plate of home fries at his elbow and a glass of beer sizzling in his hand. He leaned forward from the waist to put in his two cents: "It's a bonfire every night and that hippie music never stops. I hear they're screwing themselves raw upriver, screwing everything but the dog, and smoking drugs all day long. They really get a cabin built?"

"That one with the bones in his hair," Lynette said.

"And the niggers." Richie Oliver looked up red-eyed from his scotch and water as if he'd been dog-paddling in a sea of it for the past three days. "Don't forget the niggers."

Eight people were gathered at the bar and there wasn't a single genuine smile for him – or for Pamela either. And that hurt, because what did she have to do with it? No more than he did. Or less, a whole lot less. He tried his best to ignore Lynette and Skid Denton, who was a first-class jerk, anyway, greeted everybody by name and pulled out a chair for Pamela at the table by the window, thinking ham and eggs, or bacon, or maybe a burger, and a beer and a bump to go with it, because he'd be goddamned if they were going to chase him out of his own chosen roadhouse and bar. Pamela gave him a thin smile and took his hand across the table. "Lynette," he called, and maybe he did raise his voice just a hair more than was called for, "can we have a little goddamn service over here?"

They drank. They ate. And they took their sweet time about it. People pulled up chairs and plopped down to butt in, one after another, two at time, three, and all the news and all the burning gossip started with the hippies and ended with them too. Lynette sat right at the table with him and Pamela and watched them cut their meat and lift the forks to their mouths as if they might need instruction, and she never stopped talking, not even to draw breath. "The one with the bones in his hair and the garlic strung round his neck? Mr. Vampire, that's what I call him. He come in here and ordered a pitcher of beer and wanted to know if he could get it on credit and when I said nobody gets credit here he went around the bar and asked if anybody had any change to spare."

But Richard Schrader – the best friend Sess had on the river, the *best man* at his wedding – Richard Schrader took the cake. He hadn't been home when they came up from the canoe, and they'd skirted the tarted-up bus and the hippie out there hovering over his kiln and the shining glazed line of bowls and plates and ashtrays he'd arranged on a split log as if he was going into business in Sess's weedpatch, and now he – Richard – pulled the truck into the lot and came through the mosquitoless door and the first thing out of his mouth was "Sess, these people have got to go, they're making a three-ring circus out of my yard and I don't think I've had more than two hours sleep a night since they got here with their whooping and screaming and that unholy racket of guitars and tambourines and whatnot and did you know they took the speakers out of the bus and mounted them up on the roof so they could blast that shit out over the river and everyplace else? And I've tried to reason with them, I have, but it's Peace, brother and fuck you – "

Sess had another beer. He took his time. Wiped his plate with a slice of spongy store-bought bread. Asked about dessert. Forwent a second shot. On the exterior, he might have appeared calm, but he was boiling up inside, and he laid some money on the table, took the keys from Richard and told Pamela he wouldn't be a minute. He hadn't gone two feet out the door before Lynette was right there after him, grabbing at his arm. "And, Sess," she said, the striations of age puckered up around her lips and digging disapproving trenches at the flanges of her nose and the corners of her shrunk-down eyes till she looked like one of those dried and frozen corpses they found in the Andes, "whatever did you go and do to Joe Bosky?" She looked down at the flap of her sidearm and back up again. "I tell you, watch out for that one – "

So he drove the truck the half mile to town and eased it high up over the ruts and half-buried rocks and into the yard out front of the shack. The dust followed him in. He slammed the transmission up into park, let the engine keen a minute, then cut the ignition. What he heard then was the music, a bull-roaring voice over the guitars, drums and electrified piano, driven at such a volume the speakers couldn't contain it. The vocal settled, went slack with distortion, then settled again. Off to the right were the two cars, the VW and the Studebaker, looking as if they hadn't been moved in a month. The kiln was set in the lee of the bus, the heat of it radiating out of the seams and corrugating his view of the shack, which was in need of paint. The bus, though, that didn't need any paint. They'd been busy with that, and if there was a color they'd neglected to lay on he couldn't name it.

The air was clean, the sun going about its business. It was warmer than it had a right to be. He stepped out of the truck to the assault of the music and went up to the door of the bus and knocked at the panel of painted-over glass there. He knocked again. After a while he started to hammer at it with his fist, and it was a good thing – a good thing for them – he hadn't had that second shot. "Open up!" he shouted. "Whoever's in there, open up!"

He felt the bus give ever so slightly on its springs, and then the door cranked open and the one they called Weird George was standing there on the top step, wrapped in a dirty green blanket. He was barefoot. His hair was like a second blanket, or no, it was like the stuff Jill used to make plant holders with in her apartment, some kind of jute, rough-edged and matted, and he had half a dozen bleached-out animal bones dangling from the ragged ends of it. "Oh," Weird George said, trying to place him. "Oh, hey."

"Listen," and Sess could feel it coming up in him now, an anger pulled up out of nowhere, out of a sunny day, and heavily disproportionate to the crime, "you people are going to have to get out of here. All of you. And take all of your fucking crap with you."

Weird George made a vague gesture. He didn't look as if his legs would hold him upright another thirty seconds. "Oh, man," he said after a moment, and Sess could barely hear him for the bawling of the speakers, "you want Harmony, Harmony's the cat to talk to – "

Everybody's luck held, because at that moment Harmony came round the front of the bus, his hands dripping clay. As best Sess could figure, the man was about his age, and though he wore his dense blond hair layered like a woman's he had a fierce reddish Fu Manchu mustache to counteract the effect, and in Sess's limited dealings with the tribe he seemed the most reasonable of any of them – and a whole lot easier to communicate with than the nephew, who tended to talk in paragraphs, as if he were getting paid by the word. Harmony looked surprised. He wiped his hands on his jeans, cocked his head and gave Sess a look out of the corner of his wire-frame glasses. He was about to say "What's happening?" – Sess would have bet the farm on it – but before he could open his mouth Sess launched into a lecture of his own, enumerating the hippie infractions and the way the town felt about them and telling him in no uncertain terms that he was going to have to pack everybody up and find another place to throw his pots and blast his music and smoke his marijuana and LSD.

Sess didn't know how long he went on, but after a while Harmony was joined by his wife or girlfriend or whoever she was, a thin raggedy little woman with a serene smile and the usual hair and a pair of breasts that should have been matched to somebody twice her size, and the two of them just stood there and listened to him as if they were SRO in a lecture hall. When he was done, when he'd talked himself out and begun to think of getting back in the truck, picking up Pamela and heading into Fairbanks to celebrate life and the season and the cache that was full to bursting with dressed-out meat, the record he'd been subconsciously screaming over came to a superamplified halt, and Harmony said, "I hear you, man." He put an arm round the woman's shoulders and drew her to him. "You've been like supercool, and we all appreciate that, even Weird George. And listen, we've been maybe a little remiss in this, but Alice and I have been wanting to like show our appreciation. Here," he said, gesturing toward the long tottering line of misshapen ashtrays and bongs and fluted drinking cups set out on the naked board and gracing the tree stumps of the field, "you just take your pick – "

Three days later, when they got back from Fairbanks, the bus was still there. Of course it was – what did he expect them to do, paint it over with vanishing ink? The thing probably wouldn't even start. Why fool himself? – it was there for the duration. Maybe when the next glacial age hit in another ten thousand years the big mile-high wall of ice would creep across the tundra and grind it to dust, but for now, Sess figured, he might as well get used to it because it wasn't going anywhere. And at this point – three days on – he couldn't really get himself worked up about it. He and Pamela had had a matchless time, their second honeymoon – or first, actually – lazing in bed at the Williwaw Motor Inn, smoking cigarettes and drinking rum and Coke out of plastic disposable cups and watching the mystical flicker of the world caught and sealed in the little box everybody called by the diminutive just to express their sodality with it. They bought things. Made the rounds of the bars. And though he was disappointed to find that the dog pound had nothing with four legs and a tail that weighed more than maybe fifteen pounds – the Chihuahua meets the toy poodle meets the bichon frise in the dumped-down hills of Fairbanks – he was satisfied. He was going upriver with his wife and all the necessities and luxuries they could carry and hippie pottery too, and he didn't give a blue damn for how things sorted out in Boynton.

They got in from Fairbanks in the late afternoon, and it was blowing up cold. Sess went right on by the Three Pup, pulled the pickup into Richard's drive and backed it down to the river. "Is there anything we need out of the shack?" he wondered aloud as Pamela handed him boxes of groceries, cans of Blazo gas and two-stroke oil, a bag of brand-new socks and underwear and felt linings for his mukluks. He was leaning forward, distributing the weight in the bottom of the canoe. The wind took his hair and gave it a yank.

"Nothing I can think of," she said, straightening up and looking out over the anvil of the river. The sky was dark. Whole armadas of ice had come down to do war with the open water.

"All right, then," he said, "because I don't like the looks of that sky, not one bit."

Pamela was wearing her parka and she'd put the hood up the minute she got out of the truck. Her hands were thin gray flaps of skin working out of her sleeves, her shoulders were hunched against the wind and the tip of her nose and her cheeks were already drawing color. When she took the paddle up out of the thwarts, he saw that her knuckles showed white against the dark oiled grain of the wood. She gave him a tired smile and settled herself in the bow and he couldn't help thinking of the contrast between this and the first time they'd gone upriver together, all the way back in the fullness of June, but then a little discomfort was what the country offered everybody without prejudice, and soon enough he'd have her back in the cabin, the fire stoked and a cup of something hot in her hands. As they shoved off, the canoe shattered the spider ice that clung to the shore. No one had to tell him this would be the last canoe trip of the year.

They hadn't gone more than half a mile, the wind in their faces, when Pamela turned to him. "The keys," she said. "What about the keys?"

"I left them in the truck. Didn't I?"

"Check your pockets, Sess – you remember what happened last time."

His hand was so numb he could barely work it into his pocket, and what did he feel there taking shape under his fingers? A pack of matches, his pocketknife, the money clip – and the keys to Richard Schrader's truck. So they turned around and went back and he climbed up the bank past the battened and silent hippie bus – they must have all gone upriver, that's what he figured – slipped the keys into the truck's ignition and came back down the bank at a jog and shoved off again.

The wind was fiercer now, really cutting up, and they had to stick in close to shore to stay out of the main thrust of it, but that was a problem too because the ice was forming there and keeping them at arm's length. Twilight came down. They dug at the paddles in silence. He was thinking nothing, working on autopilot, stroke and stroke again, when the sound of the plane came to him. He heard it – they both heard it – before they saw it, and when it came into view, materializing out of the blow, it couldn't have been more than two hundred feet off the river and heading in the same direction they were. The noise exploded on them as the plane passed directly overhead and then made a wide loop out front of the canoe and came back at them, and Sess was thinking *It's Howard Walpole or Charlie Jimmy out of the Indian village at Eagle, circling back to see if we're okay –*

But it wasn't Howard Walpole and it wasn't Charlie Jimmy either. The plane was running three lights, but the one under the left wing was out of sync with the pulse of the other two – faulty wiring, a loose bulb – and as it drew nearer, swooping on them now, he saw the pontoons naked of paint and glinting dully in the erratic blue flash of light. He knew those pontoons, pontoons that would give way to skis by morning if the weather kept up, and he didn't have to see the paintless fuselage or the fading black stencil of the N-number to know whose plane it was. It was coming at them, low over the ice-flecked water, low in the dusk and urged on by the wind. He didn't have time to think, didn't have time to jam the paddle down and jerk the bow out of plumb or run for the cover of the trees, because the Cessna was right there in his face, in Pamela's face, and even as they ducked their heads and the pontoons lifted he felt the shock of the concussion and a hippie fruit bowl burst to fragments and there was water – Yukon water, cold as death – roiling in through the invisible tear in the hull.

Now he acted. He hit the water, hard, and held the paddle down till the canoe swung round a hundred eighty degrees like the needle of a compass and they were suddenly running downriver with the current and the wind. There was a dark clump of trees projecting out into the river five hundred yards ahead of them on the near bank and he shouted to Pamela to run for them even as he fumbled for the rifle amidst the strapped-down clutter of cans and boxes and hippie pottery, thinking *This is it, this is war,* thinking *Make one more pass, you son of a bitch, one more.*

The flashing blue lights faded to nothing downriver, then sparked back to life as the plane banked and reversed direction. "Dig!" Sess shouted, working a bullet into the chamber and laying the rifle across the thwarts so he could lean into the paddle and keep the stern from swinging out. Pamela's face came to him in profile, a faint pale emanation against the obscure band of the shore. "He was – " she stammered. "He didn't – ?" They could hear the plane whining for power, see the lights sharpening as the distance closed. "You better fucking believe he did!" Sess roared, driving the paddle with the piston of his shoulder, and they were no more than two hundred yards from where the shore ice was forming under the cover of the trees.

Bosky came at them too fast. He'd been expecting to find them upriver still, lagging in the current, and the roar gathered itself up and the naked pontoons rocketed past them before he could lean out and fire again, but Sess was ready and Sess let the boat swing out lateral to the current while Pamela fought for control up front and he got off three shots, three hard copper-jacketed thank-you notes hurtled up into the cauldron of the sky that probably caught nothing but air. He couldn't say. He didn't know. He was too lathered with adrenaline even to feel anger yet and outrage. He laid down the rifle and took up the paddle and a moment later they hit the shore ice and broke through it to the cover of the trees.

Everything was silent. A hard, pelting, wind-driven snow began to rush down out of the sky as if awaiting release. He heard the river then, the ice on the river slipping and squealing like two wet hands rubbed together, and he heard Pamela. She was hunched over her shoulders, a shadow amongst the deeper shadows, and she was crying so softly he thought at first it was the whisper of the hard white pellets finding their way between the last, lingering blades of grass. The bottom of the canoe had shipped two inches of water, two inches at least, and their feet – they were wearing hiking boots, ankle-high suede, the best shoes they owned for a jaunt in the city – their feet were wet. They had no sleeping bags, no ground cloth, no tent, and who needed a tent in the Williwaw Motor Inn? "It's okay, Pamela," he said, the words stuck in his throat, "it's all right, everything's going to be fine."

The first thing was a fire, but he was afraid of a fire because Bosky might see it and come back for them, so he concentrated on hauling the canoe up out of the water, unloading the wet groceries and the wet clothes and the tools and equipment and all the rest of the things they just couldn't live without, and then propping the hull up as a windbreak. Pamela worked beside him, and they didn't have to talk, didn't have to say a word, working in consonance to unload everything and cut spruce boughs to lay down under the canoe and collect driftwood to mound up for the fire if there was going to be a fire, and they would have to wait and see about that. In the meanwhile, the snow stiffened, rattling off their hoods and sleeves in pellets and granules, sifting to the ground with the soft shush of rice spilled from a sack, and soon the dark vacancy of the riverbank began to fill in with the pale glowing substance of it. "He's not coming back, is he, Sess?" Pamela said out of the void.

He looked to her, the ghostly stoop and movement of her as she mounded wood and let the phrases escape her mouth in quick snatched drifts of windblown vapor. "No," he said, "not in this, and I hope to god the son of a bitch crashes and burns till there's nothing recognizable left of him. Can you believe it? Can you believe he actually shot at us? I told you, Pamela. I told you from the beginning, and you wouldn't listen."

They waited half an hour, shivering, and then he held a match to a twist of birch bark and the fire took. They dried their shoes, their socks, their feet. Pamela dug a damp box of crackers out of a shredded grocery bag and they shared them with slices of Cracker Barrel cheddar and let their internal engines wind down a bit. What this looked like was the first big storm of the year — it had all the earmarks, what with the wind and the snow formed into pellets and temperatures in the twenties, and he had no doubt it would settle in colder and the snow turn to powder — and they had a very narrow window of opportunity here if they were going to get the canoe and all their precious stuff back to the Thirtymile before next spring. After a while, he got up and fished around through the baggage till he found a pair of his new guaranteed-to-keep-your-toes-warm-at-forty-below Outdoorsman-brand thermal socks and worked one of them through the bullethole in the bottom of the canoe till he had a plug he thought would hold. Then they loaded up again and went out on the river in the full blow of the storm, their forearms and shoulders fighting the resistance, their hands molded to the paddles as if they'd been sculpted of ice.

It must have been past midnight when they skirted Woodchopper Creek, veering far out from shore on the off chance Joe Bosky was out there somewhere laying for them, and neither of them dared even to think of what might have happened upriver, at the cabin, when Joe Bosky knew they were away from home and had the means and the motive to do them real and irreparable harm. The snow flew in their faces. A thin crust of ice formed over the baggage where the leavings of Pamela's paddle flew back on the wind and settled, and a layer of snow formed atop that. The night was a dense and private thing, working through the motions of its own unknowable rhythms, and they had no right to be out in it. Sess Harder didn't care. He was glad to be here, now, equal to the challenge, glad to be alive, glad for every furious driven bite the wooden paddle took out of the refrigerated river. And when they rounded the Thirtymile and the dogs sang out with the apprehension of their coming, he was the gladdest man in the world.

part six

old night

This was that Earth of which we have heard, made out of Chaos and Old Night.

– Henry David Thoreau, "Ktaadn"

27

It was Halloween, October thirty-first, Pan's favorite day of the year, and what did he have to show for it? Nothing – no black cats, no skeletons, not even a jack-o'-lantern. It was four o'clock in the afternoon, black dark, and the river, the big roiling silver playground chock-full of fish and game he'd cavorted on all summer, was locked up tight in a tomb of ice. Freeze-up, that's what they called it, and Pan had shuffled off down the frozen highway of Woodchopper Creek in the declining light of day to see that the last open channel had sealed up overnight. It was twenty below zero. There was a wind. He'd stood there shivering on the rock-hard bank and listening to the silence – it was mind-blowing, all that noise of buckling ice and angry water, all that *life,* smoothed out to nothing, not a whimper, not so much as a pop or burble – and then he'd hiked back up the creek to the cabin and stooped outside the door to fill his arms with firewood.

Nobody blinked. He came in through the dogtrot, slammed the outer door to, then squeezed through the heavy cabin door like a contortionist and slammed that behind him, his nose dripping, fingers numb, the sawed-off lengths of pine tucked under his arm like a stack of unreadable books. A garment of cold-thinned air came with him, and the *smell* of the cold, almost a chemical smell, and what was it going to be like when the temperature dropped another twenty degrees? Another forty? He crossed the room, poked the coals and laid on the wood, and nobody said *Hey, man, what's it like out there?* or *Did it lock up?* or *We thought maybe you were frozen to a stump or something.* They said, "Raise and call." They said, "Two pairs." They said, "Three jacks, pair of nines."

Joe was cramped in at the table with Sky Dog and Dale,

shuffling cards. They'd been playing poker for the past twelve hours at least – since they got back from the Three Pup on the snow machines, anyway – and they showed no sign of letting up. They kept a joint circulating. They were drinking beer out of the quart bottle and they threw back reds and Dexamils according to need, and he'd sat in himself for a while and made sure to look after his own pharmaceutical well-being, but he'd got to the end of that and what he wanted now was some action, some fun, some *Halloween,* for shitsake.

Joe had the generator going because money meant nothing to him and he could fly in gasoline anytime he wanted, and so the lights were on, and that was a pure and beneficial thing in one way – at least you could *read* to fight back the boredom that was already closing in like a smotherer's hand – but it was a curse too. It was curse and a royal pain in the ass to the degree that Pan, pacifist and flower child though he might have been, was considering triple homicide and maybe suicide into the bargain, because electricity meant music and for Joe Bosky music meant show tunes and country – "Oklahoma," "The Sound of Music," Kitty Wells, Roy Acuff, Flatt and Scruggs, Eddy Arnold, Gene Autry. *Gene Autry,* for Christ's sake. Ronnie couldn't let himself think about it, and he stuffed his ears with toilet paper to try to blot it out, but the corny booming voices and twanging strings and country yodeling seeped through nonetheless, polluted his consciousness till he actually found himself *humming* the shit. *The hills are alive* – if he heard the hills are alive one more time he wouldn't be responsible for his actions, he wouldn't.

Of course, the irony, sad and piss-poor as it was, was that the hills were dead and so was everything else. Joe kept talking about trapping, about the excitement of running a line and seeing what was there for you *gifted up from nature,* but he never did anything but talk. He was through with trapping, that was the reality. He was making his money flying booze in to the Eskimos in the dry villages along the Kobuk River, selling cases of Fleischmann's gin and Three Feathers whiskey and Everclear for ten times what he paid for them in Fairbanks. Ronnie had gone with him, twice, just to see what it was like, and it was the end of the world, that was what it was. Windowless shacks, chained-up dogs, dirt streets and garbage blowing in the wind, no roads in and no roads out – Boynton was midtown Manhattan in comparison. He'd made a buck or two himself, selling the odd lid of pot out of the stash he'd taken with him from Drop City – and he'd tried to *give* the shit away to Norm and Marco and Verbie and he didn't know who else and still everybody treated him like a leper, and that wasn't right, even though when he looked at it in the light of day he could see where he'd fucked up, fucked up big time, and he regretted that, he did. But the Eskimos – little half-sized scaled-down comical cats with hair like walking grease who wouldn't look you in the eye if you set their shirts on fire – the Eskimos wanted it, oh yes indeed.

"Wolves," Joe was saying over the thin toilet-paper-muted buzz of the stereo, "that's where the money's at. For a pilot."

Ronnie had been reading one of the nineteen paperbacks in the cabin – all by Louis L'Amour and all dull as silt – and he rested the book facedown on his chest and took a sip from the silver flask he'd won from some cat at the Three Pup two weeks ago, eight ball, and he couldn't miss, and looked to the table.

Dale Murray was wearing his sheepskin coat and a fur hat he'd bought off the head of some Indian woman at the Nougat for the price of three Brandy Alexanders – that was all she would drink, Brandy Alexanders, though the cream for them came from a can of Borden's evaporated milk and the brandy was grain alcohol filtered through a leftover tea bag. He and Sky Dog had about had their fill of the snowy north and for the past week or so they'd been trying to talk Joe into flying them to Fairbanks, because, as Dale kept saying over and over until it was about to stick to the walls, *California is where it's happening. Fuck this shit. I mean, fuck it.* And Joe kept saying, *Tomorrow, man. When it clears.* Now Dale glanced up from his hand and said, "What do you mean, wolves?"

Sky Dog, his eyes drawn down to blood-flecked slits, tugged at the collar of the once-white wool sweater one of the Drop City chicks had knitted for him in happier days. "You mean those big friendly dogs out there howling in the hills every night, morning and afternoon?"

"I mean bounty money, that's what I mean. You pick them out against the snow, they've got nowhere to hide. It's like swatting flies."

"I thought you were a trapper, man? What happened to trapping?"

Joe gave a shrug. It must have been about forty degrees in the cabin, but he was stripped down to a thermal T-shirt and the tattoos that twisted round his forearms like battle scars – or maybe destination scars would be more accurate (*Got this one in the Philippines, this one in Saigon, and this one, this one I got in a place so bad you don't want to even know the name of it*). "You have any *idea* the kind of work it takes to run a trapline? It's nuts. Crazy. You have to be some kind of caveman like Cecil B. Hardon to want to do that, some kind of terminal loser with his head about fifty feet up his ass. I just said fuck it and left my traps out there last winter, bones in them now, I guess, and they can just rust away to shit for all I care. No, I got smart. Took to the air. I mean, what's the sense of investing in your personal aircraft if you're not going to use it, right? Sixty-three wolves, in every shade of color from pure black to pure white, that's what I took out of the country last winter, and every one of them run right into the ground – at thirty-five bucks, per, for the bounty, that is, plus what the pelts'll bring. Who needs to pan for gold when it's out there running on four paws?"

Sky Dog snapped his head back as if he'd been slapped. "That isn't right, man, that is just not right, I don't care. If you shoot all the wolves, you've got no predators, and if you've got no predators the whole ecology is out of whack. I mean the moose and the caribou and whatnot, the rabbits, they'll eat up the forest till there's nothing left. I'm out, by the way." He folded his hand and shoved it into the middle of the table.

"Hah. That's what you say now – that's what you say when you get back to your hippie reservation in Malibu where all you have to worry about is does she have to wear that many clothes or not, but if you had to live up here you'd change your tune pretty quick." Joe leaned back in the chair and the chair creaked at the joints. He took up the quart of beer and then set it down again, leaned forward and poured himself a shot from the bottle of vodka he kept on the floor where it would chill, because if it was forty degrees at seat level it was probably about ten below down on the floor. "Wolves are nothing but trash. They'll tear the anus out of a moose and lap up its guts while it's still standing

370

there, they'll kill anything in sight, whether they're hungry or not – just for the pure pleasure of it. No," he said, pausing to throw back the vodka, "I'd kill the last pregnant wolf right here on the cabin floor in front of the governor and his cabinet if I had the chance, and you know what, the governor'd probably give me a medal."

"Who is the governor, anyway?" Dale Murray wondered aloud. Sky Dog scratched at his collar, then reached across the table for the bottle, helped himself to a shot. One minute, one of a million – a billion – ticked by.

"Fuck if I know," Joe said.

Pan, from the bed by the stove, the book spread across his chest: "Hey, people, I hate to interrupt, but do you know what day today is? It's Halloween."

All three of them just stared. The stove heaved and sucked air. It was as dry in that cabin as it must have been out in the middle of the Atacama Desert. Finally, Joe Bosky leaned over to spit on the floor. "So what do you want me to do," he said, "put on a wig and dress up like a hippie? Or maybe a woman – would that work?"

But Ronnie didn't reply – he was off someplace else, suddenly transported back to last Halloween, to Peterskill, on the banks of the housebroken Hudson, a place where there were stores and bars and clubs and head shops and where you could get any variety of dope you wanted, day or night, clothes, records, steaks, Chinese, Italian, Dunkin' Donuts, Kentucky Fried, the place where he'd wrecked his first car, the place where his parents lived. And his friends. His buddies. The people he'd grown up with. He felt so nostalgic suddenly, so lost and cored out, he had to pound his breastbone to keep from vomiting up the moose chile they'd been eating out of the pot the last three days. A ball of acid rose in his throat, burning like exile, and it brought the tears to his eyes. He and Star had really done it up that night. They were flaming, triumphant. Two majorly righteous parties, and then they went to a club with a live band, and she'd been dressed as a cat, in tights and a velvet shell that clung to her in all the right places, painted-on whiskers he'd licked off of her by the time the night was out, and she wasn't the only one – all the chicks were dressed up like sex kittens or foxes or vampires, showing off their cleavage and their legs and everything else. He wondered if anybody had ever done a study of that, some sociologist, because the chicks invariably dressed up as everybody's sexual fantasy, while the men, the cats, always went for the absurd. And what did that mean? The men could hang loose, get stoned, party, but the women – the females, the chicks – they wanted to be salivated over, they wanted *worship*.

Ronnie had gone as Pan, with a pair of leftover devil's horns painted forest brown, pipes he'd found under a pile of crap in the music room in their old high school and the hairy-hocked leggings his mother had made for him on the sewing machine, and she was handy that way, his mother. And it wasn't *that* absurd, not at all. More cool, really. People had come up out of nowhere to compliment him, and if he hadn't exactly won the prize for best costume – some asshole in a Spiro Agnew mask got first prize, a real authentic three-foot-tall hookah the club owner, Alex, had brought back from Marrakech – he didn't care. That was the night he'd left Ronnie behind, the night he'd *become* Pan for good. The memory of it pushed him up off the bed and he began shoving the felt soles down into his boots, doubling his socks, lacing the boots, layering on clothes.

"Where you going, man?" Sky Dog wanted to know. "Trick or treating?"

It was eight miles to Boynton, walkable now on the highway of the river, and four to Drop City. Two times four equals eight, that was what he was thinking, and out in the dark, in the cold, his breath going like a steam engine, Pan turned to his right when he hit the river, heading north and east, thinking of Star. They'd be celebrating at Drop City tonight, no doubt about it – Halloween, the feast of the freaks, was in the air. Norm would do it up. If anybody would, Norm would. He heard the cold rush and snap of his footsteps as he compacted the thin layer of snow over the ice, one foot in front of the other, four miles no more than a stroll in the park and he didn't feel cold at all, not in the least.

Sess Harder had once unraveled the mystery of the distances for him, in the days when he could show his face around Sess's cabin, that is – which he no longer could since he'd burned

Pamela for the five bucks, but hey, *tant pis,* as the French say. His boots crunched snow. The wind fell away and the moon was there. What he couldn't understand was why the river was called the Thirtymile – shouldn't it have been thirty miles from Boynton then and not less than half of that? Sess had been busy, always busy, mending the gangline for his dogteam, and Pan had hung over him with a neighborly beer in one hand and a smoke in the other while the mathematics played out in Sess's deep, unhurried tones. "The distance is measured from Dawson, in the Yukon Territory," he told him. "Originally, what happened was people floated downriver from there, and so you've got your Fortymile River south and east of Eagle and your Seventymile just north of it, and what happened, I guess, is somebody didn't want to call a river the Hundredmile – too daunting a number – so they just called this one the Thirtymile, because it's thirty miles, give or take, down from the Seventymile. Does that make sense?"

No, it didn't. It hadn't. They should have named it the Clothesline or the Dinosaur or the Punctured Pineapple, or maybe they should rename it after Jimi Hendrix's mother – sure, and he'd have to get up a petition as soon as he got back to civilization. He went on that way, a string of increasingly ridiculous names running through his head, the silence and the vastness of the river and the hills spiked with shadow and the moon, the *moon,* gone down deep in him – Halloween, how about that? – and he'd never felt so *connected* in his life. He bore right again at the mouth of the Thirtymile, no more concerned than he would have been turning the corner from MacDougal onto Bleecker, and when he came to Sess's cabin, to the glow of it floating against the backdrop of the trees and the smell of the woodsmoke drifting on the air like a promise, he kept on walking.

By some miracle, Sess's dogs didn't sound the alarm. If he concentrated on distinguishing one shadow from another, he could make out the line of doghouses thrust back against the ankles of the trees, but there was no movement there, no faint rustle of steel-link chain or whisper of ruffled fur, no sound at all but for the rush of the wind in his ears. The dogs were asleep, curled up tail to nose, breathing easy in the fastness of the night.

They dwelled here, they belonged, and so did he, so did Pan. He kept on walking, and maybe his toes were a bit numb – his boots weren't the best – but it was nothing he hadn't experienced before, back in New York. Colder, maybe, but not by much. He could remember five and ten below when he was a kid, ice forming in a grid of overlapping crystalline stars on the inside panes, his father kicking in the driver's side door of the Stude-baker because it wouldn't start no matter how he goosed it and the sweet metallic smell of the ether he sprayed down the carburetor in the vain hope it would come to life. His father. The image of him held for just the fraction of a second, then slipped away, a fading reel in the projector of his mind. He was walking. He walked the immensity. Thought nothing. The moon – the harvest moon, the Halloween moon – lit the way.

Drop City came to him first as the scent of smoke infusing the night air, then as a cluster of lights so pale and inadequate he couldn't be sure he was seeing them, not until he mounted the bank and came up the rise to where the five cabins described a crescent above the river. Four of them were roofed and lit from within, sailing high on the sea of the night, but the fifth was just a collection of notched logs, waist-high at best, and he thought of Mendocino Bill and Alfredo and their big hyped-up plans, make way and look out, here comes the city on the hill, the metropolis, Chichén Itzá and Taj Mahal all rolled into one. Lift that plank, man, push that saw. Still, he had to admit they'd got farther than he'd expected, because those were stovepipes projecting out from under the roofs, and that was real, honest, actual smoke trailing away on the wind, and where there was smoke there was fire and where there was fire there was warmth. He was right there in the yard – Ronnie, Pan, come back to say hello on a night like no other – and he hesitated.

He hadn't been near the place since the end of August, and though he'd run into a couple of the brothers and sisters at the Three Pup and the Nougat and Setzler's store, he really didn't know how people felt about the whole thing, whether he'd be welcome or not, forgive and forget and let's move on. Especially Norm. Norm he did not want to see, or Alfredo either. He was standing there in the cold of the moon, half-decided to slink away back to Woodchopper, and fuck Drop City, if they didn't want him he didn't want them, when something in the atmosphere shifted and he heard laughter, conviviality, somebody's voice raised over somebody else's and then a cascade of hoots and catcalls washing over both of them. He held his breath. Concentrated. And then he heard the music. There was music coming from the meeting hall, the thin attenuated whine of steel strings and the repetitive thump of drums. He crossed the yard, put his head down, and pushed through the door.

It wasn't what he'd expected. People were gathered there, all right, eight, ten, eleven faces staring up at him from the gloom of candlelight, but nobody was dancing or even talking, and nobody was laughing now. It was Buffalo Springfield on the stereo, Neil Young's stretched-wire voice working through "I Am a Child" in a way that made it seem like a dirge, the whole close stuffed-up pot-reeking room gone sad with it till Ronnie wanted to take hold of somebody by the arm and say, *Who died?* Star wasn't there, Marco wasn't there, Norm either. Or Merry. But Freak was there, and Freak at least had a greeting for him, whacking the stump of his tail and inserting a cold nose into the cup of Pan's ungloved hand, and didn't anybody recognize him, didn't anybody give a shit one way or the other? "Hey, man," he said, as faces picked themselves out of the shadows, "what's happening?"

Mendocino Bill broke the spell. He rose up off a crude bench by the stove, mountainous in a cableknit sweater his mother or his exold lady must have sent him, lifting his feet with the exaggerated care of a deep-sea diver wending his way between the killer octopus and the giant man-eating clam. "Holy shit," he said, "look who it is. Hey, people," rotating his head to take in the loft and the thermal-socked feet aggregated there like some sort of fungal excrescence, "it's Pan."

Murmurs now. Neil Young went on killing the song, killing everything, people rising like zombies out of the murk, Geoffrey, Weird George, Dunphy, Erika, Deuce, all of them squinting at him as if he were six miles away. Was it Pan, was it really Pan? But where – ? We thought – ? Holy shit! It's Pan. And there didn't seem to be any hard feelings now, soul shakes all around, and here, man, have a hit of this, and he did, he did, but where was everybody else? This was Halloween, wasn't it – or had he miscounted the days?

Angela was there, Maya, Creamola, Foster. "We're hip," Bill was saying, and he backed up against the stove to warm the big palpitating lump of his backside, "it's just that nobody really, I mean, we just didn't get it together. Plus the pumpkins were like the size of grapefruits when that first frost hit – "

"Snow, you mean," Creamola said.

"We carved a zucchini," Angela put in, and there it was on the windowsill, a collapsed green loaf of a thing with a couple of holes poked in it and a pathetic flicker of candlelight emanating from somewhere in its pulpy depths. "And Reba had Che and Sunshine dressed up like devils – they made the rounds, trick or treating here, and then at Star's cabin and the one I'm sharing with like Erika and George and Geoffrey."

He saw now that a few people – the chicks – had made up their eyes and spattered a little glitter on their cheeks and foreheads and Weird George had maybe freshened up his bones and garlic, but it was a far cry from any kind of celebration Pan could have conceived of. But what was happening with *him*? With Dale and Sky? Were they coming too?

"No," he said, "they're playing cards," and even as he said it he knew how lame it sounded. The fact was that Dale and Sky Dog were also personae non gratae here, ushered out by Marco and Alfredo after a couple of halcyon days of screwing, drinking and lying comatose in the sun, and they'd made it clear that Joe Bosky was unwelcome too – Pull Your Weight or Bail, PYWOB, that seemed to be the new motto of Drop City, and you could forget LATWIDNO. "But where's everybody else?" he asked, at the center of a wheel of faces.

Angela said: "Lydia's back."

Lydia. He felt his groin stir. "Where is she?"

"At Star and Merry's. They're the only ones that would take her in."

And he learned this: Lydia, flush with cash and laden down with scotch, chocolate bonbons and cigarettes, had blown in a week ago on the back end of some wild hair's souped-up snow machine, replete with stories about the flesh trade in Fairbanks and the temperament of the Alaskan male, and she'd burned through Drop City like a wildfire. The party lasted two days – people just wanted distraction, anything, anybody, because you could only split so much wood, chow down so many bowls of mush and play Monopoly till you wore grooves in the board before you started wondering *Is this all there is?* It wasn't even winter yet and already hard times had descended on Drop City. Factions were forming. People were terminally bored, suicidal. They had no snow machine, no way of getting out, unless they wanted to walk the twelve miles to Boynton in subzero temperatures, and Boynton itself was locked in. And what about the wild hair and his snow machine? Rain had slept with him – prostituted herself, fucked him up, down and sideways – and he'd taken her out with him in a trailing blast of exhaust and a flapping curtain of snow. She was probably back in San Francisco by now.

Pan just stared at them. The joint came round and he took it. There was beer – Tom Krishna's homebrew, and it wasn't half bad. "Hey," he said, sipping from the jar, "Tom's improving. He gets out of here he ought to go directly to Budweiser, what do you think?" Nobody laughed. People fell back into the shadows. He settled in and just *felt* things for a while, and when he got comfortable behind it he pushed himself up and changed the record, a little rock and roll to shake things up, *Excuse me while I kiss the sky*. But Bill, the big overblown Freedom busriding sack of suet and hair, Mr. Downer, said they had to conserve the battery and switched the thing off, and then he was back out in the cold, thinking Star, thinking Merry, thinking Lydia.

The thin crust of snow cracked under his boots like gunfire. It was colder now, the moon haunting the sky and the stars scattered in its wake like pustules on a broken-out face, and he had no illusions about Star, or Merry either – but Lydia, at least Lydia was mad for him, always had been, right from the first. She wasn't his type, of course, but it had been a long dry stretch living like a combination lumberjack/monk at Bosky's, humping wood, hunting, keeping the stove going when Joe was out cruising the empyrean in the Cessna. They'd brought two Indian chicks in one night and for a drunken day or two they'd gone through all the permutations, and that was all right, he wasn't complaining – or maybe he was. This wasn't what he'd signed on for, no way in the world, and if he had the bucks he'd be out of here in a heartbeat – for the winter, at least. Hawaii sounded nice. La Jolla. Ensenada.

Star's cabin was the one on the end. There was a dogtrot to break the wind, a pair of windows glowing, a curl of smoke from the stove. He stood there outside the door a minute, wondering if he should knock or what, and then he pushed on through the dark closet of the dogtrot and gave two raps at the cabin door. Nothing. He rapped again. Heard voices, the shuffle of feet. Then the door creaked open on its hinges and Marco was standing there in his bleached-out jeans and workshirt, looking noncommittal, looking stiff and unwelcoming, and there was no love lost between them, not since the pot incident, anyway, and the only thing he could think to say was "Trick or treat."

Star's voice rose from the depths then. "Who is it? Ronnie? Is it *Ronnie?*" And then he heard a squeal from Merry, or maybe it was Lydia, and a long sustained jag of laughter from all three of them, as if the very fact of his existence was the funniest thing in the world. Marco gave him a nod and the three women, exuding the close, compacted odors of the sheet, the blanket, the nightie – the odors of the flesh – were there at the door in their sweatpants and sweatsocks, cooing their greetings. "Come on in," Star insisted. "Jesus, don't just stand there – "

Inside, it was close as a prison cell. You could put your fingertips on one corrugated wall and practically reach across to the other. It was dark, hot, dry. The two built-in bunk beds dominated the place and you had to crouch to avoid the six hundred tons of crap hanging from hooks and lines strung across the room, wet socks and underwear, parkas, jeans, boots. Incense was burning. The stove glowed. There was a little table by the front window littered with cards and books and dirty plates and he fell into the chair Star pulled out for him and jerked off his gloves while the chicks hovered over him, three pairs of breasts at eye-level and their lit-up faces beaming down on him like alien probes searching for signs of life. "I can't believe it," Merry kept saying, and Jiminy was there too, he saw now, looking daggers from one of the top bunks.

Pan shrugged. "Hey, it's Halloween," he said by way of explanation. "I thought I'd stop by. See what's happening."

Nobody could argue with that, and pretty soon the three women were crowded in at the table with him, sharing a plate of sugar cookies with orange sprinkles baked specially for Halloween, firing up a joint, passing round the warmed-over jar of homebrew while Marco and Jiminy conversed in a low murmur from the upper bunks. Lydia was wearing a fur coat that fell all the way to the floor – "Cross fox, given to me by an admirer; you like it?" – and she was looking good, beyond good, and hadn't she lost some weight, was that it? "You look dynamite," he said, and he had an arm round her shoulder.

"Whoa, listen to Pan," Merry giggled. "Been without it too long, huh? Living like a what, like a goat, out there with Joe Bosky? What about me? Am I looking dynamite?"

She was sitting knee to knee with Star and they were doing each other's faces up for what was going to have to pass for Halloween, slashes of black down the bridge of the nose and across the cheekbones and everything else a pale putrescent green. This wasn't the year for sexy costumes. Or the place. "Oh, yeah," Ronnie heard himself say, "groovy. Super."

"What about *me*, Pan?" Star said. She pursed her lips and simpered and he couldn't read her eyes, not at all. He wondered if there was something there still, or if she was cutting him loose, goodbye, so long, no regrets, and so what if they were in Mr. Boscovich's class together and outdid Lewis and Clark and balled under the stars and shared every last nickel? So what?

Lydia said, "I'm surprised you never made it in to see me dance – what's the matter, baby, you lose interest? Or was I just not worth a four-hour drive?"

The three of them broke down then, poking, catcalling, gobbling, pounding the table with the shining heels of their hands. Ha-ha. Big laugh. And Ronnie – Pan – got sucked into it, trying to make excuses, and the excuses were real, they were true, because the car was, in fact, terminal and Joe flew only when he felt like it and he hadn't felt like it lately. What was he supposed to do – walk?

"So now I look dynamite, right? Now that I'm sitting two inches from you." Lydia flashed her purple eyes at him. She was joking, fooling with him, her tone light and probing, but then her face clamped up on him, just like that. "And I suppose, Mr.

Pan, Mr. Big Lover with your big dick, you want me to just roll over and make it with you as if I'm starved for it or something? Is that it?"

Ronnie was at an impasse. He was stoned, he was tired, he wanted to get laid, but Socrates would have had a hard time with this one – yes was the honest answer, but yes closed the door, and no was just another kind of groveling, and he didn't care how hard up he was, he wasn't going to grovel, especially not for Lydia. She wasn't even his type.

Out of the suspension came Marco's voice: "You took both of the rifles and the handgun too. They don't belong to you, brother, and we want them back."

"Oh, come on, Marco," Star said, her voice gone tight in her throat, "not now."

"You get your moose yet – you and who, Bosky, Dale and Bruce? They still living with you?"

"Who? You mean Sky Dog?"

"Yeah, *Bruce.* That's his name, you know, just like you're Ronnie and I'm Marco and Jiminy's – what's your name, anyway?"

Jiminy's voice, a whisper, a croak: "Paul Atkins."

"Right, Paul. Did you get your moose?"

Another tough question. Yes and you're damned; no and you're an incompetent and you give the guns back anyway. "Yes," he heard himself say. "A bull. Prime. Joe says he must have weighed eleven hundred pounds. We spotted him from the air – he was right out there in the open, this big blotch moving across the snow. I mean, we've got meat, plenty of it. I mean, if you want some – "

But what Marco said, predictably, was: "We want the guns."

"Okay," he said, "I hear you." He squinted into the gloom of the upper bunk and picked up the focused glare of Marco's eyes. There was no way he was giving up the handgun – and it was just pure luck he wasn't wearing it now – or the thirty-ought-six either. The thirty-thirty, maybe. Maybe that. "Tomorrow. I swear."

Then it was Star going on about the garden and how they'd got practically nothing out of it – they started too late, and they'd learned a lesson there – but the pot came out okay, no buds to speak of but they'd dried out the leaves and got something out of it that wasn't half bad. It got you there, anyway. And then there was a silence and Star, in her brightest voice, was saying, "Come on, Jiminy, Merry, Marco, let's go trick or treat over at Norm's and leave these two to have a little privacy for a while, what do think? Huh?"

No sooner had the outer door slammed than Lydia got up to lay a couple of sticks on the fire, though compared to Bosky's the cabin seemed as airtight as a Volkswagen and it must have been eighty-five already. She left the door of the stove open so they could watch the flames, and he appreciated the gesture, but he was sweating through his clothes and his throat was so dry he could have died for a glass of iced tea or a root beer – or a root beer float, A&W, just walk up to the window and give them your order on a muggy hot upstate New York day that scorched the skin off the back of your neck, the cicadas buzzing in the trees and the waxed cup perspiring in your hand. How about that for a fantasy? It was funny. Here he was in Alaska, in a log cabin in the middle of nowhere, snow on the ground and the temperature hovering at twenty below, and all he could think about was lemonade thick with ice in a tall cool glass, or a vodka and bitter lemon, gin and tonic, anything cold, the colder the better.

Lydia took the lantern down from its hook and blew out the flame, a thin wisp of greenish smoke rising from the aperture and an evidentiary whiff of kerosene hanging on the air. She left the candles burning. He watched her move round the room, weaving through the clutter till she found her purse hanging from a nail beside Star's navy blue High Sierra backpack, the one she'd kept in the trunk of the Studebaker all the way across country, and how about that, Pan was thinking, Star's backpack. Lydia dug another stick of incense out of her purse and came to the table to light it off the candle guttering at Ronnie's elbow. She set the incense in its holder – cloves, that was what it was, cloves and maybe peppermint – and then produced a joint from the pocket of the fox coat. She gave him a wide-lipped smile, lit it and handed it to him. Then she dropped the coat to the floor, pulled her sweater and brassiere up over her head in a single fluid motion and shook out her hair. "You want me to dance for you?" she said. "Seeing as how you missed me up onstage at the Wildcat?"

"Yeah," he said, "that would be nice."

She began a slow bump and grind, spinning an invisible hula hoop round her midsection while the big hips rotated and rotated again, and then she stepped out of her jeans and dropped them to the floor too. "What do you think, Pan, Pan the satyr, you want me now?"

She watched him from the lower bunk as he fought off his clothes, so many layers, the two shirts, the sweater, the long johns – he felt like a six-year-old undressing for his mother after a day in the snow, but Lydia wasn't his mother, uh-uh, no way in hell, and that was a good thing too, because there was nothing going to stop him now. The boots. He tore at the laces, kicked at the heels. "Come on, Ronnie," she murmured, spread out for him there, waiting, "you don't want me to get bored here, do you?"

He came for her as if he'd been shot out of a bow, and there was the usual sucking and licking and wrestling for position on the narrow slat of the bed, all good and well, all part of the agenda, love, Free Love, but she seemed to be wearing her panties still and he was pushing into her and tugging at them all at the same time, and what was this, some kind of tease? "No," she whispered, pulling away from him, "no, we can't."

"What do you mean *we can't*? What are you talking about?" He was right there, right on top of her, his hands making the circuit of her. "You didn't take your pill? Is that it? Because I don't care, I'll be careful – "

The purple eyes, the tease of a voice. "No," she said, "that's not it."

"Jesus," he said, and he might have been praying – he *was* praying. "So what, then?"

"Didn't anybody tell you? Because they've been treating me like the dregs around here, Reba especially, the bitch – she's the one that got found out. By Alfredo, I mean."

"What? What is it?"

She shrugged and the bed quailed beneath her. "Crabs," she said.

"Crabs?"

"I don't know where I got them, I really don't. And I don't think it was Arnold."

"Arnold? Who's Arnold?"

"You don't know him," she said. "He like owns this sporting goods store? He drove me back here. On his Ski-Doo. All the way out from Fairbanks, with a three-hour pit stop at the Nougat. He was sweet. He really was."

Pan felt himself shrinking.

"Nobody's got any of that ointment," she said. "That's the problem. It's not like there's a drugstore around the corner, know what I mean?"

"So big deal," he said. "It's not like VD or anything" – and it was all in the mind, wasn't it, because he came back strong now, ready to burst with it – "I mean, we could still do it, couldn't we?"

She went right to sleep afterward, down and out for the count, and by the time he pulled out of her and rubbed himself as best he could with a dry bar of soap and a towel he found hanging by the door, she was snoring. Head back, breasts flattened across her chest, all that *hair* – she snatched in the air and blew it out again, hitting all the high notes as if she were playing a trumpet voluntary without the trumpet. That was all right. He forgave her that. Lydia, his treat *and* his trick. He pulled on his long johns, but then peeled them down again and took a good long look at himself and ran the towel over his loins one more time, no problem, nothing there as far as he could see, and then he dressed in a hurry because there were four long cold miles to traverse before he could start snoring himself. He shrugged into his parka, hot, sweating, and he was about to push out into the night, relishing the idea of the cold, when Star's backpack caught his eye.

For a long time now – since he'd left Drop City, anyway – he'd been thinking about getting out, bailing, just turning his back on the whole thing and getting reacquainted with a little *civilization* for a change, and he'd written his parents three times begging for money, a one-way ticket, traveler's checks, anything, but he might as well have been dead for all they cared. So Star's backpack. There it was, hanging from the nail next to Lydia's purse. And he knew something about that backpack that Star wasn't aware of, and she should have been, because how could she ever have expected him to travel with her through all those nights on the road, in tents and motels and diners and fast-food outlets, at gas stations – Where'd you say the ladies' rest room was? – without his knowing the contents of that backpack as well as he knew his own. And it wasn't like he was stealing, not exactly, because that three hundred dollars wrapped up in a sock in the bottom of the innermost pouch was three hundred dollars she'd kept back from him, and how many times had he bought breakfast, cold drinks, cigarettes, how many times had he sprung for the motel or the campground fee? Momentarily, he felt bad about it – this was Star, after all, Star whom he loved and had always loved, at least for the past year, and these three bills were her fail-safe, her ticket out, and now she was going to be hung out to dry. But she'd hung *him* out to dry, hadn't she? She'd gone for Marco. Big mistake. And she'd set this little thing up with Lydia tonight, right in front of everybody, and if that wasn't a kiss-off, then what was?

He found the door, found the night. The smoke rose against the moon, the lights in the windows of Drop City North cut their indentations out of the shadows. There was no one out in the yard, no sound but for the crunch of his boots against the plaintively yielding snow. Pan reached in under his parka to adjust the crotch of his pants – but not to itch, not yet – and then he started off across the frozen plain of the river.

28

The air was crisp, burned immaculate with the cold, and it did him good to be out in it, breathing deep and moving purposefully across the landscape as if he belonged here, as vital as the wolf, the hare, the moose, and it was good too to escape the numbing togetherness of Drop City for a few hours at least. Most of the others were content to sit around with a deck of cards, a sketchpad, a guitar, the hours falling away like so much sloughed skin, and what's the hurry, man, be cool, but Marco was a different animal altogether. He couldn't relax. He felt bored, stifled. He needed to get out, explore the country, open up his senses, *learn* something. The washed-out faces of Drop City looked up at him in surprise, the wind in the trees, the fire stoked, Rice Carolina simmering in the pot, even the dog too lazy to lift his head from the floor. You really going *out* there? In this?

Six people were writing novels, or maybe it was seven, depending on whether the thin unspooled script crowding the pages of Alfredo's notebooks turned out to be fiction or a tract on the joys of communal living – Alfredo wasn't sure yet, but there was going to be plenty of time to work it out one way or the other once the curtain fell on the daylight, and that was coming soon, November twenty-first, according to Sess Harder. There was a lot of knitting going on. Scrabble, checkers, chess. And of course people found time to toboggan down the hill, organize skating parties on the river with the three pairs of skates in Drop City's possession, build snowfreaks with willow roots for hair and somebody's worn-out bandanna and maybe an iridescent green shirt or spangled vest thrown into the bargain. Fun and games. It was all fun and games.

The sky hung low. Through the morning the temperature had

risen into the single digits, creeping up the ladder of the thermometer in a grudging, slow, hand-over-hand ascent. There might have been snow in the air, if he knew enough to feel it, to smell it in the way Sess Harder could, or Iron Steve or old Tim Yule, who sat outside on the porch of his frame house in Boynton no matter what the weather. Marco could feel the tug of Drop City loosening as he made his way downriver, and he did look back, two or three times, just to admire the way the buildings defied the vacancy of the land, to watch the conjoined swirl of the smoke from four separate stoves twist up into the sky and listen to the fading shouts of Che and Sunshine, their figures drawn down to nothing as they hammered across the yard in their homemade snowsuits and red rubber boots.

He'd given Ronnie a week, and a week was more than he had to spare. Joe Bosky and Pan the wood sprite might have gotten their meat, and Sess Harder certainly had his and probably everybody in Boynton had theirs too and half the weekend hunters from Fairbanks, Anchorage and points south, but Drop City had nothing. And that was a concern, a real concern, because pretty soon it would be too late, the moose gone stringy and tough from the rut, and despite the protests of the vegetarians, they were going to need meat to get them through till spring – either that or they'd be trapping mice under the floorboards and boiling up their shoes like Charlie Chaplin. It was frustrating too. At the end of October, just before Halloween, he and Star had been awakened by a sound that was like the rumble of fifty-five-gallon fuel drums rolling down the hill out of the trees, a deep thump and boom that resounded through the cabin and shook him out of bed and right on out the door in his stocking feet. Two moose – bulls – were going at each other on the gravel bar, great big quaking truckloads of meat suspended on the ridiculous poles of their delicate moose legs, no thought in the world but for each other and the cow just visible in the stripped yellow crown of willow behind them, and Marco standing there with empty hands like some Stone Age hunter's apprentice, and what was he going to do, throw rocks at them? Jump on their backs and cut their throats severally while the tribe looked on wringing their hands? Ronnie had taken the rifles as if they were his alone, and Ronnie was going to give them back. It wasn't a question of ownership or even of right and wrong. It was a matter of survival, just that.

There was no sign of life at Sess's place – smoke rising from the chimney, but nothing moving in the yard – and that was all right, because he didn't intend to stop in till he was on the way back, *with* the rifles slung over his shoulder. Sess was his advisor, his mentor, the man who was going to instruct him in all the recondite ways of the country, and he'd already had to endure the humiliation of admitting to him that they had no rifle worth the name with which to go out and get their meat – Deuce had a .22 for potting rabbits and groundhogs, and that was about it – and he was damned if he was going to appear weak in front of him again. So he walked on by the Harder cabin, and though the dogs raised a noise, no one came to the door and no face appeared at the window.

There wasn't much snow – just enough to whiten the ground – and Sess had told him not to expect Santa's Workshop or whatever the people down below tried to make Alaska out to be. This wasn't a postcard. It wasn't the Cascades or the Sierra Nevada. The country around here, in the interior, was about the driest in Alaska, and if they got twelve or fourteen inches of precipitation a year, that was about it. The thing was, the precipitation *stayed*. There was no meltoff in winter, and in summer, the rains just pooled over the permafrost, which in turn created a vision of paradise for the mosquitoes – and the midges and no-see-ums and all the rest of the winged and fanged world. Marco kept on, studying the snow for sign, trying to read the country the way Sess would. It was warm now, up into the teens, at least, and he unzipped his parka and let the ends of his scarf dangle free. After a while he found himself whistling, a shrill, between-the-teeth rendition of "I Am a Child," and where had that come from? He'd been fooling around with the guitar again lately – Geoffrey's guitar – and this just might be a tune to pick up on, he was thinking, nothing too complex, a sweet lilting melody floating over the chords, but then the vocal – the vocal might be a stretch. He'd just have to take it down a key or two, that's all.

His mood changed abruptly as he rounded the bend onto Woodchopper Creek. He wasn't whistling now, and he wasn't thinking about guitars either. He'd never been to Bosky's place and didn't know what to expect – beyond trouble, recalcitrance and a shitstorm of lies, excuses and backpedaling from Pan, that is. He pictured him – Pan, Ronnie – with the little lost drawn-up bow of his lips and the tumbling chin and the eyes that always managed to look hurt and put-upon but never stopped assessing you, as if he were rating his own performance moment to moment, Ronnie the thief, Ronnie the backstabber. He steeled himself. Gulped air till his lungs were on fire. And he wasn't walking anymore, but marching, marching like a soldier going into battle, right on up the creek, across the yard and onto the porch, and he was so wrought-up he didn't even notice that Joe Bosky's ski-equipped Cessna 180 with the stripped fuselage and the crudely stenciled N-number was nowhere to be seen.

He knocked, and that was ridiculous in itself, because nobody came calling out here, no Mormons or newspaper boys or Avon ladies or neighbors borrowing a cup of sugar. Nobody had ever knocked on this door. Nobody would ever knock on it again, not if the cabin stood a hundred years. A wind settled in the branches overhead, cooled the sweat of his face. "Ronnie!" he called. "Ronnie, you in there?" Nothing. Or was that the sound of movement, of voices? "Ronnie, it's me. It's Marco."

He was about to push his way in – nobody home, and wouldn't that be a miracle – when the door swung back and Pan, in bare feet and thermals, was standing there gaping at him like a fish on the end of a hook. Pan had been asleep, that was it, a yellow crust beading his eyelashes, hair flattened to one side of his head, advantage Marco. "Oh, hey, man," he mumbled. "Hey, good to see you."

From inside, sleep-wearied, the voice of Sky Dog, of *Bruce:* "Shut the fucking door, will you? What the fuck you doing, Pan?"

Ronnie slouched back into the room, talking over his shoulder. "You want coffee? I was just going to make coffee."

Marco ducked under the lintel and entered the cabin, shutting the door behind him. It was dark, his pupils clenched round the glare of the snow and the reflective ice of the creek, and for a minute he couldn't see a thing. He could smell, though, and what he smelled was a curious mélange of overcooked meat, bodily stinks, unwashed clothes and soap – the soap and lye Joe Bosky used for tanning his wolf pelts, and there was that smell too, the smell of the skin and the dead stripped-off fur of animals. Ronnie was a ghost at the stove, then the door of the stove swung open and there was the sudden incandescence of the coals and the silhouette of a thin-wristed hand framed there laying fuel on the fire.

"No," Marco said, "I don't want any coffee. I don't want anything from you except the guns you stole."

"Hey, Ronnie, man – who is that? Is somebody here? Joe? Joe, is that you?"

"Fuck you, Sky!" Ronnie shouted suddenly, with real vehemence. "Go back to sleep, all right? Shit," he cursed, slamming the coffeepot down in the direction of the stove, "there's no peace around here, not for a fucking minute!"

Marco stood just inside the door. He wasn't moving. If this was going to get nasty, then let it. He was ready. He'd been ready for a long time now, since that day in the ditch back in California, since *Bruce* had trashed his things and Ronnie had laid his hands on Star. "The guns," he repeated.

Ronnie came into focus now, round-shouldered, big-headed, the dirty white thermal underwear clinging to him like a mummy's wrap, the depth and clutter of the cabin stirring to life behind him in a storm of dust motes and dander and two beds materializing suddenly against the back wall, one of which contained a human form: Sky Dog, the mystery resolved. "What do you mean *steal*?" he said. "I didn't steal anything. Norm gave me those guns because I was the only one that wasn't too lame to use them, and you know it as well as I do, *man*," and he snarled out the final locution as if it were a curse. "So screw you with your *steal*." The pot rattled on the stove. The dust motes settled. And then, as if they'd been having a minor philological disagreement, a matter of semantics and not substance, all over now, open, shut and closed, he added, "You sure you don't want a cup of coffee?"

Marco saw the two rifles then, a simple scan of the room and there they were, suspended from nails driven into the wall above the unoccupied bed, but what he didn't see was Ronnie reaching into the pocket of the parka hanging from the clothesline over the stove. *Enough,* he was thinking, angry, on fire with it, and he crossed the room in three strides and hooked down the top rifle, the .30-06 Springfield, and he was reaching for the Winchester when Sky Dog sat up in the bed opposite and muttered, "Hey, man, what do you think you're doing?" and Ronnie pulled Norm's uncle's long-nosed slab of a pistol from the inside pocket of the coat and said, "Put it down, man. Put it down and get the fuck out of here before you get hurt, and I'm telling you, don't push me, Marco, don't push me, man."

But he was beyond all that, beyond threats, beyond Ronnie and Bruce and the minuscule and rapidly dwindling toehold they had in his life, and he strapped the Springfield over his shoulder as calmly as if he were getting dressed in the privacy of his own bedroom, then took down the Winchester and pulled that over his shoulder too. He gave Ronnie a long look, Ronnie at the stove in his underwear with the pistol he'd worn strapped to his thigh all summer extended now in the quaking grip of his light-shattering hand with its rings glinting and fingers curled. "Don't push me," Ronnie repeated, and without knowing what he was doing, he let his other hand descend to the crotch of his thermals and he began to scratch himself, his fingers working in deep, digging hard, moving unconsciously to another imperative altogether.

And suddenly the whole thing was hilarious, a joke, as comical as any ten pratfalls, and could anyone have given a more inspired performance? Ronnie was holding a gun and Ronnie was scratching. Ronnie was in his underwear, with sleep in his eyes and his hair flattened to one side of his head, snarling *Don't push me,* and Ronnie was scratching. Marco crossed the room, shifting his shoulders to accommodate the heft of the rifles, swung open the door on daylight and paused there a moment. "Take care, Pan," he said, and it was all he could do to keep from laughing aloud. "And you too, Bruce," he called, "goodbye, man. And thanks for everything."

Outside, the light was weakening. The sky had compressed and the clouds lay curdled and pale over the tops of the trees. His breath hung frozen on the air and he moved off and left it behind, one puff after another. He'd gone half a mile before he thought to stop and check the chambers of the rifles, because what good were they if there was no ammunition? There were two rounds in the Springfield, one in the Winchester. He felt foolish, but he could hardly retrace his steps, knock on the door all over again and ask Ronnie to cough up the bullets, which he might very well have purchased on his own at the general store in Boynton and which were readily available to Marco or anybody else the next time they felt like making the twenty-four-mile roundtrip stroll into town and back. Two rifles, three bullets. The night he'd gone with Norm to visit the uncle in Seattle (and it was just as he'd envisioned it, déjà vu, the old man in the bed and the snowshoes on the wall, and though he didn't believe in karma or mysticism or any kind of predetermination at all, it was enough to chill him even now), the uncle had rattled on about using only two bullets a year, one for his moose and one for his bear. Well, all right. For the first time all fall, Marco had the means to lay in meat. And when he shouldered the rifles and came up out of his crouch, he listened to the breeze and studied the snow with the ears and eyes of a hunter.

At some point – he couldn't be sure later exactly when, whether it was half an hour up from Woodchopper or less – he saw moose sign along the south bank of the river, the neat parallel indentations of the hooves, the browsed willow, a dark scatter of pellets against the blank page of the snow, and he veered in off the ice to follow the trail. It led him inland, and there was more than one moose here – two, or possibly three, depending on how you read the tracks, and he was no expert, he'd be the first to admit it. Still, he'd hunted deer growing up in Connecticut, and a moose was just another kind of deer, six times as big, maybe, and dangerous, capable of turning on its adversary and goring him, battering him, crushing the life out of him, but for all that, a deer. He unslung the .30-06, with its two rounds, and eased through the unforgiving willow as stealthily as he could manage. There were their tracks, another pile of droppings, and up ahead, a V-shaped swath any fool could follow cut right through the center of the thicket. He went on, intent on the hunt, and hardly noticed when it began to snow.

If he'd thought about what he was doing, he might have been concerned. He was on unfamiliar ground, the light was leaching out of the sky and the snow had begun to quicken. Worse, he had no shelter, no food, not even a day pack with paper, matches, a ground cloth – he'd been out for a stroll, an hour-and-twenty-minute walk on the open ice to Woodchopper Creek in clear weather, and he hadn't felt the need to bring anything with him. He shouldn't have been hunting, not dressed the way he was and without even the most rudimentary equipment, but he had the guns, a real novelty, and he saw the tracks, and he just didn't think. In fact, as he worked his way deeper into the trees, he was thinking about Pan's itch, how funny it was, how telling, how pathetic.

Lydia had come back with crabs – lice, genital lice, hard little creeping things like ticks that were easy enough to get rid of if you went directly to the drugstore, slathered on the proper ointment and burned your underwear on the funeral pyre of intimate relations. But Drop City didn't have a drugstore, and it was a long cold walk to Boynton, and there was no guarantee you'd find what you needed there either. The crabs spread through Drop City like dye in water, and then the camps formed and the accusations flew, and the crabs – clinging, persistent, enamored of blood and secret places – became the markers in the war between Free Love and commitment. Star didn't have them, nor did Marco. But Jiminy had given them to Merry, and he wasn't saying where he'd contracted them, and Reba had infected Alfredo, fooling no one, because she'd been making it with Deuce and Deuce had – speculation now – jumped on Lydia, as had half the other *cats,* because she was back and she was available and she was new all over again. And so Lydia was the pariah, though she hadn't known what she was doing, because it took a week or so for the crabs to mate and lay their eggs and emerge to bite and suck and excrete their waste until the skin erupted and everybody *itched.*

Marco thought it was funny, *La Ronde* staged in the hinterlands. Long-standing resentments flared up. Hypocrites assailed hypocrites. People wouldn't speak to one another. They passed in the yard without looking up, dug into the communal pot for rice pilaf and meatless marinara and the person standing next to them might as well have been dead. As a result, the population of the three cabins and the meeting hall was in constant flux, Deuce at the foot of the bed one night, Angela, Erika or Geoffrey the next. Reba, as medical advisor, shrieked out over the clamor of one very contentious meeting and insisted that everybody, whether they were infected yet or not, had to shave their pudenda bald and soak their underwear in Clorox to kill the nearly invisible eggs of the things, and Mendocino Bill, himself itching, said people should forget coming to him for Dr. Scholl's because it had about as much effect as cornstarch. Norm was itching. Premstar was itching. "I know it's going to sting, people," Norm boomed out over the tidal roar of the community in extremis, "but I say a little kerosene, maybe a shot glass full, rubbed in each night for a week."

Crabs. Crab *lice*. They were one form of life on this planet, evolved to fill a niche, as the evolutionists would say. And what was the ideal form of life, one that exists independently, preying on nothing, creating its own food source through photosynthesis? The plant, the tree. Yes, but given that life form, given the tree and the leaf, evolution presupposes the insect to feed on it and the fungus to break it down, and the bird to feed on the insect and the cat on the bird. And here he was, with a gun in his hand and the snow driving bristles in his face, doing his level best to prey on another and grander form of life. And why not? If the crabs could gnaw at his brothers' and sisters' groins, then why couldn't he – why couldn't they – gnaw at the leg of the moose?

It was nearly full dark now. The trees were shadows, the tracks growing faint. Marco knelt to study them, all his senses alive, listening, watching, not daring even to breathe, and then he lifted his head and there it was, a moose, or the head of a moose, projecting in a dense clot of shadow from behind the nearest spruce in a forest of them. It was canny, this moose, its nostrils flared as it tried to pick up his scent, the bulk of its body secreted behind the trees, in no hurry to commit itself. He waited a long breathless moment for it to step out into the open, gauging where the shoulder would appear so he could aim for it, or just behind it, and do the fatal damage. But the animal barely moved, nothing more than a twitch now and again to lend it animacy, and finally, afraid of missing his chance, he took aim, the blood boiling in his veins – Do not miss, do *not* – and squeezed the trigger. The night tore open in thunder and flame, and yet, incredibly, the moose stood rooted to the spot. It wasn't until he fired the second shot that it dropped in a dark swoon to the ground and he was coming after it, coming to retrieve it with hands that trembled and legs that had gone weak.

The snow sifted through the needles with an admonitory hiss. Marco stumbled forward, one shot left, the slug in the Winchester, praying that the thing was dead, that he wouldn't have to sacrifice it all over again, because this was enough for one day, more than enough. And then he was there, by the tree with its black skirts of tightly woven needles and the bark that smelled of pitch, of air freshener and Pine-Sol, and saw that there was no moose, wounded or otherwise, lying heaped in the snow. He heard a sudden sharp heartrending cry then, the cry of a human baby spitted by some fiend on the point of a bayonet, and looked down at his feet. There *was* something there, a black weakly thrashing living form, a thing he'd shot while it clung to the bark of the tree eight feet from the ground, impersonating the head of a moose. And what was it? Weak and bristling, the life sucking out of the hole he'd put in it – a porcupine, that's what it was, the humped and hobbling old man of the woods, fit only to feed to the dogs.

For a long moment he stood there, watching the thing thrash its spiked head against the ground, back and forth, back and forth, a metronome keeping time with its agony and its unbelief – or was that its tail? All the while, the dark thumping kept time to the beat of his own unavailing blood. He felt foolish, felt lost and hopeless and incompetent, felt ashamed, felt guilty. And then, as the night deepened and the snow struck down at the unprotected flesh of his face, he hammered the dark form at his feet with the heel of his boot until it stopped moving, then hurried off to find the way he had come.

29

She'd always been a night person, or that was how she liked to think of herself. A night person haunted the clubs, slept late, sucked all the glamour out of the dwindling dark hours when the straight world was asleep and dreaming of mortgage payments. Nobody wanted to be a morning person, or at least nobody wanted to admit to it. Morning people grinned and mugged and threw cheer in your face at seven-thirty a.m. when you barely knew what your name was and your blouse with the Peter Pan collar was on inside out and the kids, the students – morning people all – were already filing into the room to let their oversubscribed hormones go to war with their metabolic disorders. Her mother was a morning person. Reba – Reba was a morning person.

Star was sitting at the table in the meeting hall preparing yet another community meal – dried salmon stew, with rice for consistency and tomatoes and peas out of the institutional-sized can for color – and she was smiling to herself as Merry chopped onions and Maya hammered at the stiff jerked slabs of fish with the butt of her knife. Night person. Morning person. The distinction didn't mean much up here, since it was night pretty much all the time now, the kind of night they gave you in the casinos in Las Vegas so you'd never stop handing over your money, the night of the POWs with the black bags pulled down over their heads, black night, endless night. It was three o'clock in the afternoon, according to the only timepiece in Drop City's possession, Alfredo's Timex with the two-inch-wide tooled-leather band that never left his wrist, and it was dark, had been dark for some time now. Somebody said it was snowing outside. Somebody else said it had been snowing for the past hour. The dog looked up briefly and laid his head back down again, as if it were too heavy a burden to bear.

People were scattered around the room in a funk of unwashed clothes and matted hair, down, dejected, disheveled, the energy level hovering around zero – they didn't even look as if they'd be able to lift the forks to their mouths come dinner, and Star had a brief fantasy of feeding them all by hand, then changing their diapers and putting them to bed one after the other. It was depressing. When they spoke, it was in a whisper, as if nobody really wanted to express their thoughts aloud, and the cramped space of the meeting hall buzzed with an insectoid rasp of timbreless voices sawing away at the fabric of the afternoon. Faces were vapid, eyes drained. It was a day for getting stoned, and Drop City had been diligent about it. Star was floating right along herself, drifting like the cottonwood fluff on the river, back when there was a river – and cottonwood. She got up to fuel the fire and get some oil sizzling in the bottom of the pot. Three steps from the table to the stove, but she saw the pale slashes of the snow against the window like interference on a black-and-white TV. Marco was out there somewhere, that was what she was thinking. He should have been back by now.

Merry was saying, "I'll never speak to Jiminy again, I swear. Not unless he tells me who it was, and I already know, I mean, I'd have to be blind not to – "

Maya, chopping: "Dunphy."

" – I just want to hear it from him, like the truth, just once. Just once I'd like to hear the truth come out of his mouth."

Both of them looked across the room to where Lydia, wrapped in her fur coat, sat against the wall leafing through one of the magazines she'd brought back as a communal offering – *Mademoiselle, Cosmopolitan, Esquire, Playboy, Rolling Stone* – along with pounds and pounds of chocolate, French milled soap and Canadian whiskey. And crabs. Crabs too.

Star threw a handful of chopped garlic into the hot oil and everybody perked up visibly because there was no denying that scent, and then she went to Merry for the onions. People froze to death up here, that was what she was thinking – and what was that story she'd read in high school, the famous one where the guy, the cheechako, can't get a fire going and tries to kill the dog to warm his hands? The dog was too smart for him, that much she remembered. But he was a cheechako, that was the telling point, a greenhorn who didn't know the harshness of the country or the implacability of the night, a tenderfoot, a novice. Like Marco. There were animals out there in the woods, wolves, bears, that writhing dark buzzsaw of a thing that jerked across the ground as if it had been set on fire – the wolverine, the glutton, the intimidator – and if it could eviscerate a goat in ten seconds flat, then what could it do to a human being? People shot each other up here too, over guns, with guns, but then Ronnie would never –

"Smells good." It was Lydia, looking over her shoulder now. "What's it going to be tonight, the salmon surprise?"

Star smiled, pushed the hair away from her face with the back of her hand. "What else?" she said, stirring garlic and onions around the snapping of the oil. "It's the specialty of the house."

She looked up then, past Lydia, to the door. She'd heard a noise, a thump at the frame as if someone had fallen dead on the doorstep – *Marco,* she was thinking, *Marco* – and then suddenly the door flung open and slammed to again, and Jiminy was there in his Salvation Army greatcoat, stamping and blowing. He was wearing a knit hat that clung to his skull and came down tight over his ears and he'd wrapped his scarf round his head and face like a chador. Snow had crystallized in his eyebrows, it was caked atop his hat and batter-spread across the padded shoulders of the coat. "Jesus," he muttered, unwrapping himself layer by layer, "it's cold enough out there to piss and lean on it."

Star saw him exchange a glance with Merry – "Hi, Mer," he said, but her eyes just bored right through him – and then it was his turn to say "Smells good" and he was crowding in at the stove, working up some friction between his palms and peering into the pot as if he were thinking about folding up his limbs and climbing into it.

"Snowing hard?" Star had inverted the Spiracha bottle over the pot with one hand while she shook white pepper out of the big rust-topped can with the other, spice for the hordes, and it could never be spicy enough.

"Snowing and blowing," he said, and everybody in the room was listening. "I was like skating? Out on the river where we cleared that nice bumpless patch for a rink? But then the snow came up and pretty much ruined it."

"You didn't see Marco, did you? Because he's been gone all day."

"What, hunting?"

"No," she said, taking up the long wooden spoon and giving the contents of the pot a vigorous stir. "He went down to Woodchopper to get the guns Pan appropriated for himself."

"I'm sorry, but Pan's a major league jerk," Bill put in. He was hunched over a chessboard with Harmony, his oversized feet dangling from the edge of the loft in a pair of candy-striped socks with turned-up toes. "Worse, he's just a scam artist, like the street people that came in and ruined the Haight for everybody. He's out for nobody but himself. Period."

"He's into me for ten dollars," Harmony said.

Tom Krishna was wrapped in a blanket atop one of the bunk beds set into the wall. He looked up from the book he'd been reading – the teachings of some guru whose name Star couldn't pronounce; all she remembered was that he'd lived on air and had achieved *moksha* after dying of brain cancer in a Tibetan lamasery. "I gave him sixteen dollars that last time, for personal items, you know? And what'd I get? Nothing. Not even a taste of that grass he says he invested in for everybody."

"What a laugh," Bill said.

That went round a while – the subject of Pan, and if she'd been depressed before, now she felt bereaved, as if he'd crawled off somewhere and died, because nobody would defend him, not even Lydia – and then Jiminy turned his fleshless backside to the stove and asked Tom Krishna if the new batch of beer was ready yet and Tom said it was and the snow fell and the dog slept and she realized she'd never had an answer to her question. Maya relit the joint they'd been working on earlier and passed it to Merry, who passed it to Star. She took a hit and passed it on. That was what communal life was all about, passing things on. But what about Marco? What about the responsibility for him, for getting seriously worried here, for organizing a search party – were they all just going to pass that on too? "Alfredo," she said suddenly, her voice too loud, "what time is it?"

Alfredo was up in the loft with Bill and Harmony, ready to take on the winner of the chess match. They were playing a tournament, twelve players, twelve matches a day, twelve days running. When that was over and the victor had been crowned, they'd play another one. "Three forty-five," he called down in a broad, matter-of-fact voice that could have belonged to an announcer in a TV studio, to Walter Cronkite or Huntley and Brinkley. Three forty-five. The real world, the mechanical world, intrudes.

"Because, I don't know, Marco's been gone since noon or something – shouldn't we, I mean, isn't anybody going to go out and look for him?"

It must have been two or three hours later when they all sat down to dinner – or when dinner was served, that is, because Drop City no longer ate as one. There wasn't enough space, for one thing. When they dragged the table out from the wall and set places around it, only eight people could be seated comfortably, if you could call balancing on a wobbly two-foot-high round of black spruce comfortable. The rest just took a plate, heaped it up with rice or beans or pasta and hunkered down on the floor or the nearest bed or climbed the ladder to the loft, impressing on everybody just how cramped three hundred and sixty square feet of living space could be. The other limiting factor was the interpersonal feuds that were always flaring up out of nothing, but never more so than when everybody was confined to four cabins with no California sunshine to massage away the hard feelings – and people shuffled in and out of those cabins in a human shell game so bewildering even Star and Merry could barely keep track of who was on the outs with whom. Half the time they'd just come in, scoop something out of the pot and run for one of the cabins with it. And that prompted a new Drop City rule: everyone was responsible for his or her own plate. People scratched their initials into the bottom of the enameled plates and bowls, and some, like Weird George, had already reached their crockery limit and had to eat out of old peach and apricot cans.

Norm blew in for dinner, trailing Premstar, Reba and the kids, and he wasn't his usual self. He didn't stamp or roar or call out greetings to the flock, just bowed his head, ducked out of his parka and got in line at the stove. There was fresh whole-grain bread laid out on the top shelf within easy reach of the stove, and butter out of the one-pound can. That and the salmon-rice dish, heavily laced with soy, and Kool-Aid and Tang to wash it all down, along with three big half-gallon jugs of Tom Krishna's yeasty homebrew and two pans of fudge brownies. Humble fare, but there was plenty of it, and the vegetarians could be glad Marco didn't have a gun, because when he did there'd have to be two meals prepared each night, the one incorporating moose or whatever, the other without it.

It was still snowing. Star wasn't given to senseless worry or the paranoia that certain grades and varieties of grass can generate – or maybe she was – but by the time dinner was on the table she was a wreck. There was no sign of Marco. It was an hour and a half to Woodchopper Creek, ten minutes to settle his business, and an hour and a half back. Three hours and ten minutes, and he'd been gone for six, six at least. Earlier, while the salmon was thickening in the pan, she'd got Merry and Maya to go out into the storm with her and shout his name into the wind. They'd taken Freak with them in the hope he'd catch Marco's scent, and they'd gone as far downriver as Sess and Pamela's place, but Marco wasn't there and they hadn't seen him. Pamela said it was probably nothing, he'd stayed on at Woodchopper when the storm settled in or he'd thrown up a temporary shelter and got a fire going, and really, Sess had camped a hundred times in much worse, hadn't he? Sess had. He acknowledged that. But Pamela was only saying the expected things, to calm her, and Star, though she was three miles high and drifting like a cloud, didn't miss the look she exchanged with Sess. They all had a cup of tea, then the three of them went out and shouted Marco's name till their throats were raw and their lungs burning. When they got back, Star went to each of the cabins in succession, thinking he might have looped round them in the storm, but nobody had seen him, and when finally she returned to the meeting hall and the smell of the food and the shot of Everclear Bill gave her to calm her nerves, he wasn't there either.

If that wore her down, the worry that ate at her with every thump of her heart and made the storm a curse and the meal as bland as boiled cardboard so that she couldn't take more than two bites of it and had to sneak her plate to the dog, what came next was even worse. It was an hour after they'd eaten. The dishes were soaking in the big washtub on the stove. People were passing cigarettes, the eternal joint. Alfredo had tried to get a sing-along going, but nobody seemed to have the heart for it, and it wasn't anxiety over Marco that had them down, it was just boredom, the sameness of the food, the faces, the night. Nothing was happening. Nothing was going to happen. This was the life they'd chosen. Voluntarily.

Norm was sunk into one of the lower bunks with Premstar, their backs against the wall, feet splayed out on the floor. He was looking old. His skin was so pale it could have been the underbelly of a fish peeled off and sewed into place, and his hair, bucket-washed, hung limp and thin around his ears. There were hairs growing out of those ears, she saw now, out of his nostrils, climbing up out of the neck of his shirt. Never repaired, his glasses looked as if they'd been thrown at his face, dirty grayish lumps of Reba's sticking plaster holding the frames together in a tentative accord with the forces of gravity. He was sniffling, victimized by the cold oozing its way through the collective mass of his brothers and sisters, his eyes red-rimmed and terminal. And he was itching, itching like everybody else. Pasha Norm. Norm the guru. Norm, the guiding light of Drop City.

He pushed himself up with a grunt, and he was just like her father struggling up out of his chair after his team had gone down to defeat, shoulders slumped, eyes vacant, one hand going to the small of his back and whatever residual ache stabbed at him there, and then he crossed the room to the table and poured himself a cup of beer from the half-gallon jug. Why she was watching him, she didn't know. She'd been playing a distracted game of cards – pitch – with Merry, Maya and Lydia, and as her gaze drifted round the room she'd somehow settled on Norm, as if she knew what was coming, as if she'd had a premonition, not only about Marco and Ronnie and the long downward slide of the night, but of the fate of Drop City itself.

Norm tipped back his head, the hair spilling loose around his shoulders, and drank noisily from the cup. "That's beer," he said, fighting back a belch. "That's the best thing about this place, our greatest achievement – Tom Krishna's beer. We ought to bottle it and sell it. 'Old Flatulence,' we'll call it. How does that sound?"

Nobody laughed. But he'd accomplished what he wanted: he had the attention of the room now, people looking up from books, games, conversations – he was working up to something, they could all sense it.

"You know," he said, talking to the room now, "while we've got everybody gathered here, or mostly everybody, if you want to discount the people harboring grudges and ill will, and I guess that's probably about *half* of us, people, half the Drop City Maniacs gone round the *bend,* and how about that as testimony to the power of brother- and sisterhood?" Still nobody laughed. "While we've got everybody here I just want to lay something on you, I mean, on behalf of me and Premstar – " They all looked to Premstar, who sat still as an icon, her lips parted in an expectant pout, her eyelids gleaming naked because she was out of glue for her false lashes and down to the last few dwindling traces of her pastel blue eyeshadow. Premstar glared back. She was out of her league here, Star was thinking, a prima donna in a community of equals, and there was no excuse for her, none, zero. She could pout all night long for all anybody cared.

"Let me guess," Bill said. "The Air Force is making an emergency drop of eighty-seven tubes of crab ointment right out on the river – "

"And six color TVs, with rabbit ears the size of the Empire State Building," Weird George cried out, thrusting up his mug of beer as if to propose a toast. "And all the back issues of *Playboy* in existence!"

There were a few sniggers, a nervous laugh or two. The stove sighed. Snow ticked at the windows. Merry looked up from her cards and held Star's eyes, as if to say, *What next?*

Norm had no problem playing to the gallery. He was like an actor – he *was* an actor – and he swung round on the pivot of his heels and threw out his arms as if to embrace everybody leaning over the rough-hewn edge of the railingless loft, the cheap seats, everybody in the cheap seats. "I only wish," he said.

Reba, who'd been sitting in the corner staring at nothing while Che and Sunshine picked sodden lumps of fish off their untouched plates and flung them at one another in a silent, dragged-down war of attrition, spoke up suddenly. "We need a Ski-Doo is what we need. So we can get into town and get the damned ointment, because this is ridiculous, and the mail, and, and – "

"And see some new faces for a change," Bill finished the thought for her.

Weird George said he'd like to hoist a few at the Three Pup.

"Toothpaste," Maya said. "Shampoo. An orange stick for my nails."

Jiminy's opinion was that they were welcome to walk – "Walking is good for you, man, like the best exercise in the world" – but nobody rose to the bait. The idea was patently ridiculous. Sure, they could walk the twelve miles, and a few people had done it since the river had frozen up, but it was twelve miles *back,* and there was no place to stay in Boynton because the bus had no heat in it and Sess Harder had refused them the use of his shack cum toolshed, even for just an overnight stay. Everybody was out here now – no more furloughs – and they were going to stay here till the river broke up in May. Count the months – two weeks more of November, then December, January, February, March and April. It was a lifetime. A prison sentence. And already they were chafing, all of them – what would it be like in three months? In four?

Everybody chased the issue around for a minute or two, any topic the subject of rancor and debate, and then there was a silence, a time-out while they each contemplated the future, both individual and communal, and then Bill coughed into his fist and looked up and asked Norm what he had on his mind.

Norm put on a mask. His face was neutral but for his eyes, his red-rimmed eyes, sharpening suddenly from the depths of the two holes he'd poked in it. "It's nothing really, no big deal, nothing to get *uptight* about, people." He paused, and though everybody was busy with something, they were all listening, all of them. "Well, it's Premstar," he said. "Prem hasn't been feeling too well – "

Again, all eyes went to her. She was glaring out of the cave of herself, bristling with some kind of animus, sure, but she looked as healthy as anybody else. And pretty. Pretty as a beauty queen. Which in itself was unforgivable.

"And I've had some news about the ranch – which I've been waiting for the right moment to share with you, good news and bad news too. The good news is we've got my attorney in there fighting the county's right to foreclose on the property – I mean, we could sell it yet, clear the back taxes, and have the bread, I mean, the *wherewithal,* to really do something here. I mean, new buildings, sauna, snow machines, something for everybody – we can really make this place work, people, make it livable, *comfortable,* even. And self-sufficient, definitely self-sufficient. That's my goal, that's it right there – "

What's the bad news? Star wanted to say, and her heart was going – she didn't need bad news, not with Marco out there somewhere in the night, maybe lost, maybe hurt – but Bill beat her to it. "So what's the bad news?" he said.

No hedging now, no going back: Norm thrust his face forward, challenging the room. "I've got to split," he said. "Me and Prem. But just for like the tiniest little running jump of a hiatus – that's what it is, a *hiatus* – because they want me in court down there, and – well, I fixed it up with Joe Bosky. He's going to fly us to the airport in Fairbanks. I mean, when the weather allows." He looked into each face around the cabin, ticking them off one by one. "Plus Prem," he said. "Prem's sick."

It took a minute. They were in shock, that was what it was. They were staggered. Punch-drunk. No one could have guessed, not in their wildest – Star watched their faces go up in flames, their eyes turn to ash. They couldn't talk. Nobody could say a word. Norm had just held a glowing torch to the roof of the meeting hall, he'd napalmed the village and scattered the refugees. She felt herself lifting out of her seat as if she were in another dimension altogether, and wasn't that the kind of thing that happened to you when you died, when you had an out-of-body experience, hovering above the scene in pure sentience? She was high up, running with the clouds, and then she burst through them into the barren night of the stars and the planets and their cold, cold heat. And now there were angry voices, frightened voices, flaring out all around her as if they wanted to shoot her down. "But Marco," she stammered, fighting to be heard, "you don't understand, you can't leave, nobody can – Marco's out there!"

She went out into the night, shouting for him, but the shouts died in her throat – he wasn't coming back, nobody was coming back,

Marco was dead, Drop City was dead, and she might as well have been dead herself. The wind spat snow at her, rammed at her shoulders, thrust a dry tongue up under her collar and down the back of her pants. She hunched herself in the parka and made a circuit of the place, up to the goat pen, down to the river and back, the tracks filling behind her even as she lifted her feet, the clouds stilled, the hills immovable and silent, transfixed on the spearheads of the trees. The snow was nearly to her knees and drifting now, picking up structure and definition. There was no feeling in her toes. Her feet were like blocks, her fingertips numb. She was freezing. She was helpless. There was nothing she could do. She went round a second time, fighting it, screaming, "Marco! Marco!" She paused, listened, called out again. No one answered.

Then she was in her cabin, laying wood on the fire. She had the place to herself, at least for the moment, because everybody else was in the meeting hall, debating, shouting, glutting themselves on the bad vibes and negativity, and the people who hadn't been there for dinner were there now – she'd seen the hurrying dark forms huddled against the snow, panic time, oh yes indeed. She tried to steady herself. Tried to talk herself down from the ledge she'd stepped out on here. What she needed most of all was to be calm, to think things through in a slow, orderly fashion. Marco was lost. Norm was bailing. *Things fall apart; the centre cannot hold*. She saw herself a Drop City widow, sidling up to Geoffrey or Weird George, peeling potatoes, hauling frozen buckets of human waste out to the refuse heap, living day by day through the slow deterioration of everything she cared about, everything she'd built and fought for, and maybe she'd pile up stones in memory of Marco, the way the Indians did, and cry over the stones and her battered hands and the whole impossible naive idealistic hippie trip she'd been on ever since she left home. What a fool, she thought. What a fool she'd been.

She thought of the money then. The three pale stiff silvery green notes wrapped up in the sock in the inside flap of her backpack, her insurance policy, cab fare, bus fare, air fare, the means to get out. Ronnie had got out, Sky Dog and Dale Murray, Rain, Lester and Franklin – and Norm was on his way. Verbie was living in town with Iron Steve in a rental with electricity and running water. Lydia was only parked here, the most temporary of arrangements, everybody knew that. And so why should she suffer? Why should she wear herself down in the thankless role of *chick* and scullery maid? She got up from the bed and went to her pack.

She dug through her summer tops, her cutoffs, sandals, a bundle of letters she'd meant to send, camping gear, books, suntan oil, three, four, five pairs of clean socks, her poncho, but when she reached into the inside pocket, deep down, at the bottom, there was nothing. It had to be a mistake. She upended the pack on the bed, went through every pouch, pocket and fold of clothing and laid everything out where she could see it, thinking she would hike the twelve miles to town all on her own, just follow the river like a highway, walk into the Three Pup and offer to pay one of the bush pilots to fly her out, Howard, maybe – he would do it, no problem. She'd offer fifty and keep the rest for a one-way ticket home – not to Florida, not to Hawaii, but home – and she saw herself sitting back in the reclining seat, eating a hot meal off the tray, prepackaged food, civilized food, and her mother standing there at the gate at Kennedy with Sam and the dog, and her father, if he could get off work. She started to cry then. She couldn't help herself.

For a long while she just sat there, staring down at the pattern of her things spread out over the bed. Then she went through everything again, sobbing deep in her chest, rubbing at her nose and eyes with the back of her sleeve. Then she got up and searched round the cabin, peering down the length of the shelves, fanning through the paperbacks, though she knew she hadn't moved that money – not unless she was losing her mind, not unless she'd been sleepwalking or dreaming herself into another dimension. She retraced her steps. Searched through the empty pack again and yet again and finally used her penknife to take the lining out of the pocket, but what she clenched in her hand was only nylon, navy blue nylon, manufactured in Taiwan.

The money hadn't vanished into thin air. It hadn't grown legs and run off. Someone had stolen it, that was the only conclusion, some thief, somebody who'd had the nerve, and the leisure, to go through her things behind her back – Merry, Maya, Jiminy, Marco. But no. She couldn't believe it of any of them, and besides, no one had known the money was there – it was her secret, her secret stash. She was desolated. This was the end of brother- and sisterhood, this was the way it played out. In betrayal. Selfishness. Meanness. In thievery. Where was the flow in that? Where was the breakthrough? It came to her that everybody must have had a secret stash, something they were holding out on for their own selfish little reasons, even Marco, even Merry, and so it was only logical that they would suspect each other and rifle – that was the word, wasn't it? – rifle each other's possessions.

Once more she went through everything, desperate now, flinging wrung-out socks and unfurled sweaters and spine-sprung paperbacks over her shoulder, and she was looking at the door and listening for footsteps as if she could hear them through the screen of the storm, a heartbeat away from *rifling* Jiminy's things, Merry's, Marco's, when she thought of Ronnie. He'd been alone here, with Lydia, and if anyone knew her secrets Ronnie did, if anyone would have gone through her things, if anyone would even have thought of stealing from her, lying to her, cheating and two-timing and offering her up to teepee cats like a prostitute and playing the unwitting victim all the while, it was Ronnie. Ronnie had her money. Ronnie.

She looked up into the devastation of the room. It was like a pit, like a cage. Smoky, stinking, everything a jumble and nowhere to escape to. The joints of the stovepipe didn't fit right, the gusts ran right through the chinking in a hundred places, the door was like a wind tunnel no matter how many layers of rags and paper they stuffed into the gaps round the frame. It was hopeless, everything was hopeless, and she couldn't seem to stop crying. Time passed – minutes, hours, she didn't know. The wood of the stove burned to coals and then ash. She was shivering. Sitting there and shivering, with no will to feed the stove or even wrap herself in a blanket. And then the door rattled on its hinges and she looked up and Marco was there.

Marco. He was a sheet of white, white everywhere, layered with it, his mustache frozen over his lips, his lips white, the flesh of his cheekbones gone the color and texture of dripped wax. He didn't unwrap his scarf, didn't remove his hat or tug at the straps of the guns slung over his shoulder – he just moved into the room on stiff shuffling feet and caught her in the deadfall of his arms.

30

Pamela was sitting at the window of the darkened cabin, lighting one cigarette off another and staring out into the moonlit yard. This was her favorite form of recreation, once the cooking was done and the dishes washed and she'd worked the furs as long as she could stand the tedium of it and patched Sess's clothes and patched them again till his pants and shirts could have stood up and paraded around the room like walking quilts – once that was over, once the wood had been hauled in and the stove tended and tomorrow's bread set to rise in the pan, she sat and watched. The weather had been clear and cold for the past week, and the moon had become her sun, omnipresent, unimpeded, lighting up the snow of the hills like a stage set. She'd been out earlier (at five p.m. by the windup clock Sess had made his obsession; the ticking drove him to distraction, he claimed, and over and over again he wondered aloud how she could possibly care what time it was anyway), and she'd watched the pulse and stagger of the northern lights going green and yellow-green and shading to purple, to red, until she'd felt the cold and come back inside. Sitting here, at the window, was better than reading a novel or laying out a hand of solitaire or doing crosswords. It was her downtime, her contemplative time, and she stared into the landscape in the way other people might have stared into a picture or a television screen. A fox in winter coat came through the yard every day, twice a day. Owls sat the trees. Ravens stirred like black rags thrown down out of the night. Twice she'd felt some inexpressible shift in the current of things and looked up to see a train of wolves clipping through the crusted snow on the proscenium of the riverbank.

As for the clock, she insisted on it. Yes, she'd given herself over to her man, and yes, she trusted his judgment, valued it, and she looked to him for sustenance and protection, all of that. And she saw his point. To live here, in the bush, was to live in primitive time, timeless time, and to have clocks ticking away the artificial minutes of man-made hours defeated the purpose, undermined the whole ethos of the natural world. But you had to make concessions, that was the way she saw it, or they'd be living in a cave and rubbing sticks together – and what about the chainsaw, the auger, the fiberglass fishing rod, the outboard engine he was talking about buying come spring? They were necessary, he argued, tools that helped them live better, because he didn't have to tell her, of all people, how thin was the wire stringing their life together out here under the immitigable sky where disaster was in the offing every minute of every day.

All right. For him it was the chainsaw and the outboard motor, but for her it was the clock, the calendar, the thermometer. If it weren't for the clock she wouldn't know if it was six in the evening or six in the morning, and people might argue that it didn't make a lick of difference, because morning and evening were artificial constructs like the days of the week and the counting out of the years from the birth of Christ, as if that mattered, as if it were real, as if God existed and the Argument from Design was a fact. She didn't care. She liked numbers, liked figures, needed to know that it was six twenty-five on December eighteenth, nineteen hundred and seventy, Anno Domini, and that the thermometer had stood at thirty-two degrees below zero when she last looked – and she might just get up again and step out the door and see how far it had dropped in the interim. She might. And she might keep a diary too, just simple things, just facts – the day, the time, the temperature, what they were eating, what was in the sky, in the trees, on the ground. That was her business, her *thing,* as Star would say, and who could deny her that? Not Sess. Certainly not Sess. So let him wake in the night to the ticking of the clock. It wouldn't kill him.

She was about to get up and do just that – check the temperature – when she saw an upright shadow isolate itself from the trees and move on up the bank toward the cabin with the slow disconnected movement of a figure in a dream. She held the nub of the cigarette to her lips, smoking it right down to the filter, and watched. The figure moved closer, huddled, kicking through the snow on limbs that separated and joined and separated again, and she felt her whole being leap up inside her: it was Star, coming to relieve her of the burden of contemplation. What was it – what would Star say? It was far out. It was party time.

She was at the door before Star could knock, afraid that she might see the darkened windows and think no one was home and turn back for the hippie camp. "Well, hello, hello," she said, sweeping her into the room, "what a surprise, what a nice surprise, and Merry Christmas, have I wished you a Merry Christmas?"

Star accepted a cup of tea, the expensive Darjeeling blend Pamela kept in a sealed tin for visitors, and Pamela found herself rocketing around the room in a high state of excitement, stoking the fire, lighting lamps, setting out a plate of crackers and cheese, bread, butter, two-berry jam, and spoons and a knife – where was the knife? – all the while talking nonstop, talking as if she'd been the prisoner of a tribe of deaf-mutes on a desert shore. She talked so much, so steadily and without remit, that it must have taken a quarter of an hour to realize that Star wasn't right there with her. Star wasn't saying anything, or hardly anything – just answering yes or no to the flock of questions she was throwing at her, nodding or grunting or chiming in with an *Uh-huh* or *I know what you mean* in a kind of call and response. Finally Pamela got hold of herself. She bit her tongue. Forced herself to take a long sip of the tea that was already going cold on the table before her. "Right," she said, "right," as if she'd just solved an equation that had been baffling a whole team of mathematicians for weeks, "why don't you tell me about it?"

She lit another cigarette. Star joined her. They held the taste of tobacco on their tongues a moment, looking into each other's eyes, then exhaled simultaneously. "Is it Marco?" she asked in a long trailing sigh of recycled smoke. "Is that it? Are you worried about him?"

Star shrugged. She was tiny – petite, a size four – and she'd never looked more lost and childlike than she did now, the hair pulled back neatly from the central parting and tucked behind her ears as if a mother had fussed over it, her shoulders thin and slumped, her eyes gone lifeless with a child's renewable grief. Marco was out on the trapline with Sess – he'd wanted to learn by doing, he said, and Sess had taken him under his wing – and they were siwashing, camping out on the trail, in temperatures that would certainly drop to minus forty or lower overnight. Or they weren't siwashing exactly – Roy Sender had built two crude timber-and-sod cabins at strategic junctures along the forty-odd miles of the trapline, and though they had dirt floors and none of the amenities of a year-round cabin, barely even a window between them, they did have sheet-metal stoves that Sess always kept in good repair, with an armload of kindling and neat lengths of stovewood ready to hand. Plus, Sess had gotten the two extra dogs he'd wanted – Howard Walpole's dogs, actually, sour as vinegar but good pullers. (Howard didn't need work dogs anymore because he was trading up for speed so he could try his hand at racing, just for the kick of it, he said – and had she heard the rumors about the Iditarod starting up again, with real prize money? – but everyone knew he'd never get off the seat of his snow machine long enough to get the dogs in harness.) And so Sess would be able to cover ground a whole lot faster and more efficiently than he would have a year ago.

"Because if that's what worrying you, honey, you can just put your fears aside – Sess knows what he's doing. He's the most capable man in the country, just ask anybody." She gave a little laugh, picturing him out there in the patched-up parka she'd trimmed with wolverine for him, best fur in the world because it wouldn't ice up with the tailings of your breath, standing tall on the back runners, his eyes squinted against the wind, the sinew pulling and muscle jumping in his arms. "That's why I picked him, you know that. And listen, thirty-five, forty below isn't critical, not really. At sixty I'd worry." She laughed again. "But only just a little. Sess is smart. He could weather anything out there. But what about Marco – he come through that frostbite okay? When was that, anyway – about a month ago now?"

It was cold at the table. The wind always seemed to find the smallest cracks and slivers, as if exposing a cabin's flaws was its whole purpose and function. She thought of getting up to fine-tune the draught of the stove, maybe lay on more wood, but something kept her rooted in the chair, something just beginning to unravel like a ball of yarn, comfortable, newsy, the news of people and their complaints.

Star just shrugged, as if that were the only gesture she knew. "I guess," she said. "But, yeah, he's okay. He's got these two white lines, they look like scars or something, over his cheekbones – but you've seen that, right? – and his toes are okay, like the two that turned black, his little toe and the one next to it on his right foot?" She stared off across the room, her brow wrinkled, thin white fingers tugging at the ends of her hair, summoning the picture. There was no sound but for the faint rattle and sigh of the stove sucking air.

"Reba said they were going to have to go and Norm said but wouldn't they just rot and fall off and Reba said you're thinking of toe*nails,* this is toes we're talking about. But they recovered. Miraculously. They're not exactly beautiful, and he did lose both nails, but there's no infection and I was like mortified because he wanted me to cut them off of him with the hatchet, I mean, can you believe it? Me? With a hatchet?"

So they laughed over the horror of that and puffed at their cigarettes and Pamela fed some wood to the fire and they both went over and sat on the bed and curled their feet under them in sympathy. After a while Star said, "That's not why I'm depressed. I know he'll be cool with Sess – "

"Cold, honey, he'll be cold."

Star gave her a weak smile. "It's Drop City," she said. "It's like the whole thing's just falling apart – did you hear Weird George, Erika and Geoffrey just walked out with the clothes on their backs?"

She hadn't heard. She knew the nephew was gone, and the little pie-face with the false eyelashes, and a handful of them kept pestering Sess – they'd pay him anything, whatever he wanted – to mush them and their guitars and she didn't know what else on into Boynton. And he was willing, why not, cash was cash, but the trapline came first because once you set those traps you were obligated by every moral force there was in the universe to tend them, if only to curtail the mortal suffering of the living beings that gave you your sustenance, because you didn't waste, you never wasted – waste was worse than a sin; it was death.

"That's terrible," she said, and she meant it. She'd got used to having neighbors, Star, Merry, Maya, Reba, people she could talk to, women, other women. Last winter she'd been in an apartment, in a city, working in an office full of people. There were movies, shops, bars, restaurants. Now there were furs, now there was Sess. She was happy – she was, she knew she was, happier than she'd ever been – but the ineradicable nights were already stacking up, the stir-crazy nights, the nights when Sess wasn't enough, when nobody could be enough. And there was something else too, something bigger than all of that, her news, her secret, and if she didn't have Star to tell it to she'd go mad with keeping it in.

Star's face floated there beside her in the soft light of the lamp, sweetly pretty, unblemished, no more a hippie face than her own. "People are eating by themselves now," she said. "And the food, they're fighting over the food."

"But I thought you said there was plenty, more than enough – didn't you tell me Norm laid in six months' worth of the basics? He spent hundreds of dollars you told me – "

"We're not running out. It's more like hoarding, I guess you would call it. People are raiding the pantry, just taking anything they want, almonds, raisins – all the dried fruit disappeared. You can forget the powdered milk too. And the chocolate." She made a face, lifted her hands and let them drop. "The flour's all full of these little black specks – I thought it was pepper at first, that somebody'd maybe dropped the pepper shaker in there when they were battering fish – but actually they were mouse turds, millions of them. And Reba – she seems to think she's in charge since Norm split, and she's always calling these meetings, her and Alfredo, to quote 'address the food situation,' but nobody comes."

"It's not even Christmas yet," Pamela said. She didn't know why she said it – she didn't want to be negative – but these people, these *hippies,* had to understand what they'd gotten themselves into here. It was like that fable her mother used to read to her and Pris when they were little, Aesop, she thought it was, about the ant and the grasshopper.

"I know," Star whispered. "I know."

Later, after they'd finished a second pot of tea and the moose steak sandwiches with sliced onions and horseradish sauce Pamela fixed for them, Star asked her if she'd mind if she spent the night

– the whole trip, the whole *scene* upriver was getting to be too much for her and she just couldn't face it, not tonight. Would that be all right? Would it be too much trouble? Of course not, Pamela told her, no trouble at all – she'd fix her up right here, in Sess's old bed, and could she believe he'd slept here alone, on this narrow little pallet, all last winter?

She gave her one of her flannel nightgowns and wrapped her up in Sess's parky-squirrel sleeping bag and her pick of the furs – they had a whole fur emporium to choose from, and what all those slinky high-heeled women in New York and Chicago wouldn't have given for even a peek in the door – and it was nice, it took her back. It was like being a child again, with Pris at her side and the tent arching over them and the comfort of their mother snoring lightly from the cot in the corner. Or having one of the neighborhood girls for a sleepover when you didn't sleep at all, not till dawn. It was past midnight when she turned out the lamp and went to her own bed in the add-on room, feeling relaxed and peaceful, and tired, gratefully tired, thinking of the neat symmetry of the arrangement – the girls were here, bedded down under one roof, and the men were out there, huddled side by side in the cold clenched fist of the night.

In the morning, they lingered over coffee, fresh-baked bread and powdered eggs in a scramble of ham, peppers and tomatoes, watching the light come up in a gradual displacement of shadow until it settled into the pale wash that served for dawn, dusk and high noon at this time of year. They listened to the radio together – *Tundra Topics* on KFAR and *Trapline Chatter* on KJNP, and learned that Olive Swisstack sent all her love to Tommy, in Barrow, and Ivor Johnson's ex-mother-in-law needed him to call her, urgently, and that Jim Drudge was radioing in from Fort Yukon to say that he was drawing breath like anybody else on the planet and very pleased about it too – and then they lit their first cigarettes of the day and played a very lax game of chess.

"You know, Star," she said, after she'd pinned down the king and announced checkmate in a soft, matter-of-fact way, "there's something I wanted to tell you all last night, but, well – it never came up, I guess."

Star glanced up from the board, where she'd been idly

fingering the king's bishop that wouldn't be much use to her now. The half-empty cup stood at her elbow. A cigarette – was it Star's or her own? – smoldered in the ashtray.

This was good, this was very good, the glow of the light through the window, the gentle respiration of the stove, the silence. A calm descended on her. She might have been asleep still or stretched out on a towel at some resort in the tropics, nodding over the glossy novel propped up on her chest. "I'm pregnant," she said. "Or I think I am. I haven't told Sess yet."

She looked past Star to the window and beyond the window to the hills and then back again, right into her friend's face, into her eyes. "So I guess that means you're the first to know."

31

What passed for light these days was just a fading gleam on the horizon, light in name only, a sorry pale tuned-down glow in the southern sky that was there to remind you of what you were missing. It was sunny in Miami Beach, dazzling in San Diego, and you couldn't put the light out in Patagonia or McMurdo Sound even if you wanted to — it was as if the whole globe had been tipped upside down and all you could shake out of it was a few shadows falling away into the grudging night of the universe. That was what Pan was thinking as the engine snarled out its dull, repetitive message — *all's well, all's well, all's well* — and the wingtips caught a glint from somewhere and the running lights pulsed out of sync till he was as tranced as he might have been in some dance club with the strobe going and the music so loud he couldn't have said what his own name was.

He was cold. Freezing to death, actually. Outside, on the ground, it was approaching forty below, and here they were up at six thousand feet where the air was thinner — and colder. Joe had the heater going full blast, but it barely registered against the wind howling in through the cracks in the doorframe and around the window, and why couldn't they make these things airtight? Why couldn't they insulate them or rig up a heater that actually made some kind of difference? He couldn't feel his toes. Under his shirt, the beads were like separate little pellets of ice. A cold clear fluid dripped from his nostrils and dampened the backs of his gloves. In desperation, he wrapped his arms round his shoulders, shivering so hard he thought his fillings were going to come loose.

Beside him, Joe was a rock. His shoulders filled the cockpit, the bulk of him made bulkier still with the puffed-up eiderdown lining of his parka. He kept a gloved finger on the yoke, stared off through the windscreen or gazed idly out one side or the other, no more concerned with the howling Arctic blast in his face than a polar bear curled up on an ice floe. He hadn't spoken – or shouted – a word for the past fifteen minutes, but then Pan didn't expect conversation, since you couldn't hear anything over the clamor of the engine anyway. So he suffered in silence, thinking only of the cabin now, of the gentle shush of the skis on the snowbound ice – of touching down and scrambling out of this torture box – and of the fire he was going to crank up in the stove. He let a long shiver work its way through him, then reached for his day pack in the backseat and extracted the silver flask.

The flask was filled with Hudson Bay rum, the same shit basically as the Bacardi 151 they used to use for flambés at the Surf 'N' Turf – tasted godawful, like kerosene, but it got the job done. Warmed you. Burned you right on down from your palate to your rectum, and he still remembered Mr. Boscovich at the board diagramming the human digestive tract – *Nine meters long,* he called out as if he were singing, *and can anybody tell me how many feet that is?* Pan gave a little laugh at the memory, then unscrewed the cap. He held the flask to his lips as the plane jarred and settled, a little spillage soaking into his beard and pinning dark beads of moisture to the thighs of his jeans, but it did the trick – it burned till he had to pound his breastbone to keep from spewing it back up – and then he tapped Joe's arm and offered up the flask in pantomime. "You want a hit?" he shouted.

Joe gave him a long, slow look, as if he were trying to place him, as if they hadn't lived in the same cabin for the past three and a half months and been airborne together for the better part of the day, and then he shook his head slowly and let a sad smile fill up the hole in the middle of his beard. "Not while I'm flying," he shouted back.

"Not even a nip?"

"Don't tempt me."

They were on their way back from Ambler, on the Kobuk River, where they'd taxied up to a shack on an island just west of town and unloaded eight cases of bourbon, rum and vodka purchased three days ago in Fairbanks. The shack was listing to the left on the uncertain prop of its stilts, sad and abandoned-looking, but there were wall-to-wall people inside, having a party, and that was a surprise. They looked at him out of their retreating eyes – all of them, men and women, trading around the same face, the face Genghis Khan must have worn after he'd got done conquering an out-of-the-way village and raping all the women and eating the dogs and sucking down the last drop of distilled rice liquor in the district. But it was cool, because they wore their hair long and spent their time getting as high as they possibly could on whatever they got their hands on and they'd never even *heard* of nine-to-five, neckties, Wall Street and Mr. Jones. They still hunted caribou when the herds crossed the river in the fall, though the hunt was reduced now to just coasting up to the animals in a flat-bottomed boat when they were helpless in the water and shooting them point-blank with a pistol, and they all had snow machines and outboard motors and bought their clothes out of a catalogue. But they ate caribou tongue and Eskimo ice cream (caribou fat whipped into a confection with half a ton of sugar and a scattering of sour berries; Pan tasted it – "Ice cream, brother, it's ice cream," Joe Bosky told him, egging him on, but he spat it right back out into the palm of his hand and the whole room went down in flames, laughing their asses off, funniest thing in the world, white man). They also ate Cheerios and Fritos and Ho-Ho's and Hellmann's Mayonnaise sandwiches on Wonder Bread, all of it flown in to the Eskimo store by the bush pilots who represented the world.

Joe told him that the coast Eskimos – the igloo dwellers, like Nanook – used to all piss in a trough and save it to wash in, to cut the grease on their skin and maybe discourage the lice too, but these people – the little sawed-off Genghis Khans with their nubby teeth and faraway eyes – didn't carry things quite that far, or not that Pan could see, anyway. They stank, though – good Christ, they stank, body, breath and hair. And their dogs were the rattiest-looking things he'd ever seen, ten or twelve of them staked out in every yard, no doghouses, no nothing. Rangy, ugly, yowling things chewing on caribou heads and moose hooves and the kind of fish remains Sylvester the Cat used to pull up out of the bottom of the trash cans in the cartoons. In a word, pathetic.

They stayed an hour, maybe. Pan sold a half-ounce baggie of

grass to an Eskimo cat he vaguely recognized from the last whiskey run, and he had a couple rum cokes and breathed the stink of the room and joined in the general sniggering laughter, and then it was back in the plane, the dual controls – yoke on the instrument panel, rudder pedals on the floor – moving in and out on his side as if an invisible presence were sitting in his lap. They shot up off the snowbound river, the shack, the village, the naked stripped willows and soft-edged firs receding and dwindling beneath them, and then there was the horizon and the promise of light to the south.

Pan had made enough runs with Joe to recognize the markers along the route home, and he checked off the white suckhole of Norutak Lake, Indian Mountain sticking up out of the hills at forty-two hundred feet like an inverted Dairy Queen cone, the Koyukuk River a mad scrawl across the face of the deepening night, and finally the lights of Stevens Village and the broad pan of the Yukon. The river flowed west here, but hooked around at Fort Yukon, where it flowed north pretty much all the way from the Canadian border, so to follow it at this point would have been a waste of time. Joe crossed the river at Stevens Village and cut inland to pick it up again at Boynton, and Pan wasn't alarmed when the river fell behind them and the dark hills loomed up again – it was the direct route, the quickest ticket to the stove and the sleeping bag and the mooseburger on a defrosted bun with fried potatoes and coleslaw on the side. In two days, he and Joe would fly into Boynton for his send-off party at the Nougat, and then he was going home, back to Peterskill in time for Christmas, and *that* was going to be something, the stories he could tell, and the weather would be nothing – he'd go around in a T-shirt, a tank top and shorts ("What, you call this *cold,* bro?"). And the concerts, the Fillmore, that new place in Portchester, John Mayall, B. B. King, Taj Mahal. Fuck Star. Fuck Drop City. Fuck them all. He was in a zone, shivering, dreaming. He took another quick nip from the flask – just for the comfort of it.

But then, gradually, he began to realize that they weren't going directly home – they passed over Woodchopper, or what he was pretty sure was Woodchopper, and came in low over the morass of creeks and cleft hills of the Thirtymile watershed. The moon had propped itself up in the sky by now, fat, cold and full, and the snow gave back the light of it till it was brighter than it had been all day. You could see everything against the snow, clearings, bogs, even a line of animal tracks. Joe banked and came in lower still, no more than three hundred feet above the ground, his eyes trained on the shapes and shadows there as if he was looking for something.

"Hey, Joe," Ronnie shouted. "Hey, man, what's up? Aren't we going home?"

Joe rotated the heavy ball of his head to give him a look, then turned back to the window. "Hand me the rifle, will you?" he said.

Despite himself, despite the cold and the misery and his essential *needs,* Pan found himself smiling. "You going to tag a couple wolves?"

The engine pulled them through the night, past the swoop of the trees and the leaping hills and falling declivities. "Check the bolt on that thing for me," Joe shouted.

No complaints, Ronnie was thinking. He was thinking, *All right, why not?* The wolves were there, money on the hoof, or the paw, actually, greenback dollars gifted up by nature, as Joe put it. They'd been out three days ago, on the way back from Fairbanks with the booze – they'd meant to fly directly up to Ambler but Joe saw wolf sign below and got distracted. It was a kill, a moose laid out in the snow in a Rorschach blot of blood-reddened loops and spiraling paw prints. The wolves were on it, six or seven of them, soapstone gray quickening to black, their eyes feasting, heads twisted round to assess this ratcheting threat from the sky, and then suddenly they were running and Joe buzzed them and banked to come at them again. Once he'd leveled the plane and angled in behind the straining dark forms below, he shouted "Take the yoke," and Pan held them steady as he hung out the window and took aim.

The snow leapt where he missed, white blooms flowering in a bed of shadow, and Pan could see it all though he was concentrating everything he had on keeping them level. *Crack! Crack! Crack!* The wolves flowed like water. A long minute, and they fell away beneath them till Joe took the controls, came round again and again had Pan take the yoke. This time, when he leaned out, sighted through the scope and fired, one of the dark streaks suddenly compressed as if it had been ground down by an iron heel, and it was a streak no longer, but a wolf, writhing. They chased on after the pack and shot a second one a mile away, then circled back and found a place to land. The snow was knee-deep. The first wolf's spine had been broken. It lay there in the snow, staring up at them in incomprehension, bred and whelped in hidden places, fed on moose, on rabbit and vole and caribou, helpless now, and staring. "Go ahead," Joe said, "but don't mark the fur. Aim for the eye."

Now Pan strained to see what Joe had picked out below even as he lifted the rifle out of the back, bought new out of the display case at Big Ray's Sporting Goods in Fairbanks with Eskimo dollars – a .375 Holland & Holland with a 4X Weaver scope – pulled back the bolt and handed it to him. There were tracks in the snow below them, he saw that now, a beaten trail that might have been made by a full-on congress of wolves, and it looped in and out of the clumps of trees, disappeared for whole seconds at a time and then reappeared heading south along the banks of the river. The moon had never been brighter, never in all Pan's experience, and he'd seen it hanging in the sky too many times to count, in the back alleys behind the clubs, through the windshield of his car, big and luminous and enhanced by the full range of the pharmacopoeia that lit his perceiving eyes. Tonight, though, tonight it ran back at them, everything silvered with it, Joe's parka, his face, the hands on the controls, but where were the wolves?

And then suddenly, out from under the trees, there they were, a pack running in formation, and Joe was hollering "Take the yoke, take it!" The air inside the cockpit went from frigid to terminal as Joe pushed open the window and the flash-frozen breeze hit them. Pan had the yoke, the plane in a bank left, Joe aiming, but wait – these weren't wolves, were they? No, no, they weren't – they were dogs, and that was a sled, and two figures separating themselves from the flowing script of the page below, people, men, and what was Joe thinking, had he gone blind or what? "Joe!" Ronnie shouted. "Joe, those aren't wolves!"

No matter. Because Ronnie was holding the plane in a steep bank and Joe was firing, once, twice, three times, the bank steepening, Joe cursing – "Fuck! Fuck and goddamnit to hell!" –

and neither one of them noticing just how close to vertical the wingtips had become until Joe dropped the gun and pulled them out of the spin and just cleared the bank of trees ahead of them. The engine screamed and there was a jolt, a sickly amplified wet hard slap as of skin on skin and the tip of the right wing had a crease in it suddenly and the whole plane was shuddering as if it were about to fall apart.

Joe fought it. Joe knew his stuff. Joe wasn't about to crash an airplane that cost him twenty-five thousand dollars just because the tip of the aluminum wing was folded in on itself like a crushed beer can, oh, no, not Joe. They must have gone two or three miles, struggling back toward the river, and where was the altitude here, why didn't he pull back on the yoke and get them up out of the treetops? before Ronnie understood that they were going down. There was something ahead, not the river, just a break in the trees, muskeg, hummocks of dead snow-crowned grass like so many fists thrust up out of the ground, and then they were down, the landing gear buckling under them and the whole fuselage pitching mercilessly to the left and into the looming impervious bark-clad shins of the trees.

Nobody much liked Joe Bosky – he was respected, feared, maybe – but he wasn't the sort of cat people would praise for his gentleness and his niceness and his manners. Ronnie dug him, though. Ronnie had a sort of younger brotherolder brother bond with him, and if you said one thing for Joe you had to admit he had his shit together, and if you looked and listened and paid attention you could learn everything there was to know about the country. About guns. About flying. He'd already given Pan half a dozen lessons and let him take the controls sometimes when they were just cruising from point A to point B, and that was something to be grateful for. Pan thought maybe someday he could come back up into the country – some summer, next summer even – and make a go of it as a bush pilot, guiding hunters and fishermen, beating the weather, riding the breeze, going in and out as he pleased. Another thing about Bosky was that while he might have been part of the war machine at one point, a Marine, no less, he had a pretty loose attitude about things – he wasn't a flag waver or any kind of fascist at all and he never ran off at the mouth about Claymore mines and gooks and all the rest of it. What was his goal in life? Pan had asked him one night as they sat at the table with Sky and Dale, picking sweet dark ptarmigan meat from the bone. To have a good time. To get drunk, get laid, raise some hell and answer to nobody. "So you're a hedonist, then?" Dale had put in. "Bet your ass I am," Joe said.

And Joe would know what to do in the present situation, except that Joe wasn't talking. He'd said one thing only after Pan had cut the seat belt with his hunting knife and dragged him out of the crumpled cockpit an hour and more ago, and that was, "Build a fire." That problem had taken care of itself, though, because when they veered into the trees the left wing folded back against the fuselage and the gas tank let loose and they were lucky even to have gotten out before the whole thing went up. Which it did. No sooner had Pan dragged Joe out into the snow than there was a flash and a thump and their ride home became a bonfire. Now it was nothing but a smell on the air and the cold was seeping back, and Joe was beyond giving advice.

Ronnie could feel his heart shifting gears in his chest. They were in trouble here and no doubt about it, but he wasn't thinking too clearly because he'd hit his head a couple times on the control panel – it just seemed to go after him, as if it had suddenly come to life with the sole purpose of beating his brains out – and that crust of frozen liquid that kept splintering every time he involuntarily grimaced over the red blur of pain that had settled in his left shoulder and made his arm trail away from him as if it didn't want to belong to him anymore, that was blood. Joe was unconscious. Not dead – he was breathing still, though Ronnie was no doctor, and even if he was it wouldn't do him much good out here with no drugs or instruments or tools beyond his knife and the dead weight of the pistol strapped to his thigh. What he did do was cut a couple dozen spruce branches and mound them up so Joe wouldn't have the exposed ground leaching the vital heat from him, and he was in the process of trying to get a fire going. He'd collected some of the dead and yellowed inside branches and snapped them across his knee to make a whole tottering pyramid of kindling, and he'd dragged a few bigger sticks out of the snowheaps as well, and he did have matches and even a few odd scraps of paper in the bottom of his backpack – the only item of survival gear he'd managed to drag out of the plane before it went up.

The moon was a terrifically heavy thing as he crouched there beneath it, baring his wooden hands for just an instant to strike a match on the uncooperative slab of the limp cardboard book – unsupportable, that moon, crushing – but though his hands were like catchers' mitts he was going to survive not only this but anything else the evil forces out there might throw his way because the match caught and the wind held its breath and the cluster of desiccated pine needles began to glower and crackle and get greedier and greedier still. He pulled on his gloves. Tore at the branches round him and built the fire till it leapt up and took over on its own. "Joe," he said, "Joe, we got a fire here," but Joe was unresponsive, Joe was cold, Joe was out for the count.

Pan crouched by the fire, beat his hands together. No one was going to come to their rescue out here. Whoever it was in the sled couldn't have been far, but why would they bother? It was Sess Harder and his old lady, had to be, unless Joe had gone completely psychotic on him, and Sess would have paid admission, premium seats, to see Bosky dead. So it was up to him, up to Pan. What he would do was wait for morning, for the half-light and the glow painted round the hills to the south – that would give him direction, and he'd work his way east to the river and then go north for Drop City. He could do it. He was tough. He was young. He knew these hills, he knew the river. He'd have to build up the fire for Joe, build the bonfire of all bonfires, and leave a mountain of wood there too so when Joe came out of it, *if* he came out it, he could stay alive till Alfredo and Bill and the rest of them – *Reba* – could get to him.

That was the plan. It was a lonely plan, a hard plan, but everything was going to be all right. The fire beat back the night. The cold began to slink away and back off into the shadows and though he couldn't feel his feet, his fingers had begun to tingle, and that was a good sign. When your core temperature dropped, the blood fed your organs to keep the machine going and the extremities were sacrificed, just another adaptation for survival, and where was that bear he'd shot the ear off of now? Hibernating, like all the moles and rodents in Drop City, and that was another way to survive. But he could feel his fingers and that meant there was no damage done, or nothing bad, anyway – he'd rather be dead than go around like Billy Bartro from high school with the two cauterized stumps on one hand and three fingers on the other because he was trying to make a pipe bomb in the basement and had to live the rest of his life wearing a pair of dove gray golf gloves like some kind of butler out of an English novel. No, he was all right. Everything was cool.

It was then that he thought of the flask. He'd left the backpack up against a tree well outside the circle of the fire – didn't want to see *that* burn – and now he pushed himself up and went back to retrieve it. A hit or two, that's what he needed. To warm him. Calm his nerves. He wasn't going anyplace, not till tomorrow morning, anyway, and it was going to be a long cold unendurable night – might as well get a buzz on. He fetched the pack, settled in again by the fire. He thought of Joe momentarily – maybe he should try forcing a little down his throat, like in the movies, see if that would bring him out of it – but he needed to tend to himself first. He'd really done something to his left arm, torn a muscle or something, and the pain of it shot all the way up into his shoulder socket and back down again when he tried to pin the flask to his chest so he could unscrew the top. The whole business was awkward, especially with his gloves on, but he managed – he had to, he had to get his *head* clear here – and in the next moment he was holding the cold worked-metal aperture with the silver inlay to his lips and taking a good long hit.

It was a mistake. And he knew it was a mistake in that instant. His throat seized and he doubled over, his whole body jolted with the shock of it. He was all ice inside, the liquid supercooled in that flask beneath the trees till it was a new kind of death he was pouring down his throat, and he only wanted it out of him. It wouldn't come. He was on his hands and knees, gagging – gagging and coughing and retching – the fire laughing in his face, Joe Bosky slumped silent on a throne of spruce cuttings, and he kept gagging till all that cellular *material* that constituted the lining of his pharynx and esophagus sloughed loose and the tensed muscles of his limbs just couldn't keep him off the ground any longer.

425

32

The first night on the trail they camped in a cabin that seemed to have been generated out of the earth itself, no different qualitatively from a cluster of boulders or a stand of trees. It had a shed roof, one sharp slope from the high end to the low, and the battens of ancient sod that composed it had sprouted birch and aspen and a looping tangle of stripped canes and leafless branches. There was a cache in the foreground, from which a hindquarter of moose wrapped in burlap hung rigid on a strand of wire, and in the flux of the moonlight it could have been something else altogether, something grimmer, darker, and Marco had to look twice before he was convinced. The dogs had no qualms, though – they made a dash for the place and then sat impatiently in their traces out front of the cabin while the moon flashed pictures of their breath rising over the dark hunched shapes of them.

He could see the doghouses now, strung out beneath the trees, crude boxes knocked together from notched logs and roofed with symmetrical mounds of snow-covered straw. There was a hill behind the cabin, soft with reflected light, a creek in front of it. Everything was still. If you didn't know the cabin was there you could have passed within a hundred feet of it and never seen a thing, except maybe for a glint of sunlight off the panes of the single window – in the right season, that is, and at the right time of day.

They'd taken turns riding the runners and jogging beside the sled, and he'd jogged the last mile or so and was sweating inside his parka, a bad thing, a dangerous thing, because the sweat would chill you to a fatal point if you didn't get yourself in front of a fire as soon as was reasonably convenient. "What do you think the temperature is?" he'd asked Sess half an hour earlier as they tossed the last of the five stiff-frozen martens they'd caught into the sled and rebaited the trap, and Sess had grinned and knocked the ice out of his mustache with a mittened hand. "I guess about minus forty," he said.

There was a thermometer nailed over the doorframe of the cabin, and after he'd helped Sess stake out the dogs and toss them each a plank of dried salmon, he consulted it in the pale lunar light. The mercury was fixed in the null space between the hash marks for minus forty and minus forty-two. "Good guess," he said, as they pushed their way into the dark vacancy of the cabin, its smells – rancid bait, lamp oil, spruce, fish, the intestinal secrets of lynx, marten, fox – stilled by the hand of the untenanted cold.

"Hell," Sess said, "it just dropped an extra degree in the meantime – but let's get a fire going and get comfortable, what do you say?"

"Sounds good. What can I do to help?"

They were standing in darkness, in the chill, and then Sess had the lamp lit and the cramped clutter of the place took on definition. "Nothing," he said. "Just sit and make yourself comfortable." Marco sat, shivering now, and watched as the kindling in the sheet-metal stove took the light from the match and the frozen kettle appeared atop it and Sess bent to retrieve a blackened pot from the earthen floor and swing its weight to the stove in a single easy motion that culminated with the sharp resistant clank of metal on metal. "Keep it simple," Sess said, "that's my motto."

They both moved in close to the stove as the fire caught and rose in a roar of sucked air and the room came to life with a slow tick and release. Smells came back. The kettle jolted and rattled, seeking equilibrium. "What's in the pot?" Marco wanted to know, and he'd never been hungrier in his life, in need of sugar, of fat, lard, sticks of butter, the basic grease of life, and no wonder the Eskimos subsisted on seal blubber – you really had to readjust your carburetor up here.

"Moose stew." Sess was fumbling around on the shelf behind the stove, looking for bowls, spoons, cups. "Made it last time through. What you do is you hack off a healthy chunk of that moose flank outside, fry it in bear fat with some flour and onions, salt, pepper, a little Tabasco, whatever vegetables you've got on hand – it was dried peas and lentils in this case – then fill it to the top with liquid, boil it down and toss your rice in. And voilà, Moose Stew à la Harder. And the beauty of it is, you just set the pot down on the floor when you close the place up and it's frozen like a rock inside of the hour." He rubbed his palms together and held them out over the stove. "Roy taught me that."

"And now you're teaching me."

"That's right. Now I'm teaching you."

If he'd had his doubts – camping, *siwashing*, in forty-below weather – the stew drove them down till he could begin to envision himself in Sess's place, at home out here no matter what the conditions, taking what the land gives you, living small and a million light-years from the suburbs and the compulsively trimmed bushes and the rolling lawns and ornamental trees, because whoever landscaped this place outside the window did one hell of a job and no denying it. The stew was delicious. He had three bowls and polished the bowl when he was done with the pilot bread Sess kept sealed in a glass jar on the shelf. There was coffee, with sugar and evaporated milk, half-thawed blue-berries in thick syrup for dessert and three shots of E&J brandy each. They sat cramped in at the little table by the window and fingered their cups and watched the way the moon dodged and shifted and went about its business amongst the trees. They talked trapping, talked snares and baits, talked Drop City, talked women.

"I'm not surprised, truthfully, to hear the nephew sprouted wings," Sess said, "considering that girlfriend of his, because she's a downtown girl if I ever saw one."

"He'll be back," Marco said, and even as he said it, out here with nothing but a makeshift stove and a half-rotten spruce wall to keep him from becoming another casualty of the country, the mortal punctuation to yet another cautionary tale, he doubted himself. When Norm had pulled out, all of Drop City went into a panic, and after the panic, they went into mourning. Norm was their rock, their founder, their guru – he'd brought them all out here into the wilderness with the irreducible power of his vision, his money, his energy – and now he'd deserted them. Star sobbed till Marco thought her ribs were going to crack. Reba ate Seconal by the fistful. Jiminy wanted to shoot the skis off Bosky's plane, handcuff Norm if necessary, anything, kidnap Premstar. Bill roared in Norm's face for a whole day and a half, and you could hear his voice starting up like a chainsaw every few minutes and falling off again till it was the defining sound of Drop City, available even to the last cabin out. And then the plane came and Norm and Premstar were gone, peace, brothers and sisters, and screw you all –

"Yeah," Sess said, "I'm sure he will. If he gets another girlfriend."

Marco shrugged. They'd put out the lantern to save fuel and to give them a better view of the night beyond the window. "I don't know," he said, "maybe we don't need him. Maybe it's all part of the greater plan."

"The greater plan? You're not getting mystical on me, are you? Here, have another shot of brandy. It's good for you."

"I mean, some people are serious about this and some aren't – Alaska, let's all go to Alaska, kids, and we'll dance to the light of the moon. You know what I'm saying? We'll see how it shakes out now that we're on our own."

"Lydia," Sess said. "She's the one. If I had my pick, she'd be the one I'd go for. But don't tell Pamela." He looked down into his cup. "By the way, just out of curiosity, did you ever – ?"

Marco shook his head. "Not my type. But I guess you heard she brought us a little present from Fairbanks, right?"

"Present?"

"Yeah," Marco said, holding his eyes. "Crabs."

Sess leaned into the table. He was grinning. "You don't mean Alaskan king, do you?"

"I don't have them," Marco said. "And neither does Star. So that says something right there."

"Oh, you're hooked, brother, you're hooked. Your wandering days are over, all she wrote." He lifted the cup to his lips, set it down again. "But seriously, you need a woman up here. If you're serious about the country, I mean. If it wasn't for Pamela, I'd be climbing a tree right now, I'd be picking fights at the Three Pup, passed out on the floor, too sick to run my traps and club that lynx today out of its misery. Which, by the way, I ought to drag in here and skin." There was a silence. "Stay tuned," Sess said after a while, "that's my advice. But listen,

429

we've got a long day tomorrow, up to the next camp on No Name Creek, and I've about had it, how about you?"

They were up with the first light, which came just after nine a.m. in a gradual dull accretion of form and shadow beyond the window. Breakfast was moose stew. The dogs had dried salmon, choked down in a fury of wild-eyed snarling and jockeying for position. The sky was low and ironclad. The temperature was minus thirty-eight and rising.

He helped Sess put the cabin in order – moose stew on the floor, water in the kettle, kindling and stove-cut lengths of birch and poplar stacked up in a crude box in the corner – and then they harnessed the dogs. To Marco's eye, the dogs weren't much – savage-tempered, erratically colored and furred, with long angular stick legs, narrow waists and big shoulders. Back home, in Connecticut, they would have languished in the dog pound for the required two weeks, unlovable, inelegant, unadoptable, and then they would have been put down one by one, a gentle stroking of the ears and then the quick sure jab of the needle. The two close in to the sled – the wheel dogs – were called Lester and Franklin, a Sess Harder reference (and homage, or so he claimed) to the Drop City dropouts he'd seen panning for water in a goldless creek one glorious summer day, and the one just behind Lucius, the lead dog, was called Sky, just to extend the joke. "Let's not make this a shaggy dog story," Marco told him when the introductions went round out front of the cabin on the Thirtymile, and Sess liked that. "I guess I should've called one Norm," he said.

But now it was thirty-eight degrees below zero and there was no time for joking. The dogs were in a frenzy to get into the traces and get going – you could hardly slow them down for the first hour or so – and Marco was bitten twice, right down through his gloves and into the flesh, as he tried to clip Sky into the gangline, and if that wasn't bad karma he didn't know what was. "Jesus," he said, raising his voice to be heard over the din of the dogs, "are they always like this?"

Sess had just waded into the middle of a three-dog fight, rearranging ribs with his moccasins and hammering the big furred heads with his balled-up fist. "You want dogs with spirit," he said, and then they were off.

That was a rush, pure exhilaration, the air so cold it burned, your lungs on fire with it, arms pumping like a marathoner's, now on the runners, now off, feeling the surge of uncontainable power that ran like an electric jolt through the spines and churning legs of the wolf-dogs and right into the sizzling core of you. Marco had never experienced anything like it. They hurtled along the trail, too energized to feel the cold, until they came to the first set and the dogs sensed it, smelled it, and pulled up short.

The bait was gone, the trap sprung, and there were lynx tracks like mortal punctuation in the snow. Sess showed him how to reset the trap, sprinkle a couple handfuls of snow over it for concealment, then nail a rotted goose wing soaked in beaver castor three feet up the trunk of a tree just behind it. And what made the best bait? Whatever stank the most. For marten, Sess used the guts and roe of the salmon he'd caught last summer – after they'd been properly fermented in a mason jar set out in the sun for a couple weeks. "No big deal," he said. "Little tricks. Anybody could learn them."

They stood there, looking down at the set, the dogs curled tail to nose in their traces, the faintest breeze agitating the treetops. "Even Joe Bosky?" Marco asked. "Even Pan?"

Sess didn't bother to answer – the question was too irritating, Marco saw that immediately and wished he could take it back. To this point, he and Sess had been getting on heroically, of one mind, and as Sess saw that he could keep up, that he was hard-driven and no tourist at all, he'd given him a larger share of the responsibilities, harnessing and feeding the dogs, mushing them, building up the coffee fire at lunch.

Sess was staring down at the scatter of tracks, hands at his hips, his parka so patched-over you couldn't tell its original color, and his face was set, engraved with suppressed emotion like a wood carving of Chief Joseph of the Nez Percé. The wolverine lining his hood took the breeze, and Marco watched the long dark hairs move and gather there, and suddenly he was thinking of the goats and the powerlessness he'd felt in the face of that implacable presence thrust up out of the woods. And what would they do if they encountered one today – or a bear? All they had with them was a .22, because Sess wouldn't let him bring the big rifle – too

431

late for moose, and it was just unnecessary weight. But the bears would be hibernating by now. Not the wolves, though. And what about the legendary *cauchemar* of the north, the winter bear, the grizzly that went into hibernation too soon and awakens desperate for the meat and fat it has to have to survive? What would a .22 do against that?

It was getting dark when they came round a switchback in the trail and the dogs slowed and began to throw quick darting looks back over their shoulders. There was a set up ahead, but something wasn't right. Something was caught there, something too big to be a marten or a fisher, and it wasn't dead and frozen like the sleeve of a fur coat hanging limp in cold storage, but alive and yellow-eyed and jerking spasmodically at the straining dun leash of its right rear leg. It was a wolf, that was what Marco thought at first, but Sess let out a low curse — it wasn't a wolf, but a coyote, all but worthless for its fur because no wrapped-up pampered matron on Park Avenue or Lake Shore Drive wanted to walk into a restaurant in a thing like that.

The dogs were crazy. They smelled the kill and they let out a furious, frustrated, caterwauling racket, jerking at their leads in a tangle of ratcheting jaws and misplaced feet. Sess tied the sled off to a tree a hundred feet away and the two of them came up to where the animal lunged and snapped at them from the radius of its trapped hind leg. There was blood in the snow. The coyote had tried to gnaw through its own fur and hide and gristle and bone to free itself, but it was too late now because there were dogs there and men and one of them had a gun and the other a stick. "Shit, I'd just as soon wade in there and knock him out and free him if I could," Sess said, "but he's got too much pep in him yet. I don't want to risk it."

The animal was pinned there, crippled, nothing but solaceless terror in its eyes, though it jerked and growled and threatened, and where was the peace and love in this, where the pacifism and the vegetarian ideal? It was the color of a German shepherd, smaller maybe, but with the same deep dun color and the black-tipped guard hairs. Marco felt his stomach clench. Could you live in the country without this? Could you live on fish alone? On what you made in the summer on a fire-fighting crew? On welfare, unemployment, on tuna casserole and macaroni and cheese? His breath smoked in the air. Sess handed him the .22. "Go ahead," he said. "Put him out of his misery."

It went dark then, or it seemed to. The coyote had stopped struggling. It crouched, panting, head hung low, the fire gone from its eyes. Marco never even brought the gun to his shoulder. "I can't," he said, and handed it back to Sess. He turned away to go see to the dogs and a moment later the hovering silence discharged itself with a single crack of the rifle.

Later, when the clouds had cleared and the moon swung up over the horizon, they found themselves in an open meadow along the river, no more than fifteen minutes from the cabin on No Name Creek that was their destination for the night. The coyote, frozen through and stiff-legged now, was strapped to the top of the sled like so much excess baggage. ("Skin it out and take it home to your girlfriend," Sess had said. "Nail it to the wall, make a rug out of it. "Call it your first kill," he said.) The dogs were lagging now, especially the two in front of Lester and Franklin. They jerked forward, then held back, hips twitching, legs kicking out arrhythmically. Marco was riding the runners, Sess jogging alongside him. That was when they heard the plane, a thin buzz of mechanical clatter on the air that was too cold to resonate.

They kept going. There was a cabin awaiting them, a fire, another pot of moose stew – or maybe it was potage of moose or moose fried in lard with defrosted potatoes and onions and maybe dried carrots on the side – and an airplane was nothing to them. It was probably somebody out of Eagle, headed to Boynton or maybe Fairbanks or Delta. Marco let the buzz fade away in his head. He was in a dream state almost, all his senses heightened as if he'd dropped acid, alive to every shading of the path ahead, to the taste and smell of the compacted air, to the swift whispering rush of the dogs' paws in the snow, to the great and marvelous engine of his own breathing and the unconquerable beat of his rock-steady heart. This was his moment, this was his connection, and he felt it in every cell of his body. He wasn't even cold. Not in the least.

But that thin unobtrusive buzz that might have been the drone of a mosquito in a sleeper's ear on a restless summer night became something greater, louder, a looming clattering presence, until he couldn't ignore it any longer. He looked to the straining backs of the dogs, to the dark line of the trees in the distance, and then he looked to Sess just as the plane broke out of the treetops behind them, no more than two hundred feet above the ground, buzzing them. Sess never stopped running. He shouted to the dogs, urging them on. And then to Marco, everything rushing in a fluid stream of night and snow and the wind they were generating in their flight – and that was what this was, *flight* – he shouted one word, "Bosky!"

They both watched the aircraft make the far end of the meadow, bank and come back at them, and there was nothing they could do about it, no time to wonder over the hate and recalcitrance that had brought them to this, no time for reason or even speech. They ran. And Bosky came at them. There was gunfire – of that Marco was sure, the snow leaping beside him and one of the dogs crying out and stumbling in the traces and the others carrying it along in a dark tide of necessity – and then there was the sharp explosive sound of something moving at high speed contacting a stationary object, a single dead whack, and they were in the trees and the plane was gone.

The first thing Sess did was halt the dogs under cover of the trees and tie up the sled. Then he pulled the .22 from the sheath he'd made for it just under the left handlebar and fired two useless shots into the night. "Fucking son of a bitch!" he shouted. "Fucking madman! Scumbag! I'll kill you!"

Suddenly it was cold. Intensely cold. The kind of cold that ran through you no matter how many layers of clothes you had on. Marco was numb, numb all over. He barely knew what had happened, gone from one dream right into the shroud of another, but he had the presence of mind to remember the dog. It was hurt. He could hear it whining, the thinnest paring of sound, like a violin careening to the top of the register. "Sess," he said into the stiffening shroud of silence, "I think one of the dogs is hurt."

It was a foot or a leg – Marco couldn't see for sure in the play of moonlight and shadow. He stood there, helpless, as Sess bent over the dog, removed it from the traces and lifted it up in his arms and carried it to the sled. He watched Sess set the dog in the body of the sled, beside the stiff-legged carcass of the coyote, and watched as Sess rearranged the dogs, the breath of dog and man alike hanging dense in the air. There came a distant sound at some point during this ordering of events – Marco couldn't have said when, exactly, whether it was a matter of seconds or minutes – and there was a flare of light some two or three miles off. "Good," Sess muttered, working in the cold, every pause and syllable an engine puffing in the night, "good, the son of a bitch. Good. I hope he's burned up and dead."

They reached the cabin in minutes, and minutes later they were going through the same ritual as the night before – unharnessing, staking, lighting the fire, settling the kettle and the big blackened pot on the stove – but they hardly spoke. They were like relief workers, methodical, bloodless, following the logic and the dictates of the moment. Sess brought the dog in – it was Sky, one staring blue eye, one deep unhurried brown – and set him on the floor under the light of the lantern. The dog whined softly and Marco saw that its right front foot was gone, or the toes anyway. Sess stalked across the room and came back with a bleached-thin flannel shirt and tore it into strips. "Can I do anything?" Marco asked and Sess said he could go out and feed the dogs, that would be a help.

Only after they'd eaten did the shock of what had happened let go of them to the point where they could begin to talk about it. Everything was quiet. The dog was back outside, its foot swollen with the knotted bandage it had no doubt already chewed off, the cabin – cruder and older than the one they'd inhabited last night, built by Roy Sender himself in a time before airplanes came to rule the country – had begun finally to hold the heat of the stove, the kettle was sending up steam and they were both staring into the residuum of coffee grounds in the bottom of their cups. Marco got up, warmed his hands at the stove. "You think they went down, don't you?" he said.

Sess looked up at him. "Yeah," was all he said.

"Think they're dead?"

"I hope so. I pray to god they are. Because if they're not, I'm going to have to kill them."

"I'm saying *they,*" Marco said, and he had to use one of his mittens to lift the kettle off the stove and pour scalding coffee into his cup, "but it could have been just Bosky, right?"

Sess held out his cup for a refill. "You can't fly and shoot at the same time."

"So it was Ronnie? You think it was Ronnie too?"

"Son of a bitch," Sess said. "Son of a hippie bitch. I want *him* dead too."

Eventually, without really discussing it or pausing to think it through, they both began to shrug back into their clothes, the two shirts, the sweater, the parka, the scarf Star had knitted, and Marco laced up his boots while Sess pulled on his mukluks, and then they were back out in the night, minus forty-four and dropping. The dogs stirred, and one or another of them let out a low interrogatory woof before they settled down again. Sess had the .22 in his hand. The snow shifted beneath their feet.

They retraced the trail to the meadow and then turned inland in the direction the plane had taken, walking at a good pace, the moon slanting through the trees to light the way. The country was dense here, off the broken trail, but they were anxious and they pushed through it as if they were passing down a long corridor in a hotel with one double door after another. Marco let his mind wander, thinking about Star, about Christmas coming and what he ought to get her, given his limited resources. Maybe he could make her something, he was thinking. Something for her hair – a barrette carved of wood or bone, or maybe bone earrings, something like that. And then he was thinking of Ronnie. Pan. If Pan was in that plane, and he had to have been, then Pan was dead, the first casualty of Drop City, the first postmortem. Norm would be back. Maybe even Weird George, Verbie and some of the others. But Pan wouldn't. The thought chilled him. Or he was already chilled – it depressed him, brought home the strangeness of all this, of walking the remotest hills anybody could hope to find on this earth beside a man with a gun in the deepest night he'd ever known. And where was his father now? And the Draft Board and General Hershey?

"Up there," Sess said, and it was as if his voice were disembodied, as if the country itself were throwing its voice, the ventriloquism of the night. "See it – see that glow?"

They climbed a ridge and looked down on the light that seemed so wrong out here, a fire, a bonfire, snapping briskly at its tether on the numinous ground, color in a colorless place. There were two figures stretched out by the fire, one on the snow, the other propped against a tree in a bed of spruce cuttings, and beyond them, the settled shape of the burned-out plane. Nothing moved but the wheel of the fire, rising up and dying back, spitting embers into the sky, wavering and flaring again.

Marco came down the slope at a run, slamming through drifts, shattering tree limbs and the grasping fingers of dwarf willow, alder, birch and black currant, heedless, in the grip of something he couldn't name, even as Sess Harder stalked behind him, gun in hand. He went to Ronnie first, to Pan, and tried to turn him over, but Pan was stuck fast to the ground in a spill of frozen blood and mucus, and he was inflexible, dead, dead for sure, as stiff and dead and frozen as the coyote strapped to the sled. He didn't like Pan. He'd never liked him. But he didn't wish him this.

He looked up at the sound Sess Harder's hand-stitched mooseskin mukluks made in the snow, the soft susurrus of his walking. Sess was standing over Joe Bosky now, and Joe Bosky's eyes were open and he was trying to say something. There was no blood on him, not a spot, his white parka as pure and unblemished as the snow caught fast to the shell of the earth. His eyes shone in the firelight and he wanted to move, you could see that, to get up, to stand and accept the challenge, but he couldn't. A term came into Marco's head then, something out of the newspaper, out of the obituaries: *Internal injuries.*

External injuries were bad enough out here, but internal injuries, what you couldn't see, didn't really offer up much hope. They would have to go back for the sled, load him into it, mush past Drop City, Sess's cabin, Woodchopper, and on into Boynton, and somebody would have to fly out of Boynton and take him to the hospital in Fairbanks, and all of that with internal injuries, the ruptured organs, the severed spinal cord, the slow seep of secret blood. But Sess had the gun in his face, had the muzzle of it resting right on the bridge of his nose, the cold kiss of the barrel marking the place where his black bushed eyebrows met, and Joe Bosky was struggling to say something, final words, and what he said, even as Sess Harder lifted the gun out and away from him and rested it over one solid moon-white shoulder, what he said was, "Fuck you."

33

At first she didn't know what to say, thinking of Che and Sunshine, their squalling faces and stamping inconsolable feet, the noise of them, the dirt – always dirty, born dirty – and she looked away, trying to compose herself. She ran a finger round the rim of the coffee mug and plugged in her million-kilowatt smile, and though she wanted to say *No, oh, no,* as she would have responded to news of cancer, heartbreak or any run of sorrow or affliction, she managed finally to murmur something appropriate, or at least compliant. And then, before she could think: "Do you – I mean, did you – ?"

Pamela took one look at her and burst out laughing – she had to set down her cup because she was laughing so hard, her eyes squeezed down to semicircular slits, her hands gone to her temples as if to keep her head anchored on her shoulders. "You'd think I'd just announced that the roof was on fire or something from the look of you – really, Star, you should see herself." She let out another laugh, slapped a hand flat on the resounding plane of the table. "God, you're funny."

Star laughed too, easing into it – sure, all right, she'd let herself in for it – but even as she laughed, as the two of them laughed, she was thinking of herself, of what she would do if it was her. She'd stocked up on birth control pills – they all had, Reba's idea, her obsession, actually – but she'd come to the end of them weeks ago. When she and Marco made love it was cautious love now, restrained love, with the threat of repercussions hanging over the act, and he always pulled out of her at the crucial moment – *coitus interruptus* – as if that could forestall the inevitable, and how many of the girls she'd gone to Catholic school with were on their second or third child already? She'd kill herself. She'd have an abortion. But where? How? Somebody told her the Indian women knew of a way, some root they boiled into a tea, or maybe they made it into a poultice that drew out the fetus like pus from an infection –

"You know, you're supposed to congratulate me. You're supposed to squeal and jump around – we're both supposed to squeal and jump around. I'm going to have a baby. You're the first person I've told and you look as if you just found me floating in the river in a sack."

She wanted a cigarette. She'd already had her first of the day and she was trying to cut back, not only because of the expense and the fact that your brothers and sisters were constantly bumming them off you day and night, but because they were a habit, and she didn't want to develop any habits except love and kindness. Pamela's pack of Marlboro's lay on the table between them. Star eased a cigarette from the pack, lit it, exhaled. "I'm sorry," she said. "It's just that I can't imagine – personally, I mean. I mean, I've got so much to live for – " But that sounded wrong – it was wrong. She tried to recover herself, because Pamela – her friend, her sister – wasn't laughing anymore. "You want a boy or a girl?" she said finally.

Pamela went off then, everything copacetic, pleased with herself, lit up with it. She wanted a girl, couldn't imagine anything else, but when she and Sess had talked about it – theoretically, that is – he'd leaned toward a boy, which was only natural. He was quiet about it, but he wanted to see a new generation in the country, of course he did, and with a boy he could teach him everything he knew about living off the land and respecting it. "He'd want a boy," she said, and she slipped a cigarette out of the pack now too. "But so did my father."

"And he got two girls."

"That's right."

And then they were laughing again.

They smoked their cigarettes and thought their private thoughts, drank coffee, played a second game of chess – which Star won – and then the rubber match, which went to Pamela. Together they made lunch, a thick cooked-down broth with egg noodles and put-up vegetables from the Harder larder, and then they settled in to read by the stove. Though they hadn't discussed it, the unspoken arrangement they'd arrived at telepathically at some point the previous night was that Star was going to stay on till their men returned from the trail. Star had washed and dried the dishes – she insisted on it – and let Pamela sit there by the window as she put everything back on the shelves in proper order. She took pride in that – she knew the place as well as she knew her own. And the pans glistened when she was done with them.

After a while she moved from the chair to the bed, pulled a fur over her legs. She could feel the nicotine and caffeine ricocheting off the walls of her blood vessels, but she wasn't nervous or coffeed-out, just steady and calm and alert. The book she had with her was by Richard Fariña, *Been Down So Long It Looks Like Up to Me,* the hippest thing going, recommended by everybody and dog-eared and chewed-over so many times it had to be the sorriest volume in the Drop City library. It was all right. Funny, wild. But the scene it described – college, dope, thumbing your nose at the straight world – just seemed alien to her now. Or remote – that was a better word. Before long, she was asleep.

She woke to lamplight, a smell of baking. Pamela was there at the stove, her hair coiled atop her head and shining with the soft flickering pulse of the lamp's wick. The windows were black. A distant voice, thin and disconnected, carried down out of the hills, and then it was answered by another and another. "What time is it?" she said, pushing herself up from the pillow. She felt as if she'd been asleep forever.

"It's early yet. Four-fifteen."

"I'll never get used to this."

Pamela was taking something out of the oven – a cake in a circular pan – and she paused, the hot pan held out before her, the sweet all-embracing scent filling the room even to the farthest corners, to give Star a look over her shoulder. "You'll get used to it," she said. "Believe me."

They were eating cake – angel food, barely cooled, with chocolate fudge icing – when they became aware of a subtle change in the tenor of the night, the faintest chink of the clip on a dog's harness, a sound as of the earth breathing in and out again, and then they were up from the table and standing at the open door of the dogtrot, peering out into the moonlit yard. The men were there – Marco and Sess – and the patient line of the dogs, sitting in their harnesses, waiting to be freed and staked and fed. Pamela turned back into the room to put the kettle on and Star followed her to get her parka, and in a moment the two of them were out in the moonlight, the shock of the supercooled air searing the nicotine from their lungs.

A quick hug, one man, one woman, and Pamela was down amongst the dogs, unclipping them individually from the gangline and leading them to their separate houses and their separate stakes. Star stood there in the cold, shifting from foot to foot, wanting to help, but she didn't know the dogs or what to do with them and so she drew back and waited. One of the dogs, she saw that much, was injured and riding up atop the sled, the frame of which seemed overburdened, piled up beyond sense or reason, and where were the furs? She'd looked forward to the furs in the way a prospector's wife might have looked forward to the jar of gold flakes brought down to her out of the hidden seams of the hills – absent the killing of the animals and the mechanics of their suffering, that is, because she didn't want to think about that, didn't want to know or even imagine it. The furs, the furs alone were what interested her. The beauty and richness of them, mink, otter, fox, delivered up from nowhere, magically, like the salmon that gorged the streams and the ducks crowding the skies. But where were they? And what was this protruding from the frame – boots? A spare pair of boots?

She was about to say something when Marco loomed up out of the blue glitter of the snow, took her by the arm and led her through the dogtrot and into the cabin. His beard was ice. His eyes were cracked and broken. The tip of his nose was the wrong color. "Something happened," he said.

There were sounds from outside, Sess's voice, Pamela's, the dogs yapping and clamoring for their food. "What?" she wanted to know, straining to read his face even as he turned away from her and held his hands out to the stove. She felt sick suddenly. There was a shadow sweeping over the ground, over the cabin, over Drop City. "What? What is it?"

"Ronnie," he said.

"Ronnie?" She didn't understand him. What could Ronnie possibly have to do with a hurt dog and three days out on the ridges and down in the ravines in forty-below-zero weather? Ronnie the thief? Ronnie the irrelevance? Who cared about him? Who cared about him, really? He'd gone to high school with her. He'd been her lover. He'd stolen her money.

Marco wouldn't look her in the face, and that scared her.

"What?" she demanded. "What happened?"

"He – they tried to, him and Bosky, in the plane. He died. He's dead."

Still she didn't understand. "Who? You mean Joe Bosky?"

"Both of them. It was a plane crash."

She had to sit down then, and Pamela was in the room now and Sess right behind her, the door slamming to, the last breath of the cold trapped and dissipating inside the furnace of the four walls, the shrinking space of the cabin crowded suddenly, shoulders, faces, limbs, three people in parkas stalking around and recoiling from one another as if they were trying to make their way through Grand Central at rush hour: *Ronnie? Dead?*

Eventually – it must have been an hour, an hour or more – she went out into the yard, her hand clasped in Marco's, to look at him there in the sled, because she still didn't believe it, didn't believe really that anybody could die – the old maybe, maybe them – but nobody she knew, nobody like Ronnie. Like *Pan.* They'd come across country together. He'd made her laugh. He'd pressed himself to her in the hush of her room, on the seat of the car, in the starched sterile drum-tight beds of motels in anonymous towns, he'd read to her, sung to her, praised her and loved her. And now he was lying there frozen in the sled, a shadow, a dead lump of nothing pressed in death to the dead lump of Joe Bosky – and those were his boots, Bosky's, sticking out of the bottom of the sled on his dead frozen feet. For a long moment she stood there looking down at the dark hummock of the sled, Sess and Pamela immured in the cabin, Marco beside her. She was trying to cry, but there was nothing there. "I want to see him," she said, and her voice betrayed her.

Marco's breath trailed away from his lips, silvered and alive. "You don't want to see him. Really, you don't. Come on, let's go inside. We'll spend the night and decide what to do in the morning. Okay?"

It wasn't okay. She stepped forward, the dogs rustling at their chains, the stars riding up and away from her till the whole night seemed to plead for intercession, and then she pulled back the blanket and the moon showed her what was there.

"That's not Pan," she said.

And it wasn't. It was something twisted to impossibility, nothing natural, nothing she could identify, no face even, because it was turned from her in its frozen cowl, just the slant of a face, that was all, and it could have been anybody. "Come on, Star," Marco whispered. She saw the hair then, spilling off the spool of his head, grown out finally to its maximum length, hip, very hip, as hip as anybody could ever have wished or dreamed, and she slipped the glove from her hand for just an instant to feel it move beneath the pressure of her five bare fingers.

On Christmas Eve, just after the light faded from the sky, it began to snow. Marco and Jiminy had cut a tree and set it up in the back corner of the meeting hall, and everybody gathered over eggnog (rum and evaporated milk, whipped with nutmeg, sugar and powdered egg) to decorate it with God's eyes made of yarn, scraps of silver foil, strings of glass beads and paper chains. The twelve-volt battery, newly charged in Boynton and retrieved on the back of Iron Steve's snowmobile, was hooked up to the stereo in the loft, and so there was music, people shuffling through the albums to find their favorite cuts, nothing religious, really, no hymns or carols, but mystical stuff, Ravi Shankar, Mahavishnu John McLaughlin, Coltrane, Rollins, Dylan.

There were four stoves at Drop City, one in each of three finished cabins, and the ancient Great Majestic range they'd brought upriver in the boat to do the communal cooking in the meeting hall, and all four were in use. They were roasting two turkeys and a goose delivered frozen from the general store in Boynton by Sess Harder, and a pair of spruce hens Marco had managed to shoot under a tree somewhere, with potatoes, stuffing and gravy, and for the vegetarians there was a broccoli and cheese casserole, meatless lasagna and mashed turnips. And cookies. A thousand cookies.

Star was in the midst of it all, juggling pots on the range, slicing, chopping, whipping, the music getting up inside her till it was like a whole new circulatory system working in symbiosis with the original one, the one she was born with, and when somebody handed her a joint, she took it and held it to her lips a moment and passed it back again. She sang to herself, hummed, made up lyrics for the tunes that didn't have any. The gravy thickened, the snow faltered. Lydia was dancing with Tom Krishna and Deuce, and Jiminy was dancing by himself, Harmony and Alice handed out personalized ceramic mugs to every one of Drop City's eighteen remaining residents – each one with a reasonably faithful representation of the recipient's face molded into it – and Marco came up and surprised her with a pair of earrings – peace symbols – he'd carved out of a scrap of caribou antler. And just when she thought it couldn't get any better, Pamela appeared at the door with two bricks of fruit cake and a bottle of brandy tucked under her arm.

There was a jabber of greeting, dishes already set out on the sheet of plywood they'd extended the table with, steam rising, the dog – Freak – looking hopeful, and then Star took Pamela's coat and flung it up to Mendocino Bill in the loft, because that's where the coats were going, no room anywhere else. Pamela stood there, giving off energy, and then she was hugging people, one after the other. She was looking good – healthy, pretty – her face colored by the wind, her hair parted in the middle and trailing down over her sweater till the reindeer dancing across her chest were hidden in a spill of honey-blond hair, and she was wearing the beaded headband Star had given her. "You know what you look like?" Star said, handing her the joint that had just appeared magically in her hand.

"No, what?"

"Like a hippie."

"You mean a hippie *chick*?"

It took her a minute. "Are you playing with my head?"

"Who me? Never."

She watched Pamela make a pretense of inhaling, then took the joint back from her. "So where's Sess?" she asked.

A shrug. "Out on the trail. But he'll be here. He'd better be." She shook out her hair with an abrupt flip of her neck. "It's our first Christmas together. I'll kill him if he doesn't make it."

The notion struck her as funny, because why wouldn't he make it? Was it that compelling out there? As far as Star could see there was nothing beyond the windows but the night and the cold and the hills that folded back into another set of hills and another set beyond that. This was where the life was, the only life within miles. There was food, music, beer, wine. There was eggnog, there were cookies. Laughter and conviviality. There were people here. Brothers and sisters. "Oh, he'll make it," she said. "I'm sure he will."

Later, after they'd eaten, Verbie and Iron Steve showed up, extending the party all the way out from Boynton, and they danced, everybody, all of Drop City, even Che and Sunshine, and there was nothing lame about it and nobody to sulk and lie and exaggerate and cheat and steal and pronounce it lame, nobody. At midnight, Bill dropped down out of the loft, got up as Santa Claus with a cotton-puff beard and every strip of red clothing Drop City owned draped round the bulk of him, and announced he had a present for everybody, right outside the door. People stirred, exchanged glances. Outside? There were groans, catcalls. "Is he for real?" Merry said.

"Believe me," Bill coaxed, "you're going to like it."

Star was drifting, nestled in beside Marco and Pamela on the bunk closest to the stove, sated, warm, letting the music infest her. She hadn't said a word in an hour. She felt bad for Pamela, because Sess hadn't showed, and that was the one damper on the evening – the bummer, the downer – the one thing that hadn't worked out. Pamela was worried, she could see that, and as the hours slipped by she'd said all the conventional things till there was nothing more to say, and then a joint went round, and a jug of wine, and she leaned back into Marco and let herself drift. But now, now Bill was in the middle of the room and people were coming back to life – it was Christmas, there was a surprise, a present. For everybody, he said.

It took a while, people fumbling into their jackets and boots, searching for gloves and scarves in the tangle of clothes in the loft, but then they were filing out the door into the cold. Bill led them. He was in the yard out front of the meeting hall, Santa with his freak's flag of hair and cotton-puff beard, his arms spread wide. It was clear now and cold to the teeth of the stars. "Here it is!" he shouted, and they lifted their eyes to the sky and saw the light pulsing there, cosmic light, yellow-green, blue, a tracery of red, indefatigable light, light that soared up out of the black shell of the horizon and burst and shattered and renewed itself all over again.

34

He was moving as fast as he could, the storm blown out now and the quarter moon slicing through the cloud tatters to illumine his way. The wind was in his face, the cold rode his shoulders like a hitchhiker. There was no sound but for the whisper of the sled's runners in the fresh powder and the faint, wind-scoured chiming of the cold steel clips on the dogs' harnesses. He was late, very late, ten or twelve miles out, thinking of Pamela waiting for him at the hippie camp, of Christmas and the present he'd kept hidden in the back doghouse since before she was his wife and just a hope flickering on the horizon. It was in the sled now – he'd snuck it in there, all wrapped in a spangle of colored paper that featured candles and bells and holly and suchlike, three mornings ago, early, when she was still in her slippers and the light hadn't yet come into the sky. He'd harnessed the dogs then, kissed her at the door and moved out across the yard and into the trees with a promise, three days, Christmas, the hippie camp.

The dogs knew they were heading home, six dogs now because Sky would never run again, and they ran as a team, as smooth and efficient as the conjoined wheels of a locomotive, streaming through the night, barely aware that he was there with them. They were going a good flat-out ten miles an hour, he guessed, and so he'd be there before long – by midnight anyway, judging from the stars. The present was nothing he'd made or bought, nothing you could mail-order or find in a store. It was a gift of nature, like the furs, the salmon, the moose, like gold. He'd found it projecting from the bank of the river after breakup had torn the earth away to leave it exposed, a bone-yellowed gleam against the flat alluvial gray of the gravel bank. He knew right away what it was – Charlie Jimmy, of the Indian Village at Eagle, had showed him one once – the curving dense-grained tusk of a mastodon, intact, earth-stained maybe, but a magical thing, a blessing, a totem to take away your fears and sharpen your prowess till you were one with the frost and the melt and the cycle of lives gone down and sprung up again.

He squinted into the wind and pictured the animal itself, the pillars of its legs, the rich red pelt stretched over a mile of hide, the tumbling sluggish winter life of the shadowy herds emerging like phantoms from the impacted ridges and wind-blown plains and then vanishing again as if they'd never been there in the first place. But would she like it? He didn't have a clue. It could be carved, certainly, made into jewelry, bric-a-brac, chess pieces, but to his mind that would be a sort of desecration. She could take it to bed with her, make use of it as a fertility charm, but she didn't need any charms, not Pamela. He smiled at the thought and the ice cracked at the corners of his mouth.

He was late because he'd had an accident, one of those things that happen once or twice a winter, no matter how careful you are. He'd been leaving the cabin on No Name Creek with the new furs he'd taken and the ones he'd had to leave behind the previous week in order to accommodate the mortal remains of Bosky and Pan, two dead men, frozen and dead, and he'd miscalculated along a stretch of the creek thick with overflow ice. It had warmed for a few days and then dropped back down to zero and the stream had bubbled up through the ice and then frozen in layers beneath it, and both his feet plunged in up to his calves before he could get back up onto the runners of the sled. He wasn't wet all the way through – the three pairs of socks and the two felt liners saved him there – but there was still nothing else for it but to stop, tie up the sled, make a fire in the lee of a rock ledge and dry everything out.

It wasn't a crisis. Just one of those things. And he'd taken advantage of the time to check the dogs' feet for ice and any scrapes or open cuts and rub them with ointment, and then there was a period where he just lay there under his tarp and watched the fire as the snow sifted down out of the branches of the trees and erased the sky overhead. It gave him time to think, because the last week had been chaotic, questions from the sheriff and the sheriff's deputy, a round of drinks at the Three Pup in memory of the dead men, more questions, papers to fill out, the life of the town, the funeral. Bosky had frozen to death, and so had Pan – after doing something so unthinking and senseless not even the wild hairs could believe it. Or maybe they could. Same thing had happened to a soldier on maneuvers out of Fort Wainwright once, oh, three, four winters ago, thought he'd eschew the regulations and bring himself a little comfort out there on sentry duty in the dead cold heart of the night. It was a shame. It was a pity. But up here planes crashed and people froze. That was the way it was.

What nobody knew, except for him and Marco, was that while the hippie – Pan – was already a corpse when they got there, Bosky was alive and breathing and aware enough to put his last two words together. It was a hard moment. The moment Sess had been chasing after for two years and more. He stood there over him with the .22, and he was going to squeeze the trigger – out of anger, sure, there was that, hate and anger – but out of something else too, call it compassion, call it habit. He brought the barrel of the rifle up to finish Bosky in the way he would have finished any spine-sprung thing caught in a deadfall or a trap meant for something bigger, death in an instant instead of an hour – that was human mercy in a place that had none to spare. But he didn't. A bullet hole would have required explanations, and those explanations would have led down a trail of deceit and dissembling he wanted no part of. And another thing: Bosky didn't deserve a bullet – better save it for the rabid skunk, the porcupine, the summer rat. What he did finally, after duly recording the man's final words, was turn his back, and he didn't argue about it with Marco – he wasn't in an arguing mood. Or a democratic one either. The two of them just backed away from the fire, the wreckage, the corpse of the one and the slowly congealing flesh of the other, and then they came back in the morning and loaded up the human weight and hauled it in. "No reason," he said to Marco, "to mention anything. The plane went down, that's all, and we brought them in."

So that was the end of it. And though he'd never gloated over the death of any man – or any creature, for that matter – he had to consider that for him, at least, Christmas had come early. Somebody, some stooped and weeping parent or aunt or black-eyed sibling, would come in the spring and take the small things of sentimental value out of the cabin on Woodchopper Creek, and then the place would stand open to anybody who wanted it, though nobody would. Over the years the roof poles would rot, the sod would give way to the pull of the earth, the walls would buckle, the floorboards subside. Birds would nest in the stove-pipe, mice in the bureau drawers. On a given night, in the still of winter, a wolf would trespass in the yard, divine the last dim lingering whiff of the scent of Bosky, Pan, Sky Dog, and lift a leg to eradicate it.

Sess could appreciate that, the natural order – let it stir, let it settle again. The wind was in his face. The northern lights were out, driving down the clouds. The snow whispered at his feet, talked to him, sang out with the rhythm of the night. He was heading home, riding the runners, breathing easy, a man clothed in fur at the head of a team of dogs in a hard wild place, going home to his wife.

a note on the author

T.C. Boyle is the best-selling author of eight
other novels including *World's End*, winner of the
PEN/Faulkner Award for Fiction, *Riven Rock,
The Tortilla Curtain, A Friend of the Earth* and *East
is East*. He is also the author of six collections of
short stories, many of which have appeared in
The New Yorker, Playboy, Granta and *The Paris
Review*. *Drop City* was a finalist for the National
Book Award 2003. He lives in California.

THE TORTILLA CURTAIN T.C. Boyle £6.99 0 7475 2572 2

'A harrowing, even horrific, tale of an immigrant couple's venture into California, and the shockingly brutal reception they receive ... a remarkable feat of imaginative empathy' *Daily Telegraph*

When Delaney Mossbacher knocks down a Mexican pedestrian, he neither reports the accident nor takes his victim to hospital. Instead the man accepts $20 and limps back to poverty and his pregnant seventeen-year-old wife, leaving Delaney to return to his privileged life in California. But these two men are fated against each other, as Delaney attempts to clear the land of the illegal immigrants he thinks are turning his state park into a ghetto, and a boiling pot of racism and prejudice threatens to spill over.

'This novel examines America's guerrilla war between the haves and have-nots with a zing unequalled since *The Bonfire of the Vanities*' *Observer*

RIVEN ROCK T.C. Boyle £6.99 0 7475 4292 9

'Early on, you want to buy copies for your friends: soon after that, you want to buy the film rights for yourself. *Riven Rock* establishes Boyle as the equal of Robertson Davies and John Irving' *Guardian*

Shortly after marrying Katherine, brilliant but highly-strung Stanley McCormick suffers a nervous breakdown, is diagnosed with a tormenting sex mania and is imprisoned in the forbidding mansion known as Riven Rock. For the next twenty years, Stanley is confined, attended to by a staff of male nurses and a succession of psychiatrists. Yet Katherine remains strong in her belief that one day he will return to her whole.

'An amazing novel – screen your calls, shun your friends, snack on cold cuts, let it become your life for a weekend ... this demonstrates where American fiction can be taken when a virtuoso grabs the wheel' *Glasgow Herald*

To order from Bookpost PO Box 29 Douglas Isle of Man IM99 1BQ www.bookpost.co.uk
email: bookshop@enterprise.net fax: 01624 837033 tel: 01624 836000

bloomsbury pbks

www.bloomsbury.com/tcboyle

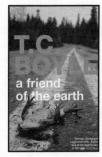